NORTHERN FIRE

CW Whitehair
Rhonda-Lee

By: CW Whitehair
& Rhonda-Lee

ISBN 0-7414-4518-2

Published by:

PUBLISHING.COM

1094 New DeHaven Street, Suite 100
West Conshohocken, PA 19428-2713
Info@buybooksontheweb.com
www.buybooksontheweb.com
Toll-free (877) BUY BOOK
Local Phone (610) 941-9999
Fax (610) 941-9959

Printed in the United States of America

Printed on Recycled Paper

Published January 2008

Acknowledgments

It would have been impossible for just two people to complete this work of historical fiction on their own. First, we would like to thank Bob O'Connor, author of the Perfect Steel Trap Harpers Ferry 1859 and The Virginian Who Might Have Saved Lincoln, for guiding us in the direction of Infinity Publishing. Often when we did book signings for Sabers and Roses, Bob would always be there to encourage and share ideas. His confidence has been an inspiration to us.

We would like to thank the historians at the Otis Gray Harrison mansion in Boston, Massachusetts for their extensive tour of this historical home. They were very informative and answered all our questions concerning Boston and its culture following the American Civil War. Also while we were in the city doing our research, Kathleen Giberti opened her home to us and gave us a tour of the Beacon Hill area.

We would like to thank the staff at the Old Charles Town Library for allowing us to go through their archives of pictures of Charles Town and what it looked like during and following the Civil War. We would also like to thank them for their assistance in providing books that were needed to obtain the history on the Jefferson County area during the days of Reconstruction.

We would like to thank the staff members of the Harpers Ferry National Park for answering questions and allowing the use of information on the history of Harpers Ferry.

Finally, we would like to commend our gracious appreciation for two ladies that helped to make this possible. First to Ronnie Osterman, who patiently read the first draft of this book and asked questions that stimulated thought for perfection, and secondly, Deborah Piscitelli of the Harpers Ferry Historical Association for sacrificing her time to see this project to its completion.

PROLOGUE

A cool breeze was blowing, the trees were green with multiple-colored leaves, and the birds were nestling along the branches filling the air with music. The surroundings were serene with only the occasional noise of an automobile passing and breaking the peacefulness of the atmosphere. Along the streets of the historic village of Harpers Ferry, visitors quietly walked toward the Hilltop Hotel for dinner, or to enjoy the panoramic view of the Potomac River and Maryland Heights. Occasionally, some of the tourists paused to question the residents of the town, who were either cleaning their yards from the previous harsh winter months, or beginning to plant their flowerbeds for the summer.

It was early spring 1960; Ann Barker sat alone on one of the wooden benches within the old bandstand near her home. It was a sunny afternoon. After being confined to the indoors for most of the cold months, she wanted to spend some time in the park, and gaze at the mountains towering over the river. At Ann's elderly age, she was very frail, although still observant and alert. This was a very special day. It was her 111th birthday. For Ann, she was not only the oldest living resident in Jefferson County, but also in the state of West Virginia. In her hands, she held tightly to the old, ragged brown diary that once belonged to her Uncle Pete Barker. As in many times over the past 35 years, she read his words over and over until she had most of the events memorized. This day wasn't any different than those previous.

For the past hour, Ann had been reading her uncle's entries he had recorded the day Katie McBride had returned in May of 1865 from Boston. After finishing, she closed the book and glanced toward Jenny's Diner that was directly across the street. Even though her eyes were failing, Ann struggled momentarily with her failing vision and gazed at the father and son departing from the restaurant. As they crossed the road toward their car parked in front of the old bandstand, Ann recognized the youngster. She anxiously called, "Danny, Danny."

Danny Rollins turned from speaking with his father and glanced in the direction of the voice. He recognized Ann. With his Father's approval he quickly approached his friend. As he neared the wooden steps, Ann smiled and jovially said, "Please come and sit for a few moments and speak with me. I haven't seen you since last fall."

Without hesitating, Danny enthusiastically said, "Miss Ann, this is my Father."

"Hi, I am Bill. I have heard so much about you, and now I'm privileged to finally meet you."

Ann gestured for them to sit. "I love it when your son spends time with me. Life can be so lonely when your loved ones live so far away." A smile radiated across her face as she turned her attention to the lad. "Danny, how have you been doing?"

"Miss Ann, you have really stirred my interest in the Civil War since I last spent some time with you. I still can't imagine what it must have been like living on a huge estate with your family and having everything."

"I recall before the war, it was the most glorious time in my life. Oh, how I miss it so."

"Where was Shenandoah located?" Danny asked.

"From here, oh, I guess maybe three or four miles west along present day 340."

Bill smiled. He took Ann by the hand, "When was the last time you had a chance to visit your old homestead?"

The words proceeded slowly from Ann's mouth as her fingers brushed her cheek. "Many, many years ago. It's been at least twenty years or more. I never owned a gasoline engine machine, or had a permit to drive one. I always depended on Mr. Roberts to take me to the store and run errands, but he has been gone for many years now."

Danny smiled and jumped from the bench. He took Miss Ann by the hand. "Miss Ann, how would you like to return to Shenandoah? I would like to see the place and I know that my Father would also."

"Now I don't want to put you two to any trouble, but you know it would be kind of nice to see the old place one more time before I die."

Without another word, Danny and his Father helped Ann from the bench. Within minutes, they were proceeding through the town toward their destination with Ann giving some of the history and knowledge of her acquaintances, who once populated the area. As the threesome drove slowly along the paved road, to Ann's astonishment, she noticed many of the changes that had taken place over the years that had passed since she last visited these particular areas. A large region of the area once owned by the Barkers, west of School House Ridge was now a limestone quarry. The property that wasn't used by the owners for industrial purpose had been allowed to grow over with thickets, trees, and underbrush. It wasn't the meticulous, plush pasture that Ann and her Mother had ridden many times on their way to Smallwood's Ridge, or better known by the locals as Bolivar Heights. She just quietly shook her head in frustration. Ann's anxiety was heightened as they proceeded through the small village of Halltown because she knew they were close to her old homestead.

The first visualization of Shenandoah that Ann observed was a dilapidated worm-shaped prototype fence. It had replaced the beautiful white-board fence that once crowned the property's borders in the latter days of her ownership. The property didn't give the immaculate appearance of the early 1860's, but only of a plain country setting. The present owners gave Ann an unfavorable impression. Apparently, they were not wealthy and unable to present the property in the fashion she once remembered. Ann smiled as she observed some thoroughbreds and their colts galloping across the open field. It reminded her of the family's prosperous business, and the days when she would sit along the fence near the house with her father. Often they watched the horses run, such as this moment. What was once the Barker estate of Shenandoah had now ceased to exist. Knowing that horse racing was a huge economic factor in the county, Ann assumed the present owners of the property still maintained the farm for breeding horses and competing at the racetrack in nearby Charles Town.

The old Charlestown Pike that ran along the boundaries of the farm was now known as Route 340. The small two-lane highway didn't offer much in the way of a pull-off shoulder along its edges, so Bill had to park his car at the farm's entrance. The long dirt lane and some of the oak trees that filled its edges still gave the appearance of the 1860's, and was the only resemblance of what actually remained of the estate. The huge antebellum mansion that Pete Barker built replaced the first dwelling that once crowned the crest of the ridge. Many of the trees that once heavily populated the property no longer existed. The lovely multiple-colored rose gardens covering the landscape had vanished. It was not as Ann recalled of the days long ago, nor she had hoped to witness on this trip. Still, it was the place she had called home.

Tears filled Ann's eyes as she observed a small girl skillfully riding a thoroughbred across the lush meadows of the once-prestigious estate. She recalled pleasant thoughts and memories of days before the outbreak of the war when life had its carefree moments. It was a time when dreams were pursued, and gave all of the hopes and appearances of life being simple instead of complex.

As Ann clutched her uncle's diary in her hands, Danny's curiosity was getting to him. "Miss Ann, I imagine life was much different here in Jefferson County when the war ended and the soldiers returned home."

Ann wiped the tears from her hazel eyes as she looked at the lad. She brushed aside her long gray hair that was blowing in her face from the strong breeze. "Yes, life was different. The reconstruction era was very difficult on all of us. Sometimes I feel it was just a continuation of the war."

Bill added, as he joined the conversation, "True, from what little history I have read it didn't end for many Southerners. At least when I returned home from the army after serving in Korea, I had a home and family to return to and could begin to pick up the pieces of my life."

Ann turned her attention, gazing at the young girl still riding her horse. "The area was vastly different in many ways after the war. Instead of the prosperous farms lining the road, all that replaced them was blackened ruins and acreage dominated by underbrush and weeds. Fences had vanished from most homesteads and the lifeless appearances depressed me."

Danny knew the conversation was upsetting Ann, but he wanted to know more, hoping someday to hand down her recollections to his family and write a book on the area's history. Cautiously he said, "If I may ask, what was life like in Harpers Ferry?"

"At the end of the conflict, Harpers Ferry was mostly deserted. Many of the buildings in the lower area of town where the two rivers meet were gone. Other dwellings along Shenandoah and Potomac Street had also suffered damage. On Virginus Island, all of the mills had been burned to the ground, and the useful industry damaged or destroyed. Surprisingly, some of the churches and schools in town met the same fate. As for the homes that escaped destruction, they were tarnished with neglect and uninhabitable. There wasn't any work with the destruction of most of the industry, especially the armory and arsenal. And as for the Negroes, many loitered along the streets, knowing not what to do with their newborn freedom. The thing I remembered the most about them was, they possessed a gaunt appearance."

Bill had been listening intently. "As I look out over this area, it's beautiful and prosperous. I can't imagine the hell everyone must have endured. As all wars, it must have affected this area in the extreme."

"Oh, it did," Ann said as she continued to share her memories. "Son, you have no idea of the extreme destitution and destruction that prevailed. It was far worse than what I remembered with the great depression of the 30's. I can still see many pictures within my mind of those times. They'll never leave me as long as I live. Some are just as if they happened yesterday. But the images that stand out the most in my mind of my experiences are the happy smiling faces that I remembered before the war." Pausing and struggling to continue her description of her past experiences, Ann continued in a broken tone. "Oh, dear God, those happy and content images I remembered before the war were replaced with worried and sadden expressions after the conflict. Many Confederate veterans discovered their families had vanished not knowing their fate or where they might have sought refuge. Only a few of the original citizens remained behind once the town became a Union military garrison."

Ann brushed her hair from her face, still clutching the diary. She was quiet as they glanced around the estate.

"It sure isn't the way you described it to Jason and me last fall. It is so much different," Danny commented.

"What happened to your family? How did this way of life affect them?" Bill asked.

Ann opened her Uncle's diary, reading an entry dated September 15, 1865. She softly and slowly spoke her Uncle Pete's words; "Life hasn't been easy since returning home from the war. Hayward and I, along with Katie, have labored long and trying hours rebuilding but met many obstacles from the radicals dominating this county. Katie has been there to give us hope and encouragement when matters don't appear promising. I know I wasted many years without her, but I'm trying to make it up to her now. Although my heart has been overshadowed with grief over Rebecca's death, we share the excitement of Mother, Caroline, and Ann returning on this day. I don't know what to expect from Mother when I see her."

Ann quietly closed the diary, glancing again toward the house on the ridge. Her mind returned to previous years when life presented many difficult challenges, life-long learning experiences, and adversities to be overcome.

Chapter 1

A lone deer stood along Barker's Ridge gazing across the once-prestigious estate called Shenandoah that was owned by the influential Barker family of Harpers Ferry, Virginia. The property had caused great controversy among family members, especially between the two brothers Charles and Pete. During the early days of the Civil War, Charles Barker, the older of the two sons of Elizabeth Barker had been the principal owner of the 5,000-acre homestead after his mother had granted him complete ownership. His mother, Elizabeth, wife Caroline, and daughter Ann occupied the premises with him. His younger brother, Pete, disagreeing with his mother's decision had departed to fight for the Confederacy serving with the 1st Virginia Cavalry.

By the second year of the war, Charles became an advisor and trusted aide to the Confederate President, Jefferson Davis. This is one of the reasons why his house and property had been marked for destruction by General David Hunter's Federal cavalry two years later in the spring of 1864. The Yankees torched the Greek revival style, huge stone, double veranda mansion that crested the lower ridge overlooking the long dirt lane. All that remained was the stone fireplace in the middle of where the parlor was once located. Everything within the dwelling such as family portraits, valuable jewelry, and heirlooms vanished in the flames. The devastation didn't halt with the destruction of the mansion. All of the outbuildings, the kitchen house, carriage house, stables, and smokehouse were all included in the destruction of the estate. In the direction of the wooded area, the partial stone wall of the barn was all that stood to remind one of the bustling industry the family enjoyed.

At one time, Shenandoah was the scene of social gaiety. Events such as political rallies, grand balls, barbecues, and equestrian tournaments attracted attention among the most prominent and prestigious families of the lower Shenandoah Valley. Often, friends of the Barkers accepted their invitation and traveled for miles to attend one-day and sometimes two-day events, but now nothing remained to remind one of such antebellum times. The only memories remaining of the prosperous and glorious days of Shenandoah Estate were the charred foundation that it once stood upon, and the stone slave quarters which were now empty. The Yankee destruction left nothing of worth that could be used by the family but an old rustic cabin near the slaves' quarters that had been built by the children's father in 1828.

During the early afternoon of September 15th, 1865, the breeze was cool, clammy, and the gray haze was lifting over the area. Along the Shenandoah River, the glimmering beams of the sun peered through the cloud cover with its reflection on the river's surface. The tall grass that covered the fields and ridgeline was still gleaming from the gentle rain shower that had recently fallen. Birds flew from the trees on the opposite shore. The crescendo sounds of the Shenandoah rushing over the rocks gave evidence to its power and majesty. Pete Barker and his close friend and worker, Hayward Cooper, were in the midst of digging rock in the vicinity of the Bloomery Mill to load onto a wagon to be used to rebuild Pete's home, Shenandoah. From sunrise, the two men had labored intently taking little time to rest.

As Pete and Hayward were about to remove a good size rock they had spent some time digging around, several crackling shots echoed from across the river, making a thudding sound against the wooden wagon. By instinct from his days serving in the 1st Virginia Cavalry, Pete ran to the front of the wagon and reached under the seat to pull out a pistol that had been smuggled into his possession by Hayward. After retrieving the weapon, he turned and looked for Hayward. He noticed he had taken refuge on the ground about a distance of twenty feet from him. Hayward was uninjured but afraid to make a dash for cover.

Pete turned his attention once more intently gazing across the river. All that he saw was thickets, underbrush, and various trees. There wasn't any evidence of human existence. Moving toward the rear of the wagon, he gestured for Hayward to make the attempt to escape to safety. Once Hayward moved and began to crawl, multiple shots filled the air breaking the silence. Even though Pete couldn't see his enemy, he returned fire in order to give Hayward the necessary cover to escape harm. It was apparent by the way the shots were directed someone wanted to kill Hayward. From a tool chest along side of the wagon, Hayward pulled out a pistol and knelt near the rear of the wagon. Looking at Pete with his dark, piercing eyes, he anxiously asked, "Do ya see 'em?"

Pete said, as he continued to scour the woods across the river, "No, but I know they are in that tree line, probably among the boulders the trees are hiding."

"How's ya know that?"

Refusing to take his eyes from the tree line, Pete answered Hayward's question. "When I was young, I use to hide there when I was mad at my father. I still remembered one incident in particular. It occurred when my Father gave my brother Charles a nice black stallion by the name of Rebel. In the worst way I wanted that horse, and thought it should be mine. But the animal was given to Charles as a birthday gift. I didn't understand why he did that. I always felt and thought that I was my father's favorite. I must admit I became very angry and ran off. As always, my father knew where to find me after I had time to think and deal with my temper. Then he and I talked about the problem and came up with a compromise. I admired my father because he was a man who carefully thought out each situation and carefully chose his words with much wisdom."

Without warning, several more shots rang out hitting some of the rock causing small fragments to hit Pete in the shoulder. By instinct, Pete knelt behind the wagon and then began to crawl underneath to get a better angle of fire. As he did so, he noticed four horses with riders departing along the opposite ridge. Pete fired twice but didn't hit any of the mysterious raiders. Standing and brushing off his pants, Pete looked at Hayward, "Someone wants us dead."

"Why? What has we done to dem people?"

"Well there are some that can't stop fighting the war. And for them, it didn't end with Lee's surrender. I guess it will never be over with."

"Other words, dey's some that wants to kill da black man."

Pete glanced once more toward the tree line. "I am afraid so."

* * * *

After hearing the muffled sound of horses, Katie McBride put aside some dishes and stepped from the cabin. As Katie stood on the porch, her green eyes followed the unfamiliar gentleman riding in the one-horse buggy among the grand oak trees lining the lane. Almost immediately, a six-man Union cavalry patrol entered the lane about 50 yards behind the buggy. As she wiped her wet hands on the apron covering her dress, she thought of the circumstances surrounding this unexpected visitation. Katie was anxious as she moved her right hand against her forehead, wiping her long auburn hair away. Stepping slowly forward from the wooden porch, Katie approached the buggy and its military escort as they brought their animals to a halt.

The soldiers and the gentleman stared as the officer rode forward. He tipped the brim of his black bell-crowned hat, "Madam, I am Captain Robert Brackett, the Provost Marshall in Harpers Ferry. And this gentleman in the buggy is Mr. C. L. Smith of the newly formed Board of Supervisors here in Jefferson County."

With her curiosity heightened, and an astonishing expression, Katie answered, "Gentlemen, I am Katie McBride. How can I help you?"

"Well, you're probably wondering why we are here on such a dismal day."

"Yes, I am," Katie answered as the rumble of wagon wheels interrupted her attention. Quickly glancing in the direction of the river road, she noticed Pete and Hayward returning with a load of rock.

"I assume the gentleman that's approaching is Mr. Barker?"

Katie remained silent and ignored the officer as Pete jumped down from the wagon. Pete knew the family had incurred some debt, so he had some idea of the visitation. "Yes sir, may I be of assistance to you gentlemen?"

With a smile crossing his face, Captain Brackett replied, "I assume you are James Barker."

"Yes sir, your assumption is correct."

"Well sir," the Captain said as he dismounted from his horse, "the nature of our visit this afternoon has two meanings."

"Go ahead," Pete answered, glancing at Katie.

"First and foremost have you heard from, or do you know the whereabouts of your brother Charles?"

"No sir, I don't. And as far as I know, no one in the family, not even his wife, has heard from him."

"I find that difficult to believe. No one just vanishes off the face of the earth."

Inwardly, Pete remained silent, but he was beginning to lose his composure. He didn't like to be called a liar, but he managed to repress his emotions.

The officer continued to look around the premises. "As you probably know, we have gathered up and imprisoned most of the Rebel fugitives from that blasted government you defended. There are only a few remaining, and one of those remaining happens to be your brother Charles. As you may well know, the paroles you rebs received are only good for the soldiers, not the cowards that dictated this rebellion. If you are hiding your brother on the property, then I would consider that a breach of your commitment."

"Yes sir, I know, but like I said, no one has heard from him. That's the truth."

Hayward nodded in agreement as Katie quickly added, "He tells you the truth. Please take the word of someone who remained loyal to the Union throughout the war. My brother Seamus served with the 1st Massachusetts Cavalry."

Captain Brackett wasn't convinced. He gestured for several members of the military escort to search the property. With each passing moment, Pete became angrier believing that his rights were being violated. As the soldiers dismounted and pushed open the door to the cabin, Pete lunged forth. As he did so, one of the soldiers pulled his revolver, cocking the hammer to fire.

Hayward used his physical strength to intervene by grabbing the young Barker by the arms. In his low gravel voice, "Yose must be calm. Deys want yas to do something foolish so deys can shoot ya."

Katie quickly approached, embracing Pete and shouted, "Stop Pete! Please!"

Captain Brackett began to laugh as he ordered the soldier to put his weapon in its holster and to continue searching the premise. Turning his attention toward Pete, he approached and grabbed the young Barker by his shirt and angrily said, "Well reb, it appears that you still have a lot of fight left. Huh? I guess you just didn't get your fill of it such as my men and me. But, you're lucky, real lucky that I'm in a humorous compassionate mood today. Because if I were not, you'd end up in the guardhouse in town or I would allow that soldier to shoot you dead. And honestly reb, I don't know of anything that would have made me happier."

After releasing Pete, Captain Brackett stepped several steps back continuing to look at Pete with a smirk covering his face. He turned and pointed toward the buggy and continued in a calmer tone. "Now to the other order of my business. According to Mr. Smith, your family hasn't paid taxes on this property since the summer of '63. This tells me in all probability they were denouncing their allegiance to the new government of West Virginia, which came into existence at that time. And that's not right." Pausing and turning to look at Mr. Smith, the officer gestured with his hand and continued in an authoritative tone. "It still means you are delinquent and owe how much Mr. Smith?"

Mr. Smith opened a little black book, looking, he replied in a loud tone, "In excess of $2,500. There was a lien placed on the property in April. It must be paid by the end of this month or we will have to confiscate your holdings, and they'll be sold at an auction in order to settle the debt."

"So pay your taxes or else lose the property," Captain Brackett interrupted.

It was all Pete could do to hold back his emotions. He knew if he said anything inflammatory he would be escorted and detained in Harpers Ferry and wouldn't have the opportunity to satisfy the debt. As for Katie, she looked on in disbelief, but Hayward was not taken by surprise by the turn of events. Like Pete, he knew it was going to be difficult for the veterans of the Southern armies to be accepted in a society that would be operated and dominated by a local government made up of individuals who were sympathetic to the Union. Their goal was only to continue to prosecute the war using emotional turmoil and economical weapons.

Captain Brackett quietly mounted his horse. Taking the reins, he said as the other soldiers filed into column of two, "I want you to remember two things. One is you best not break your parole, and secondly, if you haven't satisfied the debt by the end of the month, I'll be back."

At once the soldiers followed by Mr. Smith proceeded down the lane toward the Charlestown Pike. Pete stood quietly, observing the party, and thinking of how he could raise the funds needed to pay the taxes.

Chapter 2

An hour had gone by and many thoughts continued to fill Pete's mind. Quickly he contemplated his options. Feeling under great pressure, he struck his hand against one of the cabin's wooden porch columns. With the sound, Katie rushed onto the porch. As he turned to look at her, he noticed the fear in her eyes.

Without hesitation, Katie approached and placed her hand on his shoulder. "We'll come up with the money somehow, I know."

Pete turned around gazing in her direction. "Katie, we are broke. We have no money. Nothing at all. My family lost everything during the war and what little they had left, they needed in order to survive. As you know, it was difficult with high prices and shortages of supplies on everything."

From the stable area, Hayward had noticed Pete's actions and Katie's response. He sympathized knowing his friend's frustrations. He approached Pete and Katie. "We's have a little bit of time. We's hasn't comes dis far to give up now, has we? No! Ya must have da faith to overcome. If yas doesn't, den deys gonna git the best of ya."

Taking an advantage of Hayward's point of view, Katie quickly added, "Listen to what your best friend is saying. You won't be alone in all of this; we'll be there to help you. I'm sure we can borrow the money somewhere. I have good credit and some money that I've managed to save, and you know I'll help in anyway that I can."

Pete quickly brushed his hand through his long, brown, wavy hair. He put his ragged, brown hat on his head, still with the bullet hole through the crown from the fighting at Jefferson, Maryland in September of 1862. He tried to remain calm and optimistic. "Maybe I can speak with Mr. Larson at the bank in Charlestown. It's going to be tough, but maybe he'll grant us the loan."

Hayward turned to walk away toward the makeshift shelter where the horses were kept. "We's will come up with something. We jist need time to think and da answer will come."

Katie and Pete turned and faced each other. "I heard gunshots earlier in the direction of the river. Were you and Hayward trying to kill some rabbit for dinner?"

"No, we weren't trying to kill a rabbit."

"As I remember, there were many shots that were fired. What are you trying to keep from me?"

Pete took a deep sigh and looked at Katie. Without an answer to her question, he turned to follow Hayward. After walking a short distance, Katie stepped from the porch and followed. With her persistence for an answer, she angrily shouted. "Will you tell me what in the bloody world is going on?"

Pete turned around. "Some one was shooting at Hayward and me. I don't know why. Other than I suppose that there are those individuals that can't stop fighting the war."

"Everyone in the county knows that the Barkers were for Southern independence. Your family were leaders for secession from the Union and everyone knows you fought with a Virginia cavalry regiment. Why would they want to do bloody harm to you?"

"I don't know if they wanted to harm Hayward or myself. Probably they would like to kill both of us."

"Pete, maybe we should leave until it is safe," Katie cried.

"No. I am not leaving and running away from men that can't stop fighting the war, nor am I going to give up Shenandoah to a bunch of greedy, self-serving individuals without a fight!"

Katie knew they needed to get away and clear their minds. With his composure under control, she affectionately took Pete by the arm and the couple walked toward the peach orchard. Pete turned and allowed a gentle smile to cover his features as he removed one of the few peaches that remained. Without hesitating, he offered it to Katie.

She smiled as she accepted his gift. "I remember the day after William Pierce's reception when I came to Shenandoah to spend some time with Caroline." Katie took a bite of the peach and turned, smiling at Pete and continued, "Do you remember when she was unable to show me around Shenandoah because of feeling a little under the weather? And then you invited me to tour the estate in her absence?"

"Yeah," Pete answered as a glowing smile broke forth on his face. He paused and took a bite of the peach. "You know, I remember that day just as if it were yesterday."

Katie continued as she took his hand in hers, "It was just like today. We stopped here where you offered me some of the same fruit." Again Katie paused and began to laugh. "Oh, I remember I was so mad and upset with you, even though I desperately made every attempt to resist my attraction to you. As I stood alongside of Miss Elizabeth that day, I tried within my mind to make up every reason why I should have nothing to do with you. I don't know why, but somewhere in my heart, I really didn't believe that you were really responsible for starting the brawl in town. And over the years that I've had time to reflect on our relationship, I know there was a part of my heart that wanted to know you in a personal way."

Pete remained silent, and pulled Katie's small, shapely frame close. His eyes were fixed on her beautiful features and knew that he wanted to kiss her. Ever so gently, he pressed his lips to hers and she accepted the sweetness of his affection. They allowed their eyes to meet and share the moment quietly, just gazing at each other. Finally, Pete opened his heart and expressed his feelings. "I have to admit, I was somewhat apprehensive about being with you that day, but I wanted to have the opportunity to explain my side of the events that took place in town. I really didn't believe anything would come of our afternoon except that maybe we could be civil toward each other. The only way for me to have achieved that purpose was to distract your attention from our differences and concentrate on something else."

"Such as yourself?"

"No, no, that wasn't my intention. Since you were from the North, I wanted you to enjoy what Shenandoah had to offer. As you well know before the war, us Southerners were frowned upon because we had slaves, and we were accused of committing a great evil. But in reality, all I hoped to accomplish that day was for you to see that life wasn't all that bad on a Southern homestead."

Turning to look in the direction where the plantation house once crowned the crest of the ridge, Katie changed the subject and sadly said, "I know it still hurts to have had so much and then to lose it all."

"True, it does. But, look what I have in return. I have you, and your love."

Katie caressed his cheek and replied passionately. "And you'll always have my love. I could never give my love to another." Katie paused and continued to glance at Pete as she took his hand. "To be honest with you even though I had difficulty for the longest time admitting it, I have actually loved you from the very first time that I laid eyes on you." Pete was in awe as Katie continued to open her heart and reveal to him its secrets. "Do you recall the night of William's reception, when we danced for the first time?"

"Yes, I remember," Pete laughingly replied. "There was something about your eyes. They told a story about you, but I couldn't quite figure it out. For days afterwards, I thought about it quite often."

"I believed something was taking place in my heart as we danced that evening. The emotions wanted to surface, but I was desperately trying to deny what I was feeling. That's why there was the mysterious glow in my eyes that has remained a mystery to you for so long. Now you know why. Now you know the truth."

"Yes, I'll never forget. You don't know how many times I tried to solve that mystery."

Pouring out her emotions, Katie placed her arms around Pete's neck. "I don't know why. I just knew something was happening deep within my heart. I know it wasn't just your handsome features that attracted me. Maybe it was just that innocent expression you displayed in front of the Wager House after the brawl or your compassionate brown eyes. I really, to this day don't know. It's difficult to say. And then the afternoon when I left you in Frederick City to return to Boston, I cried the whole way home, never knowing if I would see you again. Somewhere I just couldn't accept the fact that our relationship had ended. I just knew you loved me, but I resigned myself to the fact that you must be the one to realize the truth concerning your feelings. Nothing at that point was going to make you see any different."

"I realized my love for you when I was recovering from my wound after the battle at Gettysburg. Hannah, the lady who hid me from the Yankees and nursed me back to health, planted some valuable seed in my heart. She told me I had been given a second chance in life and I should return to you and not sacrifice it. I owe her so much for what she did for me."

"I would like to meet her one day and thank her for her sacrifice and commitment. I, too, owe her so much that she gave you back to me."

"We have learned from those days. If the war taught me anything, I must confess that I learned to trust another person, face a challenge in the midst of adversity, and survive when the odds seem to be against me. My experiences caused me to grow up."

"I'm grateful that you've come a long way with your life and through such a tragic conflict. As for me, still I am troubled at times. I can hear you from the other room shouting in your sleep as if you're still fighting some battle. The killing, screams, and the horrible events that took place during that time still torment you. Often I've considered entering your room and waking you. But since it isn't appropriate for an unmarried lady to enter an unmarried gentleman's bedchamber, I refrained from taking such action."

"I respect your feelings on that matter. But as far as the war is concerned, it's going to take time, no matter what I do to forget."

A grin covered his features as some memories resurfaced in his heart concerning the lighter days of the war.

Katie was puzzled. "What's so amusing?"

Pete shook his head. "Jonathan Collins. What a friend." Pausing and looking in the direction of the river, he continued, "He was just like a brother to me. I have often wondered what might have happened to him. Often in the evening around the campfire, he spoke of his love for his wife and two sons. Like me, he declared he would live and die in Highland County. To this day, his fate continues to trouble me more then anything. With the odds so heavily against us, I am afraid he might not have survived the war. Undoubtedly, he was a fearless, bold fighter who was willing to take too many chances."

"All of you did to some extent. You were willing to die and sacrifice for what you believed in, but the same goes for those who fought for the North."

Pete stood and assisted Katie by extending his hand. "I know, but for now we must leave the war behind. We have problems we must find the answers to."

Katie and Pete began to walk leisurely toward the cabin. Katie glanced at Pete and caught his eye. Again he gently kissed her. A warm smile covered her features; she caressed his arms and attempted to make him forget about the horrors of the war, and the visitation of Captain Brackett and Mr. Smith. She knew in time they would find an answer, and any crisis that came would only strengthen their love and bond for the other.

Chapter 3

By mid-afternoon, the weather had cooperated with the cool air giving way to warmer and more pleasant conditions. Pete and Hayward had been lifting some huge rocks from the wagon. The task of the construction of the home had begun as the first row had been laid upon the foundation. The work was tedious and Pete's arms and back felt tightness from the strain of lifting. Pausing from the labor, Pete stretched his muscular, medium frame to relieve the tension. Looking toward the western sky, he noticed the sun was still high, offering the possibility of Hayward and him returning for another trip to dig more rock.

As Pete wiped the perspiration from his forehead, he was silent, gazing at the birds that filled the trees near where the house once crowned the ridge. Taking a deep sigh, he turned his attention toward Hayward. His friend paused and looked up from his labor. The perspiration was running rapidly down Hayward's face and body. At age 47, Hayward was still able to keep pace with the younger Barker, who was his junior by 21 years. Hayward waited for a word to come from his friend, but Pete ignored him and turned walking to the front of the wagon and retrieving his diary on the seat. Without an answer, he gazed in Hayward's direction; his mind was somewhere distant. When Pete didn't speak, Hayward took the initiative to begin a conversation and attempt to prod the young Barker for his thoughts.

"Yas still a thinkin' 'bout the visit of dem soldiers and us gittin' shot at ain't ya?"

"Yeah," Pete replied, "I guess I am."

Hayward asked as he wiped the perspiration from his forehead, "Well, what's ya thinkin' 'bout doin'?"

Again Pete paused, losing his concentration on the conversation with his friend. As Pete continued to write a few lines in his journal, Hayward asked again in a more urgent tone, "Well! What's ya gonna do?"

"As I said earlier, I'm going to go to the bank in the morning and speak with Mr. Larson. If I'm not successful, then I am not sure. I really don't have many options."

"What 'bout us bein' shot at? What's we gonna do 'bout that problem?

"I really don't know who is responsible. Hayward, it troubles me greatly that someone out there still wants to spill blood. We must keep a weapon handy at all times, especially after the sun goes down."

Hayward's expression reflected the despair he was experiencing. He said in a sincere tone as he leaned against the wagon, "Ya know that's a lot of money that man wants to pay off the debt. I'se has a little that ya can have, but not much."

"Hayward, I appreciate that. I really do, but I can't take your money. Since I can't afford to pay you in return, you'll need what you have managed to save for your own future now that there won't be any restrictions on what you want to purchase. Who knows, maybe someday you'll want to get married, have a family, and buy some property. As for Shenandoah and the problems I face, maybe if I made some attempt to satisfy the debt, then I could pay it gradually. If I did, then it's quite possible that Mr. Smith would give me a chance. It's a long shot but worth a try."

Katie was approaching with a wooden bucket of cold water and overheard Pete speaking. "I don't think they'll give you a chance, nor allow you relief in any form," she casually said.

"What do you mean? If they believe we are firmly committed to the Union and I could convince them Shenandoah could be profitable again, then hopefully they would see the financial advantage."

"I know Shenandoah could be profitable again, but they want to destroy you and your family in anyway they can. Look at it from their side; you fought and supported the rebellion. Radicals in this county are not going to let that issue go for some time. There has to be another way. One, which they are not prepared for and can't reject."

"Wait a minute." Hayward angrily said. "What 'bout the tax dollars that dis place can bring for dem people. We's gonna raise horses and cattle jist like we's use to. Some people jist can't git enough. Deys jist ain't da carin' kind."

Pete added after he took a drink from the dipper, "I agree with Hayward. These people are greedy and will make a buck anyway they can, legal or illegal. Shenandoah could generate a lot of revenue, possibly more than before the war. For instance, the cavalry will need good horses to fight the Indians out in the western territory."

Katie answered with a tone of confidence as her eyes were on Pete's angry expression, "I agree, but they can also make money from the property if they were to operate a business with the same idea as yours. Or, they can just sell it off piece by piece to carpetbaggers."

"Then what you're saying is that it's useless to even make the attempt," Pete said as he tossed the dipper in the bucket.

"No, I'm just saying it's going to be an uphill struggle. You're going to have to fight those in authority. And that's not going to be easy."

A serious and troubled expression covered Hayward's face. "Dey's gotta be some answer somewhere."

Katie smiled and quietly turned to walk back toward the house, allowing Pete time to ponder on the problem and her perspective of the situation.

"With Mr. Charles gone," Hayward said, "yose gonna have to make da decisions. Yose da one that must keep things a runnin'. We's can't give up now."

* * * *

After removing the rest of the rock from the wagon, Pete and Hayward paused to rest. While Hayward knelt to take some water from the bucket, Pete turned and stared in the direction of the Charlestown Pike. His mind was troubled. The words Katie had spoken continued to resurface and torment his heart. In his thoughts, he knew she was probably right, but there must be an answer; the source for the money must exist. He turned and placed his face in his hands suffering from the anguish. After a moment, he turned around and leaned against the wagon folding his arms over the top of the tool chest mounted on the side. He continued his thoughts pondering on the many citizens and Confederate veterans that lived in Jefferson County and how they had suffered greatly from the effects of the war. To some of those brave men that fought for the Southern cause, this was the only place they had ever called home. They, like him, were broke and would need to make loans if their property was going to be useful for the reconstruction and economy of the county. Hopefully, once the funds were secured, the family could rebuild the homestead and once again be eligible to compete for government contracts by selling horses and cattle.

Then Pete's mind gave thought to Charles' whereabouts. The last time the family had received news from him he had written a correspondence somewhere near Amelia Courthouse during the Confederate retreat from the Richmond-Petersburg area. He had entrusted his letter with a friend, who was an officer with General Richard Ewell's forces that had been the last to leave the beleaguered Confederate capital. In spite of the fighting that was taking place between the Federals and Rebels, Charles gave assurance of his welfare and had revealed hopes of rendezvousing with President Davis and cabinet members at Danville, Virginia. He believed under the circumstances of his service in the Confederate government, it would be too dangerous for him to return to Harpers Ferry. That was five months ago. It was the last the family had known of his welfare.

Hayward's voice broke Pete's moment of solitude. "When's ya goin' to git ready to go to town to pick up Misse Elizabeth and the family?"

Pete silently pulled his watch from his pocket. It was 3 o'clock in the afternoon. He turned around and faced Hayward. "Now, if you'll hitch up the horses, I'll put some wooden crates on the wagon for seats."

As Pete placed the last crate on the wagon for the short trip to Harpers Ferry, Katie walked from the cabin with a black parasol, shading her fair complexion. She paused, smiled, and kissed Pete on his right cheek. He grinned as he helped her onto the seat of the wagon. Hayward was silent but observant. Once Pete was seated next to Katie, Hayward tipped his dark brim hat in a farewell gesture as they departed. Pete remained silent as the horses moved slowly down the lane pulling the wagon. At the entrance to the lane, he headed the team of horses east in the direction of Harpers Ferry.

Katie knew Pete was deeply troubled. Throughout the afternoon, she had given great thought to their dilemma and the options they had for securing the necessary funds to pay the debt. She knew it appeared fruitless and nearly impossible. There wasn't anyone they personally were acquainted with that possessed that kind of money. Even the most influential and wealthiest of individuals the family knew before the war were experiencing the same problems. Though there was one idea that continued to surface within her mind, and that was Pete and her making a journey to Boston and seeking help and assistance from her family. She knew they had prospered during the war by investing in the famous Henry Rifle, which was a rapid firing weapon used by Union soldiers. Hopefully, they would be open-minded and hear her plea for help. Katie said as she turned to face Pete, "I can tell by the sorrowful expression that covers your face where your thoughts are."

Pete kept his eyes on the road refusing to look in her direction. He forced a grin. "Is it that obvious?"

"Yes, it is. It troubles you to tell your mother and Caroline the news we received earlier concerning the back taxes, and that the money needed to pay the debt doesn't exist. I believe, too, it troubles you to bring Miss Elizabeth to her home that was once so prestigious and full of life and now so barren with only a log cabin."

"You're right, it does bother me. It bothers me greatly. My concern isn't how we will rebuild the property. That's easy. But what will I do as far as paying off the debt. I had thought maybe we could secure a loan from Caroline's family, but then I remembered the correspondence that we received from her last May when she informed us of Rebecca's death and Charles' fate. At the hands of Sheridan's Yankees, her family didn't fair any better than us."

"I remember. Sheridan's forces destroying barns, buildings, and confiscating horses and livestock in this area. With what I've seen with Shenandoah and some of the rest of the homesteads in this area, I can only imagine what her family must have gone through. Probably they are just like us; barely making it. But, in our situation, it's not hopeless," Katie replied.

"What do you mean?" Pete asked, as he turned to look at Katie.

"I mean there might be a glimmer of hope where we can receive some help."

"Who? Tell me; who can help us?"

"For most of the afternoon while I was getting ready to go to town, I thought there might be a chance that my family would be willing to loan us the money.

"No, no, I don't think so. I don't want their money. Besides, if you're forgetting, I was your brother and family's enemy. Not knowing, on more than one occasion I might have been one of those Rebels who shot at him during some cavalry skirmish or battle." Shaking his head in disagreement, he continued. "No Katie, the money won't come from them."

Katie was persistent as she placed her hand on his arm. "Please listen to me. I would like to try. I was thinking over the next few days after Miss Elizabeth, Ann, and Caroline are settled, I would like for you to consider traveling to Boston with me. If we are to be married, my family will have to meet you sometime."

Pete didn't believe there was a chance of success. Looking at Katie, he was insistent. "No Katie, I wouldn't be accepted. They, like many, haven't forgotten the war and the emotional scars that it caused. The wounds are still too fresh and painful. The nation needs time to make the effort to forget."

"That's true, but unless someone takes the first step, it won't ever happen, now will it?" Pausing to wait for an answer that didn't come, Katie added, "As for Shenandoah, unless you can come up with a better idea, it's the best hope that we have."

"I'll think on it, but first I am going to the bank tomorrow morning and speak with Mr. Larson."

Katie knew Pete was battling his pride. Over the next couple of days, it would be difficult, but she believed he would consider the assistance and would accept, if it were offered. As she gave thought to their conversation, she knew he was correct concerning her family. From her last correspondence she received several weeks ago from her mother, she had pleaded with Katie to return to Boston and forsake her relationship with Pete. Katie refused when she sent her reply. Katie knew it would be a challenge with her family meeting Pete for the first time. As always, she was more then willing to accept the task.

Then Caroline surfaced upon Katie's mind. Today would be the first time in over a year since they had seen each other. This, too, would be an important step in the reconciliation process. Even though she didn't show her nervousness, there was a feeling within of apprehension. The question that continued in Katie's mind was would she meet resistance and acts of hatred from her once close friend. Could they lay their differences to the side and begin the process of rebuilding a relationship that they once enjoyed and found rewarding. It wouldn't be easy she thought. The inflamed emotional wounds from the conflict, the destruction of Shenandoah; the physical suffering and the lost of life concerning a family member, might still inflame animosity toward her.

As Katie turned to glance at Pete, she felt fortunate. Unlike the army captain and Mr. Smith, she didn't see him as a Rebel, but that of a human being with feelings and emotions. He was just one of many who fought for what he believed to be true, and now trying to pick up the pieces of a shattered life. Even though like many who lived in Jefferson County and were suffering hardship, she counted her blessings that he was still alive and was able to return home from a horrible conflict. Together again, they could enjoy a relationship, never to endure separation. To her, this was worth more than all of the gold and silver on earth.

Chapter 4

Pete and Katie were nearing the outskirts of Harpers Ferry. Pete glanced at the area known as the Lower Hall Island. In the distance, he noticed the silent, vacant remains of John Hall's once prosperous rifle factory. Before the war, it was the symbol of a promising business where 3,000 interchangeable weapons were manufactured per year. At the beginning of the conflict, Virginia state troops had stripped the facility of its valuable machinery, shipping it south to be used by the Confederacy in the war effort. It was left vacant until 1864 when Union soldiers used the nine buildings as a prison for Confederate soldiers, thus naming the area, The Island Prison.

As Pete and Katie passed the narrow channel, separating Hall's Island with Virginius Island, the first industry Pete passed was the Iron Foundry, where saws, decorative iron railings, and coal stoves were constructed. Like the fate of other factories, it too, had become a casualty of the war. In the distance, he gazed for a long time at the ruins of the huge stone flourmill. The mill had been owned and operated by Mr. Herr, a Union sympathizer. It was destroyed by fire in 1861 by Confederate raiders. Looking off to his right, Pete could see the mighty Shenandoah River flowing, and the sound of the water rushing across the rocks, echoing its presence along the street. The ample water flow was the reason why so many of the town's industries were constructed, especially the armory. Now with the conclusion of the conflict, the island's many industries would need to be rebuilt if the town's prosperity were to return.

Once Pete and Katie entered the business area of the once prosperous town along Shenandoah Street, Pete continued to take notice of the consequences from the war. There were many reminders of the destruction from the great conflict. As Pete looked around, he noticed many of the houses and businesses that had escaped total destruction had broken windows and roofs that had been partially destroyed by artillery. Most of the homes that were occupied were tarnished with neglect and almost in complete desolation while debris from the street was tossed from one side to the other by the gentle breeze. Harpers Ferry was in shambles.

Shortly the couple came upon a Federal sentry checking passes. As the guard inspected Katie's pass, Pete continued to take notice of his surroundings. He observed a company of thirty Federal soldiers marching along the opposite side of the street with a drummer boy sounding the cadence. Other than the military presence, there appeared a few men departing and entering the dry goods store. The appearance of the town was far from the busy streets filled with citizens before the war. Many of the town's Northern and Southern citizens alike departed when hostilities commenced for more secure surroundings. Optimism returned with some of the citizens over the summer months as they gradually trickled into the town they once called home. As the guard requested Pete's pass, his attention turned toward some of the Negroes that once were held in bondage. With the ruined economy and little money there wasn't a way that they could earn a living and begin a new future. For now they loitered with nothing but time on their hands.

With the sentry's nod of approval, Pete and Katie moved on toward their destination. As he moved the horses to one side of the street to allow the soldiers passage, Pete somberly said, "It's sad and disheartening to see the town in this condition. On any given day when you came here, the streets and businesses were filled with people. I can recall an evening before the war when old Preacher Case came to dinner at Shenandoah. At the time, he said there were about 3,000 people that called Harpers Ferry their home. It was due to the many jobs that were available and the vibrant economy that had drawn so many of them, even from the northern states. Now, look at the place. Even though some have returned, it still appears so lifeless and destitute."

"I know. In June of 1861 after your regiment and the rest of the Confederate army departed, many of the citizens fled out of fear of what the Yankees would do to them. If I were to guess, I would say less than 100 citizens remained in town within the first six months of the war."

Pete joking with Katie, but disguising his true intentions, replied in a most serious tone. "You mean many that were loyal to the North fled? Our boys were ready for a good fight, that's why they enlisted with the fighting 2nd."

Katie quickly turned with a displeased expression covering her face. Her Irish temper flared. "Now just you wait a bloody moment. Our boys..." Her face turned red with anger as Pete laughed. She loudly continued. "How dare you laugh at me Pete Barker? You just hold on a bloody moment and give me the courtesy of listening."

"I am just kidding." Continuing to chuckle, Pete added, "Katie McBride, my you do have a quick temper. "

Katie's eyes were looking at him, but she remained quiet, still quite angry. As Pete turned his attention to directing the horses, he said in a serious tone, "Katie, it was an ugly war, no matter which side you thought was correct. Truly, I am thankful to God you didn't see and hear some of the things that I experienced. I became so depressed. There were times after an engagement I wished and prayed that I would never have been born to witness and be a part of such carnage and horror. Many brave souls fought passionately and died out of deep conviction over the issues they believed to be righteous and just."

Katie listening to Pete sigh turned around and noticed an expression of despair covering his face. Pete continued to express his emotions; "I guess there are times when I feel guilty because I was spared the destiny with death. So many times I witnessed the deaths of so many good men on both sides." Pausing, he continued in a whisper, "Especially in June of 1863."

"Pete please tell me what happened."

"I remember one day in particular when Jonathan and I were scouting during the early morning hours near Kelly's Ford. There were several Yankee cavalrymen who took a shot at us from across the river. Jonathan's horse became nervous and threw him to the ground. As he quietly and motionlessly laid there pretending to be dead, I gave the appearance to the Yankees that I was running away and leaving him. After taking my carbine, I dismounted and quietly hid nearby among some brush. Once the Yankees crossed the ford and dismounted to check Jonathan, he immediately raised to shoot one Yankee while I shot the other from the underbrush. The Yankee that Jonathan shot was already dead, but the one that I shot was severely wounded in the chest."

Tears filled Pete's eyes as he continued, "When I turned him over onto his back, he appeared near his end. He looked up at me and asked as he struggled to breathe." 'Johnnie, can I have some water?' "I said yes. Holding his head in an upright position, I placed the canteen to his mouth. I asked him, how old he was and he replied he was only 15. I asked him how he was able to enlist into the army at such a young age and he replied he had lied. I was puzzled. I asked him why he wanted to do something so dangerous when it wasn't required of him. Struggling to life, he said his mother was very ill and bedridden. The money was needed to pay for her medical expenses and to place food on the table. I asked him why he didn't get a job elsewhere instead of joining the army. Before he could answer his life departed from him. Being a witness to the sad expression that covered his features when he took his last breath was beyond any words that I could express. I felt so guilty and tormented by what I had done. It took me weeks to revive from the experience. All I could think of was his mother receiving the news of his death and the rest of his family having to do without the necessities of life. That action took a terrible toll on me emotionally. Often during the night, even now, I can still see the tormented expression from not only his physical pain but also from the emotional pain that he had failed in his efforts to continue to provide for his family."

Katie knew Pete was still having a difficult time adjusting from his war experiences. Now composed after listening to his testimony, she said in a calm compassionate manner, "I am sorry for my temper." Pausing and giving thought as to what she would say concerning his memories, Katie continued as she looked at him. "It is difficult for many soldiers who fought in the war. I know from what I have seen from you since your return and from the correspondence I received from my mother. Everyone that participated in the conflict is having a difficult time making some kind of readjustments. She informed me that my brother Seamus was hanging out at the local pub until late at night drinking his life away. She's concerned he is becoming too fond of the spirits."

"Thank God I haven't had to rely on that way out."

"What do you mean by that remark?"

"Don't take my remarks wrong. Over the course of the war, I served with God fearing men that wouldn't even think of taking a drink of spirits. But there's something about taking another man's life. It changes you. Once they had taken a life, they began to turn to the stuff in order to escape the guilt. As I just said and know from my own experiences, it was difficult taking the life of another so I know first hand what they had to deal with. The action of destroying another individual makes you think, sometimes hours, days, or months. Something like that dwells on your mind for a long while. But then the more you fight and take a life, your heart and mind become callous, and it becomes a part of your life. It's something that you have to get use to. It's your survival. And the killing and maiming drives you to drink more and more. Whatever it takes to escape the continuous hurt, the deep pain, and sometimes the feeling of unworthiness. As for myself, after the event at Kelly's Ford, I didn't feel I could go on with this kind of life. I suppose I was beginning to think of a way out of this war. I haven't confided in you in order to gain your sympathy, or that you shouldn't scold me for the joke I attempted to play on you earlier."

"How did you deal with taking another person's life?"

"Like many events that have taken place in my life, I've learned all too well how to repress matters and allow them to build up within. After awhile you forget the little things that you've done to another, but always you remember the greater events, always trying to convince yourself that you did what was right. Again for example, the Yankee boy at Kelly's Ford. I didn't know how young the boy was or the reason why he joined the army. I just assumed as most Yanks believed, they fought to free the slaves and abolish our way of life. For me, it was fighting against an invader, protecting my family and home that justified the maiming and killing. I know I have to allow the war to die, but for now the wounds are still fresh."

"It's all right, you needed to speak your heart. You'll feel better within as you allow yourself to get those things out in the open. Life will get better for you in time."

"No Katie, you'll never know what it was like, and I wouldn't want you to."

Leaning toward Pete and placing her hand on his chin, she gently touched his face. Pete turned to look at her. "I don't want to be a part of your life in some things, but in everything. And that includes your struggle in dealing with the hurt, agonizing pain, and memories of the war. Please don't turn me away and shut me out."

"Sometimes it's difficult. It's unbearable. When it's quiet during the night and I lay down to sleep, I begin to think of the war. If I wake up during the middle of the night, it's there, haunting me and digging relentlessly at me like some kind of torture from hell. I try to keep my mind busy, but it always comes back. And I'm sure I am not the only one who is dealing with these feelings."

Katie remained quiet, but concerned. Concerns she had over Pete's emotional status with the war memories and financial problems of keeping Shenandoah out of the hands of the radical county government. Somewhere within, she still felt optimistic that in time everything would work out in its own way by prodding him to speak about his experiences. This was part of her personality.

Once they passed the corner of High Street, Katie noticed the twenty-five building armory complex area. Like the arsenal buildings that were once directly across the street, nothing remained but the charred ruins of what use to be a successful industry. The only symbol that did exist was the old engine house where John Brown and his small party of raiders sought refuge in their attempt to incite insurrection against the Federal government and the state of Virginia. As Pete turned the team of horses along Potomac Street toward the depot, Katie continued to look in the direction of where the old Wager House Hotel once stood. Memories of the brawl between Pete and Billy Smith began to surface in her mind. Katie broke out laughing.

Pete turned to look at Katie, puzzled by the sudden outburst. "What's so funny?"

"Nothing, nothing at all."

"Come on now, nobody just begins to laugh unless something triggers a thought."

"All right I will tell you. I was thinking about the first day that I arrived in town. After depositing my money at the bank, I wanted to have some lunch. I was informed by the bank teller of the meals served at the hotel."

"All right, all right, I know where this conversation is going."

"Oh do you now?"

"Yeah, I remember the first time that we met. It was very peculiar, I must confess." There was a grin covering Katie's face, as she remained silent. Pointing in the direction of the new Shenandoah Hotel, Pete continued. "We are speaking about the afternoon when you and I ended up in the mud puddle. Probably the same one that's still in front of this new inn."

"Yes, I was."

"I remember all too well. I would say we have come along way and been through much since that time, don't you agree?"

"We have. And even though I was so angry with you and could have beaten you with my parasol more then I did, still in spite of it all, I am very grateful and fortunate that I made your acquaintance."

Pete replied in a serious tone. "As I look at that mud puddle, I think of Billy Smith. I don't know if I ever told you or not, but during the fight at Sharpsburg, I saw him."

"No you didn't."

"My regiment, part of General Stuart's division of cavalry was, positioned on the far left near the Potomac protecting General Lee's army. There was a brief lull during the battle. Like many, I took rest near a wooded area behind some of our artillery. As I began to give thought to the battle's continuation and wondering what the outcome would be, I heard a groaning sound coming from the direction of some thickets and underbrush. With my curiosity aroused, naturally I began to investigate. Once I approached the brush and turned some of it back, I recognized a Confederate soldier. His face was covered with black powder mixed with trickles of blood from a gash on his forehead. I really didn't know who it was until I lifted his head and only then did I notice that it was Billy."

"What did he say to you?"

At first Pete didn't answer, it appeared to her that he was caught up in his thoughts. Then he replied without turning to look at her. "Billy knew that he was dying, so he apologized for the many disagreements we had over the past years and asked for forgiveness. His last request, that I wasn't about to refuse, was for me to take a correspondence to be delivered to Jane Powers, the young lady who created the misunderstanding between us in the first place. I promised that I would, and then I watched his chest rise for the last time, and his eyes staring into nowhere. Billy held onto the letter with a tight grip against his heart, almost as if it was the only way in his last moments that he could be close to her. Also, after the fighting, I found out about Thomas, Rebecca's suitor who had been wounded. I wasn't able to fulfill my promise. After Thomas passed on, I returned to Shenandoah to deliver the news personally to Rebecca. I forgot about the letters until the next morning and at that time I gave it to Caroline who promised to deliver it to Jane."

"At least he made peace with God before he took his last breath. He knew you weren't going to turn your back on him."

"Billy suffered greatly. At times he held his stomach with both hands groaning in pain from the wound and at the same time continuing to gasp for air. Like many I have witnessed during battle, it was a horrible sight. Even though we never got along with each other, it still took a lot out of me to be a witness to such suffering. I have always been amazed at the scene when someone was dying; how they had to clear their conscious before passing on. I know what they went through by my own experience after being wounded near Funkstown. It made death seem easier for them as well as possibly myself." Pete paused; Katie noticed tears flowing down his cheek as he continued to speak. "When I see Mother, it won't be easy. I know that she still grieves over Rebecca's death, but so do I. I don't know if it will ever be something that she will ever be able to deal with, or accept, nor for that manner, any of us. The war shouldn't have ever happened."

Katie gently rubbed her hand on his and was touched by Pete's openness and sincerity, loving him all the more.

Chapter 5

It was 4:30 in the afternoon. Pete and Katie were arriving at the railroad depot near the junction of the two rivers. The locomotive whistle was sounding; the eastbound passenger train from Winchester, Virginia was chugging to a stop. Once Pete brought the team of horses to a halt, he jumped from the wagon and assisted Katie to the ground. With anticipation, he walked with Katie along side of the passenger coaches looking toward the window for his mother, Caroline, and Ann. Many thoughts and expectations crossed his mind. Now that Katie was staying at the estate, it might cause great difficulty with his mother and possibly Caroline. Caroline may have changed her views and expressed a sympathetic attitude toward his Mother's point of view, believing Katie was the cause for the destruction of Shenandoah and loss of the family's prosperity.

Meanwhile, Katie faired no better emotionally not knowing what to expect from Caroline since their disagreement last year along the river. As for Elizabeth, she determined the worst, knowing that she possessed an extreme dislike for her. Secretly without Pete's knowledge, Katie already had made her preparations. She decided it wouldn't serve the family's best interest if she resided at Shenandoah should the family be in turmoil and division with her presence. Instead, she would move to Charlestown.

Glancing forward, Pete noticed the conductor of the train helping Caroline from one of the coaches toward the front of the train. Anxiously and without hesitation, Pete advanced quickly toward the train car with Katie still holding to his arm. Once they arrived, Pete noticed his mother and Ann also departing the same car. Pete was taken by Caroline's sad expression knowing that her haunted features reflected the emotions of her heart and mind. He knew it had been extremely difficult not knowing or receiving word from Charles of his whereabouts and welfare. But for now, most of his family was safely home and in his care.

Pete watched and was silent as the Federal sentry asked, "Madam, may I see your pass?"

Caroline quietly complied as she removed the pass from her basket. The sentry closely examined Caroline's physical description written on the back of the pass. He looked up. "I see that you are coming from Winchester? What is the nature of your business in Harpers Ferry?"

"I have returned to Harpers Ferry because this is my home."

"I see that your last name is Barker. Is it possible that you are the wife of Charles Barker?"

"Yes sir, I am."

The soldier pointing to his side said, "Over here. Once I am finished with checking these passes, Captain Brackett, the Provost Marshall of the Harpers Ferry District, I am sure will want to speak with you."

Pete defensively broke Katie's embrace and approached the guard. "She hasn't caused any trouble. Why are you doing this?"

The sentry raised his musket. "Look boy, are you going to give me trouble?"

"No, no, I just don't want my sister-in-law harmed or frightened."

As Pete approached Caroline, the sentry remained silent and didn't challenge him. Without a word, Pete embraced Caroline, kissing her on the cheek. "Caroline, I am so glad to see you."

"Pete, I too, am glad to see you. It's good to be back home even though there might not be much to return to. And of course, having to still deal with these Yankees doesn't make it any easier," Caroline answered softly.

"It's your home so there is something to return to. Several weeks ago, Hayward and I finished building another room onto the cabin. It's small, but big enough for you ladies, and hopefully it will be warm for the winter."

Pete stepped aside facing Ann. His face brightened with a smile as he hugged and kissed his loving niece. "Ann, what can I say? At the age of fifteen, you have grown into a tall, attractive young lady with such remarkable resemblance to your Mother. Countless times I've missed you and prayed for your safety. Now that you are here, I'm thankful to God that he has brought you home to me where I can watch over you until your father returns."

Ann smiled. "I am grateful for your love. It means so much to me and it has helped to sustain me during these trying times."

"I know you are troubled by your father's disappearance, but I believe that someday, your father will return. Your grandfather taught us how to survive. When it is safe, he'll return, but now, it would be too dangerous. We don't want him to be imprisoned like President Davis. Who knows what the government will do with him or those who served in his administration, such as your father."

"I know, it's just not knowing that troubles mother and me," Ann answered as tears filled her eyes.

"I know how you feel. Dealing with the void and the emptiness can be more than you can handle at times. Even though your father and I didn't always see eye to eye on matters, he is still my brother, and he is still a part of my family. I learned a lot about myself while I was away from home. Sometime soon we will sit and speak with each other, and we'll have plenty of time to talk about these matters."

As Pete's eyes looked upon his mother, he noticed that her hair had turned completely gray from its original brown and her facial features had wrinkled considerably. Her eyes were filled with tears as he embraced and held her tightly. As everyone looked on, Pete said in a trembling voice, "Mother, my heart has been constantly troubled since you left Shenandoah knowing the grief you still experience over Rebecca's death and Charles' whereabouts. But now, thank God, I can breathe a sigh of relief knowing that you are home."

Pete looked into his mother's eyes waiting, knowing the words were difficult to express. Elizabeth tried to be optimistic as she spoke. "I know I am returning to a home that doesn't exist and without family members that I love. But I agree, thank God, I have the rest of my family and that's all that I will need."

Katie followed Pete remaining silent with the exception of a cordial expression which was accepted by Caroline and Ann until she came to Elizabeth. Cautiously, and methodically with her words, Katie politely said, "Miss Elizabeth, I am glad that you are home."

Elizabeth was never fond of Katie. From the very beginning of their acquaintance in the summer of 1860, she could never respect nor accept the fact that Katie was from the North. Elizabeth firmly believed, like most citizens from the South, that Katie was one of many who didn't agree with their social views and was possessed with a desire to see change such as the end of slavery, and more control over the rights of a state by the Federal government. More importantly and personally, she was unable to forget the war and

Katie's possible role that led to the destruction of Shenandoah during the spring of 1864. Elizabeth was inflamed at Katie's presence but held her composure. She replied in a cold manner. "Oh, my, dear Katie, how are you? For some unknown reason on the trip home, I knew you would still be here."

"Well Miss Elizabeth, I am glad I didn't disappoint you."

Pete detected the subtle outburst. He quickly and calmly interrupted. "Ladies, ladies, the war is over with. Don't you think that it's time to start over with our lives?"

Elizabeth lost her temper. Some of the other people that were mingling on the railroad station platform as well as the sentry turned to listen to her loud outburst. "How can the war be over with when everything that we owned has been destroyed? Lost! Have you also forgotten that your sister lost her life and your brother can't come home and may also be dead? How! How, can it be over with! You are still like your father. The war didn't change you. Nothing can change you."

Katie was embarrassed by the public spectacle. She became very angry and unleashed her temper. "How in the bloody world"…?

"Stop it! Stop it now," Pete shouted. "The war has ended, it's over. We have to move on with our lives or we'll drown in this hate and bitterness." Pete's feelings were bruised. He realized his mother hadn't changed. The continuation of the war was still a major issue within her heart and mind. He still didn't have the equality or love that his brother enjoyed. Without another word, he took the trunks and began to place them in the wagon, occasionally glancing at the four silent ladies wondering how they would be able to live with each other.

Once Katie, Caroline, and Ann were seated in the bed of the wagon, Pete assisted his mother in the seat next to him. He was still angry and remained silent. With a gesture from the sentry, Pete started the team of horses with the sentry walking alongside the wagon. On the short journey to the Provost Marshall's office on High Street, everyone with the exception of the sentry, was silent, and he was proudly whistling "The Battle Cry of Freedom." Pete believed the only reason the soldier whistled the tune was to either provoke or in hopes of humiliating his family.

Within minutes they arrived at their destination where Pete jumped from the wagon and assisted Caroline, knowing inwardly she was as angry as everyone else was. The sentry politely smiled but was very authoritative when he spoke. "Once you enter the office, don't speak unless you're spoken to. Captain Brackett likes discipline."

Pete felt he was now responsible for Caroline in his brother's absence. "Private, I would like to escort Mrs. Barker, and if need be, represent her since I am a lawyer."

"Well Reb, that's not going to do you much good since you haven't any rights. As you well know, the town of Harpers Ferry is still under martial law, and only military law counts."

"Yes, yes I know, but can't you see that she's frighten. Mrs. Barker has been through a lot lately."

"Haven't we all." Spitting the tobacco juice on the ground, the soldier wiped his mouth. "Come on."

Once the soldier entered the office with Caroline and Pete, there was a clerk sitting behind the desk with a Sergeant nearby. The Sergeant looked at Pete and Caroline with a cold expression. He asked in a sharp, loud tone, "Private, why are you bringing this man and woman here?"

"Well Sergeant, I thought that Captain Brackett might want to speak with the wife of the fugitive Charles Barker. She just arrived on the 4 o'clock train from Winchester."

The Sergeant stepped from behind the wooden railing barrier that divided him from Pete and Caroline. He said in a calmer tone as his eyes continued to look on the two, "Oh, I see. I see." He looked in the direction of the arresting soldier. "Well done Jones. You may be excused."

"Look Sergeant, don't you see that my sister-in-law, Caroline, is scared. As I told Private Jones, Mrs. Barker has been through a lot," Pete said.

Angrily, the Sergeant pointed in Pete's direction as his eyes remained on Caroline. "Shut up or I'm going to throw you into the blasted guardhouse! Understand!"

The Sergeant ripped Caroline's basket from her hands, dumping the contents of a change purse, brush, a few hair pins, and a small wet-plate photograph of Charles and her on the floor. She remained silent, but Pete could tell by the defiant expression covering her face that she was attempting to repress her anger. Pete, too, was very angry at what he believed to be harassment and intimidation. As Pete glanced around, he was sure the

Sergeant wanted Caroline to have time to observe the ball and shackle lying on the floor next to the open rail divider and the shackles that were used to either be placed around both ankles or both hands. On a rack behind the clerk were multiple muskets with bayonets attached. He thought the Sergeant wanted Caroline to see the chalkboard hanging on the wall behind the clerk. Written on it were the many names, offenses, and punishments carried out against offenders.

As the Sergeant began to speak, Captain Brackett and several Corporals entered the front door. Immediately, Captain Brackett recognized Pete. "Well Barker, what are you doing here?"

The Sergeant quickly answered. "Sir, it's Mrs. Barker. That is Mrs. Charles Barker. She just arrived from Winchester."

Surprisingly, the Captain replied. "Oh, I see." Facing Caroline, the officer smiled and continued in a polite tone. "So you are arriving from Winchester, huh?" Rubbing his hand across his bearded face, he looked at Caroline. "Well Mrs. Barker we'll make this as easy as we can. All I need you to do is to tell me where I can find your husband."

"I don't know Captain. I haven't seen him nor heard from him since you Yankees captured Richmond."

"Oh come on now Mrs. Barker, you surely can't expect me to believe what you're telling me, now do you?"

"Believe what you want."

As Captain Brackett walked around Caroline, he said in a serious tone, "Now, I wonder if you were imprisoned for a spell if that might not take the fire out of that disrespectful tongue of yours. And it might also serve to infuriate your husband to the point that once he found out what had happen to you that maybe he just might surrender himself to us in exchange for you."

Pete calmly intervened as he placed his arm around Caroline's shoulders. "Sir, as I said earlier today, no one in the family has heard anything concerning the welfare of my brother."

Pete intentionally lied, but he wasn't ready to release any information that might lead to Charles' possible whereabouts.

The Captain asked the Sergeant, "Who are those people sitting in the wagon?"

"Well sir, that's Barker's mother and niece."

"Bring them in here now and have several of the men go through their trunks!"

With the difficult experience of losing a family member and the loss of Shenandoah, Pete knew his mother wouldn't be able to endure much more of the scrutiny and suspicion that they had lived under for the past three years. Pete tried to earnestly reason with the officer. "Captain Brackett, my mother and niece don't know any more of my brother's whereabouts than his wife or myself. Like many in the Confederate government, he fled fearing reprisal for his role in Jefferson Davis' government. Shenandoah would be the last place he would come to, and didn't your soldiers search the property earlier today?"

"Your brother, who I am sure knows these mountains could hide out in them for quite some time."

"True he could. As far as that goes, you can search them all that you want to, but you're not going to find him. It would be a waste of your time."

A smirk covered the Captain's face as he turned around and relit a cigar from the fire of a candle on the desk. Turning his attention once more to Pete, he smiled. "You know Barker you are right. He would be too smart to return to Harpers Ferry."

The Captain turned his attention to Caroline. "Mrs. Barker where have you been staying these past months?"

"With my parents in New Market, Virginia."

The door opened and a young private from the Provost detail entered with Ann and Elizabeth. Katie followed while several other members of the detachment continued to throw the ladies private possessions along the street, still searching the trunks. Pete turned to glance at Katie. Her features revealed her concern.

Approaching Captain Brackett, Elizabeth asked in a defiant manner, "What is the meaning of all of this!"

"I assume that you are the mother of Charles Barker?"

"Do you know what has happened to my son?"

Quickly Pete said before the officer had the chance to answer, "Captain, my mother believed that you asked her to come into this office because you might have had some information on my brother. That proves my point that none of us know of his whereabouts."

The officer was hesitant as he rubbed his beard. Finally after taking a deep sigh, he replied. "I am still not convinced. Maybe it was all a good show, but for now, you may all go."

By the time Pete and the ladies walked from the Provost Marshall's office, the privates had completed their duty and were throwing the clothing back into the trunks. Pete assisted the ladies to their seats and then assisted his mother onto the seat next to him. Captain Brackett stood quietly watching at the entrance to the office, smiling and continuing to puff on his cigar. Quietly, as Pete turned his attention in the direction of the officer, he noticed he was writing something on a piece of paper and giving it to another soldier, who hurried toward his horse.

Chapter 6

As they turned west on Shenandoah Street, Elizabeth glanced around the town and noticed the changes that had taken place since she departed the area in the summer of 1864. Now with her emotions calm, but unapologetic for her earlier outburst at the train depot, she said in a somber tone, "The town has really changed. It appears lifeless, nothing like it use to be when the streets were full of people mingling and speaking of the latest news. Even as unbearable as the clanging noise of the machinery at the armory could be, I must confess, I miss it. And especially Mr. Frankel standing in front of his store, as he would always do waving and speaking a kind word with the citizens walking along the street. Anymore, the town is no more than a bunch of empty run-down houses between two rivers."

"It's going to be like this until some of the citizens decide to return. Since the end of the war, I've noticed a gradual increase in the population, but I don't believe the town will ever be like it was before the war."

"What makes you say that? All things are possible."

"I really don't feel the government will ever rebuild the armory and arsenal. As you know, it was the only one in the South before the war began. And since the rebellion, it will be a long time before they will trust us enough again to build an armory and arsenal. Now that Lincoln is gone, the Johnson administration will do everything within its power to make the South pay for the war many times over; trust me, you'll see."

Now with her return, Elizabeth's first intention was to begin the process of planting seeds of doubt, mixed with half-truths to discourage the continuation of Pete and Katie's relationship. With her hazel eyes watching Pete, Elizabeth quickly changed the conversation. "My son, why are you still so possessed by that girl? Hasn't she caused us enough grief, enough loss of property and possessions, and now who knows what she'll attempt to do next to destroy this family."

"Mother, how many times will we continue to argue over whether Katie was spying during the war or not, or if she was responsible for the loss of Shenandoah. The conflict is over, it makes no difference now. And if she was, what could you possibly do to unravel all of the loss and pain that we have incurred," Pete answered in a frustrated tone.

"She was our enemy," Elizabeth snapped, "and as far as I'm concerned she still is our enemy. Because of her we have nothing, we've lost everything. We are financially ruined. Penniless! And besides, let me ask you this question. Is your family of greater importance or is she?"

Pete remained silent. As he gave thought, he knew that his mother was quite angry and unwilling to release her burden. Her behavior was unexpected, but to some degree, he attempted to understand her pain and anguish. One time of day, the family was quite wealthy from breeding horses and raising cattle for the War Department of the United States Government. They had been accustomed to enjoying great influence within the community of the lower Shenandoah Valley. Now, all that influence had vanished, gone with only memories of yesterday. Pete's thoughts continued. Not only had it been tough on the family losing its economy and the death of his young sister Rebecca, but now the attempt has to be made to save Shenandoah from confiscation by the radical county government officials.

As the wagon slowly moved along, Katie was quietly sitting directly across from Caroline. Even though she wanted to speak to her once best friend, she felt awkward knowing the toil and division the war had taken on their relationship. Katie missed the closeness that Caroline and she had once shared and cherished. In many ways, their personalities and interests were alike, and in some things identical. There had to be some way, she thought, of resurrecting the trust and love they shared as good friends. Katie's desire was to make the attempt, but she knew it would take time. Knowing that Caroline had been traumatized by the effects of the war, Katie would have to begin the relationship fresh by gradually winning over Caroline's trust and love, building stone by stone upon what was left of the foundation.

Katie remained silent until the party reached the outskirts of town. She had been pondering on where to begin a conversation with Caroline. Katie was certain with everything that Caroline had been through, she was depressed. With no word from Charles, it just compounded her fears, anxieties, and doubts of his welfare in a greater way. If they were going to dwell within the same home, they would have to come to some understanding. Katie greatly wanted the opportunity to begin a conversation.

Suddenly, the front right wagon wheel hit a hole in the dirt road. The wagon jolted to one side. Ann screamed as she clutched the wooden seat that her uncle was sitting on in order to support herself from falling off the seat. Caroline and Katie simultaneously grabbed Ann and supported her from injury. It was the opportunity Katie had been waiting for in order to break the stalemate. Caroline was the first to react. "My, child are you all right?"

Ann replied as she examined herself for injury. "I am just a little bit shaken, but to answer your question, yes mother, I'm all right."

Katie added as she too leaned forth to examine Ann, "No you're not. You've cut your finger, it's bleeding. I have a hankerchief in my basket."

Taking the cloth, Katie wrapped it around Ann's finger and applied some pressure to stop the bleeding.

Caroline was touched by Katie's compassion. "Thank you, Katie."

"It's quite all right. I was concerned and wanted to help." Noticing tears filling Caroline's eyes, Katie continued, "Caroline, Ann's going to be all right."

"I know, I know, but I should have reacted immediately."

"Mother, I'm all right. Look, the bleeding has stopped." Ann added in a concerned tone.

Caroline was frustrated and displeased with her actions. It reflected in her tone of voice as she answered. "Oh, my child my mind has been elsewhere. I must apologize to you; I haven't been myself for some months now. For too long I feel that I have neglected you."

"We all know the strain you have been through with father missing, and the suffering Grandfather and Grandmother Schultz have endured with the loss of their estate. Mother, it's all right."

As Caroline wiped her eyes with a handkerchief, Katie said, "Listen to your daughter. Everyone has suffered in some way from the horrors of this war. It's understandable that your concern for your family and Charles come first. No one likes the unknown, or the unexpected, especially after the conflict that we've endured. Your feelings and emotions are to be expected and we understand.

We'll help you in any way we can, but we must hold together in order to have success."

There was a faint smile covering Caroline's face. "Katie, you always did have the right words that brought comfort. You are such an optimist."

"I have tried to have a heart for others. It is the only way I know how to live my life."

The Katie that Caroline was witnessing wasn't the same type of person that she had envisioned on the journey from Winchester. She believed Katie would still possess animosity toward her after their disagreement along the river during the summer of 1863. After Katie's insinuations over Elizabeth's revelation and intentions for the real reason for turning over control of Shenandoah to Charles, it had sparked a heated argument between the two ladies, and was left unresolved. Today was the first time in almost two years they had seen each other. After that particular event along the river, Caroline really didn't see the possibility Katie and she could ever enjoy a relationship in the future. Now, after seeing Katie, Caroline continued to experience condemnation within her heart over the attitude and behavior that she had expressed in relationship to her that particular day. Caroline had perceived the truth of Elizabeth's intentions, but out of pride she attempted to protect her family. She knew the reality was that Elizabeth was just using Charles for her own purpose and had no intentions of ever surrendering full control of Shenandoah. In her observations, Katie was no different than the person that she had enjoyed a relationship with at the outset of the war. Pride ruled in Caroline's heart and for now she would repress the thoughts and emotions.

Chapter 7

On the journey to Shenandoah, occasionally Pete would turn around and notice his mother looking intently at the countryside. It appeared clean of existence. What were once tall cornfields, abundant orchards, and thriving farms were now totally devastated by the war. Many of the trees were barren of branches that had either been used for firewood by the soldiers of the blue and gray, or destroyed by battle. Pete knew the heaped charred wood at several locations along the road was once where someone called home. He knew all of these scenes painted a picture of horror and fear within his mother's heart. Still she kept her thoughts a mystery. From her youth, this area was where she had always called home. At 55 years of age, this is where she planned to live the rest of her life.

Pete and his family came within view of Shenandoah. He turned to notice his mother's reaction to the estate's appearance. She was quiet, though her facial features told a different story. They were troubled and appeared tense. Pete also remained quiet but continued to watch her as he brought the team of horses pulling the wagon to a halt at the entrance to the long lane. Pete knew she would become emotional and was attempting to prepare for such an event by rehearsing the words he would speak in order to comfort her. To his surprise, his mother was quiet, but he noticed the tears filling her eyes. He turned around and looked in Caroline and Ann's direction. Both were tearful. Turning his attention toward Katie, their eyes met. He noticed her concerned expression, knowing that she was sharing their pain and anguish.

As they continued forward at a slow pace, Elizabeth thought of the glory days of Shenandoah when she would socialize with some of the most prominent people in the Shenandoah Valley, inviting them to events that she hosted. The Barkers, she thought, were a family that everyone looked up to for leadership, in the county, and for their political guidance. Now, with the conclusion of the war, she feared life would never be the same again with the gracious awards that once came with the prestige of enjoying such dominance. Her pride was her strength, she thought, and again she would attempt to control events such as she enjoyed before the war. This time instead of using her oldest son Charles, she would attempt to manifest her power, strength, and influence through her younger son, Pete.

After Pete and his family arrived at the cabin, he quietly assisted the ladies from the wagon. As he did so, Hayward paused from his labor on the house. He had been laying some of the rock and the first row was now completed. He walked over and greeted everyone and then assisted Pete with the trunks. As they walked toward the cabin, Hayward curiously said in his graveled voice, "Everybody is quiet. I'se see that things didn't goes as dey's ought."

"No, they didn't. As I knew before her arrival, my mother is still fighting the war and holds contempt for Katie. She still believes Katie was responsible for the destruction of Shenandoah last year by the Yankees."

The two men paused as Hayward turned around with his dark eyes on Pete. "What matters is, does yose believe that Misse Katie did that thing? If ya does, den yose mus' make the thing right or there's always gonna be that hangin' over ya." Hayward always had a good perception of life and he himself had lived accordingly. Pete respected his opinion, but this time, he remained silent.

Pete noticed that his mother paused and didn't enter the cabin such as the other ladies. He placed the trunk he was carrying on the porch while Hayward entered with his items. Pete knew that his mother was in thought as he watched her quietly gazing in the direction where the house was under construction. He had some idea what she was thinking about and the emotions that she was experiencing. He approached from behind and said in an optimistic tone of voice, "It will take time, but Hayward and I will rebuild the house just the way that you remember."

Elizabeth continued to look at the foundation site as she spoke softly in a somber tone. "Do you know how long it took my father to build the house?"

"No, you nor father ever said. But I'm sure it took some time."

"It took six years."

Elizabeth paused and turned once more, walking to the far end of the porch to get a better view of the foundation where the mansion once stood. After taking a deep sigh, she raised her arms in a token of frustration, and continued in an angry tone. "Six years, and in less than an hour it burned to the ground. Not only was the house destroyed, but all of my family treasures were too. It was a horrible experience. The Yankees wouldn't let us remove any of our valuables, especially the items of the most important, such as my father and mother's portrait that hung for so many years in the library. My grandmother's diary that she kept during the Revolution of '76 and her opal broach that I cherished, all of it gone." Elizabeth pointed toward the cabin. "And that girl you think that you're so in love with may, and in all probability, had something to do with our loss. But you're blinded by your feelings for her. Well, the rest of us can see right through her, and we know different."

"Once and for all, when I have the chance, I will speak with Katie and once I do, this matter will be resolved."

"Do you really think she is going to admit to you that she was spying for the Union and passing information to them. No, she won't make that kind of mistake, believe me. Katie isn't a fool! She'll continue to feed you lies just like always and become angry accusing you of unfaithfulness if you are persistent for the truth."

Pete's thoughts returned to the time when Katie and he were on Short Hill Mountain overlooking the Potomac. It was last year after her escape from confinement at Winchester. He asked if she was really spying for the Union since that was the reason for her imprisonment. Her reply was, "Would it make any difference between us if I was?" Since that time when those words continued to surface in his mind, he attempted to rationalize his convictions believing that she wasn't capable of committing such a role.

Today after Hayward's comments and until he could attain the truth Pete pleaded his defense of Katie. "Mother, I know that you want to blame someone for the destruction of Shenandoah, and Katie is the most obvious since she remained loyal to the Union. Charles and you had your suspicions of her involvement with passing information, but you know that it was common practice on both sides."

"Then you do have your suspicions?"

"I have my convictions."

"Well enough for now, but trust me, she was the one who was responsible. I just hope she didn't dig out of you information that caused the death of many of our fine Virginia boys who gallantly gave their lives for a cause that was worth their effort."

After Elizabeth entered the cabin and glanced about its interior, many memories surfaced in her mind recalling the life that she lived within its walls during her youth while her father built the mansion. Looking around the cabin, the first recollection was the huge stone fireplace that was on the back wall. At one time its log mantel was covered with family heirlooms such as her grandmother's silver pitcher that dated back before the American War for Independence. Another precious item crowning the center of the mantel was her mother's wooden carved serving tray with her mother's wedding date that was made by her father as an anniversary gift. To Elizabeth, the fondest memories were in the evenings after the chores were finished when the family would sit together and speak of their hopes and dreams."

As Elizabeth continued to quietly gaze, the gentleness of a smile covered her face. She visualized her mother and herself making candles and listening to her father reading passages of scripture from the books of Matthew and John of the New Testament. Always, they would pick a verse and expound on what it meant to them personally.

Elizabeth gazed upward. The ceiling in the living area was high with the exception of the loft. There, Elizabeth stared for the longest time remembering some of the Christmases when she would attempt to peer down into the main quarters to watch her mother and father place her presents under the tree. She was always caught in the act, never being successful. The small windows she thought never allowed for much light and would cause her to be depressed during the gray winter months. This is the reason why she requested her father when he was building Shenandoah to add many huge windows.

As Elizabeth walked around, she glanced at the two small bedchambers to her left but didn't enter either one. Turning in the opposite direction she noticed the entranceway to the room that Hayward and Pete had recently built. As she entered the room, it was larger then the other rooms with a stone fireplace in the middle of the rear wall. On the opposite wall, a new bed, which was recently constructed, was adorned with new feather pillows and a multiple colored patchwork quilt that Katie had sewn. The floors creaked as she walked but for now it would have to do for shelter with winter nearing. She walked from the room. "If I may ask Pete, where will you be staying?"

"Hayward and I have fixed up one of the old slave quarters. It will be our home."

"You can't stay there."

"Mother, there won't be room here for Hayward and myself. The new room is for you, the other two are for Katie and Caroline." Pausing, he pointed upward, "The loft will give Ann plenty of room."

Elizabeth shook her head in frustration. "That girl can not stay in this house with me!"

"For as long as I am here, so shall she be with me. If she can't stay, neither can I."

Within, Elizabeth was inflamed with anger. All that she could do was just stare at her son with an expression of defiance knowing that for now she would have to learn to make the adjustment.

Chapter 8

On the outside of the cabin, Katie was walking around the foundation examining the labor that Hayward had accomplished while Pete and herself were in town. She could tell by the careful carved placement of the rock that Hayward was meticulous in his craft. As she continued to walk around the premise, the coolness of the late afternoon caused Katie to cover her arms with her blue shawl. With interest, she examined the area where the picturesque multiple-colored rose garden once blossomed its beauty. She heard a voice from behind her.

"One time of day, the most beautiful roses in the county could be found growing in this garden."

Katie turned and recognized Caroline. She answered as she slowly approached. "Yes Caroline, I agree with you." Pausing and quickly glancing at the garden where weeds and growth had overrun the area, Katie carefully chose her words, continuing, "I remember the first time I had the pleasure of visiting Shenandoah. The many-colored roses were in full blossom, giving the house and grounds a rare and unique appearance."

"We can thank old Jeremiah for the outward appearance of what the estate use to look like. He would spend long hours working around the property with many creative ideas. At one time, Mother Elizabeth would give him instructions concerning the garden designs around the house. After awhile, she trusted his judgment and allowed him to design and plant what he imagined," Caroline replied as a subtle grin covered her face.

"Maybe it can be like that again someday."

"No, I don't think so. There is only one Jeremiah, and he's probably dead by now." Pausing briefly, Caroline laughed.

"What is so funny?"

"I was just remembering the very first day that Ann and I attempted to give you your first lesson at sidesaddle riding," Caroline said as she brushed her hair to the side. "You were so frightened."

"A lady from Boston isn't necessarily subjected to riding a horse. And yes, it was quite different from living in Boston where you are escorted in a carriage everywhere that you want to go."

"Why don't we ride along the river? We still have about an hour of sunlight left. Besides, it might take my mind off some of my problems and give me an opportunity to see what the old place still looks like."

Katie agreed as Caroline and she departed for the three-sided shelter where the horses were stabled.

As Katie and Caroline rode across Barker's Ridge at a trot, Katie warned her friend of the fire pits that were dug during Federal and Confederate occupation of the estate. Once they crossed the crest of the ridge, Caroline's long blond hair began to blow in her face from the breeze coming off the river. As she brushed her hair to the side, she noticed the tall grass as far as the eye could see. Here on the southern side of the estate, the fences had been dismantled and used by the soldiers for firewood and where the potato field was once, it had surrendered to underbrush and growth, vanishing like the rest of the garden area.

Caroline attempted to visualize the vast herd of cattle and the many horses that roamed freely across these pasturelands. She turned to her right where a vast acreage of land was basically flat. It was the scene of many equestrian tournaments. Often, large gatherings of visitors and friends would appear to exhort their favorite horse and riders onto victory. She remembered the last horse race that was held at the estate. It had been a warm, sunny, spring afternoon in 1860 when the family had invited a number of prestigious families from across the lower and upper region of the Valley. After a social period and a barbecue of beef, the men mounted their horses to compete in the racing tournament. As she sat with Mother Elizabeth and the Russells of Turneysville, she cheered her husband, Charles, on to victory. She could still visualize the excited expression covering his features, just as if it were yesterday. Now, as she looked around the area, there was nothing left but wide-open space, which appeared lifeless with the exception of a few rabbits running through the tall grass.

Caroline remained silent as the two ladies trotted to the next elevation, which was known as Applegate Ridge, named after Elizabeth's grandmother. Once there, Caroline and Katie brought their horses to a halt. The sun was setting along the western horizon. Katie admired the beauty of the wide-open country with the river snaking along the mountains in the background. Katie said in a serene voice, "During my life I have had the opportunity to travel and witness many places of splendor and beauty, but none of those regions can compare to the majesty of Shenandoah, even though it has been shattered by war."

At first Caroline didn't answer but just gazed. Breaking her silence, she softly answered, "It's still difficult to see the estate in this condition and to know what you once possessed was gone."

"I know, but isn't a relationship with someone the most important, and their life spared from such horrible conflict greater than all of this?"

"Yes, I agree. Having your loved one home with you is the most important. For Ann and me, it's been very difficult with the disappearance of Charles. Shenandoah appears lifeless without him." Caroline paused; tears filled her eyes. She continued, "Who knows if he will be able to come home to me, or if he is still alive. It's the unknown that's difficult for me to deal with. I would feel better about the whole thing if there was just some way that he would let me know of his welfare. I could hold on. I just don't know how much longer I can go through this ordeal." Pausing and taking a deep breath, Caroline continued in a broken voice. "And then too, it's difficult for Ann. She hides her feelings and emotions when she is with me because she knows that it will cause me to become emotional. Although, in the quiet of the night, I've often heard her sobbing in her room."

"I, too, share your concern for Ann. I hope you won't take this in the wrong way, but over the years I've loved her as if she were my own child. There is something about her sincerity and innocence that allows me to be close to her."

"No, I'm not offended. I know how she feels about you. She is the best thing that happened to Charles and me."

The ladies dismounted and allowed their horses to graze on the meadow. Silently, they walked along the tall grass. Caroline looked toward the mighty Shenandoah River. "I can still remember Charles and I occasionally riding out here at this time of day. We shared our thoughts, dreams, and even differences of opinion. It was just good to have some privacy."

"You are much like me in that way."

Caroline turned to gaze in the direction of the glowing sun dropping behind the dense woods in the distance. "In many ways we are alike. I guess that is why we were attracted to each other and became such close friends."

"I agree; we share much the same interest." Suddenly, the thought surfaced when Pete and she were escaping from pursuit by Daniel. She remembered the conversation they shared as they were resting on the mountain trail after ascending Short Hill Mountain. Pete had informed her that Caroline really didn't believe that she was a spy for the Federal army or responsible for the family's misfortune of losing Shenandoah. If there was any lingering differences on Caroline's part, she wanted to resolve them. This would be the opportunity while they were alone. It would be important to her if there were any chance that they could pick up the pieces of their broken relationship and make the attempt to restore their friendship. Katie had cherished the sisterly love that Caroline and she had enjoyed. Over the past year with their separation and the conflict, Katie had felt the void of its absence. She continued speaking with passionate emotion. "Last year Pete helped me to escape from prison in Winchester."

"In prison? For what?"

"For spying."

"All of this time, was I wrong about you?"

"No, no, you were not. I was visiting with Miss McDonald and her sister when I was arrested at their home. The Confederate Provost Marshall drew his allegations on a visit that I had paid the previous evening when I visited the camp of the 1st Virginia Cavalry, Pete's old regiment."

"Why, why did you go there?" Caroline asked angrily.

"I went there only with the intention of finding out some information from some of the soldiers concerning Pete's death. That's all. The next thing I know, I'm in jail and William Pierce shows up to escort me back to Richmond. It's difficult for me to say this, but it doesn't stop there. He tried to have his way with me. When I wouldn't submit, he abused me physically."

"I never did trust William. It would be just like him to do something that desperate."

"Caroline you must believe that I wasn't spying and had nothing to do with your loss."

"How does Pete feel?"

"It's the one thing we don't talk about."

Caroline paused for a while and continued to look at the river. Finally, she turned. "Katie, I believed then and I still do that you were not involved with the destruction of Shenandoah. Today, I'll stand by my beliefs regardless of what anyone else might believe."

Katie breathed a sigh of relief. It was her intention to continue the conversation as she folded her arms. "That's not all. After a long ride, we paused along a trail on the mountain. Pete told me some very important information that I've held close to my heart for these past months concerning you."

"What did he say?"

"After we had our difference along the river and lost contact over who was really in charge of Shenandoah, Pete told me that you still had old Jeremiah keeping an eye on me. Of course not out of suspicion, but out of concern. You wouldn't believe the hope those few words gave me. I have held them close to my heart all these months."

Caroline turned to face Katie, pausing to consider the right words to say. She knew within her heart she wanted to continue the friendship she had missed over the previous years. Caroline had enjoyed the closeness of their relationship and experienced the loneliness of their separation. It could be part of a new beginning. Caroline wanted to be honest with Katie. "It's true; it's all true. From the very beginning, I knew there was something different about you that my other friends didn't possess. Katie, I am not the kind of person that just allows anyone to walk into my life. Maybe it was your sincerity or openness, I am not sure, but there was a difference. Once Charles became involved with President Davis and his government, he believed that it would be too much of a risk if we continued our friendship."

"Then he was concerned that I was spying and would pass on any information you inadvertently gave me."

"That's right, he was just being cautious and protective. I understood and respected his feelings so I did become somewhat concerned knowing your views about the war and that you, too, had a brother fighting for the North. Therefore, I was always finding myself guarding what I said during a conversation with you."

"So, Charles really believed that I was spying."

"Oh yes. He did. Matter of fact, when we were in Richmond, he insisted that we not maintain contact and break off our friendship." Caroline raised her arms in the air and became frustrated. "That was difficult for me to accept. I was broken by his persistence."

Katie continued to search for the truth now that Caroline was opening up. "Pete believed Charles was applying pressure to you about our friendship."

"Katie, I am sorry for the stiffness and coldness that I showed you, but I truly believed I had to be loyal to my husband's request and I did so out of my love for him. You must understand my marriage and family was placed in jeopardy." Caroline took Katie by her hands "Can you ever forgive me, I was so ever wrong."

"All of us must be willing to put the war and the emotions that it caused behind us. It will be difficult for some such as Miss Elizabeth, but in our case, it's a blessing."

Both Caroline and Katie smiled knowing that their best days together in their friendship were still ahead of them. In spite of the hardships, tribulations, and difficulties that they might endure, both believed within their hearts that they would find strength and endurance. Their bond as friends would become cemented in the love that they knew still flourished.

Chapter 9

It was early morning. The sun had risen and Pete was standing on the front porch of the cabin while the ladies remained inside preparing breakfast. Glancing, he noticed Hayward at the stable tending to several of the horses. He would be departing to the river to load rock on the wagon for the continuing construction of the family's home. As he turned, he continued to lean against one of the wooden porch supports. His concentration wasn't on the Union cavalry patrol heading east in the direction of Harpers Ferry but distant in thought concerning the answer for paying the delinquent debt that the family owed on Shenandoah.

Pete's thoughts consumed him on the presentation for Randolph Larson, President of the Jefferson Trust Bank in Charlestown. The family had carried out its financial business with this bank before the war and enjoyed a prosperous relationship with its president who was also a social friend. Often, Mr. Larson and his wife Pauline attended the social events hosted by the Barker family. Charles served on the bank's Board of Directors before the war.

Pete had his suspicions of the Larson's loyalties to the Southern cause. For one thing, they didn't allow their son, Lucas to fight for the Confederacy like many of the families living in the county. Instead they sent him to Pittsburgh to escape forceful enlistment. Mr. Larson did not support Vice President Breckinridge during the 1860 election for President of the United States, but instead he cast his allegiance to Stephen Douglas from Illinois.

Pete continued to ponder on the loyalties of Mr. Larson. It was known throughout the area and the rest of the South that no one that was loyal or sympathized with the Southern cause was able to vote, teach school, and hold political office. More important, the radical government officials loyal to the Union would have disqualified any prominent position such as a bank president where one held the responsibility over the monetary funds within the county from someone of Southern Loyalties. Hopefully, Mr. Larson if he was truly as Pete suspected, a Union loyalist, would display a heart of compassion such as Abe Lincoln had desired to promote throughout the South if he had lived.

If that option failed, then there was also Katie's suggestion of visiting her parents in Boston and possibly securing their assistance. He still maintained his doubts since most of the majority of the citizens living in the North that had loved ones who perished, or were wounded and missing, still harbored resentment over their loss. Katie's parents were probably like many, and didn't feel any different, desiring some kind of punishment enacted against those who fought and governed the rebellion. He still had some options, but few. First he thought he needed to inform his mother and Caroline about the debt against the property and prepare them for the worst that might befall them should he exhaust all of his options.

Pete's mind turned toward thoughts of how he would approach his mother and Caroline. The $2,500 debt was a lot of money for a family that was financially ruined. Even if they raised the funds, the Radicals would continue to cause their life to be miserable in spite of their compliance to their authority. If Katie's assumption was correct concerning the Radicals confiscating the estate for their own desire and financial prosperity, then there might not be much that he could accomplish even though he had been educated as an attorney prior to the war. He knew since the conclusion of the conflict and the formation of the new state of West Virginia, which Jefferson County was a part, the laws were different from the commonwealth laws of the state of Virginia. One consideration if everything else failed, he thought, would be, to sell some of the estate to raise the funds. It might not be possible even under the best conditions to maintain nor financially provide for such a mass amount of property. With the slaves receiving their freedom, labor would be costly until they could negotiate and possibly receive a government contract as before the war. The Federal government might refuse to accept or allow a family who patronized the Confederate government and fought against its army any chance to regain its business.

Pete's thoughts were interrupted as the door to the cabin opened with Katie standing at the entranceway. Pete turned. "Is breakfast ready?"

Katie noticed the despondent look covering Pete's face. She closed the door and approached. Touching his arm with her hand, she said in a concerned tone, "I know what is bothering you. You're thinking about going to see Mr. Larson today and you sense failure. And not only that, but also telling Caroline and Miss Elizabeth."

"It must be done and there is no hiding from the truth. I've tried for as long as I can to avoid breaking the news to them because I know what it will do to my mother. Shenandoah has always been her home and property. She hasn't known any other place."

"It surprises me she hasn't said anything about it all. Surely Miss Elizabeth must have known there were back taxes and that they hadn't been paid in the last two years."

"Well, my mother is the type that doesn't like distressing news and if she feels that it is coming, she will avoid a confrontation with it for as long as she can. She doesn't deal with matters good when she isn't able to control the situation. Unfortunately, in life we can't always have things go our own way."

Katie's tearful eyes met his. "Does all of this mean that we will have to postpone our marriage?"

The words were difficult to speak because Pete knew the dissatisfaction that it would cause. Marriage and a family was something Pete and Katie had been expecting and planning. Now with the current circumstances he knew all of their plans would change, and for how long, Pete wasn't certain. Until their life could have some stability, it wouldn't be using wisdom entering into a life-long relationship not knowing where your home might be or how you were going to support a family.

Pete placed his hands on Katie's shoulders and replied in a calm and assuring tone. "Katie, my love, I strongly feel that it wouldn't benefit us to marry until this matter is resolved. I don't know what's going to happen with us possibly losing the estate. This was where I hoped to build us a home and raise our family, but now I don't know what to expect."

"Somewhere in my heart I knew that this would happen. It's just like the war, something always arises to divide us and prevent us from being together," Katie replied in a quivering tone.

"I know that it hurts and you feel the anguish but I promise it's only temporary, not permanent. We'll still have our family just as we had planned. Besides, the most important consideration is that we love each other, and there's nothing on this earth that will stand in the way of those feelings." Pausing and gazing into Katie's eyes, he spoke in a reassuring tone. "It's not like the war where there weren't many options and I was always finding some reason to resist your love. As I said that day along the river when you returned from Boston, I'll say it again to give you reassurance, we will never be separated again, I promise."

As Caroline opened the door, Pete and Katie's eyes continued to meet. Katie took heart in the words Pete spoke, trusting him.

Caroline smiled and cleared her throat. She noticed the sadden expressions as Pete and Katie turned their attention in her direction. Not wanting to intrude, she said, "Breakfast is ready." Then she returned inside closing the door behind her.

Pete remained silent as his eyes looked into Katie's. He ran his fingertips across her cheek, gently kissing her.

Chapter 10

As the family sat at the table, the fire was crackling in the fireplace, giving off warmth as discussion centered on the estate. Pete was sharing with his family the efforts that had been accomplished since Hayward and he had returned from Maryland at the conclusion of the war. Most of the family was talkative but Elizabeth quiet. Her expression was somber and reserved. As Pete glanced in her direction, he noticed that her mind was elsewhere. He knew living in the cabin was degrading for a lady of her stature and was causing her great anxiety and depression. Thus far it had been difficult for all of them to try and readjust to the style of life that had been dealt to them by the consequences of war. Though now, there was the opportunity to develop and create a new beginning without the possibility that this event could ever happen again.

Ann was dominating the conversation at the table. She was reminiscing of the times she and her mother would ride to Bolivar Heights and watch the sunrise between the mountains at Solomon's Gap. "I know it troubles all of us to return home and see what life has done to us but thanks to you Mother, I am attempting to deal with my feelings concerning our hardship and troubles."

Caroline somewhat bewildered asked, "What do you mean?"

"You remember before the war, you and I use to take morning rides along Bolivar Heights. I remember one morning how you had such a peaceful expression on your face. It wasn't like you had a care in the world. I made a remark concerning your expression and you explained to me that this was where you found solitude and comfort. You continued by explaining to me that I was too young to understand the problems of adults. Now that I am almost 16, I have a greater appreciation for what you might have been experiencing during those times." Ann continued as Caroline's eyes brightened. "This morning I rode over to the heights and it was as if all of my problems didn't exist. As I watched the sun rising in the gap, I experienced some peace in my life and it gave me time alone to reflect on my life and the hope of a future."

"Are you suggesting that I should practice what I preach?"

"Maybe Ann is right," Elizabeth replied as she stared at both of them, "You should go with her just like you use to. You two need time alone. Haven't you been through enough with Charles' absence and Rebecca's death? Not to say what the blasted Yankees did to your parents' property?"

Caroline took a deep sigh as she clutched both hands around the tin cup that was filled with coffee. Looking at it, she lifted her head and looked at Ann. "Yes, you're right, maybe I should practice what I preach. It might be good for all of us."

Pete glanced at Katie sitting across the table. From her troubled expression, he knew the news concerning the debt on the estate had been delayed for too long. It was time to tell his mother and Caroline about the visit from Mr. Brackett and the amount of the debt. The news would destroy the only peace and contentment that the ladies had found since their return yesterday. It was too serious of an issue to delay any longer. Everyone looked on silently as Pete stood and pushed back his chair.

"Pete, you are quiet," Elizabeth said in a serious tone. "After all of these years, I know by your troubled expression, there is something wrong."

All Pete could do was silently gaze at his mother and know the news was going to cause her great emotional trauma. He answered in a calm tone. "Yes, I am afraid there is something wrong, and what I have to say is going to affect everyone sitting at this table."

Caroline, concerned that he had received news of Charles and had been withholding it from her added in a nervous tone, "Please, what is it? Tell us the truth."

Pete took a deep sigh. He attempted to repress his nervousness. "Yesterday we had a visitor from Shepherdstown, a Mr. C. L. Smith."

With her face suddenly turning red and features tense, Elizabeth was burning with anger. "Ah yes, I remember that traitor. He claimed to be a friend of the family, but during the election of 1860, he suddenly turned against Charles and attempted to undermine and manipulate the election in this county. That's why Breckinridge couldn't carry the county because of the lies that he spread. What does he have to do with all of this anyway?"

Pete walked toward the fireplace to pour more coffee. "Well, now, Mr. Brackett is a member of the Board of Supervisors. He showed up here with a cavalry escort yesterday morning to inform us that we haven't paid taxes on the property since 1863. Unless we raise $2,500 before the end of the month, then Shenandoah will be sold."

Elizabeth jumped to her feet. "No! They can't do this to us. Haven't they punished us enough by burning our home and destroying our business? Now they want to take what little bit we have left. Our property!"

Caroline hid her face within her hands sobbing. Katie and Ann attempted to comfort her.

Pete gestured with his hands, "We still have some time."

Elizabeth fired back. "Well, what are we going to do?"

"This morning I'm going to see Mr. Larson at the bank and try to persuade him to give us the loan."

"I don't trust him either," Elizabeth snapped. "Once the war began, he wouldn't take a stand for the Southern cause when it came time to choose sides. He's a loyalist!"

"I know, but we must try."

"Do you have any other ideas?" Elizabeth asked.

"Yes I do. If I'm not able to secure a loan at the bank, then Katie and I are leaving tomorrow afternoon for Boston."

"How will a trip to Boston help us? I don't understand," Caroline said in an astonished tone.

"As you know before the war, my father was and still is the president of Citizens Trust Bank," Katie answered in an optimistic tone. "I was hoping that maybe he would be willing to help us with a loan or could place us in contact with someone that could do so. I know the odds are against us but we have to try if you want to hold onto Shenandoah."

Elizabeth said as she shook her head in frustration and loudly answering, "No, no, no, I don't think so. The Yankees have done enough to ruin our life, we will get along just fine without their charity."

"But the war is over. There is no need to continue the hatred and animosity. Can't we make the effort to live in peace?"

"Hatred! Animosity! After all that my family has been through. The death of my beloved daughter! My son can't return home and he might even be dead! Plus the loss of everything that I own! Hatred! Animosity! You're going to try and tell me that I am not entitled to feel this way. How dare you!"

Elizabeth approached Katie with her right hand raised to strike her cheek, but Pete stepped in between them. With his eyes glaring at his mother, he warned, "No, you will not strike her." Choosing his words, Pete continued, "Do you feel you're the only one that feels the loss of Rebecca?" Elizabeth remained quiet as Pete continued. "Well you're not. Everyone in the room, with the exception of Katie, knows the void that it has caused in our lives. She was my only sister whom I loved in spite of her faults and sometimes outright bitterness. And as for Charles? No we didn't always agree on matters, and many times we fought, but he is still my brother. He is still a part of my life. I want his safe return just as much as everyone else in this room would like to see. But maybe Katie's right. It's time to stop the bitter feelings, and work together. The continuation of hatred isn't going to save Shenandoah. If you really want to fight, then save your anger for the Board of Supervisors."

Katie ran from the cabin with her hands hiding her face crying. Caroline was very displeased. She jumped from her seat staring with coldness. "Mother Elizabeth, I hope that you're pleased!"

Elizabeth turned and looked at Pete for sympathy, commenting as Caroline followed Katie, "Now, she is against me."

"With that type of outburst, I guess so. Mother, you've never liked Katie from the very beginning. Her only crime is that she is from the North and holds different views than us. Before the war and all through this conflict she never exerted her views on this family. She didn't attempt to change us from the way we lived but yet in some way you have constantly punished her. Well, you better get use to her being around because once this matter of the taxes is resolved, then Katie and I will be married. With or without your blessings!"

"It will never happen while I am living here."

"If that is the way you want to act then once the issue of the taxes is resolved, Katie and I will leave."

Caroline was on the porch where Katie was sobbing uncontrollably. Immediately, she placed her hands on Katie's shoulders and turned her around where she embraced Katie, allowing her to continue to cry. Caroline remained silent, but she thought of how verbally ruthless Elizabeth could be with her choice of words and her fiery anger. Someone exerting his or her temper had always been intimidating to Caroline. She had witnessed enough of her father's anger when she was a child. Often her younger sister Mary and herself had been physically subjected to his wrath and punishment.

Once Katie stopped sobbing, she stepped back. Still sniffling, she said in a whisper, "Thank you."

"I can recall whenever my father was angry with my sister Mary, I would do just as I did with you. It seems sort of natural to reach out to your younger sister that's suffering."

"Do you feel that way about me?"

"I guess I have always thought of you as a sister even though we have had our differences but then who does always see eye to eye."

Katie wiped her eyes with her handkerchief. "I have always felt that way concerning our relationship. Since the beginning, I've had the utmost respect and admiration for you. The one thing I've missed the most in my life is not having a sister. After my mother gave birth to me, she wasn't able to have any more children. In reality, my parents only wanted the one child, they didn't plan for me."

"But you are here and you're a blessing to Ann and me."

Pete opening the door interrupted Caroline and Katie. Caroline turned, nodding an affirmation that Katie was all right. Smiling, she stepped from the porch and proceeded in the direction of the foundation where Hayward was cutting some of the stone that was to be used. Katie was silent as her eyes met Pete's. Pete placed his hands on Katie's shoulders. "I want to apologize for that incident. I guess there is no changing my mother. She is blinded by her emotions. I am afraid that mother will always feel this type of hatred and bitterness over her losses."

"She didn't have any bloody right to treat nor speak to me in that way. Here I am willing to travel to Boston. Make the effort to save her precious Shenandoah and hopefully she can have a normal life again with some of what she lost, but she is too bloody ungrateful and wants to continue to fight that bloody, bloody war."

"Katie, Katie, listen to yourself!"

"No, no. As long as I am here, there will never be peace in your family. She has ruled for too long. Too many years in this family thinking that everyone should be subjected to her will.

Besides, I don't intend on continuing to live here if all that she can do is deal out her abuse."

Both paused, remaining silent to regain their composure. Pete took another sigh. "The whole mess isn't worth it. If by chance we can't hold onto the property, then life for us will go on. Like many, we are just going to have to start over again, whether it's here or elsewhere. Shenandoah doesn't fill the void within my heart; it's you. The most important thing in life is that we are together, you and me."

Calmness inwardly began to rule Katie's facial features. Pete remained silent, taking her by the hand as they walked to the far end of the porch, gazing in the direction of the mountains that caressed the shoreline of the Shenandoah River.

Chapter 11

It was nearing mid-morning as Pete glanced at his gold watch that his father gave him before his death. He had just arrived in Charlestown, once the seat of the County's government, and the town in Jefferson County that was the most adamant for secession from the Union at the outbreak of the war. Pausing on his horse at the corner of Washington and George Streets, the short five-mile journey from Shenandoah had consumed but little time.

Glancing around, there were many reminders prior to the war and the devastation from the conflict. To his right, Pete glanced at the old Market House that had been constructed in 1809. It was once the symbol of prosperity, and a main gathering area prior to the war for citizens to discuss or argue the events drawing the nation in the direction of hostilities. Now with reminders of the great damage suffered by Union forces from the war, it would be a reminder for generations to come of the great rebellion. As Pete gazed at the structure, he could still recall and visualize within his mind his father, and him entering the dwelling to conduct business with Mr. Humphrey. Jackson Humphrey was a surveyor that had overseen the boundary markers for the family's new property acquisitions, but he was mostly a trusted friend who on many occasions would visit on an early morning at sunrise to fish with his father. Pete was sure if he dismounted and examined the walls, he could still find where bullet holes penetrated the brick giving evidence of the skirmishes that took place in the streets of the town.

As Pete continued to marvel at the town's appearance, he looked to his right where he noticed the Jefferson County Courthouse which had been rebuilt after a fire destroyed it in 1837. It was during that early period of Pete's life after observing a controversial trial for murder in 1855 involving a petty thief by the name of Henry Lake that Pete decided to study law. The red brick walls of the Courthouse were sorely damaged by what appeared to be artillery fire leaving the building too severely devastated to be of any constructive use. He turned once more; this time toward the right and glanced at the brick two-story structure that stood along the corner. The dwelling once occupied a figure of inflammatory circumstances, the infamous John

Brown. Brown was confined within its walls in 1859 while awaiting trial after committing insurrection by seizing the Federal armory at Harpers Ferry. Later, he was executed on grounds not far from the jail.

During the war, the jail was left intact, probably used by the Provost Marshall while Federal forces occupied the town. Still, with all of the scars of war, the town's appearance was more acceptable and livable than the war tattered town of Harpers Ferry.

As Pete continued to glance around, he heard a voice from behind him. "Pete, Pete Barker." Turning in his saddle, Pete recognized John Morris from his old cavalry regiment, the 1st Virginia.

Quickly dismounting from his horse, a smile beamed from Pete's face. He shook his comrade's hand. "How have you been John?"

"Since returning home, I've been doing good, I guess."

"It's been a long time. I guess the last time that I saw you was when we were trying to beat back that Yankee attack near Gettysburg," Pete jovially replied.

"Yeah, that was a sad day for the army." Shaking his head in frustration and reflecting on the past, he continued, "You can't help but to think what might have happened at Gettysburg if Pickett's boys would have been able to take that stone wall fence and us cavalrymen coming in from the rear of Meade's army. The war might have had a different outcome."

"It might have prolonged the conflict, but unfortunately it didn't happen that way. I guess for as long as we live, we'll always wonder what might have been."

John had been residing in the Charlestown area for most of his 23 years and was a member of Company F of the Shepherdstown Cavalry, the same unit that Pete had enlisted in the spring of 1861. Tears began to fill his eyes as he recalled. "Pete do you remember Ambrose Reilly?"

"Come to think of it, yes I remember him. He was with Company D from Clarke County. Berryville if I recall."

"Well back in 1862 he and I were fighting side by side as we were moving through Boonsboro covering General Hill's retreat from off the mountain, you know, just before the big fight at Sharpsburg?"

"Yeah, I remember."

"Well my horse became nervous and threw me to the ground. I tried to regain the reins but wasn't able to." Beginning to chuckle, John continued, "From out of nowhere here comes old Ambrose yelling 'come on boy, ya's gonna git killed if ya don't take my hand and jump on.' Without thinking, I did as he said. Well that was the beginning of a close friendship. We fought side by side and we confided in each other. Even though I never met his family, I felt like I had always known them until Gettysburg. And that day, things changed."

"What happened?"

"Oh... I was on the ground so involved with trying to strangle the life out of a blasted Yankee that my buddy Ambrose was shot from behind. He didn't know what hit him. After Boonsboro, when we were in a fight, I never let him out of my sight but the one time that I did he's gone." Continuing in a whisper, "Gone for good."

"I know what you mean. My cousin Lester Tyler took a saber blow to the head. And yeah, it happened when I was pointing my gun at the Yankee and it misfired. All that I could do was helplessly watch the saber come down across the side of Lester's scalp. In the worst way, I wanted to kill the Yankee, but another comrade had already mortally wounded him and I was persuaded by my friend Jonathan not to finish the job. Fortunately for Lester he survived but has become an invalid. Bedridden for the rest of his life; which might not be that long."

"It was a tragic war. Maybe it shouldn't have happened. If the Yankees would have stayed home then we might have never fought such a horrible war." Suddenly, John's expression turned to one of anger and his voice reflected the emotions of his heart. "I still hold my hatred for what the Yankees did and the life I have been robbed of. All the Yankees wanted were to free the darkies and to ruin our homes and families. I wasn't ready for Appomattox nor the surrender of the war. If I had the chance, I would continue without a second thought to kill every blasted Yankee and darkie that I could find. What will the South do now that the darkies have their freedom and our economy and homes have been destroyed? What do they expect us to do? "

The thought surfaced in Pete's mind as to the affair along the river yesterday when he and Hayward had been working and was fired upon. Was it possible that John could have been a part of such an act, or maybe he knew who might have been responsible? It was known that organizations had formed consisting of former Confederates wanting to continue the war in a partisan fashion. Pete continued to ponder as he looked at John. Was his former comrade possibly one of the individuals who tried to kill Hayward and him, or was he just displaying his trapped emotions to an old comrade?

It wasn't Pete's desire to continue the war in any fashion. As far as he was concerned, it was over with and time to rebuild and move on with his life. "John, the war has ended, and there is nothing that we can do to change the outcome. All of us that fought with Jeb Stuart as well as the other Southern forces are going to experience many changes that are going to affect our life and some of them we are not going to like. You're not the only one who is suffering from the effects of the war. It's difficult for members of my own family who are trying to make the changes. For instance, when Richmond was evacuated my younger sister Rebecca was killed. And it wasn't by the Yankees but by someone else. My brother Charles had to flee from possible imprisonment for his part in Jeff Davis' government. To this day, I don't know if he is alive or dead. The toll that it has taken on me emotionally has had a great impact on my life. And at times when I think on the past and the war, we would have been better off if we wouldn't have been so quick to want to fight. We just weren't prepared to fight a long war such as the Northerners."

"I just don't agree with you. Why did you fight? Maybe you should have just stayed home," John answered in a rough tone.

"I must admit I was hesitant. But such as yourself, once the war began and the North was determined to invade Virginia, I, like most felt that it was my obligation to my family and state to defend our property and rights. I didn't want changes anymore than anyone else. But, I knew it was a mistake to bomb Fort Sumter and to open a conflict we had little chance of winning. Maybe, if we had been patient, there would have been some kind of compromise instead of force. Things might have been a lot different for all of us."

Again John remained silent staring at Pete. Pete knew hatred and animosity was destroying John's heart and mind like some disease that ravages the body until death brings relief.

The thought surfaced in Pete's mind concerning his close and dear friend from Highland County, Jonathan Collins. He hadn't seen nor heard from him since the night that he helped Katie escape from confinement in Winchester, Virginia. Pete gave thought to Jonathan's whereabouts and his welfare. His curiosity was heightening. "Do you remember Jonathan Collins?"

"The big, jovial guy that loved to play poker and who use to wipe everybody out of their money the same as cleaning a chicken bone?"

"Yeah, yeah, he's the one. Do you know if he survived?"

"The last that I seen of him we were retreating from the Farmville area. We were guarding a wagon train when Gregg's Yankee cavalry hit us hard. The fighting was heavy and we suffered great loss. To be honest, the last that I saw of Jonathan, he was bleeding from his shoulder and falling from his horse and then I witnessed a Yankee fire at him while he was lying on the ground. We were able to drive off the Yankees, but I didn't see Jonathan again."

Pete's spirit was broken by the revelation that John shared about Jonathan's fate. Immediately, the thought surfaced concerning the evening on the outskirts of Winchester when Jonathan assisted him with helping Katie to escape from jail. Pete remembered pleading in vain with his friend to return home because the war was lost. For three long years they had served together in the cavalry. The bond and closeness that Pete shared with Jonathan was as if he was his older brother. He knew Jonathan was a prideful individual and it was characteristic of his friend to say that he wasn't ready to stop fighting even though it was his desire to return home. Jonathan's convictions were deep concerning issues and his loyalty was unchallenged.

Turning around, Pete softly said as he walked away, "Thank you, John, for the information."

Pete paused as he looked around town. He grieved deep within his heart. He wondered what might have become of Jonathan's wife and two sons. Like many who fought this terrible war, they were probably struggling to survive with little hope of success or a future.

Chapter 12

Within the next five minutes, Pete was walking through the front door of the bank. After asking the teller if Mr. Larson was available, the teller nodded in the affirmative. Escorting Pete to the small office in the corner of the establishment where the bank president was signing some documents, the teller announced Pete's presence but was ignored. As Pete waited, Mr. Larson didn't acknowledge his presence. It was as though he didn't exist. Pete thought, usually his brother Charles was the one to handle all the business transactions for Shenandoah and he wouldn't have tolerated such an inconsideration but times have dramatically changed and that advantage ceased to exist any longer.

Pete waited patiently for a short time. Mr. Larson pushed the papers to the side. Looking up at Pete from his seat, he said as he removed his bi-focal glasses, "It's been sometime Pete. How are you doing these days?"

"Struggling like many I guess."

"The last that I heard, your mother was in Richmond and your brother had disappeared."

"My mother and Caroline returned yesterday from the Upper Valley. After the fall of Richmond, they went to New Market where they spent the summer with Caroline's parents. As for Charles, we don't know where he is."

"I guess Caroline's parents didn't fair any better than your family did. I mean as far as the destruction of property. It's a shame that Sheridan and Hunter's boys didn't show some mercy toward the farmers. They really didn't think what the cost would be afterward, you know, once this war ended. But I guess I can understand they had to do what was needed in order to end the bloodshed."

"This war has been hard on everyone. In some way, everyone has lost something whether it was their property, their livestock, or the lives of a family member or a neighbor. I guess most of all a civilization has passed into history and that is our way of life."

"So, I guess you are here looking for start-up money? But what puzzles me the most is that your brother owns Shenandoah. Why are you here?"

"Charles is family even though he isn't home, and now I am the one who must assume the responsibility in his absence. And to answer the rest of your question, I am looking for money to pay off back taxes."

Silently rubbing his hands across his long beard, he replied, "How much?"

"I need $2,500."

"Son, that's a lot of money." Mr. Larson stood and walked to the window, looking out onto the street and remained silent. Turning around, gazing in Pete's direction, the bank president continued, "This war has been tough on everybody including banks. Unless we have financial stability from investors from up North, we ourselves won't survive. I guess what I am saying is that this bank is having its share of financial problems just like everyone else. Not only us but also all the banks in the region. One time of day I could have easily have given you that kind of money, but times have changed. There is just no way I can make that type of a loan."

"Or are you just saying this because you don't want to do business with a rebel."

Nervously gesturing with his hands, Mr. Larson said in a conciliatory tone, "No, it's not that. Not that at all. I must confess, I wasn't for Virginia seceding from the Union and I supported force, if necessary, to maintain that she remain a part of this country. And even though I had many friends in this county that were loyal to the Southern cause, I feel no animosity toward them. But I can't do what I can't do. My hands are tied."

As Pete stood, so did Mr. Larson, saying as he stepped from behind the desk. "There is one more option that you might consider. It's not the best and probably not what you want to hear."

"I know, sell off some of the property."

"Son, see it from a business point of view," Mr. Larson suggested as he placed his hand on Pete's shoulder. "It would be more beneficial to sell let's say, 1,000 acres to a businessman from the North than try to use it as collateral on a loan." Turning around and returning to his seat, Mr. Larson continued, "You would still end up with something rather than nothing. Even if we could use some of the property as collateral and something unfortunately happens that you can't satisfy the loan, then I wouldn't have much choice but to seize it anyway."

"But you would end up making money because they would open accounts with your bank, which means that you'd have more money to loan. Am I right?"

Mr. Larson had a grim look on his face, as he remained silent. Pete wasn't ready to submit to what he believed would be defeat or have Shenandoah stolen out from under his family. He knew his family would have a difficult time of resigning themselves to the cold reality that Shenandoah would have to be sold piece by piece in order to maintain some of the estate. He wasn't ready to surrender just yet. He would exercise all of his options.

It was a long ride home. His mind had been consumed on resolving the problem of raising the funds to pay off the debt on Shenandoah. Once he came to the lane, he looked around to witness what little had been accomplished in the way of progress over the months toward the property's restoration. The absence of slave labor was evident. In the past, they were the ones chiefly who had been instrumental in maintaining such a large estate. At the end of the estate's lane, he noticed Hayward diligently laboring on the foundation. From the progress of his work, Pete knew that Hayward took great pride and satisfaction in his task. Around the cabin all appeared to be quiet with the exception of a few chickens running around. Once Pete dismounted, he walked through the door to find the place vacant with the exception of his mother, who was sitting alone by the crackling fireplace gazing at the wall. She either didn't hear him, or her attention wasn't focused on her surroundings. Pete walked to the front of where she was seated. "Mother are you all right?"

Elizabeth looked up and he noticed the saddened eyes. She answered in a calm tone. "No my son, I am not. I know that your trip to see old man Larson was in vain."

Pete knelt in front of her rocker and placed his hands upon hers. "I knew also, but I had to try."

Tears flowed from her cheeks. She was in great despair as she whispered, "Oh, dear, my beloved Shenandoah. What will we do now?"

"Mr. Larson made some suggestions."

"I know, sell off some of the property. Only carpetbaggers can afford to buy. There's surely no one around here that can afford to." She gripped the arm of the chair. "Oh dear God, what would my father think knowing that I have lost everything that he worked so hard and so many hours to accomplish?"

"Mother, my father knew trouble was on the horizon and there was the possibility of the risk of war. Do you remember when Mr. White and Mr. Hunter begged him to run as a state legislator in the election of 1854 and he refused?"

"Yes, I was the one who opposed him running because he didn't share my views, but Charles did. I told your father one night as we were sitting in the drawing room that it would be too embarrassing if he believed one thing and I believed another and it became public. You know how opinionated that I can be. I felt it was more important to raise you boys and Rebecca and leave the politics to someone else. He reluctantly agreed and walked from the room. I never did know what his thoughts were that night when he walked away and it wasn't something that we discussed again. It just faded away. I guess that's why I was so opposed to Charles being involved in politics. I could see that Caroline didn't share all of his views. If you are going to be a candidate for office, then everyone that's close to you must share your vision."

"Maybe Mother, he knew that war would come and didn't want to be in a position of voting against something that he didn't really believe to be the answer. We all know now that it was to be secession. He knew he would cause more strife at home with you than what it was all worth. I know that often you and father didn't see eye to eye on matters. He had a tremendous amount of respect for you and a tremendous amount of love for you and our family. But with all of that said, still we are a family and we have each other even in his absence. Isn't that more important than holding onto Shenandoah? I feel father would have been content to have his family near and alive after such a horrible ordeal such as the war. It wouldn't have made a difference because we could have started over again with a smaller homestead."

Without warning, Caroline walked through the front door. After witnessing the scene between Pete and Elizabeth, Caroline knew the news was grim. "What happened? What did Mr. Larson say?"

Pete looked at Caroline as he stood to his feet. "There is no hope. The money just isn't there."

"Oh God. Dear God; what are we going to do? Where will we go?" She asked as she held her hand over her face.

Ann and Katie came running through the door. Ann asked in a frighten tone. "Mother what is wrong?"

Turning around, Caroline was full of emotion and couldn't speak. Instead, she placed her face upon her daughter's shoulders and wept uncontrollably. Katie stood near her friend gazing at Pete knowing the situation appeared hopeless.

Elizabeth said in a frustrating tone as she looked up from her chair at Pete, "This wouldn't have happened if Charles were here. Somehow, somewhere he would have gotten the money."

"Yes mother, we all know Charles would have been the salvation of Shenandoah," Pete fired back. "Ask yourself the question, how would he have raised the money since we are broke? After all, it was his idea to sell off all the horses and livestock and then foolishly spend the funds purchasing worthless Confederate promissory notes."

Elizabeth jumped to her feet slapping Pete across the face. "Don't you dare speak of your brother in that tone of voice! At the time he made the investments, it looked like we were going to win the war. The risk would have paid off. And for us that would have meant a new government which your brother would have played a prominent role in."

Pete rubbed his left cheek. "Dreams, dreams, dreams. That's all that this family was living on. There wasn't any way we could win the war unless the Yankees and citizens from the North had their fill of the whole thing. Man for man we couldn't match them because there were too many. And no one knew that more then General Grant." Pausing and regaining his composure, Pete added, "But that's in the past. It's not going to help us now in retaining Shenandoah. We must try every opportunity available to us, and that means if the money is in the North then that's where I have to go."

Excusing himself, Pete departed from the cabin slamming the door behind him. Everyone in the cabin remained quiet and reserved. Once Katie was satisfied that Caroline's emotions were under control, she walked out to the front porch. There she watched Pete slowly walking in the direction of the orchard. She knew his feelings had been bruised by the words that his mother had spoken. She always knew by what he said and by his actions that he always held his mother's feelings in high regard She also was beginning to sense there was a change that was taking place within his life. She wasn't sure of the cause. Most likely, he was determined to be his own man instead of trying to please others.

Pete heard the sounds of footsteps quietly approaching as he turned. Katie's features appeared worried and tired as if she had been emotionally driven to her limits. As he reached to place his arm around her shoulders, he said, "I can tell by your expression that all this is beginning to take its toll on you."

"True it is, but you know me, I like a challenge. I've never run from one yet.

"This, too, has been challenging for me. It's no different than trying to stay alive during some fighting. Only this time, it's a different kind of war. I guess tomorrow, we'll leave for Boston."

Chapter 13

It was 2:00 o'clock in the afternoon as Pete glanced at his watch. From the window of the passenger coach, Pete quietly glanced in the direction of the busy Boston Harbor with its many assorted vessels. As he continued to look around, he noticed the area was surrounded with many distinctive homes that were constructed close together and multitudes of various businesses filling the streets. As the train was gradually coming to a halt, he glanced at Katie's excited expression. After four days of traveling from Harpers Ferry with only a brief stay in New York, Katie and Pete were finally arriving at the Boston and Providence Railroad's Public Square Depot in Boston, Massachusetts. Even though he wouldn't confess his anxiety because of his pride, Pete was quite uneasy at meeting Katie's family, especially her brother Seamus.

Pete knew before the war that Boston was the foundation for the abolition movement and from here the rest of the Northern states rallied around the call for the abolishment of the institution of slavery. In 1861, many of the leaders from Boston were just as inflamed about ending slavery as the Southern leaders of Charleston, South Carolina were inflamed over protecting the institution's legitimacy. Pete's suspicions led him to believe that in all probability, the McBrides had been actively involved in the abolition movement even though Katie and he had never discussed the issue.

As he turned to glance at Katie, Pete admired the peaceful expression covering her face and the way that she had dressed. Katie had made the best effort possible with her clothing, but it fell short of the fashionable way that she was accustomed to dressing due to the lack of money. Today, she was wearing a gray-stripe dress that she made from material she had managed to purchase at the dry goods store in Harpers Ferry. The jewelry she cherished the most, her Grandmother McBride's gray cameo broach, was pinned to the white collar around her neck. Pete quietly touched Katie's hand and smiled, drawing her attention as she returned the gesture. Often, they would remain silent and just allow their eyes to meet and gaze at each other. The firm influence that Katie had displayed in Pete's life since living at Shenandoah provided him with the trust to allow him to love her all the more.

They were very compatible with each other and very seldom were they separated from each other's company. It was his hope while in Boston, they would be able to get away from the problems involving Shenandoah and the family and to just be able to spend time with each other and share their love and affection.

Suddenly, Pete's mind returned to reality as the train jolted to a halt. Once Pete stepped down from the train coach, he turned and smiled, taking Katie by the hand while she held firmly onto her black hat with its white plume. After assisting her onto the platform, Pete gathered their carpetbags containing their clothing and proceeded to the four-seated, open barouche carriage that was waiting to take them to her home on Mt. Vernon Street.

Katie was just as apprehensive about visiting her parents with Pete, as she knew that he must be. As with most of her correspondence that she received from her mother, the family had pleaded with her to return to Boston and to forsake her relationship with Pete. To her mother and father, Harpers Ferry didn't offer opportunity and was still a dangerous place to be and shouldn't be the home of a lady of culture. Their rejection of Pete only caused her to become more persistent in her challenge to be her own person and to make her own decisions and have her own identity. It wasn't that she was attempting to be rebellious against her family but she had become very independent and serious minded; something that she had learned from her mother during her rearing. It was also due to this education that Katie's personality was quite different than the more conservative type of lady that lived in Virginia.

Katie believed that her family, with maybe the exception of Seamus, would be hospitable toward Pete, but she knew that it would take time before they would accept him. It could be, she thought, a long road once she broke the news to the family of her intentions of marrying Pete and continuing her life at Harpers Ferry. Katie had found happiness and in time she firmly believed that her family would accept the relationship with Pete and come to terms with her decision. It would require much patience and understanding on her part as well as Pete's.

As the coachman loaded the couple's possessions on the back of the carriage, he began to move the team of two horses in the direction of Beacon Street. With her black parasol in one hand to shade the sun's rays, Katie took Pete by the other hand. "Pete my love, I too, feel your uneasiness."

Pete turned around as a grin broke forth over his face. "Is it that evident, huh?"

"Yes it is and trust me I understand. I felt the same way last week when Miss Elizabeth and Caroline returned from New Market. The evening before their arrival I was very anxious and even sometimes a little snappy with you as I remember. I guess it was due to the fact that I didn't know what kind of reception that I'd receive from them, but fortunately it worked out. I am so glad Caroline and I have made amends over the past. We have promised to put the war behind us and move on with our relationship. It has relieved such a burden that I've been carrying around for the past year even though there were some things you said that gave me comfort. Though I wish I could say the same when it comes to Miss Elizabeth. She really has a difficult time with dealing with matters."

"I would be lying to you my love if I said that I wasn't a little edgy. I guess such as yourself with my family, I don't know what to expect, but I promise that I'll make the utmost attempt to be on my best behavior."

"Pete Barker, I'm counting on it." Pausing and changing the subject in a serious tone, Katie expressed her desires. "There is much that I want to accomplish in the little time that we'll be here. First, I'd like you to speak with my father; asking him for my hand in marriage, and of course, his blessings."

"Which he'll reject."

"In all probability, yes. I know my folks all too well. They'll try to persuade me to stay in Boston, meet an up-standing gentleman at one of the socials."

Pete interrupted gesturing with his hands, "And give you many, many reasons why you shouldn't be tied down to a rebel, such as myself, who can't possibly give you the life, which you so dearly deserve. If I were to guess, I'd say the greatest dislike they have for me is that I fought for the Confederacy. I really don't believe they'll ever give me the chance to prove my worth. Like many, they'll judge the outward appearance and not the inward appearance. It's the same old mistake that people make over and over."

"That's not bloody fair of you to say Pete Barker."

"Oh yes it is Katie McBride."

"Who made you judge, sir?"

Pete said, as he raised his arms, "No one, but...."

Katie interrupted in a calmer tone. "Pete, my love, please, you must try and understand that the war was just as difficult for them with my brother taking an active part in the conflict. I ask that you would think of me if they say something inflammatory and please make the attempt to withhold your temper. And if you do, then maybe they'll be more receptive to loaning you the money to pay the back taxes on Shenandoah."

"As I have said before, this whole trip will be a waste of time with the exception of you visiting your family."

As the horses trotted along the cobblestone road pass Bowdoin Street, Pete glanced at the huge yellow-gold building with the gray dome and a large veranda with huge white columns as support. With his curiosity heighten, he asked, "What is the importance of this building?"

Katie said without any thought and without looking at the structure, "Oh, it's the State House. Originally, it was designed by Mr. Bulfinch, who designed many of the homes in this area. Today, my father is in all probability in that place determining how the good people of the Commonwealth of Massachusetts will live."

Immediately, Katie knew that she had blundered. She wasn't concentrating on the question when asked but instead pondering on their little disagreement that had just occurred. Katie became so frustrated with herself for not providing the opportunity to speak with Pete before the trip. Knowing his pride and stubbornness, she knew that he would have probably refused to have made the trip with her. Originally while in New York, Katie had planned on telling Pete about her father's election to the Massachusetts House of Delegates but she feared he would have returned home. Then she thought of telling him once they arrived in Boston. No time seemed right for Katie. She was beginning to feel guilty over compromising his trust that he had so graciously given to her.

Pete was surprised by Katie's words. He turned and looked, remaining silent with a stunned expression covering his face. "Why didn't you tell me or were you not going to do so?"

Katie placed her hand over her mouth. Pausing, she answered in an excited tone. "Pete, I am sorry." Continuing to be remorseful, she placed her hand over her heart. "Oh, I am so sorry. There were many times that I wanted to tell you but I was afraid it was going to affect our relationship and how you personally felt about me. I believed that if you found out about his election that you would have judged me unfairly as well as your family. At the time the war was still going on and you were still a part of that conflict. As you know we didn't see much of each other and when we did, I tried to keep matters at a safe distance."

As Katie paused, Pete silently stared at her waiting for her to continue. In a broken tone, she said, "And that's not all, you must know the rest. My family were strong abolitionists believing that everyone should have the opportunity to determine their destiny and live in freedom including the Negroes. Often they attended meetings at the old Baptist Church on Joy Street and listened to speeches and testimonies from those who experienced the cruelties of slavery. Naturally, after sometime, they actively became involved and were vigorous in the campaign to end slavery. They supported the Underground Railroad and helped runaway slaves begin a new life in the North. On different occasions, my father spoke to other groups across the Northeast that were rising up and speaking their voices against the evils of slavery. My father became so zealous over the issue that he believed that he shared the vision of many of the citizens living within the city and that their voices and expressions could be represented through him. So he ran as a Republican and was elected, such as Lincoln, receiving the support from soldiers fighting with Irish regiments made up mostly from Boston as well as most in the Irish community."

Frantically, Katie continued to express her feelings. "Even though you and I didn't often speak of the issue of slavery because of the possibility of arguing, I know you must have suspected that I also shared their views. Granted, I never tried to impose my feelings about slavery on your family or you; nor did I ever look upon you and your family as some kind of low-life for treating the dark-skinned people the way that Southerners did."

"I was so blinded by your beauty and charm that I didn't put two and two together and realize that your father was Thaddeus McBride. Oh yeah, the Virginia newspapers use to draw cartoons of him and the darkies." Shaking his head in frustration, Pete continued, "Why didn't you tell me all this before you returned to Boston last year after I helped you to escape from prison?"

"I think that was quite evident. I was in love with you. Besides, it would have brought greater condemnation upon me because it would have given your family greater suspicions that I had an agenda against the Southern people. With haste, they would have implicated me in the loss of Shenandoah and also passing information to Federal forces."

As Pete turned away and silently glanced in the direction of the Commons, he watched a young couple walking along the path arm in arm, smiling, and appearing to speak with each other in a pleasant way. He wasn't angry with Katie, but quite frustrated with her for withholding a secret. Then the thought surfaced within his mind over the discussion that he had with his mother concerning her continual suspicions of Katie's possible spying adventures during the war and the destruction of Shenandoah. He didn't believe Katie was really an agent, but again the words that she had spoken on Short Hill Mountain continued to torment his memory. At times he totally ignored the words when he asked Katie of her involvement and she replied, "Would it make any difference?"

Now with Katie's new revelations concerning her family could it be possible she was lying to cover up her real intentions and only wanted to help rebuild Shenandoah out of guilt? Trying to shrug the thought, Pete possessed his convictions that she wouldn't have committed such a treacherous act against his family, especially him whom she loved. But then again, if family members could fight against family members and be in such division out of strong conviction during the war, then anything was possible. It was an issue that continuously confused him.

Now Katie's words changed all that. Pete wanted to know while they were alone before their arrival at her home. He didn't want any surprises revealed to him by her father or any other family member. The truth must come from her and her alone before they arrived. As he turned to look at Katie, she was looking aimlessly at some of the people leisurely walking as the carriage made the turn onto Walnut Street.

Katie glanced at Pete and said, "We'll be there soon."

"Is there anything else that I need to know before I meet your family?"

"What do you mean by that statement?"

"I mean is there anything else that I should know about?"

Katie didn't answer. She gazed at Pete with a frustrated expression covering her face. She was beginning to feel there was a question concerning her trust and loyalty in their relationship. Maybe, she thought, Pete was over reacting and really feeling a greater unease than what she expected about meeting her family, especially not knowing how they would respond or how Pete would react. The most troublesome issue she thought would be the problems involving the black man's freedom and the reconstruction of the Southern states. It was sure to be discussed and to complicate matters. Not only these issues, but now Pete really knew who her father was. For now, no other issues surfaced in her mind that she thought could stimulate such a response, but it was enough to arouse her suspicions that not everything was right between them.

Chapter 14

The rest of the short journey had been quiet between Pete and Katie after their discussion over her lack of honesty and the new revelations concerning her family. Pete had concerns over Katie's dishonesty but knew she was probably attempting to protect her family's image for as long as she could, and prolong the disagreement they were now experiencing. Seldom, did Pete and Katie disagree on any subject, but instead would talk the issue over until they were able to compromise on a solution. Pete didn't like the feelings of separation and lack of communication, but he believed at the first opportunity, Katie and he would have to settle the issue and move on with their life.

Once the carriage came to the end of Walnut Street, the coachman turned the team of horses onto Mt. Vernon Street. In an attempt not to dwell on their differences, Pete had been glancing around and was impressed with the many fine, decorative charming mansions that he saw along the way. This area of Boston was known as Beacon Hill where the cities wealth, prosperity, prestige, and national voices were displayed. Many notable leaders lived or had some point in time lived in the area. The most notable that Pete thought of was former Senator and Secretary of State, Daniel Webster, who was now deceased. It was Webster's famous speech on the floor of the United States Senate that Pete had studied at the University of Virginia when he was studying to be a lawyer. As he remembered, it was Webster in 1828, who had supported the High-Tariff Bill, which placed a tax on states that would export cotton abroad to England. Southern leaders became inflamed with anger, especially Senator Robert Young Hayne from South Carolina. He believed that his state had the right to overturn any particular piece of legislation. It wasn't until the most famous words that Webster uttered in a speech given in 1830, "Liberty and Union, now and forever, one and inseparable," that the Southern politicians and leaders enhanced their views and framed their arguments for the justification of states' rights. It was only the first of many sparks igniting the fire that caused various small skirmishes to a larger battle resulting in all out civil war.

Another person of interest that came to Pete's mind from the area was, Julia Ward Howe. She authored the famous patriotic song of the Civil War, "The Battle Hymn of the Republic," which was composed in 1862. Pete remembered on occasions scouting along the Rappahannock River in the spring of 1863 listening to Yankee bands playing the Howe's selection or Yankee soldiers singing its words to boost their morale.

Shortly, the carriage came to a halt in front of the residence. Pete stepped down from the carriage and adjusted his black John Bull hat and brown frock coat as he looked at the huge brownstone-brick, four-chimney mansion that crested a slight elevation. Turning around, his eyes were on Katie's troubled expression. He took her by the hand, helping her from the carriage. "Katie, as soon as possible we will do as we have done in the past concerning troubled issues. We'll talk about it and resolve this matter."

"It's serious, I know. I feel so guilty for not telling you about my family, especially my father. But I guess what troubles me the most is if we can't settle this issue. What then, my love?"

Again as Pete looked at Katie, he struggled with the thoughts that continued to surface in his mind. Was the woman that he was looking at really a spy during the war and all this time she had been secretive because she inadvertently fell in love with him and couldn't reveal the truth.

As the coachman walked to the back of the carriage and was removing Katie's trunk, Pete said, "In a way I do feel betrayed. It's not like you to withhold something of importance from me. I must also admit it's difficult for me because I really felt that if you knew that I truly loved you then you could have confided in me with anything that you needed. Don't think of my love for you as being something that is shallow and that it doesn't have any depth to it because it does."

Katie remained silent, though a faint smile broke forth over her features giving Pete the impression that she was relieved by the words he had spoken. Pete took Katie by the arm as they walked up several steps and through the iron rail gates leading to the mansion. As Pete glanced at the house, he was impressed with the Corinthian style fluted pilasters and the hipped roof with its outer edges trimmed in the same black decorative railing that surrounded the front of the property and gates. In the center of the roof was an octagon glass dome that caught Pete's attention. It was very similar to the description that a Yankee prisoner from New Bedford, Massachusetts spoke of during the Gettysburg campaign. Once Pete and Katie stepped under the four column semi-circle portico, the butler of the house opened the huge mahogany door. They stepped through the entrance and Pete was amazed with the amount of sunlight due to the web fanlight above and along each side of the door.

Pete handed the butler his hat as Katie said, "Robert, how are you doing?"

"I am doing well Miss Katherine."

With a grin, Pete replied, "Katherine, huh."

Katie ignored Pete and asked Robert in an excited tone of voice, "Is Mother or Father home?"

As the butler was beginning to answer the question, a soft voice came from the direction of the elliptical stairway that was to the back of the huge atrium. "Katherine my dear is that you?"

Pete remained silent as the tall, slender, gray-haired lady, who was dressed very fashionably with a violet hairdressing approached the bottom of the stairway. Katie quickly glanced at Pete looking for his approval. He turned and smiled but felt very uneasy not knowing what kind of reception that he would receive. Without hesitation Katie walked over and embraced her mother. Pete could tell by Katie's mother's acts of affection that Katie had learned well by her role model. With a smile that covered all her face, Katie spoke softly to her mother. Taking her by the hand and escorting her to where Pete stood, Katie said in her introduction. "James Pete Barker, I would like to have the honor of introducing you to my mother, Margaret McBride."

"Mrs. McBride, it's my pleasure to make your acquaintance," Pete answered as he cordially kissed her hand.

After acknowledging Pete's words, Margaret curtseyed and suggested, "If you would, let us go into the parlor where we can visit."

Turning around, Margaret gave the butler an order. "Robert, I would like for you to bring some tea and lemonade for Katherine and Mr. Barker."

As the butler left the area, everyone walked into the large parlor. Pete was impressed with the white ornamental molding surrounding the perimeters of the wall and ceiling. The room was furnished in a contemporary style with a huge pocket door leading into a second parlor. All the windows recessed archways were trimmed with dentil molding forming a semi-circle decorated with light blue brocade hangings. The light brown colored carpet with various colors of roses and flowers covered the length and width of the room. After the ladies were seated in several chairs near the marble fireplace, Pete sat on the sofa. He noticed to his front the wooden mantel that surrounded the fireplace had various ornaments resembling the Roman culture. Over the mantel was a mirror that covered the length of the fireplace with four little fluted pilasters surrounded also by engravings of Roman culture.

Suddenly, Pete's thoughts were broken once Margaret posed a question. "Well Mr. Barker, I must say that every time Katherine has written me, she has always spoken fondly of you. I will not hesitate to say that often during the terrible conflict, my husband Thaddeus and myself pleaded with her in our correspondence to return to Boston where she would be safe. Knowing Katherine as I do, she was naturally so obstinate in her behavior. But that is all behind us now." With her blue-green eyes staring at Pete, she continued confidently, "I just want to thank you personally for watching over her and bringing her home to us safely."

As the butler was pouring the tea, Pete answered in a cordial tone. "And Mrs. McBride, I want to thank you for the gracious honor and privilege of knowing Katherine. She has been an inspiration and blessing in my life."

As Pete took a sip of the tea, Margaret suggested, "Mr. Barker, maybe you would like to rest from the long trip before my husband returns from his business, and then you may have the honor of meeting Katherine's father before dinner."

"Thank you, I would like to rest. I know that you and Katherine would like to speak privately."

As Pete followed the butler from the room, Katie noticed the serious expression covering her mother's face. With a flare of anger and quickness, Katie said, "I know Mother, you have already judged him and you don't like him. Am I not right?"

"No, no my darling Katherine. Listen to me. Please understand how your father and I feel. We don't believe that you should live in an area where it's so dangerous and the behavior of many of the individuals that fought for that rebellious cause couldn't admit that they were defeated. They are so unpredictable. We have read in the newspapers how some still prosecute the war by attempting to destroy the Negro race. Such atrocities as hanging men and women, shooting and stripping their bodies and burning their homes is so unstable and uncivil. You are right there where you are in the middle of this bloody mess and might get harmed. I am sure Mr. Barker has the most admirable intentions for your safety and convenience, but it's not the place where a young lady such as yourself will ever find happiness and have the opportunity to progress with your profession."

"Mother, I can sincerely appreciate your concern for my welfare and safety and I take comfort in your words and thoughts, but I am 25 years old and my life and future is with Pete."

Margaret became frustrated and angry as she jumped from her seat and paced the floor. "Katherine, how can you possibly say that your life and future is with someone that has lost everything and has nothing to offer you? If I may ask, how would he provide for you? For example, just look at the way you are dressed. It's not the wardrobe that you are use to wearing and it's certainly not the fashion that you'd wear if you were living here in Boston."

Inwardly, Katie felt like she was beginning to break down with emotion from her Mother's verbal scolding. She said in a sorrowful tone, "I am sorry Mother, I know I have fallen short of what you expected. Honestly, I know that you must be shocked by my appearance. But I had no other choice but to use my clothing for chores around the farm."

Margaret was stunned. "Chores! Katherine, your father and I never raised you to work like a farmhand. What is wrong with you? Have you lost your dignity and pride?"

Realizing the conversation was getting out of control, Katie said defensively, "Mother, I can't expect Pete to do everything. I really don't feel you understand what many of the Southern people have gone through and experienced as a result of the war. They have nothing. They have to rebuild with the little that they possess."

Margaret was calmer and said in a pleading tone. "Katherine, don't you see my point? My darling, life is going to dramatically change for those people in Virginia with restoration of the Southern states. I don't know why you could or would possibly give up everything that life has to offer here in Boston to live in some old cabin with no possible hope in sight."

"But I do have opportunity. As you know, it's my desire and dream to educate the Negroes, and to help them have a fair chance at life."

"Oh Katherine, Katherine." Margaret snapped in a frustrating tone, "When, my child, are you going to stop dreaming? For one moment do you think that he's going to allow you to teach the Negroes?"

"Mother…"

"No, Katherine he's not going to. He fought for the rebellion. He fought to keep the Negro in bondage while your brother battled to give them their freedom."

"Mother stop it! You don't understand!"

"Oh, yes I do Katherine. You're so innocent and will believe anything that you're told. Are you so blinded that you can't see he has lured you with his charm and many promises? Oh, and let's not forget about his lies? And he has probably deceived you with his gracious words in order to have his way with you."

Katie was stunned and shocked by her mother's outburst and anger. In an attempt to defend Pete she angrily replied, "No he hasn't even tried to have his way with me. Even though we've been alone on many occasions, still Pete has respected me and been nothing short of a complete gentleman. He's not like some of the other men who have professed to be something that they've proclaimed, such as a gentleman, only to fall short of their confession."

"Are you trying to tell me that your former suitor Doctor Edward McVey wasn't an honorable man? He had one of the most prestigious practices in the city. Katherine he loved you dearly, God Bless his dear soul."

"Mother I can say now what I couldn't say at the time when Edward and I were together."

"Katherine, what are you saying?"

Margaret had a surprised expression on her face as she once again sat in the chair and listened to Katie.

"Mother, Edward was a gentle and compassionate man when the family was present, but he had an ugly angry streak. At times I was fearful that he could possibly become physical with me. There was one particular occasion that stands out all too well in my mind."

Katie turned from her mother looking at the fire dancing among the logs of the fireplace as she continued to speak softly. "It happened late on Christmas night in 1858 after we had dined with Edward's family. After we exchanged gifts, we returned here. You and father were in the upstairs chamber. I am not sure where Seamus was. Edward and I came into this very room and a fire was burning in the fireplace such as now. For a while we exchanged cordial conversation and then his behavior changed. Edward had been drinking brandy heavily at his family's home; I, of course didn't have any. While we were alone, Edward tried to have his way and was very persistent. At first I thought that if I discouraged him, he would stop his challenge, but the more that I did, the angrier he became with me and the more physical were his attempts. I pleaded with him to stop. Of course we had words but he kept on trying. Finally, he was on top of me pinning me down on this very sofa. I wanted to scream but I didn't out of fear that it would be too embarrassing for all of us. With no other choice, I took my open palm and struck him in the face near his eye. You don't know afterwards how physically and emotionally sickened I was by his act. After that incident, I began to have doubtful thoughts about out future together."

"But you told your father and I that Edward and you were robbed by two men with a gun near the corner of Cambridge and Hancock Street. It supposedly happened while you two were on the way here from his family's home, and that is how Edward received a bruised eye, trying to defend you."

Katie turned once more toward her mother. "No Mother, I lied to you. I guess it was out of embarrassment. Maybe to protect his good image, or maybe just out of shame."

"But you two were to be married."

"I know, but it would have been a relationship that would have pleased Edward and his family as well as you and Father. But what about me?"

Katie gazed at her mother and paused for a moment to give her the chance to respond. Katie continued as she again took a seat opposite her mother. "I could never love Edward again after he tried to have his way with me and the physical behavior that he exerted. If he wouldn't have had his accident several weeks later and have died from his injuries, then in all probability I would have done what was expected of me and married him, reared his children, and lived a life of pure hell just to please everyone. And what is even worst, I've painted his love for me to others to protect his reputation. I know you would like to make accusations against Pete and find fault with him. True he isn't perfect, he does have his faults, but he is the one that has accepted me for who I am. Mother, try and understand that our relationship is based on honesty, trust, and mutual respect. We have many of the same interests, but all of that would be meaningless if it wasn't on a foundation built from our love toward each other. Over the years and through my experiences, I have discovered that all of the other qualities would come tumbling to the ground if it weren't for that one essential element. Too many relationships prevail for only a short time because there isn't any root to them. Remember when you taught me from the Good Book that when a seed is planted into the ground that unless the soil is fertile and good, there will never be a harvest from it. Again, love is unselfish and it's sacrificial. There have been too many times during the war when Pete and I have been together that we've shared or learned to share that experience. Mother love is a good seed."

After Katie finished there was a silence that came over the room. The only sound that existed was the clattering of horses' hoofs coming to a halt in front of the residence. Katie's mother continued her silence, staring defiantly at her daughter. At the top of the stairway, Pete quietly stood, hearing all the conversation that took place between Katie and her mother.

Chapter 15

Without hesitation upon the arrival of the carriage with its male passenger, Robert, the butler opened the front door. The gray haired-partially bald, well-dressed gentleman walked through the door, acknowledging the butler, handing him his brown bell-crown top hat and ivory handled cane. Afterward, he glanced in the direction of the parlor where his face brightened at the presence of the two special ladies that were seated. After a tense morning with business issues at the bank and an emotional meeting at the Governor's residence with the Speaker of the House, his heavy heart, troubles, and concerns were replaced with joy and satisfaction.

With the sound of someone entering the room, Katie turned from staring at her mother. Her face glowed with the gentleman's presence. As he rapidly approached, she said, "Father, I am so glad to see you."

Katie's father placed his hands on her shoulders and kissed her on the cheek. He marveled at his daughter's appearance. "My Katherine, my Katherine, oh how good it is to see you. Ah Katherine, you're as beautiful as ever. Whenever I look at your mother, I can't help but to see your Irish face. I can never express in words the void I have felt in my Irish heart since you've been gone. Even though I didn't mention it in my correspondence to you, I've had many sleepless nights with your absence."

"Now Father."

"No, no Katherine. Almost constantly since you've been gone we've burned a candle at the church for your safety and requested Father Murphy to say prayers for your prompt return home. And now you're here and that's all that matters." After kissing his wife on the cheek, he continued in a jovial tone. "Oh my dear child, wait until your brother sees you when he arrives tomorrow from his business in Hartford."

Margaret possessed a less then merry expression as she approached, "Thaddeus, there is a young gentleman that arrived with Katherine this afternoon who I am sure will want to meet you."

With a smile covering Katie's face and in a tone of excitement, she said, "Father, I have waited a long time for this moment and I want to be the one to make the introductions. Please grant me this request?"

"Fine, Katherine, that will be acceptable." Turning around, Thaddeus nodded his approval to Robert, who was standing nearby. At once the butler complied with the request and summoned Pete to the parlor.

Thaddeus was speaking with his wife and Katie as Pete entered the room. Suddenly, everyone ended their conversation and the room was filled with silence. Pete assumed by the stern expression covering Katie's father's face, he was being judged. Pete remained calm and walked upright in a military fashion. As he slowly approached, Katie smiled. "My loving Father, Thaddeus McBride, I would like to introduce you to my suitor, James Pete Barker from Virginia."

In a most cordial and gracious way, Thaddeus replied. "Mr. Barker, I finally have the honor of meeting you. Katherine has written so much about you as well as her life in Virginia, excuse me sir, West Virginia."

"And sir, I too consider it an honor to meet you. I have heard many great things about you from Katie, ah, I mean Katherine."

"Ah, my Katherine is the apple of my eye. From the very first time that I laid eyes on her, I knew she would be my favorite. It's not that I don't love my son, Seamus, but my Katherine, like a thief in the night, stole my Irish heart the very first moment that she came into this world."

Pete glanced at Katie and said as he began to smile, "I know, for she has stolen my heart also."

Katie laughed and bowed. "Please, please gentlemen, I am flattered by your love and gratitude toward me. Before it becomes too much for me, maybe you gentlemen would like to speak with each other and become better acquainted."

Thaddeus cleared his throat. "Yes, yes by all means. I would like very much to speak with Mr. Barker."

Katie smiled and bowed. "Well then, if you'll excuse Mother and me, we will retire to my chambers where I'd like to show her the new material that I purchased in New York to make a dress."

Once the ladies departed, Robert walked into the room and offered the two men some spirits. Thaddeus took a small glass and turning, he asked in a cordial tone, "James, would you like to share a brandy or whiskey?"

Pete took a seat on the sofa. "No sir, I haven't had any since the end of the war."

After taking a sip of his drink, Thaddeus said, "Ah, whiskey helps me relax after a troublesome day at the bank. And I've had many lately. As you know with the emancipation of the Negro, many have moved to this city and are looking to start up a business. It's my desire to help as many Negroes as possible, but unfortunately, I can't loan money to everyone that comes into my bank. Mostly the ones that are the best educated and of the best character, I will consider. For those Negroes that are still illiterate, unless an individual of means will stand behind them, then there isn't much that I can do to help them but refer them elsewhere. I hate to admit it, but like all other businesses, I have to pick and choose whom I will trust to pay back their debt, and in doing so I am fulfilling my obligations to the banks investors. In my world, banks only stay in business with sound investments and individuals who are willing to pay off their loans."

"I see, and I know that feeling. I guess just as it is for the Negro's attempt to survive and get started here in Boston, times are just as difficult in Virginia, I mean West Virginia. Many of the citizens are wondering where the help will come from and how soon."

As Pete boldly spoke, Thaddeus took a seat. After taking another sip of whiskey, he replied, "I can imagine that it's difficult for you to be living in Jefferson County. I mean I am sure that money is hard to come by since the banks were drained of their financial means due to the war, and no longer any Negro sweat being poured out to gain profits from. It must be difficult for you, especially since your home and business was destroyed and your Negro labor gone."

"Yes, I must admit it's difficult but we've begun rebuilding with what money we do have, and of course it's going to take time. In the future, Shenandoah might not be the farm that it once was but it will be close." Pausing and looking Thaddeus in the eye, Pete continued confidently, "With or without Negro help."

"James, how can you be so sure of success when there is so much instability in the South? You people are going to have to undertake readjustments without free Negro labor, and that is going to be troublesome for many. To be honest with you son, in many ways your family was bloody fortunate that you were still able to hold on to the property since your brother was serving the Davis government in this bloody rebellion. As I think about it, I don't understand how the Treasury Department overlooked the confiscation of your family's property."

As Thaddeus pondered on his last comment why Shenandoah hadn't been taken from the Barkers, he noticed the surprised expression covering Pete's face with this new revelation.

"Sir, what do you mean by that statement that my family is fortunate to still have our property. I don't understand?"

Rubbing his hand across his gray beard and believing that Pete didn't know what he was truly speaking, Thaddeus said in a surprised tone, "Ah, Mr. Barker, I can see by your bewildered expression that you really don't know what I have spoken of, do you sir?"

"No sir, I must be honest with you, I do not."

"Well let me explain to you Mr. Barker so that you'll have a clearer understanding. In June of 1862, the United States Congress passed a law that levied a tax on property owned by Southern families in the rebellious districts such as northern Virginia where you live. Commissioners were chosen and empowered so that in case of default, they could confiscate and sell the property. In order for the owner to hold onto the property, he had to appear in person and pay the taxes himself. If he didn't appear then he would lose the property. Even if someone else in his absence attempted to satisfy the debt for him, they would have been also refused and their payment wouldn't have been acceptable."

Thaddeus took another drink of his brandy. "But now Mr. Barker, with the conclusion of the war, your problems are more severe. Because under President Johnson's new plan for reconstruction of the Southern states, anyone that owns property in an excess value of $20,000 is going to lose their holdings anyway. I am sure that even though property in your area has deflated with the war destroying much, still your property is worth considerably more. With Johnson's plan, I'd say it still looks very troublesome. Not only for you but also for many of the plantations and farmers in the South that didn't have their holdings confiscated during the war. I am going to be the first to tell you that once your property becomes available, there will be some prospective Northern businessman with the money who will be there to buy up your holdings, that is, if the Negroes don't end up with it first." Pausing and waiting for a reaction that didn't come from Pete, Thaddeus continued, "Matter of fact, as I understand from Katherine, your family, I believe owns somewhere around 5,000 acres?"

"Yes sir they do."

"If the Northern opportunist doesn't take advantage of your misfortunes, and the Negroes don't take their spoils, then it's going to take a lot of money to keep the place running and profitable."

"True sir, times are difficult and we have been fortunate on many occasions but I am going to beat the chances against me. I will use every method and recourse available to me to hold onto the property."

With a surprised expression on his face at Pete's determination and answer, Thaddeus asked in a pitched tone as he raised his hands into the air. "How? You are in circumstances that you can't overcome nor control. Son, you are living in some kind of denial. You are part of the defeated rebellion. There are many out there that want to make you pay, and pay dearly for what you have done to this nation. Do you think that you can just pick up and start all over again like it was before the war? Ah, no Boy, that's not going to happen. And just remember this; that Thaddeus McBride told you so."

"Sir, with all due respect, although my family was wealthy one time of day, no one ever gave me anything. I've always worked for what I have, and I am a firm believer in hard work and persistence. With those qualities, I believe there is the possibility of an agreement with the War Department and loans from Northern investors. If so, I know I can make the farm profitable again."

Thaddeus rudely interrupted. "Like I said, maybe."

Pete wasn't discouraged by his comments; he continued to express his optimism. "I have a friend, a Negro, by the name of Hayward whom I have known for years and who worked for the family before the war. He is more than willing to contribute to the effort of rebuilding the estate. Sir, whether you chose to believe it or not, he shares the very same vision as I do."

"Even if you can hold on to the place, how will you pay him if you don't have the money?"

"I have given it considerable thought and I am going to give him several hundred acres to do with as he sees fit. And I will pay any other Negro who is willing to help me."

Thaddeus nodded his head in approval and was impressed by Pete's generosity. He said as he lit a cigar, "I must admit your offer would appear to be more than fair and it's very compassionate of you. Matter of fact, it surprises me. I would have thought that you held the Negro in the utmost contempt and hatred and like many living in the South think of them as an inferior race."

"No Mr. McBride, I don't hate the Negro. Personally, whether you believe it or not, my views on slavery were considerably different from my family. I didn't agree with stripping the Negro of his voice and freedom to do as he chooses. I have always tried to be fair and do the right thing even if his skin was a different color. Maybe you good people that have pushed the abolition movement may have just judged some Southerners unfairly. Not all of us have used the whip on the Negro to get him to work or to gain his respect and trust. Some of us didn't fight the war because we wanted to keep the Negro in bondage." Thaddeus tried to interrupt, but Pete gestured with his hands to allow him the opportunity to continue. "No sir, when it comes to the Negro, you're wrong if you think such a thing. Sir, many of us fought for the Confederacy because we didn't want the government intruding on our way of life, or our rights as free individuals. Like many, I fought the war to preserve those rights against a people that I felt was invading our state and declaring how we would live. But now with the war behind me, like many of the Confederate veterans I have personally spoken to, desire to have the opportunity to start over again, and put the animosity and hatred from the war behind us."

"But James, not everybody shares your sentiment."

"No sir, unfortunately they don't; some will always continue the fight beyond Appomattox."

Pointing his finger at Pete, Thaddeus said in a pitched voice. "Son, maybe you still don't understand. You're still paying for the bloody rebellion that you took part in and you're going to pay for it for many bloody years to come. With the radical behavior of some of those former Confederate soldiers who still want to destroy the Negro, it's only going to make things more difficult for you, and it's going to make things more difficult for the citizens of the South who desire to live in unity with the North. The reconstruction of the Southern states will be prolonged until those groups are dealt a blow. Until then, you'll continue to suffer from it."

Pete stood and began to pace. "Yes sir, I agree with you." Turning, he looked at Thaddeus. "But I can't let that stop me or destroy my dreams. Sir, hear my words, Shenandoah will be rebuilt."

"I am sure that you're determined," again pointing his finger in Pete's direction, he continued in a raised tone, "but whether it will be or not, it's still not the place for Katherine to be residing. She deserves better than what she has been given of you. And if you are able to hold onto the property, where will the money come from to operate the place?"

As Pete glanced out the window at the rose bush in front, he was reminded of the red rose that Hayward and he found after they returned to Shenandoah for the first time at the end of the war. That special rose was the only one that existed on the bush which was a mystery for that particular time of year. The rose was so full of life on the McBride's bush. It was the very same color and shape of the rose he gave Katie along the river when she returned later that same afternoon from Boston.

Pete's thoughts were broken, as Thaddeus demanded an answer. "Well, Boy come on, how are you going to come up with the money?"

Turning around, Pete looked at Thaddeus, sighing and approaching, he said, "Sir, as I am sure that you'll remember my words from a few minutes ago, I expressed the idea that it would take money and an agreement with the War Department and Northern investors. Again sir, individuals such as myself can only hope for the generosity and business opportunity presented from businessmen such as yourself. Without the assistance, maybe it will only be a matter of time before some of the farmers lose their property and homes because of debt and taxes. In truth, I've already felt the effects and received the threat of confiscation of Shenandoah. Sir, during the war, my brother owned the homestead, not my mother. He broke his contract with the government and invested the money from the horses and cattle he sold into worthless Confederate notes. Now, with his absence, I am trying to keep from losing the place."

After taking another puff form his cigar, Thaddeus replied calmly. "I take it that you want my help."

"Yes sir, I do. It would be greatly appreciated. Sir, my way of making Shenandoah profitable again would be through the War Department. They are going to need horses for the army. They will need the best, and I know how to breed them. Not only will they need horses but they'll also need good cattle for beef."

"What would you charge?"

"I have given it considerable thought and I feel the prices per pound for beef would be fair if we charged the same price as we did at the outset of the war. With the horses, it wouldn't be any different. It would hopefully make it easier for us to deal with the War Department since the nation went into great debt supporting the war effort For them it would make any agreement more desirable. Also, I would give them a guarantee we wouldn't raise any of the prices for the first three years."

Thaddeus was silent, his piercing gray eyes staring at Pete. Suddenly, he stood, puffing on his cigar; he walked over to the fireplace. Continuing his silence, he placed his arm on the mantel in continuous deep thought. Pete quietly observed him, looking for some indication from Thaddeus' facial features for his prospects for success. After flicking some ashes from the cigar into the fireplace, Thaddeus turned to look at Pete and asked, "How much to you owe?"

"Our back taxes amount to $2,500."

"I see that's quite an amount of money." Pausing from the conversation, Thaddeus stopped in the middle of the floor with his arms crossed and grinned. "James, I know my daughter all to well. It was probably her idea to come to Boston and ask for the help that you need. Am I not right?"

"Yes sir, you're correct. "

"She is always trying to help someone in some way. Ah, my Katherine is an amazing individual who will do just about anything within reason to see someone happy. Ah James, she could never stand to see someone who was without. I guess now I know that is one of the reasons why she went to Harpers Ferry, to help the Negro whom she's always felt a burden for." In a more serious tone of voice, Thaddeus cleared his throat. "Getting back to the point, as I understand from her correspondence, I knew things had been extremely difficult for you. Even though she didn't mention it, I knew there was the probability of a lack of money on your behalf and that you would be looking for help somewhere." Hesitating, he took another puff on his cigar and chose his words. Thaddeus began to pace and continued in a serious tone. "But to be honest with you due to political considerations and my influential Negro friends, mainly Mr. Douglas, I am not in the position to make that kind of loan to you. As you well know, my family strongly supports the rights and the equality of the Negro. Let's just say that I am offering a strong voice for them. But not only that issue alone, we strongly opposed the peace movement in the North that supported General McClellan's campaign for the presidency last year. It was on these fundamental reasons that I was elected as a representative to the Massachusetts House."

"In other words, you can be let's say, influenced?"

"Well let me ask you, if you were in my political position, how would it look to my supporters if I was to help you monetary or in any other way? Not bloody good, right?"

Pete remained silent as Thaddeus continued to explain his feelings. "I thought that you might agree. Besides to make my position known on the matter and to set the record straight, I feel the South should pay for the rebellion against this nation and be severely punished for the lives that were lost in putting down the Southern cause. My good and dear friend, Francis Shaw lost his only son, Robert, in 1863 near Charleston, South Carolina. As you may well know, he was the noble Colonel of the 54th Massachusetts Infantry who proved that the Negro soldier would fight if given the opportunity."

With Pete's eyes fixed and remaining silent, Thaddeus continued his indignation. "And if every bloody blasted one of you loses what you have for what you've done then so be it. Maybe, it's God's righteous judgment against you people, I don't know. But Mr. Barker, I want you to personally know the anger that I feel not only over that issue but also over the death of one of the most noblest and greatest men that I've ever had the pleasure of making an acquaintance; Abraham Lincoln. He was a man that I visited on numerous occasions when visiting Washington City and could call my personal friend. In history, he'll be recorded as one of the greatest presidents that ever lived because he fought to keep this country together. And I know what I am about to say will anger you even more and I truly hope that it does. But you must understand that I too have my convictions also on these matters. When the authorities catch up with your bloody brother, I pray they'll hang him along side of Mr. Davis just like they did those bloody infernal scoundrels that helped to kill Mr. Lincoln."

Pete was angry and ready to leave with such inflammatory comments but instead he repressed his emotions. As he had promised Katie, he wouldn't lose his temper and embarrass her. He had been prepared for such an encounter. Pete wasn't taken by surprise by anything that was said. His suspicions were confirmed that the McBrides did desire to see a punishing blow delivered against the Southern people. As Pete thought about the matter, he couldn't understand what possible constructive means could prevail from such an attitude and action. With people such as Thaddeus McBride, it would only prolong recovery of the Southern economy and unity within the nation. Pete tried to reason within his heart the political position of punishing the South that Thaddeus McBride was taking was one that was favorable through many circles in the Northern states. It would gather him the attention he needed to remain a voice within his state. Pete's thoughts were broken as Robert made the announcement that dinner was being served. For now he would withhold asking Thaddeus for Katie's hand in marriage and instead prepare for Seamus' return tomorrow.

Chapter 16

The next afternoon, Pete and Katie enjoyed some chowder at the Parker House Hotel located on School Street. Afterward, they departed and toured the city where Katie and he journeyed to the old State House, located near the waterfront on the northeastern side of the city. Walking around the hollowed grounds, Katie explained to Pete that the brick structure with its glass cupola was built in 1713. From its balcony, was the site where British troops in 1770 massacre some of the colonists for their protest and revolt against taxes on imported goods. She continued to emphasize that before the great revolutionary, Samuel Adams and other patriots used the dwelling as a meeting place to argue the issue for independence and arouse momentum for the great rebellion against England. Another important aspect of the state house she expounded on was where the Declaration of Independence had been read annually since July of 1776.

From there, Pete and Katie's journey took them to the oldest house of worship in the city, the North Church, which was built in 1723. On their approach, Pete was impressed with the brick-Georgian style architecture and the very tall steeple crowning the building. It was here in 1776 that Paul Revere received the first warning concerning the movement of British troops against the colonists in putting down the rebellion for independence from England. Once Pete entered the church, the appearance of the two brass chandeliers with doves mounted hanging above the center aisle, caught his attention, but the most lasting impression was the old clock that was constructed in 1726, hanging in the rear gallery. Pete marveled at the clock for sometime as Katie spoke of its history and the poem that Henry Wadsworth Longfellow wrote in 1860, Paul Revere's Ride, which spoke of the old North Church.

As Pete and Katie continued back through the city toward Beacon Hill, Pete noticed many of the residents going about their business or mingling in conversation along the street. He could tell by the way many were dressed that they were already or had become very wealthy from the war by making wise investments. As the horses moved at a slow pace, he noticed there were many shops and merchants to choose from and anything one might desire could easily be found. Boston was a city with over a

100,000 citizens. Soon Pete and Katie arrived at Faneuil Hall. It was a huge brick structure with many windows, doors, and a dome along the front crest of the building. What captured Pete's attention were the Doric brick pilasters surrounding the building, and the Ionic pilasters on the third floor. According to Katie's history, a wealthy merchant by the name of Peter Faneuil funded the construction of the building. It was used not only as a marketplace but also a meeting hall. The only history Katie withheld from him was the fact that prior to the Civil War, such notable leaders as Frederick Douglas and William Garrison used the dwelling as a place for arguing the evils of slavery and its abolishment.

After the informative tour of the historic city, Pete and Katie arrived at the corner of Beacon and Walnut Street. To their left was the area known by the locals as the Commons. Without warning, Katie suddenly instructed, "Shane, can you stop here and let us off?"

Pete turned to look at Katie. "Why?"

"I thought that you and I might spend sometime alone and walk along the path over to the pond where we can speak concerning private issues between us."

Pete assisted Katie from the carriage. "Shane, "Pete said, "You may return, we'll walk the rest of the way."

Pete watched the carriage move slowly in the direction of Walnut Street. Without hesitating, Katie took Pete by the arm and held her black parasol over her head to shade her eyes from the brightness of the late afternoon sun. As they quietly walked along the path, Pete knew their relationship had suffered a considerable amount of strain. This was probably the opportunity they needed to speak privately and settle the doubts of some issues that had recently been plaguing them. Turning to glance at Katie, he noticed the troubled expression covering her face. "I see the leaves on the trees have a tint of autumn mixed within," Pete said.

"Yes, they do. It probably means there will be an early winter. Snow and coldness generally comes early to Boston." Hesitating for a moment, Katie changed the subject and asked in a curious tone. "I know there hasn't been the chance to ask with mother or father being around most of the time, but how did things go between father and you yesterday?"

"In my opinion, not well. Personally, I hope what I am about to say you'll not be offended, but I really don't feel that your parents care for my presence. Since I fought for the Confederacy, I guess I can understand their emotions and all that they've been through. The war makes it very difficult to bury the past with everything that happened. The way that many families had to suffer, it will be this way for some time."

"Then I guess my father isn't willing to help you with a loan to pay off the taxes. "

Pete remained silent, shaking his head, indicating the answer was no. Katie glanced at him. "Why? What reason did he give you?"

"Your father feels he's in a political position that won't allow him to make such a loan or even to support one. With the abolitionist and Negro leaders that supported his election, and I am sure the leadership of the Republicans, it would place him in a troubled situation. Actually, I don't know of any politician that wants to jeopardize his chances of re-election. They want to continue to possess the kind of power and authority that the people gave them."

"No it's not that, I know my father all too well. The problem is, it's just his bloody Irish stubbornness."

Pete noticed the disappointment covering Katie's features. "I do have to admit, at times on the trip here, I felt some confidence with your optimism, but now I don't know how we'll be able to hold onto Shenandoah."

Tears began to trickle down Katie's cheeks. "I am sorry. Maybe, I gave you a false impression concerning what my family would be willing to do for us. I really believed my father would do this for me. I will speak to him when we return."

"Katie, it won't do any good. His mind is made up whether it is his stubborn behavior or if he is telling the truth. His hands are really tied."

"Pete Barker, blood is thicker than water."

Pete grinned at Katie's determination even though he believed her father's position was firm. Pete had come to know from his own experiences that Katie didn't always accept no for an answer. She would continue her quest until all of the options had been exhausted.

Within minutes, Pete and Katie were standing by the pond. Katie watched some of the fish near the surface. In anticipation of coming to this area after lunch, Katie had taken half of one of the dinner rolls that was left and pulled it from her basket. Tearing small pieces from the roll, she tossed it into the water toward the fish. Turning around and glancing at the surprised expression covering Pete's face, Katie smiled. "Why do you appear so surprised?"

With his hands on his hips and shaking his head in acknowledgement, he replied in a humorous tone of voice, "Katie McBride, you always continue to astonish me. You know that it's not appropriate to take leftovers from the table. And not only that but you placed the roll in your basket?"

Katie chuckled as she continued to feed the fish. "I am not always prim and proper when it comes to etiquette. Right?"

"How did you manage to place that roll in your basket without me noticing?"

Katie smiled, rolling her eyes around. "Oh, it happened when I had your attention and was speaking about visiting the State House. Actually, at the time you were looking me in the eyes."

"But still, I would have noticed."

"You weren't watching my hands." Finally, they were silent just looking at the fish and the water. After several minutes had passed, Katie said in a more serious tone. "I wish life could always be as carefree as we just experienced."

Pete removed his hat. "I share your views, but life has dealt us an unfair hand and we must accept the challenge and make the best of the circumstances. If we don't, then Katie it's over with, we will never survive."

"What do you mean by those words?"

"Simply this. I feel with the circumstances surrounding our possibility of losing Shenandoah, somewhere the strain of trying to survive is going to take a toll on us emotionally. It's difficult because we can't accomplish the ambitions that we have set for ourselves and eventually it might destroy what we have between us."

Katie became frustrated, pointing in the direction of her home. "Were you or were you not the one who said yesterday that your love wasn't shallow and had depth to it?"

"Yes, but..."

Katie interrupted and fired back in an angry tone. "Then wait a bloody minute Pete Barker. Let it never be said that Katherine McBride wasn't willing to give her all. And that means not only my effort, time, and loyalty but most of all my love and affection."

"Katie, it's going to be tough. It's going to be an up hill struggle with many obstacles and challenges. And we may have to prepare ourselves for a struggle that we might not win. Try to see it from my side. Your father is correct in his perception that Harpers Ferry is still an unsafe place to be. Besides, look at what happened to Hayward and me; we nearly got killed along the river. And if that isn't enough, then also for just a moment, think of yourself. You have to look at pursuing your dreams and desires in this life."

Pausing and approaching Katie, Pete placed his hands on her shoulders and continued to express his words and emotions. "Katie, you're still young and I know there is much that you want to have in this life such as a home. Maybe if you're fortunate, something like what your family owns, and hopefully, the nice things to go with it. But most of all, I know you want a family and stability. I don't know that I can offer all of those things to you right now, even though I would like to, even though it's my heart's desire. I guess what I am saying is that you deserve better then what you're getting and what I am able to give you at this time."

Katie's features showed her frustration as she quickly answered. "I am not fooled for one moment. It sounds like something that my father said to you. Pete, my father just wants you to feel guilty. My parents are attempting to dominate me through you. All they want is for me to return home and be something that they desire. Truly, I don't feel they really care about my hopes and dreams nor my happiness."

"Katie, I must admit, I want you to have only the best that life can offer."

"Pete, my love, please don't try to run from me again like you did during the war. Listen to me my love. I have found the desires and wishes of my heart with you. My trust is in you and the relationship that we share. The challenges we are facing are ours together. My survival doesn't depend on whether we will live at Shenandoah or the nice things that you want to give me, but it depends on your love and commitment to me. It's that one thing I have drawn strength from and it's the one thing that encourages me and I depend on for my survival."

As Katie gazed at Pete's somber expression, she quietly caressed his cheek with her hand. Tears filled her eyes as she gently embraced Pete, kissing him passionately. Afterward, she continued to gaze into his eyes hoping for a reaction to her affection that wasn't expressed. Again, she caressed his cheek. This time she noticed tears filling his eyes. Somewhere within her heart, Katie was beginning to fear she was about to lose the only man she had truly loved. For the past five years, the closeness that they shared made her feel that she had known and loved him for a lifetime. Now their relationship was in jeopardy and she could see it vanishing such as a vapor on a cold winter night.

Chapter 17

It was late in the afternoon. Seamus McBride was dining alone on fresh scrod and potatoes. Seamus spent the last five days in Hartford, Connecticut and had just arrived home. He was exhausted from raising money for a business enterprise that he had engaged in with several of his comrades from his former cavalry regiment, the 1st Massachusetts.

As Seamus sat in the dining room, he thought of the many settlers that were moving west across the plains as far as California looking for property to begin a homestead or a new business venture that would serve the needs of the new settlers. With the conclusion of the Civil War, some of these settlers were Confederate veterans and Southern civilians that had lost everything during the conflict and had nothing left. Not only those issues ignited the movement westward but also the chance to escape the oppression of reconstruction.

With the outbreak of Indian hostilities against settlers during the Civil War in the Dakota and Colorado territories, the problem now was becoming more troublesome. More recently the Indians fought against Mormon frontiersmen in Utah. With no other alternative, the regular army had begun to increase its strength in these regions. This is the reason why Seamus and his comrades had traveled to Hartford to secure more funds from a potential investor, Patrick O'Malley, who was another prominent Irish businessman.

After their presentation, Seamus and his investors offered O'Malley the opportunity to join them in patenting and manufacturing a repeating rifle such as the Henry and Spencer weapons for the army's use. O'Malley was exuberant over the idea of developing a weapon that would fire with a greater accuracy, possess a greater caliber, and be lighter in weight for easy firing. O'Malley accepted their invitation. He pledged thousands of dollars into the venture. Before departing, Seamus wired the first of those pledges to his bank account in Boston. Seamus was delighted and possessed great expectations for this business enterprise. With his father's mentoring on business issues and now with another investor, the future appeared promising and full of hope. Seamus and his investors possessed the ability to outbid and prosper over their competitors. If all was successful, as he had planned, Seamus knew that over the next three years he would be in a position to buy out his partners.

Once Seamus finished his meal, he slowly sipped on hot tea. His green eyes scanned the latest headlines in the Boston Courier newspaper. His father and mother had gone to a reception held at the Governor's mansion for one of the representatives that was retiring for health reasons after serving in the Massachusetts House for over thirty years. After wiping his mouth, he stood and walked to a desk in the family library where he began to compose a correspondence to a friend, Captain Augustus Williams formerly of the 4th Pennsylvania Cavalry.

In the campaign against the Confederate Army of Northern Virginia in the spring of 1864, Seamus and Williams had served together in the 1st Brigade of Brigadier-General David McMurtrie Gregg's Division. Seamus had met Williams under the most peculiar circumstances when both were captured while battling Confederate General Fitzhugh Lee's cavalry during the Trevillion Raid. Both men knew that being officers meant their destiny would be Libby Prison in Richmond. Since 1862, Seamus and Williams like many had heard the rumors and testimonies throughout the Union Army of the Potomac concerning the living conditions and the horrors of confinement at this particular prison. It was quickly decided by them that the effort to escape was worth the risk. After darkness the day of their capture, the two officers, along with five other soldiers of less rank, attempted to escape but only Seamus and Williams were successful. The other men of lesser rank where either recaptured or killed while making the attempt. From that time on, Seamus and Williams had bonded, becoming the best of friends until their separation after the Confederates surrendered at Appomattox. Since then, they had continued their communication by correspondence.

After finishing a few lines of his correspondence to Augustus, Seamus paused to ponder on what to write next. Without warning, his thoughts were interrupted by the noise of the main door being closed. He stood and walked toward the entrance of the room where he noticed his sister Katie had just entered and was handing her parasol to Robert. Seamus' eyes brighten as he quickened his pace to greet his sibling. He stretched forth his arms. "Katie, Katie, I am so glad to see you."

Katie began to smile as she embraced her brother. After kissing him on the cheek, she said, "Seamus, it too is good to see you." Katie looked at her well-groomed brother's appearance. "Seamus McBride in the past two years you haven't changed at all. I have missed you more then you'll ever know, and I thank God that you made it home safely."

"Ah, Katie, you haven't changed since the last time that I saw you in that hell hole of a forsaken bloody town in Virginia called Harpers Ferry," Seamus laughingly added.

Katie looked at Seamus and said in a joking manner as she removed her white gloves, "I was hoping after your visit to that hell hole of a bloody forsaken town as you call it that you would have kept in touch with me like you promised. But as usual, you didn't. Seamus McBride, you always make promises that you don't keep. If I heard anything about your welfare it was from Mother whenever she wrote me."

Before Seamus and Katie spoke another word, Pete entered the front door. A surprise expression covered Seamus' face. He recognized Pete from the Battle of Antietam Creek. Swiftly, his mind drifted back to the day after the bloody confrontation when both Federal and Confederate forces had agreed upon a truce. For Seamus and Pete, it was a rare coincidence that both of them should meet in this manner since they both had a relationship with Katie. On that September afternoon in 1862, Pete was hungry and without anything to eat. He reluctantly made an exchange with Seamus for the ruby jeweled birthstone that he had received from his mother as a gift. During their brief exchange of conversation, Pete asked Seamus if he knew Katie. Seamus confirmed Pete's suspicion that Katie was indeed his sister, but before the two men departed they went to blows with each other verbally and almost physically. Now that the war was concluded, Seamus still didn't care to meet Katie's suitor and he suspected that the feeling was mutual as far as Pete was concerned. Now they were both looking each other in the eye with Katie standing between them.

Inwardly, Katie was nervous and frightened knowing the dislike Seamus and Pete possessed for each other. Katie knew she had to maintain her quiet manner and hoped that the gentleman that each proclaimed to be, would remain calm and composed, not only for their own pride and dignity but also their confessed love for her. Without asking her brother's permission and without hesitation, Katie took the initiative and boldly acted by formally introducing Seamus to Pete. "My brother Seamus, I would like to introduce you to my suitor James Pete Barker."

Knowing that he had no other choice in this situation, Seamus out of respect for his sister reluctantly stretched forth his hand, "Mr. Barker, again we meet. Let's say this time it's under more pleasant and peaceful circumstances rather then on the field of battle."

Pete was just as reluctant as Seamus. As they stood less then seven feet apart, Pete and Seamus' eyes remained on each other. Pete hesitantly stretched forth his hand. "Yes, I agree, and now I finally have the chance to meet you under let's just say, reduced emotional distress."

After the introductions, Pete, Seamus, and Katie quietly walked into the parlor. Immediately, Seamus summoned the butler asking him to rekindle the fire in the fireplace. After stoking the embers and placing a few more logs on the smoldering fire, Robert quietly poured Seamus a brandy while serving Pete and Katie water.

Pete continued to be very cautious of Seamus, knowing that he had an explosive temper and like some of the Union veterans, he didn't believe that Seamus was ready to commit himself to putting the war behind and burying the past. In a bold manner to break the tenseness that filled the air, Pete was the first to speak. "Seamus, as I understand from Katie, you have been in Hartford on business."

With his piercing eyes blazing, Seamus placed his liquor on the small marble-top table and answered in a boastful tone. "Yes sir Mr. Barker, several of the officers that I served with in the past rebellion have entered into a business arrangement with me in producing a rapid firing, high caliber rifle for the army's use in the western territories. As I see it, if everything progresses, as it should, then this time next year, we shall be able to outbid our competitors and hopefully develop a monopoly on the small weapons industry. We are close to our goal and hopefully within the next six months, will be in a position to present our rifle to the army for their approval."

Katie looked at her brother. "That is good news. I am sure that you must be excited and encouraged by your progress with this new invention."

Desiring to say little in the conversation, but wanting to remain cordial, Pete added, "Yes, Seamus, I must agree with your sister. It appears that you have an open door for opportunity."

Inwardly, Seamus was burning with anger at Pete's presence and his sister's aggressiveness for bringing him to their home. What inflamed matters is that he knew Pete was the youngest brother of Charles Barker, an aide to the Confederate President Jefferson Davis. Seamus was like his father because he also desired harsh punishment for the rebellious Southern states and for the treachery toward President Lincoln. For these reasons, it was all that he could do to maintain his composure. In some way it was his desire to humiliate and disgrace Pete in some fashion before his sister, and at the same time drive him from his presence and home. He decided to look for such an opportunity. He knew his actions and words would upset Katie. The resentment of seeing many of his men wounded, killed, and sometimes never given the opportunity to surrender during the fighting fueled the hatred that dominated his heart and mind. When he gazed across the room at Pete, all that he saw was another rebel who was responsible for the anguish and misery inflicted on the soldiers' families that had fought with his regiment. Seamus knew from his father the misfortunes that Pete was experiencing with the destruction of Shenandoah and that Pete's family was fighting for its survival.

Seamus took a sip of his brandy. "As I understand from my sister's correspondence your property was destroyed by Yankee raiders during the war, and now you are in the process of rebuilding or should I say attempting to rebuild your homestead?"

"Yes, you are correct. At the moment, we are rebuilding the house, but I know that it's going to take sometime."

Katie's eyes came to life. There was enthusiasm in her tone. "Oh, Seamus, if you could witness the beauty and experience the sound of the river running alongside of the property. The multitude of rolling green slopes, the tall mountains, and experience the tranquil life that I have had the honor of being blessed with, then you, too, would have fallen in love with Shenandoah such as I did."

"Yeah, I am sure that I would have. Honestly, I don't mean to be belligerent, but I have seen all of Virginia that I desire to see in this lifetime."

"Oh Seamus, I must apologize. Please forgive me for being so thoughtless. I didn't take into consideration your feelings because as mother wrote me, you are still experiencing the wounds from the war." Quickly, Katie turned her attention to Pete. "And I know also that it's still difficult for you my love, but what I have to say comes from the depths of my heart, and I want both of you to hear me out."

Pete and Seamus paid Katie the courtesy of remaining silent. Finally after gaining her thoughts, Katie continued in a soft and serious tone. "The war has been difficult on everyone that played a part in it, whether they were actually fighting on some far off battlefield in Virginia or remaining at home waiting for a loved one to return from conflict in Pennsylvania. I know from my own experience with both of you." Looking at her brother, she said, "Seamus you fought with a Northern cavalry regiment. You served the Union for the principles that you believed to be right, which was its preservation and the abolishment of slavery."

Turning to face Pete, Katie continued, "And you, Pete, fought with a Southern regiment against an army of men from the North that you believed was invading your homeland with the intentions of enforcing their ways and principles upon you and your family."

Looking at both men once more, Katie continued to pour out her heart. "I want both of you to know that it tore my heart to shreds to see you two men that I dearly love, fighting against one another, not knowing if you were safe from harms way. Day and night, both of you were constantly in my prayers and thoughts. I didn't know from one day to the next what news to expect when reading the newspapers, or by correspondence from mother, or most often the news that would be posted on the bulletin board at the telegraph office. I lived in constant fear for your welfare so much so that many nights it was difficult for me to sleep, especially knowing that the armies were on the move and would soon be engaged in some terrible battle. As I am sure, both of you have seen and heard things during battle and afterwards that will always leave a scar on your mind. You both have been compelled to act in a way that was unimaginable in order to survive, but now you both must make the attempt to move on with your lives. Now that the great conflict has ended and both of you by God's grace have been given the gift of life, there is the opportunity for reconciliation. Once the war ended, I must confess that I was living in some kind of dream thinking that life would rapidly return to normal and that many of the people from the North and South would be able to make amends and put the past behind them. But I guess I was just kidding myself. I now know that it's going to take some time; maybe a lot of time, but I hope and pray that it can start in this room here today with this family."

Seamus fired back once more in a skeptical tone of voice. "Ah Katie, living in Virginia near this bloody Johnnie has poisoned your precious mind."

"Ah Seamus, Seamus, why..."

"Katie you don't bloody know for one moment what I went through, and the experiences that I endured fighting the bloody Johnnies. It's a horrible nightmare to have another soldier's brains and blood splattered all over your face, and body, and still another soldier crying with pain asking to be put out of his misery. There isn't a night that doesn't pass by that I don't still see their faces when I sleep. Katie McBride, it's easy for you to try and lecture me on forgiveness and all of those religious virtues, but you didn't see the war as I did. If you could have witnessed the wretched features, the stench from the blackened-bloated bodies that were not buried, and the bloody screaming and cursing from some soldier while a surgeon removed an arm or leg, you would feel the same as me." Seamus' features were tense as he continued to speak his heart. "Katie, what I experienced was enough to make one sick to their stomach and leave an unmanageable impression upon one's mind that he will never forget."

"I have some knowledge of what you're going through from my own experiences. I know that it hurts," Katie replied in a sympathetic tone.

Seamus quietly looked at Katie and Pete in a defiant manner. Abruptly, he turned and threw the brandy glass toward the fireplace. "No Katie, you don't have the least amount of understanding as to what I went through. I couldn't wish that kind of hell on anybody." Seamus pointed in Pete's direction and continued to verbally pour out his anger. "A lot of good men from my command would be at home today if it hadn't been for those bloody Johnnies such as that one sitting there."

Pete remained silent knowing the situation could quickly get out of control. But not Katie, she was willing to continue to plead her convictions. "Seamus McBride, you're not the only one that has suffered."

Seamus' temper was spiraling rapidly out of control. Again he shouted as he swiftly approached Katie. "I am not going to have you bringing this bloody low life into our house and causing differences in our family."

Pete continued to observe Seamus' tense features. He feared Seamus might unintentionally strike Katie a blow with his fist that was already clinched. Without hesitation, Pete jumped from his seat and placed himself between Katie and Seamus. He said in an authoritative tone as he raised his hand gesturing for Katie's brother to halt. "No, Seamus!"

Once Seamus saw that Pete was ready to intervene, he paused and said angrily, "Katie, I don't know why you want so much to defend this Johnnie. You are betraying everything that you believed in when you left home to go to that bloody hell hole in Virginia."

"Seamus I was just as loyal to the Union as you were, but now that the war is over, I can't see the reason why this bitterness should continue."

"Come on Katie, the game is over with."

Rapidly becoming frustrated with the bickering, Pete said in a serious tone, "What do you mean by that Seamus?"

Seamus looked at his sister and Pete laughing as if someone had shared a humorous joke with him. Again, he pointed at Pete and asked Katie, "Does he know why a young lady from Massachusetts such as yourself would travel so far away from home to live in of all places Virginia? No, I didn't think so. Apparently he doesn't know the real truth of who Katie McBride really is." Turning and pointing at Pete, "Aye, Johnnie she is very smart. Smart enough that she kept you in the dark with her innocent, charming charismatic ways, but in reality Katie McBride is not the person that you think that she is."

Turning his attention once more toward Katie, Seamus began to laugh loudly. "I guess you've never told him you were spying for our cause and you were passing information across the lines to your contacts living in Sandy Hook and Frederick." Pausing and assessing the verbal damage, Seamus continued in a taunting tone. "What is this you said earlier that we have to get over the war? Katie, Katie, my sister, are you not the one who was playing both sides of the game? I am sure that probably on more than one occasion you were able to garnish information from Mr. Barker on Jeb Stuart's cavalry positions in the lower Shenandoah Valley or other Johnnies." Turning once more and facing Pete, Seamus continued, "Mr. Barker you must be the biggest, bloodiest fool on this earth, or blinded by love and passion." Shaking his head and continuing to laugh, Seamus added, "Mr. James Barker, you should have been able to put two and two together. If you had been smart enough, you could have figured it all out."

As Seamus looked on, Pete turned to look at Katie for an explanation. There was a bewildered expression covering her beautiful features. "Are these accusations true? Were you using me?"

Katie was silent by her brother's outburst of words, wild accusations, and Pete's demand for an answer. The only emotion she shared was a tear trickling down her left cheek.

As Pete looked Katie in the eyes, he witnessed the pain and betrayal they reflected. On past occasions when her world was falling apart around her, she desired his embrace and comfort. Due to his distrust, he couldn't. The thought of her passing information harming the Southern effort and possibly causing the destruction of Shenandoah as a result was once again resurrected within his mind. Pete shook his head, turned and walked away.

Chapter 18

After the verbal confrontation with Katie and Pete, Seamus left the residence for the northeast end of the city where he wanted to enjoy a few beers at his favorite pub, O'Rourke's. Seamus was still troubled over the incident when he walked into the smoke filled, dimly lighted establishment, which was located near the waterfront.

As Seamus looked around, many of the men were sitting at tables playing cards. A few were arm wrestling for money, and near the entrance where he was standing, several men that had a little too much to drink were arguing with each other over a lady. Nearby, the jovial sound of patriotic songs and hands with beer mugs raised caught his attention from a number of men wearing blue kepis. Seamus knew by the Maltese Cross covering the crown of one of the kepis that the individuals were wearing that these men were former members of the Irish 9th Massachusetts Infantry. The soldiers served under the command of Colonel Patrick Guiney, and were one of the regiments that made up the famous Fifth Corps of the Army of the Potomac. For a brief moment, Seamus pondered on the extensive and difficult fighting that the regiment undertook from Mechanicsville in June of 1862 to Cold Harbor in June of 1864. He knew from his own experience that many were fortunate to have returned home to their families.

Continuing to look toward the rear of the establishment where the bar was located, Seamus noticed an acquaintance from the war was seated at a table in the far corner. Without hesitation, Seamus made his way to the rear through the crowded tavern to where his old friend Patty Adair was seated. Once Seamus approached, he caught Patty's attention by patting him on the back, "Ah, Seamus, my Boy, you look like you need to have a few beers with the old boys and me."

A smile radiated from Seamus' face as he took a seat opposite of his friend. With Patty, were several Irish laborers, who were rough and muscular in appearance from the local shipyard. Seamus didn't personally know them, so Patty introduced Seamus to the two individuals as his major during his time in the military.

With a cigar pressed tightly against the left side his mouth, Patty opened the conversation. "Ah, Laddy, you seem to be in a jolly mood this evening. Why might that be?"

"My sister has just returned home and believes that she is in love with some bloody Johnnie from Virginia. Ah, but Patty my friend, I pitched into them and gave them the devil for their bloody sin. You know how I feel about the Johnnies and other things."

Nodding his head in agreement, Patty looked up from the table. "Ah Seamus, my Boy, you should have invited him along for a few beers. What are friends for?"

"Patty, you need to take me bloody serious about this."

"Yeah, Laddy, I know. You must forgive old Patty for being so rude. But I must say, that it was very bold of Miss Katherine to bring him here, especially this soon after the war. Why Laddy it might not be bloody safe for him, at least ways on this side of town."

Seamus lit a cigar. "Oh, that won't happen, but I must be honest with you, I saw bloody red when that blasted low-life entered my home. If it wouldn't have been out of respect for my sister, I would have tore into him and sent him back to Old Virginy with his tail between his legs. Remember Patty. Just like we did the rest of those bloody rebs when they retreated from Petersburg."

Over the past months, Patty had grown weary of listening to Seamus boast about his money, prosperity, and now this evening his conquest over another individual. Patty quickly changed the subject to one of interest to him. "So your sister has returned home you say?"

"Yeah, Patty, Katie returned yesterday afternoon. I must admit, I haven't seen her for quite sometime, but the sight of that Johnnie sort of dampened my enthusiasm."

Patty asked as he puffed on the cigar. "Tell me Laddy, is Miss Katie as pretty as she was when I saw her before she left for Virginia?"

Before Patty could continue, Seamus interrupted, "Patty, your thirteen years older then Katie. Besides, she is so blinded by this bloody rebel's charm that she probably wouldn't look at another man, even a good Irish gentleman such as yourself."

Everyone seated at the table broke out in laughter. After taking another drink of his beer, Patty placed his hand on Seamus' shoulder. "Seamus, Seamus, my Boy, you and me, we go back a lot of years. Long, long before the war. Don't you think that as your good Irish friend that old Patty is entitled to make a run at your sister?"

Seamus knew that Patty and the other two men had been drinking beer for some time and were beginning to feel its effects. Even though Seamus didn't agree with Patty's comments, he laughed just as jovially as they did.

Chapter 19

At the McBride residence, Katie sat alone on the sofa in the parlor while Pete was upstairs in his bedroom. As she listened to the crackling sound of the fire burning in the fireplace, she wiped the tears from her eyes with her handkerchief. She thought about how unprepared she was to face her brother. She underestimated the resentment that he still possessed within his heart and mind. Katie was hurt and in deep anguish over his verbal assault and his abuse toward Pete. She knew that Seamus' behavior had always been unpredictable ever since they were young and growing up in Boston. Often, the academy where Seamus attended had threatened him with expulsion for fighting, but his father always intervened and persuaded the superintendent of the school to take him back. Katie had always believed that in time Seamus would learn to control his emotions and refrain from acting so carelessly and negligent. With his actions this evening, she didn't see any difference nor was there any evidence that he had even made the attempt over these past years to change. Unfortunately, his cockiness, cynicism, and sarcasm had increased with time and age.

Seamus, like Katie, had always been given everything that life had offered. In Seamus' case, he took it for granted but with Katie, the material wealth and possessions were not the things that brought about the fulfillment that she needed in her life. Katie always wanted to be loved and it was the most important virtue that she needed and strived to accomplish. At one time, the actions came from her mother but since midway during the war, much to her despair, her mother had become so indifferent and bitter. She was not the same person that Katie once knew. As for her brother Seamus, he also had grown cold and stern in his demeanor toward not only others but toward her. When it came to the family, it was the one attribute that didn't change over the years. Their critical observation of another person was something that Katie had discovered early that she abandoned in her own life. Now disgusted after everything that had happened thus far with this particular visitation with her family, Katie was ready to return to Harpers Ferry. Even without her father's blessings on her forth-coming marriage.

Katie's thoughts turned toward Pete. She knew from the very beginning of the trip that they had begun to experience difficulties within their relationship. His trust in her was compromised since she didn't inform him of her father's stately position prior to the war and now in Massachusetts's politics. Katie knew for sometime that Pete had been struggling with his pride. He was barely able to provide for her and now his family. After possessing an exuberant life style and having any possession that one desired, his life now was a humbling experience and he was having a very difficult time of living and accepting its terms. Now with Seamus' revelations and accusations of her passing information across Southern lines to Federal authorities, Katie now feared that the end of her relationship with Pete would be terminated. All of the trust and challenges they both had built their life upon and the tribulations they endured together over the last five years was poisoned by Seamus' words. Maybe, had she listened to Pete and not have made the journey, their life together would be different.

Katie's thoughts were interrupted by the sound of Pete's footsteps entering the parlor. She quietly and tearfully looked up from gazing at the floor and stared at him. He, too, was quiet as if waiting for a word to come from her, though Katie remained silent. After a minute had passed, Pete approached Katie. Katie continued her silence, but her eyes followed him walking across the floor. For the first time since their acquaintance, Katie was afraid to speak out of fear of what Pete might say, especially the words that "it's over with between us." Pete quietly sat next to Katie. She continued to look at him waiting for a word of reassurance such as he had spoken on past difficult situations.

Finally, knowing that something must be said, she spoke with softness and trembling in her tone. "Pete, I must say something to you. First I'd like to apologize to you." Tears began to rapidly flow from Katie's eyes. She continued to attempt to control her composure as she spoke. "Please understand that it is very difficult for me to speak at the moment but I feel that I must. I know your visit to Boston with my family hasn't been a pleasant experience for you. The rejection that you must feel by them must cause you considerable hurt and bitterness, especially from my brother. In my opinion, all of them have judged you unfairly. Seamus' actions and anger were uncalled for and I feel so hurt and betrayed by all the words he has said to you and me on this evening. When someone hurts you, they hurt me also. Maybe it would be best if we leave tomorrow and return to Shenandoah."

"I must admit that I came here with many doubts about receiving any help from your family. At times Katie, I feel that both of us were kidding ourselves when we trusted that with the end of the war that amends would begin to take place between our families, but I guess that's not to be the case. There have been many things about this trip that have disturbed me, but the accusations that Seamus made concerning your role during the war troubles me more then anything. Often since we spoke that afternoon on Short Hill Mountain concerning your possible involvement with passing information and spying for the Federals, the question has continuously raised many doubts within my heart. I don't know why you've never admitted or disclaimed your role."

With her composure under control, Katie said at the conclusion of his sentence, "And I remember that I asked you, would it make any difference."

"Yes, you did."

"Well would it?" Pete remained silent as Katie continued to speak her heart. "But more important to me at this moment is, are you doubting the sincerity of my love for you. Haven't I proven over and over again my commitment and loyalty to you?"

"Katie, there is something that you don't know, but that I do."

"And what don't I know?"

"The evening that Shenandoah was destroyed, I was there after the Yankees' raid."

"Why didn't you try to make the attempt to see me?"

"It was because I was afraid of first compromising my identity and secondly the truth of my assignment. At the time, if the Federals had found out that I was one of Mosby's men, and what I was doing in Harpers Ferry other then posing as a preacher they would have hung me. But I must confess, I did see you walking from the school to the church. I knew then you must have known about my supposed death at Gettysburg. I must confess, it hurt and depressed me that I couldn't see nor embrace you and tell you that everything would be all right. But I couldn't. During that time, I was struggling with my feelings for you, trying desperately to repress what I knew to be true, even hoping that you'd find another gentleman that was more worthy of your love than me. I thought of the great pain and anguish that you were going through but again I was afraid of getting caught. All of this happened the afternoon just before Shenandoah was destroyed."

"Is that all or is there more?"

"Yes, I am afraid so. Once I arrived at Shenandoah, there wasn't much of anything of value left after the burning. My mother and Caroline tried to understand how this could happen to innocent civilians, but they were too terrified and stunned by what took place."

As Pete continued to reveal his secret from the previous months, he noticed the anguish in Katie's expression. "Within thirty minutes of my arrival, Daniel appeared after making a trip to Charlestown. He informed us that he had seen you earlier in the afternoon at Harpers Ferry accompanied by an officer that you met at the train depot. From there, he was very suspicious of you and followed the officer and you to the armory paymaster's home, used by General Howe as his headquarters on Fillmore Street. Daniel said that he continued to stay hidden from sight and observed you and the two officers speaking on the front porch of the General's headquarters. Before you departed, a courier approached your party and spoke with the general. From there he rapidly departed. Later that evening, General Hunter ordered the torching of homes near Charlestown and then Shenandoah. Over the next couple of evenings, the Yankee cavalry continued its warfare on innocent civilians by destroying Congressman Boteler's home, Fountain Rock near Shepherdstown and Mr. Lee's home, Bedford. The destruction of private property would have undoubtedly continued if it hadn't been for General Early sending McCausland's Confederate raider into Chambersburg and setting the town on fire."

For a moment, Katie remained silent, her teary eyes staring at Pete. She was taken by surprise by his revelation and understanding of events that took place last year. "And you believe that I am responsible in someway for your loss as well as the others that you just named?"

"To be honest with you Katie, I don't know what to believe anymore." Pausing and looking at Katie for a reaction or a word, Pete continued in a determined tone. "I know that it has been a difficult evening for you, so for now I won't press the subject. Instead, I am going to find your brother and speak about these things with him. Afterward, you and I will speak again."

Chapter 20

After Pete finished speaking with Katie, he inquired from Robert, the butler, where Seamus usually passed the evening. The butler informed him, that Seamus and his friends on most occasions enjoyed a few beers at the establishment of O'Rourke's. Immediately, Pete decided this would be the place where he would begin looking for Seamus. Before departing, Robert also informed him that it could be dangerous along the waterfront where O'Rourke's was located because of the amount of robberies that had taken place over the past five months. Pete thanked Robert and turned once more looking into the parlor where Katie quietly sat gazing aimlessly at the flickering fire in the fireplace. Without saying another word, Pete quickly departed the residence and saddled a horse.

Pete rode a short distance along Washington Street. There, he noticed some of the citizens entering the Boston Theatre where Katie and he had planned on attending this evening. But now, with the change of events taking place at the McBride residence, Pete found himself instead going into an unfamiliar area after dark without a weapon for protection. From Washington Street, Pete turned his horse east along Franklin Street, passing the Washington Gardens, continuing to proceed in an easterly direction. After little difficulty finding his way around the huge city, he soon found himself at the corner of Olive and Purchase Street. He paused and gazed around trying to determine whether he should proceed in a northern or southern direction along this particular street.

Nearly three hours had passed since Seamus had confronted Pete and Katie. Like Patty and the other two men that were with him, Seamus was feeling his liquor. He paused from the conversation he was enjoying with his Irish comrades and removed his fancy gold-leaf timepiece from his pocket. According to his timepiece, it was nearing 7:30 in the evening. He rubbed a hand across his face. "Ah, my good, good Irish friend, I hate to depart from such good company, but I must leave you. I have some business that needs my attention early tomorrow morning."

With Seamus buying one round of beer after another, Patty pleaded as he grabbed his arm, "No, no Laddy, you can't go, the evening is just beginning."

Seamus pulled more money from his pocket and placed it on the table. "Patty, you and the boys have another round on me."

Seamus looked at Patty, saluted, and turned toward the entrance of the establishment. As he did so, Patty turned to look at his two silent comrades. As he began to grin, he nodded in a gesturing fashion for them to follow Seamus. Quietly, they both stood and left the table knowing the meaning of the gesture.

Once Seamus departed O'Rourke's, he paused and lit what was left of his cigar. After looking around, he turned and began to stagger along the street. Finally, after finding his horse among some others, he untied the reins. As he was about to mount the animal, he heard a voice calling, "Ah, Laddy, wait for a moment?"

Seamus turned around and attempted to recognize the two male figures. He paused as they approached. Once they had his attention, they quickened their pace.

"What can I do for you?" Seamus asked in a slurred speech.

One of the men pulled a knife from his coat pocket and placed the blade against Seamus' ribs. "Laddy, if you know what's good for your bloody soul then you best go along with us."

Once the second man seized Seamus by the arm, Seamus was ordered toward the alley between O'Rourke's and an adjacent building. The two Irishmen escorted Seamus in an abrupt fashion about ten feet into the alleyway when he made the attempt to break their clutch and make his escape. One of the men took and struck Seamus in the back of the head with his fist, but as Seamus turned around to defend himself, he struck the Irishman with the knife knocking it from his grip.

Trotting along near O'Rourke's on his horse, Pete heard the sound of the commotion coming from the alleyway. As Pete quickly dismounted, he noticed and heard the sounds of the two men beating unrelentlessly upon a male victim who was unable to defend himself against the physical onslaught. Without hesitation, Pete raced into the alleyway and struck one of the two men a blow alongside of his face as he was pounding away at the helpless and almost unconscious individual. The second man dropped the victim to the ground to protect himself, but Pete unleashed a series of blows against his body and face. From behind, the first attacker struck Pete with his fist while Pete contended with the second attacker. Pete turned quickly striking the individual with several blows to the chin, knocking him against a stack of wooden barrels and to the ground where he failed to rise. With both men on the ground agonizing in pain, Pete knelt down alongside the helpless individual only to notice that it was Seamus. As Pete examined his injuries, he noticed that his lip was cut in several places though the most severe injury sustained was the deep wound that was above his left eye. The blood was flowing profusely from the wound down his forehead and against his red hair. By now, Seamus was completely unconscious and breathing very heavy. Pete looked around for help but there wasn't anyone to be found.

Quickly, Pete placed Seamus' body over his right shoulder and emerged from the alleyway. Once he had Seamus positioned on his horse, he grabbed another and led Seamus' horse behind his back toward the McBride residence. For fear that Seamus would implicate him in the fight, he traveled in another direction, remaining inconspicuous so that suspicion wouldn't arise that he was the attacker. After arriving at the McBride home, Pete removed Seamus' body from the saddle. Again, Pete carried Seamus' body into the residence where he was immediately met by Katie and her parents.

"Oh my God, what has happened to my son?" Margaret screamed after noticing her son's bloody appearance.

"Someone needs to send for a physician, Seamus has been badly injured," Pete quickly answered.

"Please take my son upstairs quickly," Margaret commanded.

Katie followed Pete upstairs with Seamus' limp body still over his right shoulder directing him to her brother's bedroom. After she opened the door to the chambers, Pete quickly entered and gently laid Seamus upon his bed. Pete noticed the anxiety and troublesome features covering her face.

Katie anxiously asked as she looked at her brother's motionless body, "Oh Pete, what happened?"

Pete answered the question as Katie examined the head wound. "Seamus was being beaten by two men when I arrived at O'Rourke's. I believe they were trying to rob him."

"I can tell from the blood on your lip that you must have been involved." Katie said as she glanced at Pete.

"Don't worry about me now."

"It appears that by the size of the wound and the way that he is bleeding, whoever did this must of used some kind of sharp object as a weapon. I can't be sure because of all the blood."

"As I was dragging him from the alleyway, I noticed there was a knife lying on the ground several feet from where he was lying. Once I fought off his attackers, I managed to escape with him before they regained consciousness."

Katie paused and looked at Pete. Her mother and father rushed into the room with plenty of clean linen and a pitcher of hot water. "Thank you, you'll never know how much this means to me."

Pete didn't answer Katie but instead stepped to the side and allowed her mother to place the warm wet linen on Seamus' forehead. As Pete observed Seamus, he noticed Katie's father out of the side of his eye staring contemptuously at him. With his lip still bleeding, Pete was wondering if Thaddeus believed that Seamus' injuries were a direct result of a physical confrontation that he was responsible for and was now making up an alibi to cover his complicity. As Pete turned to leave the room, Thaddeus followed.

Once in the hallway, Thaddeus asked, "Mr. Barker, how in the bloody world did this thing happen to my son?" Pete remained silent, as Thaddeus' eyes were ablaze with anger. Again Thaddeus asked, "Now Lad I say, how did this thing happen to my son? From your bloody appearance, you must have been involved."

"I am not sure. I guess that he might have been robbed shortly after he departed from the tavern. All that I know is that two men were struggling with him when I arrived," Pete replied as he maintained his composure.

"When Seamus comes to and I find out who is responsible for this treachery, then there will be bloody hell to pay for this deed."

"Mr. McBride the smell of spirits was so strong on your son's breath, that I have my doubts that he'll even be able to remember what happened to him, let alone who was responsible," Pete replied as he cleaned his lip with a handkerchief.

Before Pete and Thaddeus could continue their conversation, Robert the butler and the physician were climbing the long stairway toward their direction. Once at the top of the stairway, the elderly physician quickened his pace as Thaddeus quietly gestured and escorted him to Seamus' bedroom. Quietly, Pete followed as far as the entranceway of the chamber and paused, watching the physician examine and clean Seamus injuries with some brandy that was in a bottle on the stand next to the bed. Katie turned to glance at Pete with a troublesome expression. Pete turned away and walked over to the window and began to observe aimlessly into the darkness of the night. He knew somewhere within his heart that Katie's parents would somehow try to implicate him for this misfortune cast upon the family. He needed to leave Boston as soon as possible.

As Pete removed his bloodstained frock coat, he heard Katie say as she approached from behind, "How are you doing?"

Pete turned around to face Katie. "I guess as well as can be expected."

"It's not your fault you know."

"In a way it is my fault, because if I would have stayed in Harpers Ferry instead of coming here on some wild goose chase looking for help from your family, maybe all of this wouldn't have happened. Today matters between us would be different."

"Are you trying to tell me that you don't love me anymore?"

"Honestly Katie, I don't know what to believe anymore. For some reason, you haven't been yourself since we've been here. I don't believe everything that took place and was said earlier this evening is just the main reason, but sometimes I feel that you've been distant from me. Are you hiding something that I am not suppose to know, or maybe you just can't bring yourself to tell me the truth. The only thing that I am sure of is that your family dislikes me, and now, they probably feel that I am the reason for your brother's troubles."

Before Katie could answer, Thaddeus appeared. "Yes, maybe you did have something to do with this. More then once since you have known our daughter, Katherine, my son has voiced his displeasure of your acquaintance to her and has greatly disapproved of the relationship that you have pursued. We all had hoped better things for Katherine."

"Father, I am not your little girl anymore. I am a grown lady, and I want to be treated as such. I love you and mother greatly, but at times it's so difficult for you and her to understand and respect my feelings."

"But Katherine…"

Pete was beginning to lose his temper over the false accusations against him. He abruptly interrupted in a pitched voice. "Quite honestly sir, I have heard enough of your insults and insinuations against me."

Katie raised her hands into the air. "Pete, you don't have the bloody right to speak to my father in that tone of voice."

Pete addressed his reply angrily toward Katie as he pointed at her father. "I don't, do I? But yet it's all right for him to degrade me and think of me as your brother does, some kind of low-life breed from the South. Sorry sir, Katie, but I have more pride than to stay here under these conditions. So if you'll both excuse me, I will leave.

"Please Pete, don't leave me."

Pete turned and said as he walked rapidly toward the stairway, "It would be better for both of us if you stayed here among your own kind."

As Pete jolted hastily down the stairway, Katie ran down part of the stairway crying for him to return. Although Pete heard her plea, he refused to acknowledge her or answer. The door slammed shut and he was gone.

Katie paused knowing any further effort on her part would be fruitless. She sat on one of the steps and began to weep uncontrollably knowing her father was watching from above.

Thaddeus refused to act or speak any words of comfort that might assist his daughter in controlling her grief. He was relieved that Pete was gone and that Katie was home.

Chapter 21

Several hours had past since Pete departed from the McBride residence. Katie was in her room sitting in front of the warm fireplace, dwelling on all of the events that had taken place over the past several days involving Pete and her. As she briefly glanced out the window, she noticed the ocean breeze was tossing the trees to and fro. Turning her attention once more toward the sound of the crackling fire, many thoughts raced through Katie's mind. Staring at the dancing flames, she continued to ponder on her brother's recovery after being beaten so badly and on Pete's whereabouts. It was her heart's desire to see Pete return once he regained his composure but somewhere within her heart and mind she had the premonition that he would return home to Shenandoah.

Katie thought of what she should do next. If she stayed in Boston, then she would be submitting to her parent's wishes and would be admitting and consenting that the relationship with Pete was terminated. She greatly desired to be with him. Even under the tremendous hardships of living at Shenandoah and submitting to the oppression of readjustments that all Southern people were under going, Katie was certain that her love for Pete would compel her to be with him once more. Katie knew her heart and had learned long ago to listen to its nudging. She was also sure it would cause differences with her mother and father once she announced her intentions of returning to Harpers Ferry. Her parents were the kind of people that would receive this decision as a rejection of their respect and love. It could have severe consequences for Katie such as banishment in return. But their disapproval wouldn't be a factor in her decision. Her mind was made up. Once she was certain of Seamus' welfare, she would immediately depart on the first available transportation to New York.

With this decision, Katie pondered on the unresolved situation concerning Shenandoah. It was close to the end of September, the deadline given to Pete by the Board of Supervisors for payment of the $2,500 debt against the property. Where could the money possibly come from to satisfy the taxes? Katie knew Pete and his family would be devastated if they lost the estate. The animosity that already consumed them over the destruction and now the threaten confiscation of the property would be more than they could endure. The only option that remained for the Barker family would be for her to speak privately with her father and attempt to convince him of the importance of the resolution of this financial problem, and the benefits of what it would mean to her and hopefully still her future with Pete.

After several hours of solitude, Katie heard the clock in the downstairs hallway chime eleven times. She rose to depart from her room. Katie peered through the door where she noticed her mother in deep thought walking toward her carrying Seamus' bloodstain clothing.

Katie wanted to catch her attention. "Mother," she softly said.

Margaret paused, "Katherine, why are you still up at this late hour?"

As she approached, Katie took Seamus' clothing from her Mother's arms. "I just couldn't sleep with everything that has taken place this evening."

"Your father is extremely angry and at this very moment, he is speaking with the Chief of Police, Mr. Connor, in the parlor."

"I hope they catch those men who were responsible," Katie added as she glanced toward the stairway.

"What men? You saw the cuts on Mr. Barker's mouth and face. Isn't it obvious to you, Katherine, that he was responsible for Seamus' beating? That's why he departed so swiftly out of fear we would have him arrested for the crime."

Katie spoke softly to her mother so that her father and Chief Connor wouldn't overhear the indignation in her tone. "Yes, Mother, Seamus, was in an angry mood with Pete and myself when he departed earlier this evening, and yes Pete did follow him after about an hour, still, I don't believe that Pete was responsible for Seamus' injuries. You know as well as I do that Seamus always goes to the taverns near the piers and drinks spirits with his war buddies. It is a place for trouble, and you know that is true just as I do."

"Katherine, with what I've witnessed of Mr. Barker's actions over these last several days, he is, in my opinion quite capable of committing any hideous transgression upon this family," Margaret answered angrily.

With the police involved, Katie was fearful they would arrest Pete if he returned to the residence. She was appalled by her mother's words and actions. She understood her parents were very annoyed over the mauling that happened to Seamus. Hopefully, once he regained consciousness, he would remember everything or at least some of what happened to him and vindicate Pete of any complicity in the affair.

Without hesitation, Katie followed her mother down to the first floor. Mr. Connor and Thaddeus were both smoking a cigar and discussing Seamus' welfare with Doctor Brown.

Once Katie and her mother entered the room, the physician and police commissioner stood at once and acknowledged them. "Ladies."

After being seated once more, Mr. Connor looked at Katie. "Miss Katie, I know that it's been a trying evening for you, but if I may, I'd like to ask you a few questions about the events surrounding your brother's incident."

As Doctor Brown walked from the room to the stairway, Katie replied cordially, "Mr. Connor, I would like to help you in any way that I can."

"Is it not true that your brother and suitor, Mr. Barker, were involved in an argument earlier this evening?"

"My brother was the one who was doing all the arguing, but it was with me. Mr. Barker remained cordial and calm with the exception of when he thought that Seamus might harm me. At that time, he stood between Seamus and me to protect me from any physical harm. With Pete's actions, Seamus refused to approach any further, but instead, he hastily departed."

Margaret became furious as she gestured with her hand. "Katherine, that can't be true. Seamus isn't that type of person. You are only trying to defend that rebel by lying to protect him. Does he mean more to you than your own flesh and blood?"

"No, Mother, I am not saying that at all, and furthermore, I am not trying to take sides. Instead, I am telling the truth to how the events happened."

Thaddeus puffed on his cigar. "My, Katherine, you don't think for a moment that your brother would strike you or harm you in any way, do you? He has a humble Irish heart, just like me."

"What was the disagreement about?" Mr. Connor asked.

"The past rebellion," Katie replied. "I have known the resentment and animosity that Seamus felt concerning those who fought for the Confederacy, but I must admit, I don't believe that Mr. Barker was any happier about the meeting than my brother was. Knowing these feelings, I wanted to take advantage of the situation by trying to help Seamus see that the war was over and that it was useless to continue to hold onto those types of feelings. I believe Mr. Barker was more acceptable to the idea than my brother. Seamus wouldn't have anything to do with it but instead he began to verbally attack Mr. Barker and me by making all types of accusations. When I attempted to intervene by explaining to him that everyone in some way suffered, he became even furious, to the point to where as I said earlier, he was beginning to angrily approach me when Mr. Barker intervened."

Out of frustration, Margaret walked over to glance out one of the front windows while Thaddeus remain seated, shaking his head in disagreement.

Mr. Connor continued, "But Mr. Barker left the residence at some point, am I correct?"

"Yes, he did. After sometime had past, Mr. Barker and I had a brief conversation in this very room," Katie softly answered.

"About what?"

"About our relationship, which appears from this evening to be over. Mr. Barker wanted to find and speak with Seamus about the accusations that he made against me before he departed in his fit of anger."

"What did your brother accuse you of doing?"

Again, Katie was hesitant to speak. As she walked over to have a seat on the sofa, she said once more in a composed and soft tone. "Of spying and passing information to sources that were loyal to the Union."

"What!" Thaddeus shouted as he jumped from his seat. Margaret turned around with a shocked expression covering her face.

Mr. Connor pursued the matter. "Well, did you?"

With her answer already in mind, Katie's reply was immediate. "If you were from some place like Boston and living among the Virginia citizens such as I was at Harpers Ferry, Virginia, wouldn't you be suspected of spying or passing information that was going to help your cause?"

Chief of Police Connor remained quiet but nodded in agreement as he gazed at Katie. With her answer, he didn't pursue questioning Katie any further.

Thaddeus accepted Katie's answer, but it was her mother, who continued to question the reasoning. Why, after so many correspondences, pleading with her daughter to return home, did her daughter remain in an area where there was such hostility and instability? During those turbulent times, she didn't fully accept Katie's explanations that she desired to remain at Harpers Ferry because of her love and feelings for Mr. Barker and her close friendship with Caroline Barker. Margaret McBride determined within her own heart there might just be some truth to what her son Seamus had revealed about Katie. As Margaret walked to the door with Thaddeus and Chief Connor, she turned and glanced once more at Katie standing quietly facing the fireplace.

"Thaddeus, within the hour, I will have my men looking for Mr. Barker. If he's at the train depot or any place else within the city believe me we will catch him. And when we do, I'll inform you without delay," Chief Connor said to Thaddeus.

"I would appreciate that Andrew. Please send Abigail and the children our love."

After Chief Connor departed, Margaret and Thaddeus stared at each other puzzled by Katie's answers to the police chief's questions.

Chapter 22

Once again, Margaret glanced into the parlor where Katie was still standing near the fireplace. Without saying a word, Margaret quietly preceded upstairs to Seamus' room to see if he had regained consciousness but not Thaddeus. Instead, he stood quietly by the entrance of the parlor gazing at his daughter.

For the past three hours, Katie's mind was consumed by Pete's absence. Where could he be hiding or staying within the city at this late hour in the evening? It was apparent to Katie that if Pete witnessed the police chief's arrival and visitation and an officer guarding the perimeter of the house, he wouldn't dare return for fear of being captured and imprisoned. The only answer that she could figure was that he was attempting to escape the city and return to Harpers Ferry by any means of transportation that was available. What would he discover once he arrived at Shenandoah? The new county government had given Pete and his family until the end of the month to satisfy their debt. There were only six days left before the deadline. The only question that continued to surface within her mind was, would they maintain their integrity and word, and honor their pledge, allowing the Barker's time to act? Katie would make one more attempt to persuade her father. If her efforts failed, then she would travel to Washington City and ask for an audience with Secretary of War Stanton, another close friend of the family.

Katie wasn't aware of her father's presence; instead, she continued to gaze, deep in thought at the flickering fire. Thaddeus patiently waited for his daughter to turn and acknowledge him but she didn't. Finally, he entered the room, clearing his throat as he approached. Once he captured Katie's attention, his eyes were unmovable. He said in a curious tone, "So that's some revelation that you shared with Chief Connor, I mean about your supposed spying activities. How in the bloody world did Seamus come up with that crazy idea?"

"Like I explained earlier, if you were from Boston such as me, and living in a place such as Harpers Ferry, wouldn't you raise suspicions among the citizens of the town? Doesn't it make sense?"

"Yes, I guess you're correct."

Thaddeus noticed Katie's features becoming tense and by her actions, she was showing visible signs of anxiety and frustrations.

"Father, I really don't want to discuss this anymore, instead I have something that's of greater importance to me," Katie said.

Thaddeus urged his daughter to continue, "Katherine, please come and sit with me and we'll talk about what troubles you." After taking Katie by the hand and being seated, he asked in a concerned tone. "Now my child, tell me what worries you?"

"Father, regardless of how you feel about Pete Barker and his family, I want you to know that I love you and mother very much. Somewhere in my heart I really don't believe we are going to agree on what I am about to say."

"What troubles you?"

"From the first time that you and mother laid eyes on Pete, I don't believe either of you wanted to make the attempt to accept him for who he was. Instead, all that you have seen was just another rebel that should be punished for taking part in the rebellion. As much as I love Pete, I didn't for one moment side with the Southern cause while living in Harpers Ferry. Pete knew this, respected and accepted me, knowing how I felt and also knowing that Seamus was fighting with the Army of the Potomac. Father, the war is over and it's time to start over again."

"True, your mother nor I cared for Mr. Barker's presence in our home. All my life, I have worked long hours so that you and your brother could have the best of things, and we had hoped for a better life for you once you were older and on your own." Thaddeus paused and a grin radiated from his face. He continued, "Oh, my precious daughter, I remembered when I came to this country aboard a ship in 1816 from Dublin. I was looking for challenge and opportunity and after taking some financial risk with what little we were able to accumulate, I found it. I must say that this country has treated me with respect and given me a chance at success that I couldn't have found if I would have stayed in Ireland."

"I know that you've worked hard and long hours, investing your money wisely but so have the Barkers, only they lived in an area that was affected by war and unfortunately they lost everything. It wouldn't have made any difference if they fought for either side. They would still have lost everything."

Thaddeus shook his head in disagreement. "Katherine, I want you to understand this war was going to happen whether we wanted it or not and it was going to affect everyone no matter where you lived. For many years as you know, the atrocities of slavery had to be brought to an end, and the Southern leadership are the ones who chose war. We attempted to compromise with the stubborn leaders of the Southern states and their bloody representatives in Congress in an attempt to end the evil bloody institution and its expansion into potential territories, but we couldn't. This war had to be fought, and only with the shedding of blood could the land be purged of the evils of slavery. And now, the Southerners have to be punished for splitting this Union and for the men that died trying to preserve this wonderful land that we love and call home. Shouldn't their blood be avenged? These are the convictions that I stand for and believe in."

"This was only a politician's war," Katie answered as she jumped from the sofa.

"There is probably some justification in your views. But at least the land will be better off now than what it was five years ago."

"Except for the Southerners, such as Pete and his family. They are about to lose everything that it has taken a lifetime to build. Father, you are in a position to help with the rebuilding of Shenandoah. Pete and his family could use your help. All that they desire is a chance to begin a new life and make a living. But in order for that to take place, they need to retain their property and be allowed to live and work on it without molestation from the authorities."

Thaddeus swiftly replied as he stood and looked at his daughter, "No, we can't interfere with the local authorities, especially in that particular area. It would be too delicate of an issue. Besides, those people that fought for the Southern cause are going to have to learn to submit to the laws of this country."

"Well then I guess I am going to have to learn to submit to those laws just the same as the Barkers."

"What do you mean by that?"

"What I mean father is this. I am going to return to Harpers Ferry as soon as I know that Seamus is going to recover. As much as I love you and mother, I too love Pete, and hope to be his wife if he is still willing after coming to Boston and being humiliated by this family. And if Pete will marry me, then I intend on having his children, your grandchildren. Now if I may ask, do you desire them to grow up and live in an impoverished area where their parents are unable to financially support them?"

Thaddeus raised his hands and pleaded, "Oh, no Katherine, by no means."

With tears beginning to flow from her eyes, Katie approached her father. To his astonishment, she said, "Then father, understand that I am desperate and I have only one recourse."

"And what is that?"

"On my way back to Shenandoah, I am going to pay Secretary Stanton a visit at the War Department and plead my case to him. Maybe he'll do something for the Barkers that this family refuses to do, and that is, intervene and help them," Katie answered in a challenging tone.

"Oh no, Katherine, you don't understand. With my political views and power, you could ruin me if all of this comes out in the newspapers. Please understand that Secretary Stanton is a man such as myself. He shares the same views and vision. It would be useless of you to make the attempt to persuade him and would cause me great embarrassment in the process."

After her father finished speaking, Katie remained silent, just gazing in his direction. She was determined to carry out her threat even without his approval. Once he finished speaking, she stormed upstairs angrily passing her mother, who was standing near the bottom step listening to the argument.

Thaddeus and Margaret were both bewildered by their daughter's behavior. They stared at each other, attempting within their own hearts and minds to reason with this issue that appeared to plague and divide their family.

Chapter 23

Early the next morning, the first rays of the sun beamed into Seamus' bedroom. Katie had been sleeping in the huge chair next to her brother's bed when she was awakened by the brightness of the sunlight. After only a few hours of sleep, she slowly rose and wiped her eyes with her hands. She paused and stood by her brother's bed gazing at his motionless body and then placed another quilt on him for warmth. It was cool in the room and she noticed there were still some glowing embers in the fireplace. Instead of calling for one of the servants, Katie walked over to the hearth and immediately placed several logs upon the grate, and meticulously stoked the embers. Once she was satisfied with the fire, she walked over to a small marble stand and poured some cold water into a basin and began to wash her face. Stepping to the side, she gazed into the mirror on the face of the armoire, examining her tired features as she combed her long hair. Katie pondered on the conversation that she shared with her father late last night and her intentions of paying Secretary Stanton a visit on her arrival in Washington City. Katie knew that her father was correct in his views concerning Secretary Stanton. Not all of the radical Republican politicians were in favor of leniency toward the Southern people, such as President Lincoln had envisioned. Instead, they believed that Southerners had to endure some kind of punishment for their treachery against the Union. Hopefully, Secretary Stanton, who had been a Democrat, would have a soft place in his heart concerning the Barker's family's problems once he heard her plea. If he didn't, she would attempt to use the family's friendship to manipulate the Secretary of War to gain his favor.

Once Katie finished placing her hair in a bun, she heard a faint sound coming from her brother's direction. At first, she thought her hearing was deceiving her or that she was imagining things. Katie slowly turned around. She cautiously walked over to her brother's bedside where she gazed for evidence of consciousness. As she continued to examine for any response, he again faintly moved his lips and made a few whispering sounds. Without hesitation, Katie leaned over the bedside near his ears. "Seamus, I am here. Can you speak to me?"

At first there wasn't a response. Katie began to feel the disappointment of failure. As she continued to observe her brother, Katie held both of her hands in a praying gesture against her face. Suddenly, she noticed the twitch of an eyelid. She thought Seamus was attempting to open his eyes. Again, Katie leaned over his body. "Seamus can you hear me? Please answer me by gripping my hand if you can."

Instead, Seamus slowly struggled to open his eyes. As he did, Katie began to caress his face with her hand. Tears filled her eyes as she spoke. "Seamus, it's me, it's Katie. Can you see me? Can you hear me?"

As Seamus quietly rolled his eyes in her direction, Katie lost her composure and began to openly weep. Through her tears, she noticed the glimmer of a smile radiating from his bruised and scarred face. Inwardly, she was full of joy and praise to God that her brother was conscious and recognized her. At once she knelt over him and began to kiss his forehead still weeping with joy. As she turned around, she heard the sound of someone walking up the long stairway. Turning toward the doorway, Katie dashed from the room to the edge of the stairway where she noticed her mother approaching. With the excitement of a child, Katie shouted, "Mother, Mother come quickly! Seamus has regained consciousness!"

Without hesitation, Margaret called into the dining room for Thaddeus, who was having his breakfast. She proceeded up the rest of the stairway as quickly as possible with Thaddeus closely following. Once Margaret and Thaddeus entered the bedroom with Katie, they broke forth in tears embracing their son and each other. As Katie looked on at the joyous occasion, it reminded her of the reception that she should have received from her mother when she returned to Boston several days ago with Pete. Not the cold response that she did receive. In a greater way, Katie missed the warmth and love that her mother had shown on so many occasions when she lived in Boston. Now, her mother appeared so distant and withdrawn from her, almost as if at times she didn't exist.

As Seamus' health continued to progress favorably through the morning hours, Katie pondered on returning to Harpers Ferry. Finally, finding the time alone to have a breakfast of eggs and a biscuit with tea, Katie knew that she had a major task and challenge awaiting her once she arrived at Shenandoah and confronted Pete with the truth concerning her role during the war. It appeared that no matter what explanation she presented, he would continue to be troubled by the words spoken and the events that took place yesterday evening when Seamus presented his accusations against her. In Katie's mind, first things first, and that meant the assurance of Seamus' recovery. Even at this very moment, Doctor Brown was upstairs with her parents examining Seamus. If his prognosis was favorable, then Katie would carry out her plan of traveling to Washington City to visit Secretary Stanton and then on to Harpers Ferry.

Katie's thoughts were interrupted as she heard the sound of voices and footsteps in the upstairs area. She quickly wiped her mouth with the white linen and anxiously proceeded in the direction of the stairway. Looking toward the upstairs, she noticed the physician and her Father beginning the decent down the stairway.

"Doctor Brown how is Seamus? Please tell me, is he going to be all right?" Katie asked.

Doctor Brown smiled as he looked at Katie. He confidently answered, "Well Katherine, thank God now that I was able to move him, I couldn't find upon examination any broken bones. He'll be a little sore for a while, but your brother will be just fine. He's young and very strong."

"How long will he need to rest?"

Doctor Brown answered as he rubbed his hand across his gray beard, "I guess he'll be up and about in three to four days."

"But we won't force him," Thaddeus added.

With the good news, Katie's mind was made up; she'd return the next morning on the passenger train to Providence.

As Thaddeus was speaking and escorting Doctor Brown to the front entrance, Margaret slowly descended the stairway. Katie quietly watched. Once her mother had finished descending the stairway, she turned with a cold expression. "Your brother wishes to speak to you."

Without hesitation, Katie ascended the stairway. On the way up to her brother's bedchamber, she thought of the words that she might say after last evening's disagreement. If possible, she wanted to question Seamus concerning the identity of who might have been responsible for attacking him in hopes of clearing Pete of any wrongdoing in the event. Once she entered her brother's room, without hesitation he turned to look at her. He made the attempt to smile, but Katie knew by the tenseness of his expression that it was painful.

"How do you feel?" Katie asked.

"Ah, a little painful. But you bloody know that not much can keep Seamus McBride down." He paused gazing into his sister's troubled eyes. "Katie, I just want to thank you for being with me. As I understand from mother, you were the one who sat by my bedside throughout the night, and I am grateful for your love and sacrifice."

"What is family for if they can't love and help each other when they are in need?"

"You are making me feel bloody ashamed of myself after the way that I spoke to you last night. Though, I guess from what I understand from father that my remarks accomplished what I had hoped for."

Katie bluntly interrupted, though holding her temper. "Yes, Seamus, they did. Pete left after he brought you home unconscious."

"He what? You mean to tell me that the bloody Johnnie was the one who brought me home? Besides, what was he doing at O'Rourke's? Was he responsible for this?"

"No, don't be foolish. He didn't have anything to do with this."

"That's not what father said."

"I don't care what Father said," Katie said in a defensive tone. "Pete followed you to O'Rourke's last night after we spoke concerning our relationship. All that he wanted was to speak to you concerning your accusations and treatment against me. He meant no harm which brings me to this question. Do you remember anything that happened?"

"No, no, I don't. And it bloody bothers me. Over and over all morning I've tried to recall the events that took place last night after I left O'Rourke's." Lifting his hands slightly in a gesture of frustration, Seamus continued. "But I must have been too full of spirits to remember anything. What did the Johnnie tell you anyway?"

"It was late when Pete carried you through the door on his shoulder. We immediately brought you upstairs and called for a physician. Pete explained to us that on his arrival at O'Rourke's he noticed two men beating you in the alleyway. At once he intervened in your behalf and took up the struggle, beating the assailants off. Afterward, he placed you on a horse and brought you home."

"No, no," Seamus said as he shook his head in agreement. "Father said that he had blood over his face from a cut on his lip. It appears that I put up a good struggle and he took advantage of my drunken condition to avenge himself of his hatred and frustration against me. Katie can't you see that his actions were deliberate?"

"No, Seamus McBride; that is a lie. None of this is bloody true." Tears began to fill Katie's eyes. She continued in a pleading tone. "You must believe me! I know him! He's innocent of this crime against you!"

"I am sorry Katie, but I can't. You're trying to defend him, and it's not going to work."

Katie paused looking at her brother. The tears were flowing rapidly down her cheek. Without another word, she raced from her brother's presence to her bedroom. There, she dropped to the bed sobbing.

Chapter 24

During mid afternoon, Katie had cried herself to sleep from exhaustion and frustration after her disagreement with Seamus. Her heart and mind were greatly troubled because no one in her family believed her defense of Pete. It was almost as if they were attempting to draw her into a position to where she would have to choose between Pete and her family. As she gave thought to her situation, there appeared no way that she would be able to avoid such a dilemma. Once she departed and returned to Harpers Ferry the choice would be obvious and she knew it. In all probability to punish her, she would be banished by her family from returning home. Also, with Katie returning south, she knew that she would be taking a great risk because there wasn't any indication that Pete would accept her and be willing to continue their relationship. Even after their argumentative encounter last night, there was a compelling nudge that continued to dominate Katie's heart. She knew no matter what anyone thought or said concerning Pete, she still loved him and she would never give up the quest for his love and affection that she had personally experienced.

As Katie continued to ponder on matters, the thought that troubled her most over their discussion was the idea that Pete believed that she had been distant and somewhat reserved since arriving in Boston. Katie thought that maybe this had intentionally happened because her mind had been constantly on the idea that her family wouldn't accept him now with the war's conclusion. She knew that coming to Boston with Pete possessed a great risk and it wasn't one that she had planned to happen this soon after the war. Because of the financial problems that surrounded the Barkers and their desperation to save Shenandoah, there wasn't any other choice but to take the chance.

After combing her hair, Katie walked the short distance to her brother's bedroom where she found him alone gazing out the window and finishing some hot tea. Unannounced, she walked into his room and stood by the side of his bed. Seamus turned and quietly looked at her. Apparently from her first observations of Seamus' expression, he was allowing his pride to rein over him once again. Katie knew that she would have to be the first one to speak. In her causal soft voice, she said, "I see that you must be feeling much better."

Placing the cup on the saucer, Seamus answered with confidence," Yes, my recovery is much quicker than what I thought."

"Well, I just wanted to see how you were doing."

After speaking, Katie turned around and began to walk toward the doorway. "What now Katie? What will you do now that the Johnnie has left you?" As Katie turned, Seamus continued, "Will you stay here with us or will you return to him?"

Katie walked slowly over to Seamus' bed "Why does it make any difference to you or anyone else in this family as to what my intentions are? All of you accomplished your purpose."

"Yes, I guess we did. But I asked the question because I wanted you to know mother and father are hoping that you'll stay in Boston and make something of yourself."

Katie grabbed Seamus' empty cup and saucer from his bed stand and answered in a sarcastic tone. "And not be as you all say, like one of those low-life Southerners?"

A grin covered Seamus' expression as he continued in a confident tone, "But as for me Katie, I know you all too well. You have to be the most stubborn and determined female that I've ever known. As I was lying here and recalling the past when we were growing up and the times that we shared together, I can still remember the many arguments that took place between us. Most of those disagreements were because you would never submit to taking no for an answer even when the reasoning was sound advice. Even though you're one of the most loveable and humblest persons that I've ever known, once your mind is made up about something you refuse to compromise your goals until you have your way. You're sort of like that bloody old bulldog that Uncle Clancy once owned."

Katie brushed her hair to the side. "I guess Seamus I realized a long time ago that if you want something bad enough in life you have to continue to go after it until you have achieved your purpose."

"And that means you're going to leave Boston and go after that Johnnie?"

"Yes that is exactly what I intend on doing. Matter of fact, I am leaving early tomorrow morning."

Seamus took Katie by the hand and pleaded. "Katie listen to me. You know as well as I do that leaving here tomorrow morning could possibly be the greatest mistake you'll ever make. Why give up a chance to have everything that you could ever dream of possessing to return to Harpers Ferry where the area has been so bloody ravaged by war. The Johnnie has nothing to offer you. I know that's the only reason that he came here with you was to beg for money. It certainly wasn't an attempt to make amends with our family for the transgressions that he and the rest of the Southerners were responsible for."

"Seamus, let me ask you a question. Have you ever been in love before?"

An astonished expression appeared on Seamus' face as he quickly answered. "No!"

"Then you have no idea how I feel. Am I not correct?"

"Well, yes, yes, I guess you're correct, but you know that I've never had time for such foolishness."

"Well Seamus McBride I don't believe that your explanation has an ounce of truth to it. For four long years you allowed the rebels to shoot at you and take the risk of being killed but never challenged a relationship with a lady." Seamus remained quiet and defenseless as Katie continued to scold him. "I'll tell you what your problem is. You're too bloody afraid to take the risk and accept the challenge. And then too, maybe you're afraid of the commitment. Aye, that is it!"

Quickly, Katie turned around and left the room. As she did so and out of sight of her brother, she began to quietly laugh knowing that she had placed her brother in a peculiar position. Katie made the comments in hopes that it would provoke Seamus to thought. Then maybe with his own experience in a relationship, he would know what she was feeling emotionally and why she had to return to Harpers Ferry and Pete Barker.

Chapter 25

As Seamus and Katie were speaking in the upstairs chambers, Thaddeus was softly humming a ballad while looking through some business papers in the library. After finding one in particular, he began to scribble some notes in the margin. Without warning, his attention was interrupted when Margaret entered the room. Thaddeus looked up from his work and removed his bifocal glasses, watching silently as his wife approached. He noticed the troubled and tense expression covering his wife's face.

"Is there anything wrong my love?" Thaddeus asked.

After pausing, Margaret quietly walked over to the edge of his desk where he was seated and answered in a troubled tone. "Possibly."

"Do you mean our daughter?"

"Yes Thaddeus. It concerns me greatly that Katherine wants to return to Harpers Ferry. As you well know, there isn't a future in that place or anywhere in the South for that matter for a lady such as her. She is only going to ruin her life and any chances of success to pursue some false dream." Walking toward the window away from her husband and with her hands raised, she continued to exert her frustrations "I have repeatedly questioned myself as to what I did wrong in rearing her. Oh, Thaddeus, you don't know the sleepless nights that I have experienced since she left home. Night after night I have prayed that she would return and desire a normal life, but my daughter must feel that there is some void in her life. Something drives her to do and act as she does, though I don't know what it could be. Oh dear, Thaddeus, we must do something."

Thaddeus took a deep sigh and shook his head in frustration. He was quiet for a moment as if in deep thought. He turned his attention once again toward his wife. "I, too, have had many sleepless nights over her absence, and I'd do anything under the sun to keep her here with us. But Margaret, you know as well as I do that Katherine will go against our wishes just like she did five years ago when we pleaded with her not to go to Harpers Ferry because of the possibility of war. But no, she wouldn't hear of it. She had to have things her own way, just like now." Thaddeus silently leaned forth placing his head in his hands.

Margaret walked around the desk and placed her hands on her husband's shoulders. "Isn't there something that we can do?"

Thaddeus shook his head.

"Do you really believe that she'll visit Secretary Stanton?"

"Oh, yes, that girl will do as she promised. You can bet on that."

Thaddeus looked at his wife. Margaret's mood had changed.

"Well for me," Margaret said in a frustrated tone, "I've already made up my mind as to the position that I am going to take if she returns to Harpers Ferry. For me it's one that I had hoped not to exercise but it's the only thing that I can do."

"And what is that, if I may ask?"

"Thaddeus, I don't expect you to agree with me and you might feel that it's harsh but, I will insist that she doesn't return in the future. I will insist that she asks for nothing and that I am breaking off any correspondence with her. I've had it with Katherine and her rebellious conduct."

Thaddeus turned and looked up. "Margaret, you can't do that to Katherine. She is our daughter."

"You may say that I can't, oh, but I will."

As Margaret and Thaddeus turned and looked in the direction of the doorway, there stood Katie. With her eyes on them, she quietly and slowly entered the room. Katie continued to gaze at her parent's surprise and tense features. By her mother's words, she was emotionally bruised and disappointed but most of all the cold tone left her with an impression that she wasn't loved by her. As those words continued over and over in her mind, piercing her heart, she raced from the room.

"Katherine, Katherine," Margaret called.

Katie continued to race up the stairway ignoring her mother's plea.

Without another word, Margaret turned and looked at Thaddeus. Thaddeus struck his fist against the desk in frustration and jumped from his seat walking toward the window where he stood looking at a carriage with its occupants heading in the direction of the Commons. After a moment of reflection, he turned and walked over to where Margaret was standing. "If Katherine is persistent in leaving tomorrow for Harpers Ferry, then I'll escort her as far as Washington, and maybe I will have the chance to speak to her and straighten this whole mess out. I just can't let her leave here feeling the way I know that she must feel. I love her too much for that to happen."

Thaddeus swiftly departed the library and left his wife to ponder on the issues surrounding their daughter.

Chapter 26

In room 103 of the Willard Hotel located at the corner of 14th Street and Pennsylvania Avenue in Washington City, Katie was standing in front of the huge mirror meticulously placing her blue hat with its veil upon her head. As she continued to gaze at her appearance, she was particularly concerned that her green dress with black piping completely covered the lower portion of her white hoop. Once satisfied, she walked over to the window where she paused and briefly glanced at the gray, dreary sky while placing her white gloves on. She observed some men of color with a limp horse pulling a dilapidated cart behind carrying goods for delivery to sell at the market. Turning around, she glanced at the clock on the mantel of the fireplace. Walking over to a small marble-top table beside a chair near the bed, Katie grabbed her basket, paused and glanced in the mirror one final time. With a deep sigh and many thoughts racing through her mind concerning her anticipated visit to Secretary Stanton, Katie departed from the room somewhat anxious to meet her father in the hotel lobby.

As Katie left the room, a hotel messenger approached with a note from her father informing her that he was paying Colonel Lafayette C. Baker, the chief investigator in the assassination of President Lincoln, a visit in his office across the street from the hotel. Katie's father requested that she meet him by the fireplace in the lobby in fifteen minutes. Already, her heart was racing with anxiety at meeting with Secretary Stanton concerning help for the Barkers. Stanton was a man of unpredictable and fierce emotions and she didn't relish the meeting. Even though the family had known the Ohioan for some years before the war, Katie knew from past experiences that the Secretary of War could be difficult to deal with in any manner of business. Still, there weren't any choices in the matter. She would have to play out the option in hopes that she could overcome the odds against her in this sensitive matter.

Once Katie arrived in the downstairs hotel lobby, she noticed the area was full of visitors coming and going. As Katie made her way through the hotel area, she noticed some of the men were mingling, their faces aglow with laughter and indulging in jovial conversation as they sipped on brandy and smoked expensive cigars. Katie knew from her father's conversation and frequent visits to Washington that the Willard Hotel was the place where one wanted to stay or gather if it was in your political or business interest. Many of the most promising and hopeful individuals from across the country congregated with influential and prominent senators or representatives in Congress in an attempt to gain their favor or promise.

While looking around, Katie accidentally walked into a well-dressed, handsome gentleman. She was startled, and embarrassed by the incident. As she looked up at the tall middle-aged man, she apologetically said, "Oh, I am so sorry. This was so awkward and rude of me. I guess I need to watch where I am going."

"Madam, that's quite all right." Pausing and taking notice of Katie, he continued to speak. "I know that it might not be appropriate for me to ask but I can't help noticing what appears to be a troubled expression. If I may say, you must have many thoughts on your mind?"

"I do have some things on my mind."

"The circumstances I know are somewhat awkward for both of us, but please let me introduce myself. I am Robert Bateman from Harrisburg, Pennsylvania."

"I am Katie McBride from Boston."

"Your name is all too familiar to me. By chance are you related in any way to Major Seamus McBride, who served with the 1st Massachusetts Cavalry? I ask because I served with him in many cavalry engagements throughout May and June of last year."

"Yes, he is my older brother."

A grin covered Robert's face as he answered in an astonished tone. "Well, I'll be. What do you think of that for coincidence? Often, Seamus and I sat around the campfire with some of the other men playing cards, drinking coffee, and reminiscing about life at home. As I remember, he spoke quite often about his family, but said little regarding a sister."

"My brother and I don't always see eye to eye on matters."

"I guess I can understand those situations." Robert knew by Katie's expression that the conversation was a sensitive one so he changed the subject. "Has Seamus said anything about me since he returned home?"

Katie answered as she looked around the hotel lobby for her father, "I don't know since I haven't lived in Boston for the last five years."

"Oh, I see. Then you must be here in Washington with your husband on business or pleasure."

"No, I am not here on a pleasure trip with my husband. Actually, I have come to Washington City with my father on business. When I accidentally walked into you, I was looking for him so that we could leave to take care of our business." Pausing, Robert's brown eyes met hers. Katie felt uncomfortable with being caught up in the moment. "Now, if you'll excuse me, I must go."

"Must you leave? Can't you sit and chat for a moment longer? I'd like to know more about you if that's permissible?"

Katie was more persistent in her tone. "No, really Mr. Bateman I must go. Now if you will excuse me," Katie turned and walked away.

As she began to walk away, her father approached from behind calling her.

Katie turned around at the sound of his voice. As he walked to where she stood, Robert once again joined her. Without hesitation, he took the initiative. "Sir, if I may have the honor of introducing myself, I am Robert Bateman. Your son Seamus and I served together with General David Gregg's cavalry brigade in the Army of the Potomac."

Thaddeus' eyes glowed revealing his pride and joy as he answered, "Well Lad, I am honored to make any acquaintance with someone who served with my son and fought to preserve the Union. But how do you know my daughter Katherine?"

Robert took the blame and wanted in some way to impress Katie. "Well sir, I know her as Katie. But to make a long story short, I awkwardly bumped into her not watching where I was going. And the gentleman that I am, I apologized to her for the mishap and my discourtesy."

"Oh, I see."

"Sir, if I may ask, are you the same Thaddeus McBride that has so valiantly fought for the abolishment of slavery and the Negroes' emancipation prior to the great rebellion?"

Thaddeus began to laugh. "Yes Lad, I am one in the same."

Katie remained silent gazing at Robert as he continued the conversation, "Mr. McBride I must say that I have heard so much about you from Seamus when we had free time and were not fighting, and I'd like to say to you personally, I have the greatest admiration and respect for the efforts and labor that you've put forth for the Negro race. I am sure that it has given you its rewards and gratitude to be such a leader in such a noble cause."

"Mr. Bateman, the work is just beginning. Now we as a nation must make the effort to integrate the Negro into our society and help them to feel that they are needed to make a contribution economically, and that they do have worth. All the years that they lived in bondage have stripped them of their pride. That needs to be restored in a constructive way."

"Oh, yes, sir, I agree with you one hundred percent."

Thaddeus quickly glanced at his watch and then looked at Katie. "Katherine, we must be going or we'll be late."

"If I may ask one more favor of you?" Robert asked.

"Certainly. What is it lad?"

"Will Katherine and you join me this evening for dinner? I would like to here more on your views concerning the Negroes and their new freedom."

Thaddeus knew this might be the opportunity for Katie to get to know someone else and begin the process of putting James Barker and Harpers Ferry in the past. "Well, sir, we accept your invitation."

"Let's say around seven o'clock?"

"That will be fine."

As Katie and her father walked in the direction of the front door, she knew that her father was making the attempt to raise her interest in another gentleman. Already, she was feeling somewhat guilty allowing Robert to consume her time in conversation when she should have ended it with his apologies and moved on. Katie was attempting to repress the thoughts that were plaguing her mind over her new acquaintance.

"Mr. Bateman is a very nice gentleman don't you think?" Thaddeus said to his daughter Katie as they departed the Willard Hotel.

"Yes, Father, I agree." Katie calmly replied and continuing as she glanced and smiled at her father. "But I know where this conversation is going and I am not interested in him. You know how I feel about Pete and that isn't going to change."

Thaddeus pleaded as he paused and looked at Katie. "Katherine, Katherine. Child when will you see the light of day when it comes to Mr. Barker and realize once and for all that he isn't doing anything but using you for what he can get out of you. Katherine, listen to me, you have too much to offer someone. You're a loving and committed soul who would do anything for anyone. That bloody Mr. Barker sees your Irish heart how soft that it is and he's playing the devil on it."

"Now Father, that's very wrong. You know there is not a bloody word of truth in the words you speak!"

As Thaddeus stepped up into the coach and sat next to his daughter, he insisted on making his point and his wishes known.

"Katherine, now you listen to me, I've been around long enough to know when someone is getting used and being deceived. I can see into Mr. Barker's mischievous eyes and know that he's up to bloody no good, especially now since he's been to Boston and saw where you live. I'll say over and over again Katherine until I get the message through to you, the bloody Rebel has nothing to offer you now, and he'll never have anything to offer you in the future. I beg of you as your Father to reconsider your options."

Thaddeus paused waiting for an answer from Katie, but she just stared defiantly at him. He noticed the tense expression covering her face. He knew she was more determined in her resolve then before. "I guess you're not going to listen to me," Thaddeus said. "My advice is worthless. Am I not correct!"

"No, Father, I have the utmost respect for you and mother, but my feelings compel me to return to Harpers Ferry and to my life at Shenandoah as long as Pete will have me."

"Katherine, sometimes I just don't understand you even though I make the greatest attempt."

"What do you mean Father?"

"I mean that someone comes along such as Mr. Bateman and it's quite obvious that he's interested in you. Now you're going to throw away the opportunity to have the dreams, possessions, and prestige that every young lady your age can only dream of."

"Please father," Katie snapped as she held her hands up. "I've heard enough for now. We must let the matter rest."

Turning around to look out the window, Katie was experiencing emotions of guilt for being so abrupt with her father. She knew he had the most honorable intentions in mind for her success in life. For the past two weeks, Katie's mind continued to be troubled and confused with all the events that had taken place since leaving Harpers Ferry. She was emotionally and physically exhausted. Somewhere she knew that she needed to find the strength to continue her efforts.

Chapter 27

As the coach noisily rumbled at a slow pace along Pennsylvania Avenue, Katie quietly looked out the window. She noticed the light rain had ceased. Occasionally, the coachman had to slow the vehicle due to the rails running along the middle of the street and some of the ruts in the cobbled-stone pavement. Many of the shops that she noticed had their windows dressed with various displays and were offering bargain prices, but today, she didn't have time to browse or purchase. Placing her dark blue shawl more snuggly around her shoulders, she noticed many of the shoppers entering and leaving the establishments were not stifled by the cool dampness that covered the city. The sounds of geese and the cries of fish peddlers filled the air as the coach paused to allow some citizens to cross the street near the grounds of the Executive Mansion. This brief delay caused her some anxiety at being late.

As Katie continued to look around, she wasn't impressed with the more modern and elite side of the city. To her, Washington was quite different in appearance and culture then Boston. On the journey to Washington, her father attempted to paint the most optimistic description of the city by explaining to her that the northern side of the city was the most influential and prestigious with the most to offer. She knew on various occasions, he attended several of the Grand Balls at the Willard during the war when he was looking for Republican support for his candidacy to the Massachusetts House. She played ignorant. Little did her father know that she had visited the city in the summer of 1861 and discovered for herself that the capitol had little to offer.

Once Katie and her father passed the Executive Mansion and grounds, the appearance sparked memories of the environment and atmosphere around Shenandoah during the antebellum era. As she observed the gardeners laboring among the multiple flower gardens and fruit trees, she recalled many fond memories of the activities around the Barker's estate prior to the great rebellion.

Looking at the lawn, Katie envisioned President Lincoln walking over to the War Department late in the evening. On her few trips home during the war, she heard her father speak of the President's dedication and habit of daily examining or answering telegrams coming in from the battlefront during the war. Katie quickly gave thought of the leniency President Lincoln had envisioned for the people of the South and the hopes of a smoother transition back into the Union. Maybe it would have been easier for the Barkers and many like them that had suffered such terrible lost, if Lincoln had lived.

Katie's attention returned to the executive mansion. She looked at the mansion's front where a long row of black ornamental railing with huge gateways separated it from the street. Many pathways crossed its grounds to the Treasury Department and other various government buildings. To Katie, the executive mansion gave the appearance of a Southern plantation, but it left an untidy impression. Still, it was the home of President Johnson. Across from the Executive Mansion in Lafayette Square, Katie gazed at the bronze equestrian statue of Andrew Jackson. She had to turn her head once more in the opposite direction to escape the offensive odor coming from the old city canal that was on the opposite side of the park.

The coachman turned the horses onto 17th Street where the War Department and State Department were located. Once the coachman brought the team to a halt, he opened the door and assisted Katie and her father from the coach. Without hesitation, they walked up the few steps and entered the brick structure.

As Katie walked through the doorway of the War Department, she noticed the small reception room was empty with the exception of a lone clerk sitting behind a desk and a provost guard standing at the door of an office. Katie with her father closely following approached the clerk. The young man paused from scribbling on some paper and looked over his wire-rimmed spectacles. "Yes Madam, what may I do for you?"

"I would like to speak with Secretary Stanton on a matter of urgent business."

This time the clerk looked up from his work and answered rudely, "That's impossible. He has already given his time and spoken with petitioners several hours ago. You're late, come back tomorrow at 10 o'clock, and don't be late."

"Excuse me sir," Katie answered in a flare of anger, "that is no way to address a lady. Now, I insist on you informing Secretary Stanton immediately that Katherine McBride is here to see him!"

"As I said before, you can not see Secretary Stanton. You must return tomorrow." The soldier stood and continued to speak in an authoritative tone and pointed in the direction of another soldier. "If you continue to insist, then I'll have that guard over there toss you out of here. Do you understand me?"

As the guard turned and looked in the direction of the confrontation, Katie's father shouted, "Now look here sir, I am Thaddeus McBride, a good friend of Secretary Stanton! See here Lad, I will not have you speak to my daughter in this bloody tone of voice. Do you understand me?"

As Thaddeus was reprimanding the young clerk, Katie's attention was diverted as an officer, that she recognized, walked through the main entrance and approached the provost guard. Not wanting to be recognized by the officer, she quickly turned her attention to the conversation taking place between her father and the clerk. The arguing between them wasn't going anywhere and it appeared that not much would be accomplished. Katie scrambled for an idea. If she could only get through the door to the office, she believed Secretary Stanton would make the exception and hear her appeal. Once the soldier began to speak with the officer, Katie saw an opportunity to race by the guard and enter the Secretary's office. With two separate conversations taking place, it was a natural diversion. Katie believed the effort was possible and the risk would reap its dividends. Without hesitation, Katie quickly dashed for the door and jolted through with the guard and officer following and grabbing her by both arms. Thaddeus quickly intervened shouting as he followed. "You bloody fools, let my daughter go."

Secretary Stanton jumped from his seat and shouted. "What is the meaning of this intrusion?" Pausing and recognizing that it was Thaddeus McBride, Secretary Stanton commanded the guard in a calmer tone, "Never mind, never mind! Let the young lady go."

The officer looked at Katie and whispered as he released his grip, "You are lucky Miss McBride, this never happens."

Katie turned and looked at the officer but remained quiet.

Pointing to the two soldiers and gesturing with his hand, Secretary Stanton commanded, "You two out and close the door behind you and furthermore don't let this happen again."

Secretary Stanton walked from behind his desk and approached Thaddeus and shook his hand. "Well Thaddeus, how are things going in Boston?"

"Ah, Edwin things couldn't be better."

"Word has it that you're thinking of running for Congress next year."

As Katie looked at her father with a surprised expression, he jovially answered, "That word could be correct. Mr. Frederick Douglass and some of the other Negro leaders have approached me trusting that I could represent their views and voice very well in Congress since they are not able to run for office yet. Also, I have the Irish community in Boston who would undoubtedly support my candidacy."

"Well Thaddeus if it should be known by me, I believe that you'd make an excellent candidate. And with my blessings, I encourage you to run."

"Thank you Edwin, I appreciate your support."

Secretary Stanton paused and looked over his wire rim spectacles at Katie. "Now Katherine to you. Something must be very important for you to come busting through my door in the manner that you did."

"Yes, Mr. Secretary." Pausing and looking at her father's troubled expression and knowing with the words she just heard spoken between her father and Secretary Stanton that things could not possibly change with what she was about to say.

Secretary Stanton started to become impatient. "Well…"

"Mr. Secretary for the past five years, I've lived in Harpers Ferry. During that time, I became acquainted with and hope to marry an individual, who fought for the Confederate army. My suitor's family owned a large estate on the outskirts of town where they raised horses and cattle for the army before the rebellion. As it was, Union soldiers burned the property, destroying everything of worth. Now, since the end of the war, my suitor, Pete Barker, has been trying to rebuild and go on with his life, but the county government demands that they pay back taxes of $2,500 or else they will confiscate the property."

Secretary Stanton continued the sentence and added, "And you want me to step in, correct?"

"Yes sir, I would. Like many in that area, they need a fresh start. I would consider your intervention a great favor."

Secretary Stanton rubbed his beard as he repeated the name. "Barker, Barker. I know that name." After pausing, he looked Katie in the eye. "Ah, Charles Barker. Am I not correct Katherine in saying that Charles Barker is maybe the brother of your suitor?"

"Yes sir, you're correct."

"No Katherine, I can't help you nor would I advise anyone that I know to do so." Secretary Stanton replied in an irritated voice.

"Why? The war is over with. The Union has been preserved."

"Yes, and at a great price!" Secretary Stanton shouted. "Many thousands of brave men fought and died to protect this Union and it cost the highest official of the land his life. Abraham Lincoln didn't deserve to die in the manner in which it happened. No, it was the Southern leadership that had to strike one more blow. Capturing Richmond and Lee's surrender at Appomattox wasn't enough to call it finished." Pausing and regaining his composure, Secretary Stanton continued in a more subdued tone, "No, no Katherine. Trust me, we will find Charles Barker and when we do, he'll have to pay up just as Jefferson Davis will. Charles Barker won't need the land any more."

"I am not asking this petition on Charles' behalf, but on Pete and his family's behalf. Shouldn't they have a fair chance at starting over? If these feelings of animosity continue between Northerners and Southerners, then doesn't the war also continue? What is the difference than lobbing cannon shells and bullets at each other. There isn't. Right! Now instead it's words. Don't your words and actions speak loud enough to continue to fuel the resentment?"

Thaddeus interrupted. "Katherine, I insist, that is enough!"

Katie turned and looked at her Father. "No, Father, it isn't enough. All that the politicians are looking for now is to reap all of the punishment possible on people that are already broken and ruined. You two are politicians, tell me then, how are you going to reunite this nation so that its citizens can live in harmony once more?" As Secretary Stanton and Thaddeus McBride looked on at Katie, she continued. "Well! Can you tell me?"

Neither Secretary Stanton nor Thaddeus McBride answered Katie's question. Katie rose from her seat and quietly departed the Secretary's office.

Chapter 28

As Katie raced through the reception room of the War Department, the officer that she had previously recognized noticed and followed her out the front entrance. "Katie, Katie, wait a moment."

Katie paused, turned and snapped. "Now is not a good time to talk."

"Please Katie. It's been some time since I last saw you."

The young officer approached. "I remember the first time when General Scott introduced me to you here in Washington City. Do you recall? It was Independence Day 1861, several weeks before Bull Run."

Katie answered as she looked into his gray eyes. "Yes, Colonel Bradley Longsten, I do. You were commanding the troops assigned to guard General Scott."

Bradley chuckled as he looked into Katie's troubled eyes, "You do remember." Pausing, allowing Katie to calm her emotions, Bradley continued to reminisce. "I can still remember that day, just as if it were yesterday. As I recall, many of the good citizens of the city turned out that morning to support the troops as they marched with pride along Pennsylvania Avenue. Many were rallying around the battle cry: On to Richmond. On the flag-draped platform, President Lincoln and his cabinet watched the troops pass by in review but as for me, I was touched by your emotions and sensitivity. I can still visualize the dramatic expression that covered your face as members of the New York regiment, the Garibaldi Guard tossed flowers in the direction of the President and his staff. But after our introduction to one another by General Scott, all that I could do was watch you. In all honesty, I must admit, I was captivated by your beauty." Pausing after his confession, Bradley asked Katie in a confident tone, "Do you remember what we did after the review passed?"

"No, Bradley. Forgive me, but I don't remember."

"Come on Katie, I am sure that you do."

"No Bradley. I really don't remember."

"If I may, let me refresh your mind. From the reviewing stand we walked to Franklin Square where we first visited the camp of my good friend, Colonel Ezra Walrath, of the 12th New York

Infantry. While we were there we enjoyed the bands playing patriotic music such as Yankee Doodle. Don't you remember? We even joined in on the singing with many of the other citizens and soldiers that were present."

"It seems so long ago. Please Bradley, really, I don't remember."

As the officer removed his tall-brim black hat and ran his hand through his black hair, he continued the attempt to refresh her mind, "Do you recall when I walked you back to your hotel room that evening?"

Katie interrupted and turned away. "Yes Bradley I do. Please stop, I've heard enough!"

Bradley reached out and took Katie by the shoulders turning her around to face him. Looking compassionately into her eyes, Bradley said in a more subdue tone. "I really thought maybe something was happening between us. It had the opportunity of growing into a friendly relationship, or let's say, something more permanent. But I guess I was just fooling myself. And then the next day when you departed the city without leaving a word, I was heart-broken and saddened. Constantly, while I was away from you after our acquaintance in Washington, I thought of the day we shared together. No matter where I marched and fought with the Army of the Potomac for those two long years, I was unable to get you out of my mind. The correspondences that I sent you were never answered. I guess I knew then that all of my hopes and dreams of being with someone as beautiful as you was just a fantasy. I didn't hear from you again until you met me two years later at the railroad depot at Harpers Ferry. I was carrying some very important dispatches for General Howe. I was very surprised when I learned that you were escorting me to the general's headquarters. On the short ride to Fillmore Street, I remember, you were very cordial, but distant much like you are now."

Pausing and continuing to look at Katie's sad eyes, Bradley continued to speak, "Katie, the one thing that puzzles me the most is, I couldn't quite figure out why you were at the depot, and no one could tell me your business once I inquired. But anyway Katie, for just a moment in time, you made me forget that there was a war going on."

"Bradley, I am sorry if I hurt you in anyway. At the time, someone, who was very special to me, had departed with the

Confederate army to fight for what he believed. In July of 1861 when I came to Washington to visit Mrs. Greenhow after the death of her daughter, I met you the next day for the first time, I was lonely and felt a void in my life which I was trying to fill. But it was in the wrong way and with the wrong person. Forgive me for giving you a false impression." Pausing with tears flowing down her cheeks, Katie continued in a whispering tone. "I don't know what got into me. I was sorely tempted by my loneliness."

Bradley and Katie were distracted by her father walking through the front entrance to the War Department. As Thaddeus approached, Katie managed a smile and said to Bradley, "Colonel Bradley Longsten, I would like to introduce you to my father, Thaddeus McBride."

Bradley reached to shake Thaddeus' hand. "Sir, it's all my honor. I have heard many great things about you."

Sensing by Katie's expression that matters were troublesome for his daughter, Thaddeus said out of courtesy, "Thank you Lad. It's my honor and privilege to make your acquaintance since you fought to preserve this great Union of ours."

Bradley smiled and answered as he looked at Katie. "Sir, the privilege has been all mine."

Again Thaddeus glanced at his daughter. "Well Katherine, if you are ready, then we must depart."

"Yes Father, I am very exhausted."

"Miss McBride, may I call on you this evening?" Bradley quickly asked.

"I am sorry Colonel Longsten, but I already have a prior engagement."

As Katie and her father were walking down the few steps to the coach that waited to return them to the Willard Hotel, an army captain passed and looked in their direction tipping his hat and speaking in a friendly gesture to Thaddeus. "Sir."

Thaddeus remained silent, continuing to walk, but nodded his head in acknowledgement.

Once the Captain reached the top step, he recognized Colonel Longsten. As Bradley gazed at Katie and her father boarding the coach, he smiled and said to the captain, "Phil, that is a very attractive woman. Don't you agree?"

Phil looked at Bradley and then again at Katie and said in a brisk tone as he rubbed his beard, "Bradley, I'm not sure."

Pausing and continuing to watch Katie, Phil continued his thought. "I believe I know that lady from somewhere. And if she is who I think that she might be then she is deadlier than a copper snake."

Bradley became irritated and raised his voice. "How can you say that? What grounds do you have to make such an accusation?"

"I just said that she looks like someone that I've met. I am not sure. It was several years ago."

"Where?"

"Oh, at a little hole in the wall called Berlin, Maryland, about six miles east of Harpers Ferry."

"Can you still recall the day?" Bradley asked Phil as they watched the coach depart from the War Department.

"Oh, yes, I still remember it all too well. The incident happened in early March of 1863. At the time, I was a Lieutenant assigned to provost detail in Baltimore. The accused, Captain Ford had jurisdiction over Berlin and also the ferry that crossed the Potomac into Virginia. As the story goes, Captain Ford and Lieutenant G. W. Benjamin along with a lady detective from Baltimore, who was working for the government were arrested for charging civilians for passes to travel either North or South. Anyone, who was loyal to the Union or disloyal to the Union were issued the passes as long as they paid the required fee. After numerous complaints of the activities of these officers by some of the loyal unfortunate individuals to Colonel Baker at the War Department, an investigation began."

"How does Katie fit into all of this?"

"Well, the young lady, Miss Katie as you call her, arrived at Berlin several days before the arrests were made and was posing as a young lady wanting to travel south to Culpepper with an older lady posing as her mother. Their excuse for the passes was that her mother's older sister was ill and possibly dying. At the provost headquarters, the lady detective, a Mrs. Frances Able attempted to persuade Miss Katie and her supposedly mother into paying a hefty fee to obtain the pass. With Ford's complicity and after Miss Katie and her mother met the requirements and were searched, they proceeded on their own way with the purchased passes."

Bradley interrupted. "That still doesn't prove anything concerning Katie."

Phil held up his hands in a gesture. "Wait! You haven't heard the rest of the story yet. Shortly thereafter, the two officers and Mrs. Able were arrested and brought to Baltimore. After being confronted by the two female government agents and Colonel Baker, the two officers along with Mrs. Able were sent to the Old Capitol Prison."

"How can you be certain?"

Phil smiled. "I was there."

Bradley Longsten remained silent. He was stunned and surprised at the eyewitness account that Phil had shared with him. His thoughts returned to the day that he met Katie and some of the conversation they shared. She was particularly interested and asked many questions when he spoke of his good friend, Captain Thomas Jordan, who had resigned his army commission in May of 1861 to serve with the Confederacy. Jordan was later known to have formed a spy ring in conjunction with Rose Greenhow and other prominent civilians living in Washington for the benefit of the Confederacy. Had Katie and his meeting been intentional? Was her only interest in being with him that day for the purpose of acquiring information about Mr. Jordan or Mrs. Greenhow, who was later imprisoned at the Old Capitol building? After all, she had admitted to him earlier of her visit with Mrs. Greenhow, and Bradley knew that Rose Greenhow was a friend of Thomas Jordan. Bradley continued to think that maybe he had been a suspect. Bradley was bewildered because Katie appeared so innocent and didn't impress him as the type of individual who was capable of being involved with such dangerous activity. Maybe Phil was mistaken; but one thing that Bradley was sure of from the conversation with his friend and that was, there appeared to be a dark side to Katie McBride that he didn't know and couldn't figure out.

Chapter 29

For the past several hours since leaving the War Department and her unexpected encounter with Colonel Bradley Longsten, Katie had been suffering from a terrible headache due to emotional strain. Although it had been a difficult and unpleasant afternoon for her, she didn't complain to her father or give him the impression that she was sick or that she wanted to cancel the evening with Robert Bateman. After several hours of rest, the pain had only slightly subsided; still out of respect, she was committed to the evening with her father and Robert.

While Katie was walking toward the lobby area with her father, she remained silent. For most of the late afternoon, she was very much deep in thought over the troublesome events that transpired this afternoon at Secretary Stanton's office. After failing to convince the Secretary of War that Shenandoah could be profitable again, it appeared to Katie just to be an echo of the discussions that she had with her father before making the trip. Secretary Stanton's blunt refusal complicated matters in a greater way for her because it was the last possible effort that she could undertake on the Barker family's behalf and it had miserably failed. Unless someone came up with the necessary funds to pay off the delinquent tax burden, then it would only be a matter of time before the county would confiscate Shenandoah and sell it piece by piece to the highest bidder at an auction.

Not only did Katie have problems with trying to raise the necessary help and funds for Shenandoah and attempting to salvage her strain relationship with Pete, now even greater trouble loomed on the horizon. The reappearance of Colonel Bradley Longsten and his flamboyant nature caused her great pain and turmoil in her mind. His presence would complicate matters in a terrible way in her life; possibly cause more trouble and hindrance due to his inability to surrender to his pride and admit defeat. The sight of Bradley earlier had caused many old memories to resurface with his reminiscing; events that Katie had blotted out of her mind long ago. Again, they troubled her to the point she wished that she could just run away. Katie believed now with Bradley knowing that she was in the city; he would be persistent in his effort for her attention. Katie knew that the challenge of her conquest compelled him to further continue the effort in his attempts for her heart and romance. Katie knew the only way that she could escape him would be for her to depart early in the morning on the train to Harpers Ferry. For now she would make the attempt to repress her troubles and concentrate on this evening outing with her father and Mr. Bateman.

For the past thirty minutes Robert Bateman had been seated near the fireplace glancing over the headlines of the Evening Star newspaper. As the clock chimed seven times, he glanced above the paper, where he noticed Katie and Thaddeus entering the lobby area. Promptly, Robert stood to his feet and with a smile approached the McBrides. "Miss McBride, the pleasure of you accepting my invitation to dine with me has made me very happy." Turning his attention to Thaddeus, he continued, "And of course sir, it's good to see you again and I hope that all is well with you."

Katie smiled. "Mr. Bateman…."

Robert interrupted, "It's Robert."

"Robert…. The pleasure is mine. You may call me Katie."

Thaddeus smiled. "Thank you sir, for inviting us to your table this evening."

Robert held out his arm toward Katie. "Shall we."

Katie smiled and took him by the arm. His compassion and warmness made her want to forget her troubles and the trials of life. She felt an attraction to Robert but her feelings for Pete continued. As Robert and Katie walked in the front with Thaddeus following, the headwaiter took them to their reserved table near the corner of the large dining room. Without hesitation, Robert pulled the chair from the round table, assisting Katie as she was seated and then Thaddeus and Robert took their seat.

Robert directed his first question to Katie. "I hope your business this afternoon was prosperous and successful for you."

Katie half-heartily smiled and answered. "No, not really. I had hoped for greater success and understanding, but I failed."

"Well maybe there's something that I can do. I have many influential friends in this city and also back in Harrisburg. Maybe we should discuss the matter further and determine the needed assistances that I may lend.

Swiftly, Thaddeus answered as the waiter approached the table, "Mr. Bateman, Katherine is just a little disappointed. I am sure that in time she will be just fine and will find another way of resolving this problem."

Robert's heart was moved with passion. "Oh, but sir, you don't understand. It's important to me that I help Katie in any way that I can."

There was a pause in the conversation as Robert directed the waiter to bring Thaddeus and him bourbon. Again Robert turned his attention toward Katie. "Please Katie, tell me the circumstances that trouble you. I would like to help in some way."

"I have some close and dear friends that live near Harpers Ferry. As many in that area, they were affected by the past rebellion..."

Thaddeus interrupted Katie, "Please Katherine, we shouldn't trouble Mr. Bateman with your problems."

Robert gestured with his hand to Thaddeus. "Oh, but I must try. And how did they suffer?" Robert asked.

"In May of '64, Yankee raiders appeared at their home and burned the main house with all of the outbuildings and barns. Then they confiscated what cattle or horses that they had left. And to make matters worse, they left the family homeless. They just stood there and watched a lifetime of effort go up in smoke. What angers me the most is that the Yankees would not allow my friends the common decency to remove any valuables or heirlooms that meant so much to them. They were innocent civilians deprived of any dignity or respect. To this day, they haven't recovered and they are still having a difficult time surviving. Financially, they are ruined and struggling like many in that area. The banks don't have the funds to make loans and my friends owe a sizeable tax burden."

There was a somber expression on Robert's face. As the waiter poured the bourbon, he asked, "Were these people that you speak of sympathetic to the cause of the Confederacy?"

Katie didn't speak. She just nodded her head in the affirmative.

Robert took a sip of his bourbon and looked at Katie. "If I may ask, were you sympathetic to the Southern cause?"

"No." Pausing and looking Robert in the eyes, Katie continued to speak softly. "I wasn't. The five years that I've lived at Harpers Ferry, I've been loyal to the Union."

"Then why did you stay knowing I am sure that Harpers Ferry was an unsafe place to be? As for myself, I have never been to the place but from what I understand from others who have been, it's not a safe and desirable area to be living. And I guess from what you're telling me I can't help but to ask myself the question as to why a woman of your stature would continue to live there."

"Like many I guess, I had my reasons; but for now, I wish not to discuss them. They are personal to me."

A surprised expression appeared on Thaddeus' face with Katie's remarks although he remained silent.

Robert knew that Katie was hiding something from him, but he didn't wish this early in their re-acquaintance to press the issue and drive her away. There would be time later to find out what she was hiding. Instead, he simply said as he glanced at Thaddeus, "I can respect your wishes."

After pausing briefly to order dinner, Robert wished to continue the conversation with Katie. "Katie, I would like to find out more about the situation that your friends are engaged in. How many acres do they own?"

"I believe they own approximately 5,000 acres."

"What did they do before the war that required that much property?"

"They were in the business of breeding horses and cattle; selling many of them to the army."

Nodding his head in agreement, he answered, "I see. They must have had many Negro slaves." Katie remained silent as Robert tried to get as much information as he could. "Do you believe that they would be willing to sell some of their holdings to pay off their debt?"

"I don't know."

"The reason that I ask is that I have several businessmen who might be interested in purchasing some of their property."

"And I assume that means you too?"

Robert was surprised at Katie's little outburst, but answered honestly, "Yes it does."

Thaddeus saw an opportunity to try and direct Katie in another direction by presenting the Barker's problems of sustaining the ownership of Shenandoah appear as hopeless. He interrupted the conversation. "As I understand from some of my friends, who are taking advantage of such opportunity, you can acquire property fairly cheap in that area as well as much of the South. It will be better for the family to sell off most of their holdings rather then lose it all when the government under its reconstruction policies do it for them. If that happens, then they'll lose everything and have nothing to show in return."

"Father, that's not going to happen," Katie fired back.

Robert took Katie by the hand. "Katie, listen to your father. What he is telling you is the truth and it will happen. The war has changed things greatly for people living in the South. Their life will never be the same."

"Then what you're telling me is that you want to legally steal their property?" Katie angrily asked.

"No, no. Please don't misinterpret what I am saying. But matters do look gloomy on the horizon for them and at this point, something is better then nothing."

After Robert's statement, everyone became silent. Katie casually looked around the large dining room, trying to get her mind off the conversation that just transpired. She looked several tables from where she was sitting. Out of the corner of her eye, she noticed Colonel Bradley Longsten gazing in her direction as he feasted on steak. Immediately, Katie began to feel quite uncomfortable and nervous, but she maintained her composure and didn't reveal outwardly her fears to anyone at the table. Once her dinner was served, she quietly ate while Robert and her father spoke of his acquaintance with Seamus and the reconstruction policies that would be imposed on the Southern people.

As Katie inconspicuously looked from the corner of her eyes in Bradley's direction, she could tell his attention was constantly focused on her. Even though she was very angry and felt she was being spied on, she knew there was nothing she could do in this situation. It would be unwise on her part, she thought, to approach him. Instead, she would ignore Bradley and begin to take part in the conversation on a safe level. Hopefully since Bradley had seen her with Robert, he might just disappear if she was to give him the impression that she was interested in Robert. She began to carry out her idea. It wasn't a struggle within to play the game.

Chapter 30

Occasionally throughout the evening, Katie continued to glance in the direction of Colonel Bradley Longsten's table. Over the past several hours she had frequently noticed Bradley watching her every move and his actions were causing her to grow uneasy with his presence. Every time that Bradley caught Katie glancing in his direction, he smiled, which irritated her greatly. Maybe, she thought, she didn't play the game of romantic interest good enough with Robert to discourage Bradley to give up the quest and leave the premise.

According to the clock near the far wall, it indicated that it was 9:30 in the evening. Robert and Katie's father were still enjoying their conversation on reconstruction politics and the integration of the Negro into a free society. As for Katie, she was looking for an excuse to leave the dining area and return to her room to escape Bradley's gestures.

"Father, Robert, if you'll excuse me," Katie interrupted. "I am feeling a little exhausted from this afternoon and I have a slight headache. I really feel that I need to return to my room."

"Yes, Katherine, by all means," her father replied.

Robert saw an opportunity to be alone with Katie. "Please, if I may, Katie, I would like to escort you to your room?"

In an attempt to try and control her attraction to Robert, Katie replied, "Thank you Robert, but that's not necessary. I know that father and you still have many things to talk about."

"No, now I insist on walking you to your room. Besides, I'd consider it an honor and privilege."

After reassuring Thaddeus that he'd like to continue their conversation, Robert stood and pulled back Katie's chair.

Katie easily surrendered to the idea of Robert walking her to her room. Somewhere within, it was the fantasy that she wanted to bring to life. Hopefully, it would discourage Bradley Longsten.

As Robert and Katie departed the dining room, Katie took Robert by the arm and knew that Bradley was watching. Hopefully, this would have some effect on Colonel Longsten, but she had her doubts.

Once Katie and Robert were totally alone walking toward her room, Robert said, "Again, I am sorry that you have friends that are suffering from hardships caused by the war. Often I have thought had there been some kind of an understanding between the leaders of the Northern states and Southern states this rebellion could have been avoided. Unfortunately many lost their lives and others will bear the scars for the rest of their lives because of politicians' stubbornness. I guess I was fortunate that I saw the fighting for only a short time during the spring of '64."

"I thought you said that you served with my brother Seamus?"

"Oh, yes, but it was for only a short duration."

"Did you leave the army for some reason?"

"No, no. After the fight at Cold Harbor, I was chosen to serve on General Grant's staff. I didn't see any fighting after my promotion."

Katie was impressed with Robert. She, too, spoke of her experiences. "I remembered in September of 1862 when Stonewall Jackson's forces surrounded the Federal garrison at Harpers Ferry. I had taken shelter in a wet cellar in town. I could hear the loud sounds of the bombardment of Confederate cannons from the heights surrounding the town. Sometimes it sounded like the shells were exploding close by and when they did, it was terrifying. After sometime, there was a young artilleryman from New York that was wounded and took refuge with me. It was the first time that I had actually witnessed someone being injured from combat. After tending to his wounds, we stayed until the next morning. By then, the fighting had ended. After the surrender that morning, I watched Stonewall Jackson with his staff riding through Harpers Ferry. By his appearance, you couldn't really tell that he was a general, but you knew when you looked at him that he was a very stern and pious man."

"Did you know your friends at that time?"

"Yes, I knew them shortly after arriving at Harpers Ferry. The Barkers are a very congenial and warm family. Caroline was and still is my closest friend."

An astonished expression covered Robert's features. "Did you say the Barkers?"

. "Yes, I did."

"Then you could only be speaking of Charles Barker and his family. As I recall, he lived in the Harpers Ferry area."

"Yes Robert, he did. What is wrong with that? Robert, what is wrong?"

"Senator Lloyd and myself were just speaking of him earlier this afternoon. It is believed by some here in Washington City that Charles Barker may be back in this country. Senator Lloyd told me that they were certain that Barker had made good his escape before Jeff Davis was captured in Georgia."

Quickly realizing Robert had a greater amount of influence and inside connections with many prominent officials, Katie probed for more information. "Do you know where he may be?"

Robert was more then willing to share his information with Katie. "Actually, it's only speculation that he is in this country but this we do know; Barker had connections in Liverpool, England. This is apparent from the journey he made there in '62. So after escaping at the conclusion of the war, he may have hid there among friends and former enemy agents. If he is back in this country, he's probably in the western territories or being hidden by the Confederate underground until it's safe. Who knows? Maybe he has hopes of his destiny with punishment being forgotten. But I don't believe for one moment that Secretary Stanton is going to let him go."

Believing that Robert had more information than what he was revealing, Katie wanted to play this game a little further to acquire as much from Robert as possible.

"Do you feel the only reason the authorities are putting his property up for auction is to try to get him to come out of hiding?" Katie asked in a naïve, innocent way.

Robert chuckled as he looked at Katie. "What useful purpose would that serve?"

"Well maybe, he would be willing to make some kind of deal such as turn himself in to the authorities in return that Shenandoah would remain in the possession of his family until he has served out his punishment."

"No, I don't think so. Barker's too smart and he isn't about to play the role of some kind of hero. No Katie, it's only a matter of time before they catch Barker. They believe that he'll only be able to stay away from his wife and daughter for so long." Pausing and glancing at Katie once more, he smiled and continued. "Somewhere he'll make a costly mistake of believing that Federal authorities have forgotten about him and he'll communicate in some way with his wife. Once she makes the attempt to see him, I am sure that Mr. Pinkerton and his comrades will be watching and eventually she'll lead them to him and they'll be able to make the arrest. No Katie, time is on our side."

Robert must be telling the truth, Katie thought, because it wasn't mentioned in their conversation that the Barker's had a daughter. Katie remained silent and disguised any true facial expressions. Inwardly she was joyful in the knowledge that Charles was still alive. She knew that once she could share this information with Caroline, it would relieve some of the pressure that Ann, Elizabeth, and Caroline were experiencing; but too, she must caution Caroline not to go to Charles if contacted by him. What Caroline had been experiencing over these past months at this moment caused Katie to look back on her own experiences. The emotions that she endured when she saw the casualty list after Gettysburg and had believed that Pete had been among the war's dead.

Robert and Katie arrived at her room. As they stood in front of the door to her room, Robert softly said, "Katie, I have enjoyed this evening more then you can imagine. In the little time that I've known you, I have found that you are a very remarkable woman with much to offer. Quite honestly, I find myself attracted to you even though I am a little older than you. And, I must admit, I am quite fond of you and would like to see you again, if I may?"

As Katie looked into Robert's eyes, she discerned the sincerity and passion they revealed. Robert took her by the hands. "I don't know Robert. At the moment, I am confused and unsure of myself concerning my feelings for you and someone else. There is a part of me that wants to see you again and be with you, but I must make amends with someone that I've loved for the past five years."

Before Katie could say another word, Robert embraced Katie gently and kissed her. Katie responded by placing her arms around his neck and embracing him. Robert likewise held her close to him, stroking her hair with his hand. Katie paused, her heart was racing. She looked into his eyes and again she kissed him passionately. Afterward, Katie remained silent gazing into his eyes.

"May I come in?"

"No, you better not." Pausing and looking at Robert, Katie continued in a whisper, "it would be for the best for both of us if I were to go."

"May I return later?"

Even though it was difficult for Katie, she hesitantly replied, "No, I will speak to you in the morning before I leave for Harpers Ferry."

Robert was greatly disappointed and it reflected in his tone. "I see." He paused and step forward once more embracing Katie and kissing her again.

Katie felt tempted to allow him into her room but instead, she insisted, "Please, Robert, you better go."

Robert nodded in agreement and began to walk along the hallway. Once more he turned and smiled at Katie.

Katie stood silently watching him walk away. For just a moment, she was teased by the thoughts of what the night could have been like had she invited him into her room.

Katie entered her room, closing the door and leaned against it in deep thought. Almost immediately, Katie's heart began to condemn her and she felt guilty of betraying her commitment and love to Pete. Since she had betrayed her love to Pete with Robert, she began to experience emotions of worthlessness because she knew that she would end up hurting the one and rewarding the other. For a long period of time, her loyalty and trust for Pete had been unbroken and unshaken by the disagreements, trials, and tribulations that they had faced together over the past years. As she explained earlier to Robert, she knew that she was confused and unsure of herself. Another incident like this had happened with Bradley Longstsen in the summer of 1861 after Pete departed Harpers Ferry with the Confederate army. Bradley tried to press the situation more vigorously. Again Katie rejected his challenges at Harpers Ferry in 1864 after he made various attempts for her affection.

After Katie prepared for bed, she sat in front of a small vanity brushing her hair. As she looked into the mirror, her thoughts returned to the time that she first danced with Pete at the reception for William Pierce in August of 1860. Whether either would be willing to admit it, this event was the beginning of their relationship when both of them were attracted to each other even though they shared social differences. During the middle of the war when Pete came to the church one evening while she was praying, it was a turning point for both as they spoke openly and embraced each other. For Pete it was the first time that he truly shared his emotions with her. For Katie it was the first occasion when she told him that she was in love with him.

Since Pete angrily left Boston five days ago, Katie knew that she missed him. In many ways, Robert reminded her of him. Robert was compassionate and considerate just as Pete. Both possessed the same humbleness, but Robert lacked that innocence and flamboyance that she had come to know with Pete and most, the emotion that filled his eyes. Her condemnation grew as she thought of how some in the Barker family accused her of spying and had forsaken her company, but Pete was the exception. It was Pete who had remained loyal to their relationship and was the one who was willing to risk his life for her freedom when she was imprisoned at Winchester, Virginia. It didn't make any difference to him if she was spying or just the innocent victim of false speculation. His commitment to her was firm and he wasn't willing to judge her such as others.

Katie knew that Robert had entered her life at the wrong time and also in a moment when she was very vulnerable and experiencing loneliness. Pete's absence had created a void in her heart. Instead of dealing with her emotions, she made the mistake of trying to fill the void with Robert's presence, affection, and attention. Katie began to wonder if her only attraction to Robert was out of anger toward Pete for leaving Boston. At 25 years of age, Katie was troubled by her family's expectations and the social standards of the day. She was expected by her family status in life to be married and already rearing her children. Now, with all the problems that Pete and she had been experiencing, she wondered if she wasn't trying to escape reality and forsake the one she really loved.

Katie pondered on ways how she would approach Pete tomorrow when she arrived at Harpers Ferry and the explanation that she would share with Robert before departing. Again, Katie thought of her first attraction to Pete and the first evening that she danced with him at Shenandoah. It was while the string ensemble played the ballad "Lorena." Tears began to fill Katie's eyes as she remembered a phrase from that particular song. She hummed most of the ballad, but she softly murmured the words, "Thy heart was always true to me."

As Katie laid the brush to the side, she glanced into the mirror one more time. Noticing a figure quietly standing in the shadows behind her, she was stunned, shaken, and paralyzed with words. A frightened expression covered Katie's face as she instinctively placed her hands over her mouth. As the mysterious figure moved into the light, Katie turned around and whispered, "Oh dear Lord, it's you."

Chapter 31

Along the Shenandoah River it was quiet and serene as Hayward Cooper cast his fishing line into the murky waters at the vicinity where he and Pete had often leisured and shared personal conversation. For Hayward, his time of solitude was important for him because it was a time of reflection and thought concerning his life. Often after he escaped danger in the spring of 1862 where he helped runaway slaves in their flight to freedom, Hayward had envisioned himself returning to this region of the Shenandoah estate and being able to once more spend time at an area he considered almost heaven. Sometimes for Hayward being alone was a blessing, giving him the opportunity to enjoy and dream of a future where he was given the occasion to come and go as he pleased. The chance of someday owning a piece of property and feeling useful in a greater way toward society than previously when he lived at Shenandoah before the war, gave him a sense of security and expectation that was never possible before under the old rule of law. Even though before the war when he was a free man of color, and still had to acknowledge Pete as his master in accordance with Virginia law, he rejoiced inwardly knowing that being looked upon by another man as a possession had ended.

As Hayward observed the deer roaming freely on the opposite side of the river, he thought of how the old establishment of slavery was forever ended, and by law could never be resurrected in the future. Although the emancipation of his race came at a terrible and horrible expense, Hayward on many occasions had given God the praise and glory for all that was accomplished. He, like many of his race believed that they were being persecuted, mistreated, and held in bondage against their will such as the Israelites experienced under Pharaoh of Egypt in the biblical times, and that President Abraham Lincoln had been used by God as their deliverer such as Moses had been for his people.

Since Pete and Hayward had returned to Shenandoah, they had constantly labored to get the estate up and running, working from dusk to dawn seven days a week. Although Pete couldn't afford to pay him for his labor, Hayward believed that in times past before the great rebellion that Pete had protected him from the scandalous attempts of the estate's overseer Daniel Johnson, and Pete had treated him with the utmost respect and dignity.

On many occasions, Pete and he would come to their special place along the river and speak of joys and pleasures that they experienced. They also expressed their concerns and troubles that attempted to besiege them. It was a relationship that most people of color never shared with the white folks and Hayward was thankful for the opportunity and friendship that they had shared. With those emotions and firm commitment to each other, Hayward would stay for a while longer and help his best friend through troublesome times.

Hayward knew the difficult emotional strain that Pete was experiencing. He believed that Pete needed to endure the hardships and tribulations to mold him into a person of greater integrity concerning life and to determine who he was as an individual. Even though Pete had learned to survive the deadly game of war, Hayward knew now with the absence of his brother Charles, that the challenges that Pete would have to face would bring about personal wisdom, which stimulates growth, and the advantage to discover his priorities in life.

Since Pete and Katie had left for Boston, Hayward had continued to build the house. It had been a slow and tedious task but with Ann's help, it had been amusing with her determined curiosity, attentiveness, and sometimes dealing with her high-strung emotions. Now with skill, she knew how to lay a plumb-line and mix mortar in the building process. As for Caroline, Hayward thought, she was attempting to re-adjust and make the best that life offered by trying to stay busy and keep her mind occupied with chores and knitting. At times she gave the impression that she was happy, but the sadness and heaviness that her eyes revealed told a different story. Hayward shook his head in sadness as he thought of her riding along the river most evenings knowing that she needed to speak her troubles to someone and talk the process of grieving through to a positive conclusion. Knowing the optimism, encouragement, and constructive spirit that Katie possessed, he thought she would be of benefit and help in this area of Caroline's life. Occasionally Ann would accompany her mother, but more often, she had buried herself in Katie's educational literature, making the attempt to study English literature, French as best as she could, and with her grandmother's help, the social graces that a young woman of culture was expected to learn.

As for Charles, his whereabouts and welfare was still unknown. Hayward hoped the family would soon receive news from him; something that would give everyone hope, or if he was dead, then conclusion and finality. It was the unknown that was keeping the family on edge. As for Miss Elizabeth, the short time that she had been home, it was apparent to Hayward by her words and actions that the war was still being waged. Hayward was sure that she had refused and was determined within her heart not to make any changes or accept its verdict, but to continue to live in bitterness and resentment. Miss Elizabeth had possessed many dreams and expectations of the future before and during the first half of the war, but with Rebecca's death and the destruction of the property, and worries over Charles, it was the issues that drove her the most to exercise her unpredictable behavior. His hope for Miss Elizabeth was that she would be able to pick up the pieces of her life and accept its consequences and move on to hopefully a brighter destiny.

The greatest issue that Hayward had with her was, since Pete's absence, she had made some offensive remarks concerning the Negro race and Northerners in general, but Hayward knew that his patience would sustain him and give him a greater strength in an area of his life where in the past he had experienced some weakness. He had learned long ago that when she was in an angry mood, to turn and walk away and allow her the time alone. He knew the war had changed the family's way of life in many ways. Now, everyone would have to find some kind of common ground and continue to make the best of it at rebuilding not only an estate but also a business that would prosper.

Some time had passed when Hayward glanced toward the western sky. He noticed the sun was beginning to set along the horizon. There were still a few chores he wanted to accomplish and then turn in early so he could begin his labor on the house at first light in the morning. Slowly rising from the slated rock, and whistling the "Battle Hymn of the Republic," Hayward kneeled along the riverbank and removed his catch of carp and catfish from the water. He grabbed his fishing pole and placed his net of fish over the front of his saddle and turned his horse in the direction of Barker's Ridge.

As Hayward proceeded at a slow trot across the tall grass, he glanced in the direction toward the western pastureland. He counted five riders advancing in his direction at a steady pace. Pulling back the reins on his horse, Hayward paused and stared intently in the direction of the mysterious riders. At first he thought it was a Yankee cavalry patrol, but as the riders continued in his direction, he noticed they were dressed in regular civilian clothing, with the exception of one, who was wearing a white duster. After the skirmish that he and Pete had experienced two weeks ago, he had good reason to be cautious and fearful of the approaching riders.

Once the horsemen were within a hundred yards of him, Hayward heard a cry come from them such as he had witnessed from Confederate cavalrymen in the early spring of 1862 when they charged a Yankee patrol near School House Ridge. Suddenly, there was the popping noise of gunfire and the whizzing sound of bullets flying by. Immediately, Hayward placed the heel of his boot against his horse's ribs and riding close to the animal's neck, he dashed toward the cabin across the ridge. Hayward looked back and noticed that the five riders were gaining ground. Birds and rabbits made their flight in fear as the echoing sound of multiple gunshots continued to fill the air. Hayward's heart was racing with anxiety. Perspiration was dripping from his face and neck as he looked back to see if they were continuing to gain ground on him. Convinced that they were, Hayward struck his horse on its hindquarter but the animal couldn't respond. He believed the gelding was older than the horses that the five men were riding. Many thoughts of survival raced through his mind.

Hayward suspected these people were the same individuals who attempted to bushwhack Pete and him along the river when the two of them were digging for rock for the house. Once he reached the top of the ridge, he paused and looked back thinking that they would by now have given up their quest, but three of the riders continued toward him while the other two went in a different direction toward the Charlestown Pike.

Hayward noticed the wagon near the construction site and turned his animal around and headed in that direction knowing his loaded pistol was in the toolbox. As he neared the wagon, the three riders came over the ridge continuing to fire their weapons. With the sound of gunfire, Caroline was the first to step out onto the porch from the house. Hayward dismounted and shouted. "Git in the house now 'fore yas gits kill."

Before Caroline could turn around, Elizabeth came running from the cabin shouting, "What is the meaning of all of this?"

There were several more shots fired at Hayward by the approaching riders only this time he began to rapidly return fire. Again and again in desperation, he turned in Caroline and Elizabeth's direction yelling for them to go back into the cabin.

Elizabeth was infuriated with anger shaking her fist in defiance believing the raiders were Unionist who were trying to intimidate the family into selling their property. Caroline grabbed Elizabeth by the shoulders and attempted to physically control her, but Elizabeth continued to vigorously resist Caroline's attempts.

Hayward kept up a steady fire and at the same time waving for the ladies to take cover. By instinct, he returned his attention to one of the riders advancing close to the wagon when he discharged his pistol dropping the individual from his saddle near the rear of the wagon. Hayward glanced one more time in the direction of the two ladies only to notice Elizabeth clutching the right side of her chest and collapsing in Caroline's arms. Hayward began to race toward the two women. "No, no dear Lord! Please!"

Chapter 32

Within the hour, Pete had arrived at Harpers Ferry aboard the 3:15 passenger train on the way to Wheeling, West Virginia. After the events surrounding the terrible attack against Seamus McBride, the turmoil that followed at his residence, Pete's escape had been a tiresome and at times difficult task. Traveling by foot through an unfamiliar city such as Boston, and finally a three-day journey aboard a cargo vessel across turbulent waters to Baltimore, it was a reprieve to return to the Shenandoah Valley. Pete knew in all probability, the Boston police had most likely been hunting him like some fugitive, and once captured, they would have imprisoned him for the attack on Seamus. Pete was quite convinced by the words and actions of the McBrides that they believed he was responsible for the assault on their son and had implicated him in the affair.

The whole issue with the McBride family didn't trouble Pete as much as the indifferences and confusion surrounding Katie and him. Even though Katie expressed her love for him, he knew since their arrival in the city, she had been reserved and distant in their relationship. Katie wasn't the optimistic and confident individual he knew before the trip to Boston but quite the opposite. Instead, she appeared to be unsure and not confident in her life and was attempting, he believed, to regain her family's favor. It reminded him much of the experiences he endured before the war with his mother and brother Charles.

Thoughts resurfaced in Pete's mind of the time last year when he had helped in Katie's escape from prison in Winchester, Virginia. While waiting for the train in Frederick City that would return her to Boston and safety, they had shared some intimate moments in conversation before her departure. Pete had confronted Katie with the real reason why she hadn't returned home at the beginning and during the civil war. She admitted that it was because her parents had banished her return to Boston for going against their wishes in the first place and beginning a new life far away from home in Harpers Ferry as a schoolteacher. When she returned to Shenandoah at the end of the conflict, it probably increased the family tensions. In many ways, Pete discovered that Katie was a rebel in her family just as his family knew him.

Pete knew Katie was struggling with the way of life that they had been enduring at Shenandoah. The oppression was increasing upon Southern citizens by the unfair laws that were implemented, and the Unionist that were rigging the elections and taking control of the local government had become a heavy-laden yoke of burden. Since her return from Boston at the conclusion of the war, they had been experiencing many hardships in their attempt to rebuild the estate and re-establish the Barker reputation and standing in the community. They continuously met some kind of obstacle.

As far as a successful life goes, Pete wanted Katie to have the opportunity to fulfill her dreams and take advantage of all the prospects that would be available with living in Boston or some place that was far away from the barren region of Jefferson County. Katie's father was correct concerning Shenandoah and living in the south. It was still a dangerous area and she deserved more then he was able to give. From Pete's impression of Boston and all the advantages that the city offered, if Katie continued her life there, then eventually, maybe, she'd forget about him and Shenandoah, and be able to fully reconcile with her family.

Once Pete came upon the lane at Shenandoah, he heard the noise of gunfire. His heart began to race with anxiety and his fear that the men who attempted to ambush Hayward and him several weeks ago were making the attempt to finish the job. Without hesitation, he smacked his horse on the hindquarter and galloped at a full pace toward the direction of the cabin. On his arrival, the fighting had stopped and the intruders were disappearing over the ridge. Pete noticed that Caroline and Hayward were kneeling beside his mother. Pete was surprised as he jumped from his horse and raced to his mother's side. Immediately, he noticed the bluish color of her face. She was semi-conscious. As he looked at his mother, she was holding her hand across her chest and gasping for breath. It was a scene that Pete had witnessed many times on the battlefield but this incident was totally different, the fight had become personal, and unexpected. This time, it was his mother, an innocent individual, who was unable to defend herself against an enemy.

Pete glanced at Hayward and believed by his gloomy expression that the wound was fatal. Tears began to run uncontrollably down Pete's cheeks as he brushed his mother's hair from her face. He began to feel guilty and emotions of failure began to surface. Thoughts crossed his mind that if he had been here to defend his family, this wouldn't have taken place.

Pete looked at Caroline as she cradled his mother in her arms and was crying. "Oh no, no, why does the fighting and killing have to continue? Why?"

Again, Pete looked at Hayward. "Who did this?"

Speaking with a quiver in his voice, Hayward answered with a stutter. "I'se, I'se, was finish fishin' and on my ways back here when dose men charge at me and started shootin'. I'se didn't have a gun, so I'se headed this way to git it from the wagon. Miz. Elizabeth come a runin' from the house a shoutin' at them when she fell hurt. Dey's took off towards the river when dey's seen yose a comin'."

"Was it the same ones who shot at us along the river?"

"I'se think so 'cause one of them was wearin' a white coat."

Suddenly, Pete remembered John Morris's friend Benjamin Watson use to occasionally wear the same type of coat when the 1st was about to go into combat. Pete remembered the time when the cavalry regiment was nearing Catlett Station with General Stuart in August of '62 just before the fighting at Manassas that he personally had warned Benjamin against wearing the coat because he would make an easy target. Like many times in the past Benjamin refused Pete's request and wouldn't even heed the warning of those who were much closer to him. Why would Benjamin Watson hold a grudge against him since they were friends fighting for the same cause? Was it because he was one of the few that couldn't accept the reality of the Confederate defeat and surrender at Appomattox, or was there some other hidden hostilities that Pete wasn't aware that Benjamin might want revenge?

"We need to move Mother Elizabeth to the inside to a bed where it will be more comfortable," Caroline urgently requested.

"Yes, I agree," Pete replied.

As Pete and Hayward gently lifted Elizabeth from Caroline's arms, Pete noticed his mother's bloodstained gray dress. He attempted to repress his anger and keep his emotions under control until he knew his mother's outcome with this injury. Caroline dashed in front of them and opened the door directing Pete and Hayward to where they should place Elizabeth. After placing his mother on the bed in her room, Pete turned to Hayward and commanded, "Go into town and bring Doc Marmion as quickly as possible."

Hayward nodded in acknowledgement racing from the cabin and mounting Pete's horse.

Pete turned his attention once more examining the wound that his mother received.

As Hayward galloped off in the direction of town, Ann arrived by another route from riding along the northern pastureland. Once she dismounted, she became concerned as she noticed that Hayward was galloping down the lane at a brisk pace. Within her heart, she knew that something terrible had happened because she had heard gunfire.

Quickly entering the cabin and looking around, she heard her mother. "Ann we are in here."

Racing toward her grandmother's bedroom, she entered and cried. "Oh no, Grandmother."

As Ann began to break down with emotion, Caroline commanded, "Ann, please there is no time for that now, I want you to start boiling some hot water and cut up one of my undergarments! Hurry!"

Ann was still in shock and sobbing by all that she was witnessing. Again, Caroline commanded in an authoritative tone. "Ann, please go now and hurry!"

This time without hesitation, Ann raced from the room praying as she complied with her mother's request.

Pete was applying some pressure to the wound. He had witnessed surgeons in various field hospitals doing that after a battle in the attempt to save a life. As he became tired and removed his hand, the wound was still slightly oozing. Immediately, Caroline took his place and followed through on the same process that she noticed Pete doing. With all the turmoil and confusion taking place, Caroline had not missed Katie until she glanced around. She looked at Pete and asked surprisingly, "Where is Katie?"

Pete remained silent looking across the bed at Caroline. Again, Caroline asked, "Where is Katie? Didn't she return with you?"

"No, she stayed in Boston."

"Why isn't she here? Did something happen?"

"Caroline, please, now is not the time nor place to discuss this matter."

"Pete Barker, I want to know now. Is she all right?"

Pete didn't desire to discuss the situation about Katie and her family to Caroline so he lied in order to delay telling her the truth, especially under the current circumstances surrounding the incident involving his mother. When the time was right, he would tell her the truth knowing that she'd be very emotional and angry. "Yes, Katie is fine. But can we talk about this later?"

Caroline nodded her head in agreement and dropped the subject.

As Pete stood and continued to observe his mother's shallow breathing, his heart became troubled knowing there was a possibility that she could die. He glanced at Caroline as she was attempting to withhold her emotions. There was a sigh of pain coming from Elizabeth as she continued to struggle to live. Pete knew she was suffering but couldn't accept the reality that she might not live another hour.

Chapter 33

Nearly an hour had passed since Hayward's departure for Harpers Ferry for help. On her mother's request, Ann was outside the cabin drawing water from the well and boiling it over a huge fire she had started. Ann heard the sound of horses and turned her attention toward the Charlestown Pike where she noticed Hayward returning with the physician and three Union cavalrymen. As she removed the wooden bucket from the rope and poured the water into the large black kettle, she paused and wiped her hands on the apron tied around her waist. As the horsemen quickly approached, Ann stepped onto the porch of the cabin and opened the door. "Mr. Hayward is returning with Doctor Marmion and some Yankees."

Pete had been continuing to apply pressure to his mother's wound. He was exhausted but with Ann's warning of the soldiers' arrival his adrenaline began to flow. Both Pete and Caroline's eyes met; their astonishment was evident with Ann's news. Pete gestured to Caroline. Without hesitation, she took his place while he walked to the window and glanced. There were three Yankee cavalrymen dismounting and one of them was Captain Brackett whom he disliked. Pete knew the officer was probably up to no good and most likely didn't care if his mother lived or died. He believed the army captain knew that his mother was very passionate and supportive of the Southern cause for independence. She had never at anytime during the Great Rebellion attempted to hide or disguise those passions. Pete continued to think, maybe, the army captain had arrived to order the family to vacate the estate since he recognized him earlier at the train depot. Still, Pete thought, there was another day left in the month before the foreclosure on the property.

Hayward, Doctor Marmion, and Captain Brackett quickly dismounted and entered the cabin while the rest of the cavalry detail remained mounted. As the physician entered the room where Caroline was continuing her efforts, Captain Brackett did also. Hayward remained in the other room.

Doctor Marmion knelt over Elizabeth's motionless body. "What happened?"

Caroline stood and chose her words methodically knowing the army Provost Marshall would be listening to every word. "Mother Elizabeth and myself were in the cabin making a few candles to carry us through the week when we heard the sound of horses approaching. We were the only ones at home at the time. Naturally, out of curiosity we opened the door and walked outside when all of the gunfire began. Mother Elizabeth…"

Doctor Marmion interrupted and finished the sentence. "Yes, I know all too well Elizabeth's behavior. She lost her temper and was going to try and take on the intruders herself."

Tearfully and in a broken voice, Caroline answered. "Yes, that is the way that it happened. I tried, but I couldn't stop her."

"Elizabeth must be the most stubborn woman I've ever known. But, I guess no one can be as successful as she has been if they weren't."

Pete was impatient as he stood near the head of the bed watching and listening to Caroline speaking with the physician. He glanced defiantly at Captain Brackett, who was still standing silently in the doorway observing Doctor Marmion as he placed his finger in Elizabeth's wounded chest area searching for the bullet.

"Doctor Marmion, how is she? Is my mother going to recover?" Pete impatiently asked.

The physician paused his examination and turned his attention toward Pete. "The bullet has to come out now." Pete was silent as the physician continued, "My greatest concern is that she is so weak from the loss of blood and the position of the bullet that she might not survive. But on the other hand, if I don't do anything and delay the attempt, she'll die sooner. At least this way if something happens, we know we made every attempt to save her."

"Then that means we have to get started and not waste any more time," Pete anxiously replied.

Doctor Marmion took Pete's answer as consent to remove the bullet. He commanded as he searched his satchel for a probe, "I need hot water and plenty of it."

Hayward was standing by the doorway with Captain Brackett. "I'se will git it now."

Pete assisted the physician as they gently positioned Elizabeth for the procedure. Doctor Marmion gestured with his hand for

Pete and Captain Brackett to leave the room while Caroline and he removed most of Elizabeth's clothing.

With tears flowing down his cheeks, Pete glanced once again in the direction of his dying mother as the physician was rolling up his sleeves and preparing to wash his hands with the hot water that Hayward had poured into the washbasin.

Pete and Hayward stepped out onto the porch followed by Captain Brackett. Pete leaned against one of the porch columns staring at the two cavalrymen that remained mounted on their horses. Without a word, Captain Brackett stepped from the porch and walked toward the other two cavalrymen. Pete continued to watch the officer speak to them and pointed in the direction of the wagon and stone foundation of the house. Pete knew they would be searching for weapons. Then Pete slowly turned his attention in Hayward's direction. Hayward was seated on one of the porch steps. As Pete glanced at him staring aimlessly at the ground, he noticed the tears flowing from Hayward's cheeks. He knew Hayward was blaming himself for all that had taken place with the wounding of his mother. Pete watched as Hayward covered his face with his hands and shook his head in frustration. Pete wasn't angry at Hayward but knew that he did everything possible to defend the ladies and him from the attack of the intruders. He needed to reassure Hayward there wasn't any choice in the matter.

Walking over to where Hayward was seated, Pete sat beside him and placed his arm around his friend's shoulder. "Hayward, I don't blame you nor am I angry with you over what happened today. There wasn't any other choice."

Hayward turned and looked at Pete. He shook his head in disagreement. "No, no, I'se should have gone another way. Deys would had followed and this thing wouldn't have had to happen. I'se jist didn't think, I'se jist didn't think."

"I remember when I was fighting during the war, it seemed that everything got crazy and confused when we were fighting at close range. I found out very quickly that you don't always think, but instead you act by instinct. It's your nature to survive in any way when your life is being threaten."

"I'se know, I'se know, but I'se had the time to think and I'se got scared. I'se was thinkin' that deys was comin' to git me and hang me cause I'se was the one who for many years 'fore the war help the black man escape to freedom. Deys hadn't forgotten.

Maybe I'se best move on after I'se know's the outcome with Miz. Elizabeth?"

Pete wasn't planning to reveal any of his intentions so soon with Hayward. "No, I'll need your help. After I know how things go with my mother, I will tell you of my plans."

Anger covered Hayward's features as he fired back in a scolding tone. "Now's boy, yose better not do something foolish. Yose hear me?"

Again, Pete glanced in the direction of the officer and the cavalrymen. He watched as the two cavalrymen dismounted and with Captain Brackett they approached Hayward and him. Pete knew that there would be questions.

Captain Brackett said in a sympathetic tone as he looked at Hayward and Pete, who were still sitting. "Barker, I am sorry for what happened to your mother today, but I need to know what has been going on around here that you people continue to fight the war."

Pete answered as he looked up at the officer with a cold expression. "I don't know what you're talking about. As you well know, I have been in Boston."

"I know Barker, but neither am I a fool. Something such as this doesn't happen over night. Now, what has been going on?"

In an effort to protect Pete and the rest of the family, Hayward replied, "I'se tell yose whats a goin' on. I'se was a fishin' along the river when dese men come along, a chargin' and a yellin' like some kind of a demon. I'se run like de scare rabbit cause I'se was scared." Pausing and choosing his words, Hayward continued in a defensive tone. "I'se wasn't thinkin' when I'se decided to come back here to git my gun. Deys was close. I'se didn't have the time to git away from the cabin. I'se shot back. I'se might have hit one. Mr. Pete, he's come when deys men was a runnin' over the ridge."

"Which way did they go?" Captain Brackett asked.

Without a word, Hayward pointed toward the ridge that leads to the river.

Captain Brackett turned his attention toward Pete. "Well Barker, I guess you didn't have anything to do with this." Turning and pointing in the direction of one of the cavalrymen carrying a pistol in his hand, the officer continued, "But it is apparent that you people keep weapons on the property." Maybe this wouldn't have happened if there hadn't been any gun play on your part."

Pete became furious with anger as he jumped to his feet. "And what are we suppose to do sir, allow these renegades the right to come on our property and harm us and destroy what little that we have! No sir, not for one moment will I allow my family to be tormented by them or anyone else."

Captain Brackett replied in an authoritative tone. "Well, maybe you need to spend sometime in the guard house to cool off."

Pete remained silent and attempted to repress his anger and remain calm. He knew he had to be here with his mother and the rest of the family. The raiders might decide to return and finish the job and then if something happened while he was imprisoned, then he'd never be able to live with himself. He quickly said, "I am sorry. I guess I've let this whole matter get the best of me."

"I understand Barker. Although I am not convinced that you or your darkie friend are telling me the truth, apparently, there isn't much that I can do at this time, but restrict you to the premises. But I'll warn the both of you now, that if anything else happens such as occurred today, I'll toss both of you in the guard house myself and let you rot there. Understand!"

Pete and Hayward remained silent, but shook their head in agreement.

"Then I guess we have an understanding." As the officer departed, again he turned around. "By the way Barker so that you'll know that not all Yankees are tyrants and evil human beings, I will see that the foreclosure of your property will be postponed for one week until we know how your mother will fair. But until then, I'm placing a guard here to keep watch on you."

As Pete watched Captain Brackett and the other soldier depart, he glanced defiantly at the other guard quietly taking a seat on the porch. Suddenly from inside of the cabin, Pete heard the sounds of a loud scream.

Chapter 34

As Pete raced through the door, he noticed Ann standing at the bedroom doorway with her hands covering her face and sobbing uncontrollably. Perceiving the meaning of his niece's actions, Pete frantically dashed for the doorway where his mother was lying. He paused and watched Doctor Marmion listening to his mother's heart with his stethoscope. Pete's attention turned toward Caroline. Tears were streaming down her cheeks as she too observed the physician searching for any evidence of life. Pete's heart was racing, his mind was thoughtless, and he began to perspire from anxiety as he entered the room. Without words to express his anguish and pain, he just stared at his mother's motionless body.

Once Doctor Marmion removed the stethoscope, he turned around and looked at Pete and Caroline. Shaking his head in frustration. "Her heart stopped beating momentarily, and quite frankly, I thought that I had lost her. But Elizabeth is tough; she's not ready to give up. She's breathing again but very shallow."

Pete took a deep sighed as he brushed the tears from his cheeks. "Were you able to remove the bullet?"

Doctor Marmion once again shook his head in frustration as he answered. "No, I wasn't able to. As I entered deep into the wound, your mother's breathing became very shallow and occasionally she would stop breathing. Out of fear of losing her, I decided that it would be best to terminate the procedure. And then suddenly, she stopped breathing altogether for about a minute. I really thought that I had lost her."

As Pete stood over his mother's body, he was quiet, thinking of the times when he was a young lad growing up at Shenandoah. He could still visualize the smile that often covered his mother's face when she and father would walk hand and hand around the mansion and property, speaking and pointing to the different wonders of nature. Pete remembered some of the greatest moments were the social events held at the estate. Elizabeth was always in her glory and at her best when guests would attend one of the events. Even though she still had her faults during that time such as her domineering nature and being very outspoken, it was still a joy to witness her jovial expressions. Pete had noticed the dramatic change in her personality and life shortly after his father's unexpected death. He knew she was still angry over her loss and maybe was taking it out unintentionally on someone else.

Caroline stood from kneeling alongside the bed and quietly walked over to where Pete stood and placed her arms around his shoulders. She kissed him on the cheek. "There is nothing we can do now but wait and see. I'll make Mother Elizabeth as comfortable as possible. She will not be alone; Ann and I will take turns staying with her.

"I appreciate all that you are doing. I know that over the years it's been difficult for you and Charles living with her..."

"But I have always loved her regardless of her faults. Mother Elizabeth accepted me as part of this family and has always made me feel at home. Under no circumstances will Ann and I leave her."

Pete and Caroline walked slowly from the room and sat at the table sipping on the coffee that Hayward had prepared. Thoughts of revenge surfaced once more in Pete's mind.

* * * *

After several days, Elizabeth's condition had not improved nor had she regained consciousness. Caroline had awakened early and was sitting in a chair near the fireplace trying to keep warm while sipping on some coffee. Pete entered the cabin after helping Hayward tend to the horses. Caroline looked in his direction and asked the question that had continuously been on her mind, "Pete, we still have some unfinished business to talk about you know." When Pete didn't answer, Caroline continued, "I want to know why Katie didn't return with you?"

Pete walked over and poured some coffee and sat in the chair opposite Caroline. He looked aimlessly into the flickering fire. "Even though I hadn't planned on saying anything yet, I just as well tell you now. Sooner or later I am going to have to be honest with you anyway."

"What is wrong? What are you keeping from me?"

Pete turned from looking in the direction of the fire. "Katie isn't going to return to Shenandoah."

"Why? What happened between you two?"

"Have you ever felt that the world was collapsing on you and there wasn't any way out?"

"Yes, quite frankly, I do. There still isn't a day that doesn't go by that I don't think of Charles. I've experienced many sleepless nights since we left Richmond just before General Lee surrendered. Often I wonder if Charles is dead or alive, and if he'll ever come home to me. So to answer your question, yes I know all too well."

Pete took another sip of coffee and began to explain in a troubled tone. "From the time that Katie and I arrived in Boston until I left, nothing could go right between us or her family. Our differences began to happen just before we arrived at her home."

Pete turned and gazed at Caroline as he continued. "The first of many surprises was the fact that Katie had never told us that her father, Thaddeus McBride, had been one of those great leaders behind the abolitionist movement in Boston. I found out on the way to her home that he was elected to the Massachusetts House of Representatives in '64 where now he is a leader among his party. And then when I had the opportunity to speak with him about possibly helping us financially, he was against the idea because of political repercussions and he, like many in the North, wanted to see harsh measures taken against us Southerners. If that wasn't enough, Katie's brother Seamus tried to discredit and humiliate not only me verbally but also his own sister. He made some serious accusations against Katie; accusing her of being a Federal agent during the rebellion. And the only reason for our relationship was to play me for some kind of fool to gain as much information as possible."

Caroline jumped from her seat and fired back. "I don't believe for one moment that Katie was a spy or agent for anyone! She isn't that kind of a person. It's lies, it's all lies!"

Pete was silent, allowing Caroline to calm her emotions. He stood and quietly walked to the fireplace and placed his arm on the mantel. Again he gazed at Caroline's troubled features. "I don't know about that Caroline. When I questioned her after Seamus left the house, she didn't say much in her defense. It was like she was totally taken by surprise, betrayed by someone who loved her. The only thing that she said in reply was, 'would it make any difference between us?'"

Caroline was astonished at Pete's words. Pete continued to speak of his experiences in Boston with the McBrides, as she remained silent and listened. "I knew that I had to find out the truth because it was eating at me. Was Seamus straight forth with the truth or was he lying to try and come between us? So, I followed shortly thereafter, only to find some thugs beating on him in an alleyway near the wharfs. After beating them off and returning him home, his family began to accuse me for the beating that he received. I tried to explain to them all that had taken place, but they already had their minds made up. As far as they were concerned, I was guilty. When I tried to verbally defend myself against such accusations, Katie defended her father. Naturally, I was angry and stormed out of the house not allowing her the opportunity to say anything."

"From what you've said, this isn't the Katie that I've known and loved. I still find it all hard to believe because Katie has always been so open and honest. I can't imagine that she was just putting on a disguise to deceive us."

"What troubles me the most is that she was so distant and reserved toward me. We've always been close since the end of the rebellion. We haven't kept anything from each other. It was almost as if sometimes we didn't know each other. But what puzzles me is that she professed over and over her love and loyalty for me." Pete looked back at the fire and shook his head. "Maybe I let my temper get the best of me. But I don't know who Katie McBride is any more."

Caroline knew Pete was greatly troubled. She stood and walked over to where he was. "All of us have been through many things over the past four years. People grow and change through what they've experienced. And you know for us, the war hasn't ended, especially if people such as Katie's father feel the way that they do toward us. But in spite of the hardships that face us, the most important thing that you need to answer is, do you still love Katie enough to forgive her for everything that has happened?"

"I don't know. I need time to think on matters."

"I understand. But when this matter is settled with Mother Elizabeth then you might think of returning to Boston and making amends with her. And I mean away from her family. Maybe she was just confused and unsure of herself in returning to Boston with you. I'm sure that she must have had some idea of how her family would accept you. Katie was unprepared to be placed in the middle of people who are still fighting the war. She just didn't handle it well."

"What do you mean?" Pete said as he looked at Caroline.

"I mean, she apparently returned home in desperation trying to help us out. I don't believe she was ready to return to Boston and face her family, especially since she was planning on marrying you. For now, think about what I've said and don't allow your pride to rule you in this matter. You're much like Charles in that way."

After spending some time alone thinking about Katie, Pete stood and walked over and looked in on his mother. Again his anger over this situation surfaced and continued again to rule Pete's thoughts. Now he believed was the time to hunt down those men responsible for this incident and pass judgment upon them. He had already devised a plan to draw the soldier's attention away from the front entrance of the cabin where the Yankee had been observing the horse shelter area. Pete would use Ann as his decoy since the young soldier had made various attempts to be friendly with her. Once Hayward and he secured a horse from the shelter, they would move with haste in the direction of the river so that later they would be difficult to track by Federal cavalry.

Again, Pete remembered Hayward previously had mentioned the possibility of Ben Watson's involvement in the fight at Shenandoah since he was the only one that Pete knew that wore a white duster. Pete knew Ben and his family lived across the river against the base of the mountain. This is where he decided he would begin his quest for revenge. At the first opportunity, he would lay out the details with Hayward and Ann. He planned on leaving at first light the next morning.

* * * *

As the first rays of sunlight hovered over the mountain, Pete was up after a restless night, and along with Ann, prepared to carry out his plan. After looking in on his mother, he glanced at Caroline and nodded farewell to her. There was a gloomy appearance upon her beautiful features as she rose quietly from her seat next to the head of the bed. With a shawl around her shoulders and her arms crossed, she approached him. "Pete, please, won't you reconsider going after those men and allow the Yankees to do justice?"

"No, I'll take care of matters myself and my kind of justice will be served."

As Pete turned to walk away, Caroline grabbed him by the arm and pleaded. "Is your kind of justice right? Do you feel it's going to change Mother Elizabeth's condition?" Pete noticed the sincerity in her eyes but just stared coldly at Caroline as she continued her effort. "No, it's not going to. You're just going to get yourself in more trouble by taking the law into your own hands. Ann and I need you here with us, not in jail or dead."

Pete continued to look at Caroline. He wouldn't answer her because he knew that she was correct and stoking coals of guilt upon him. Caroline's plea was her ability to use good common sense, but his anger was compelling him to act differently.

As Hayward was standing next to the fireplace warming his hands, Pete gestured for him to proceed for the door and to the shelter as planned. Hayward would give the guard the impression that he was feeding and watering the horses. After about ten minutes, Pete glanced quietly out the window to see how things were proceeding. The sight of the Yankee soldier sitting near the window watching Hayward tending to the horses aroused Pete's anger. Several more minutes passed and Ann was instructed by her uncle to proceed with her participation in the plan. She walked out the door toward the well to draw water, as was her chore every morning. Once she lowered the bucket into the well and filled it, she acted as though she was having difficulty in raising it to the top.

"Miss Ann, may I help you with that bucket?" The Yankee asked as he approached.

"Yes, please, I'd appreciate the help."

Once the Yankee had finished raising the bucket of water to the top of the well, he allowed it to rest on the flat stone surface.

"Thank you for your help," Ann smilingly said.

At first there was a smile that glimmered on the soldier's face. Ann knew by this expression that the Yankee had swallowed the bait.

The Yankee was quiet, not knowing how to handle the opportunity of knowing Ann in a personal way. Finally, he asked, "May I help you into the cabin with this full bucket. I mean since you had a difficult time with it."

Ann led him on by saying as she grabbed the bucket, "Well, I don't know."

"Please, I insist, let me help you." The soldier asked as he lifted the bucket from her grasp.

"I guess it will be all right with my mother."

As Ann was speaking with the soldier by the well, Pete quietly departed by the rear door to the cabin. He quietly moved from the rear of the structure to the side of the dwelling. Standing near the corner of the front porch and out of sight, he glanced at Ann and the soldier walking toward the cabin. Pete looked in Hayward's direction for the go ahead signal that the horses were ready. Finally after Ann and the Yankee soldier entered the cabin, Pete moved swiftly in the direction of the shelter where Hayward was already mounted and holding the reins of the other horse for Pete to ride. Once Pete mounted the horse, the Yankee walked onto the porch of the cabin with Ann.

After noticing Pete and Hayward's actions, the soldier grabbed his pistol and shouted. "Halt, halt, or I'll shoot."

Pete and Hayward ignored the command as they proceeded from the shelter area with the Yankee soldier's horse. The Yankee raised his gun and fired one round into the air, but Pete and Hayward ignored the warning. Again the Yankee went to discharge his weapon, but this time he aimed at Pete. As he cocked the hammer of the weapon Ann took her hand and struck his causing the weapon to fire toward the ground. As Pete and Hayward rode out of the pistol's firing range, the soldier placed the weapon at his side. He remained quiet, but looked angrily at Ann. Ann turned around and quietly walked back into the cabin.

Chapter 35

Once Pete and Hayward ascended the crest of Barker's Ridge, Pete brought his horse to a pause and turned to look back in the direction of the cabin. He glanced at the Yankee soldier still standing a few feet from the porch. Pete knew the soldier had to be frustrated and once he had to answer to Captain Brackett concerning Hayward and his escape, the soldier was probably going to receive the Captain's wrath. For the first time in days, there was the glimmer of a smile covering Pete's features. Again as many times during the war, he out smarted his foe. He turned and glanced at Hayward, who was continuing in the direction of the river still holding onto the rope that was used as a bridle and rein for the Yankee soldier's horse. Once again, Pete glanced in the direction of the cabin and then slapped his horse on its hindquarter, proceeding with haste to overtake his friend. By the time Hayward reached the riverbank, Pete was riding beside him.

Hayward quickly dismounted while Pete held onto the reins of the horses. As Pete turned around and looked in the direction of the cabin, he hoped and prayed that Caroline and especially Ann wouldn't receive punishment for their participation in his plan. Pete was still anxious as he turned and looked at Hayward. "Hurry we don't have much time to waste."

Hayward paused, looked at Pete, and pointed. "Young man, yose wait de minute, I'se will not be hurried."

Once more, Hayward turned and continued patiently walking along the riverbank searching for a birch tree with two hatchet marks on its trunk. Suddenly, Hayward fell to his knees and began to dig away the dirt with his hands. Within moments, he pulled out of the ground and from the base of the tree an old brown granter sack. Kicking the dirt to refill the hole, Hayward carried the sack and handed it to Pete. "Here dis is where I'se hide the thing."

Quickly Pete opened the sack and peeled back the newspaper. From the paper he pulled out its contents and found a pistol and two boxes of ammunition.

"Boy, what's ya gonna do with dis'?"

"Well done. Mount up, we'll go over to the Watson home and start there."

Hayward didn't have a good feeling in his heart and mind about this whole situation but remained silent. He decided that he'd go along with Pete and make his best attempt to keep Pete out of trouble.

Without delay, Pete and Hayward headed in an easterly direction along the river masking their tracks some twenty yards distance from the riverbank. Cautiously proceeding, it didn't take long for them to arrive near a bend in the river where Keyes Ford was located. It was the only shallow area that the river offered along the estate's borderline. Before crossing, Pete paused to look around the area to insure their safety. As he did, he quickly thought of the afternoon several weeks ago when Hayward and he were ambushed in this same area. He was sure within his heart that there couldn't be peace for his family until this matter was resolved, and it had to be his way, right or wrong.

Hayward was quiet as he removed his old black hat and rubbed his hand across his forehead. Pete glanced at Hayward and then the two crossed the river to the opposite side. After Pete turned the Yankee soldier's horse loose, Hayward and Pete headed westward along a trail that led to Vestal's Gap where the Watson homestead was located.

Once they began to ascend the steep mountain road, they came upon an area where there were some rock outcroppings and trampled underbrush that caught Pete's attention. Once Pete brought his horse to a halt, he pointed. "Hayward, look at the color at the base of the trunk of the sycamore tree near those outcroppings."

Hayward dismounted as Pete held the reins of his friend's horse. Hayward knelt and then was on his hands and knees moving some of the brush from around the base of the tree. Then his attention turned toward one of the rock outcroppings. He turned with a surprised expression covering his face and said as he pointed, "I'se did hit one of dem. Dis is dry blood on the bark of the tree and deres some on dis rock."

"Yeah, Hayward, you must have done some serious damage to one of them. The way I see it, they definitely headed in this direction and are probably holding up at Ben's cabin until they are sure that it is safe. Come on, mount up. We have to find them before the Yankees find us."

As Pete and Hayward were riding side by side, Hayward asked, "I'se hadn't heard yose say anything lately 'bout Misse Katie?"

"She stayed in Boston with her family."

"May I'se ask why?"

"Well Hayward, it's a long story, but I don't think that we'll be seeing each other again. When we have time, I'll tell you everything." He paused and shook his head in frustration. "Besides, she'll be better off with her own kind rather than living under the conditions that we'll have to endure with Yankee occupation of the South."

"No's no's, not Misse Katie. She's loves ya too much to keep away from ya. Old Hayward knows that she's love ya and was too devoted to ya to keep away. I'se knows, I'se always see the brightness in her eyes when she was with ya. Dey's has life." Pete remained silent as he looked at his friend. Hayward chuckled and shook his head as he continued to speak. "No's, no's, ya's not bein' honest with me 'bout dis. Ya's should know by's now that ya can't fool old Hayward."

"Tell me about it."

Within the next fifteen minutes, Pete and Hayward were within an area where they could see a small cabin in a clearing overlooking the river. Both men dismounted and tied their horses to the limb of a nearby tree. Pete removed the pistol from his belt and looked for any evidence of Ben or his family and friends around the cabin. After a period of time, a heavyset woman departed from the dwelling in the direction where the hogs were kept. After feeding them from the pail she was carrying, she returned to the cabin. From Pete's observations, it appeared she was the only person home.

Pete and Hayward moved quietly through the wooded area until they came within a short distance of the rear of the cabin. As quietly as possible, Pete moved closer to the rear of the structure where he glanced into the small windows to see if there was anyone at home other than the woman. He noticed three small children, two girls and one boy, sitting around the table eating. Pete gestured for Hayward to follow. Once Pete moved to the front of the dwelling, he glanced around before stepping onto the porch and opening the front door.

Pete cocked the hammer on the pistol and kicked open the front door of the cabin. The woman and the three children sitting at the table screamed with terror. Pete knew the woman didn't have a weapon within reach so he placed the pistol to his side "Shut up and you won't be harmed."

After the woman and children regained their composure, Hayward entered with an expression of astonishment covering his face.

"Hayward, start searching the house," Pete commanded.

The woman began to protest, "You can't do that! This is my home! That darkie and you jist can't come in here and order us around and now search my home. You jist wait until Ben returns. He'll fill ya..."

Pete interrupted. "So you are Ben Watson's wife? I hope that he does come back while I am here. It will save me the trouble of hunting for him."

Hayward entered the bedroom.

"That darkie can't go in there. My husband will kill ya both for sure," Mrs. Watson shouted.

Pete gave Hayward a hand gesture to continue. His attention returned to Mrs. Watson.

Hayward carefully looked around the room. He opened an old trunk at the foot of the bed where he sorted through the family possessions until he came upon a Confederate uniform. As he continued to sort through the clothing, he noticed the white duck coat at the bottom of the chest. Without hesitation, he removed the item.

Pete turned and noticed that Hayward had the coat in his hand and was looking down at the wooden floor. There, Hayward pulled back a small rug and knelt to examine the floor.

"What did you find?" Pete asked.

Hayward looked up and answered. "I'se think that I'se found blood stains on the floor."

Pete coldly gazed at the woman. "Whose blood is on the floor?"

"I don't know what you talkin' about," Mrs. Watson fired back.

Pete walked to where Mrs. Watson was standing. He grabbed her by her straggly-dark brown hair. He cocked the hammer of the weapon and placed the barrel of his pistol against the side of her head.

Hayward raced from the bedroom. "No's no's yose can't do that."

"Tell me or I'll blow your worthless head off!"

As Mrs. Watson attempted to speak, Pete removed the weapon and again placed it at his side. He commanded in an irritated tone. "Now tell me everything that has taken place here over the last few days? If you do, I promise that we'll leave you and the children unharmed."

Knowing that she didn't have any other choice and desiring to protect her family, Mrs. Watson consented. "All right, but only if you will leave us alone."

Pete nodded in agreement as he patiently listened to Mrs. Watson explain. "Several days ago, Ben and some of the boys were butchering a couple of the hogs. They was drinkin' pertty heavy that day and talkin' about the war and how's they should a kept fightin'. Well one thing led to 'nother and then, Ben went into the cabin and returned with that coat on. I knew that there was gonna be trouble. They talk of shootin' and scarin' some of the Yankees or more so, some darkies. I begged him and those foolish boys not to go, but he was so drunk up that he wouldn't listen to me." Mrs. Watson paused. Tears filled her eyes as she looked at Pete and continued to speak. "Hours had passed and they returned, but one of them was shot in the stomach."

"Who was wounded?" Pete asked.

"Aaron Dean."

"Is that his blood on the bedroom floor?"

"Yes, he suffered the rest of that day and passed on sometime durin' the night. So he is buried over there jist as you go into the woods."

Pete gestured for Hayward to go and confirm her statement. Pete asked, "Where's your husband?"

"Why? So you can go and kill him?"

Pete remained silent but continued to gaze at the troubled expression that covered the woman's face and the tears that filled the children's eyes. He answered, "Several days ago, he shot my mother. For all that I know she even now might be dead. So to answer your question, if I have to, I'll do just that."

"My mama told me that two wrongs don't make a right," Mrs. Watson sadly answered.

Pete noticed Hayward in the distance approaching with the horses. He walked onto the porch with Mrs. Watson. "I am sorry for all of the difficulties that I've demonstrated toward you and your children today, but you must try and understand how I feel concerning matters."

"I do. You a Unionist, huh, still wanna fight the war?"

"No, I rode with the 1st Virginia the same as your husband. We fought together from 1st Manassas to Gettysburg. So to answer your question, I am a rebel."

"Then ya has a score to settle with him, huh? I told Ben some months ago that he had to git the killin' and craziness of the war behind him, but all that he's done is drink, get angry, and cry. Sometimes, he's takin' his anger out on me and them kids over there, beatin' us until he was jist too plum tired or drunk to keep on."

"Where is he?"

"You might try Milford Pomeroy's farm near Myers's Ford. Ben likes to drink and talk about the war with his buddies from the 1st."

"Thank you and again I am sorry for all of the pain I caused you."

Pete glanced at Hayward and asked, "What did you find?"

"I'se find the grave all right."

Pete mounted his horse, and rode in the direction of the Pomeroy homestead, which was about six miles from Charlestown.

Pete was quiet and feeling guilty for the way that he had treated Mrs. Watson and the children but because of his desperation for information about Ben Watson, he felt compelled to act as he did. His actions with the woman and her children caused war experiences to resurface once again and trouble his mind.

Chapter 36

Within the hour after leaving the Watson farm, Pete and Hayward paused to rest at an area along a steep cliff that overlooked the Pomeroy homestead and the Shenandoah River. As Pete gazed in a westward direction toward Myers's Ford, his mind returned to an engagement that took place in this same area last year.

Hayward was also quietly looking around and admiring the view of the fall foliage covering the mountain and the valley below. From the clearing along the ridge near the crest of the mountain, Hayward marveled at the scenery, and for the first time, he could fully appreciate the majesty and beauty of the Shenandoah Valley. As he turned and glanced at Pete, his mind returned to Pete's actions at the Watson farm. He knew his friend was quite angry and emotional over the serious events of the last several days. Hayward knew Pete needed to express his emotions but not in the manner that he displayed with Mrs. Watson and in full view where the children could witness what was said. They also had observed all his aggressive actions.

Hayward was troubled greatly by the change that he was witnessing in Pete's life; it was as if he had become a different person. He knew both of them were being sought after by the Yankees and if found were probably going to spend some time in jail for violating their trust with Captain Brackett. If Pete continued to act irrational, Hayward knew they could be spending a lot of time behind bars; something that he'd have to intervene and prevent from taking place, if possible. Again, Hayward turned and noticed that Pete was continuing to look in the direction of the river. "It sure… is pretty up here. I'se never knows that this place could be so beautiful."

"I agree with you. Now it's peaceful, it's not always been so."

"What's yose thinkin' 'bout?" Hayward asked as he rubbed the horse's mane.

Pete pointed in the direction of the ford. "This time last year I was fighting my last battle with Colonel Mosby and for the Southern cause."

"I'se sees. Then yose saw a many good fellas lose their life on both sides."

"Yes, I did. The day was much like this, warm, cloudless, and pleasant. Most of us in the command had been constantly fighting the Yankees for days with little or no rest. When we arrived here on our way toward Charlestown, some of our men were ordered to cross the river to scout the area. I was suppose to ride with them but my horse was just too lame to continue so I stayed on this side with the men that were left behind. I was alone about thirty yards from many of the men looking at the left front foot of my horse. Looking back at where the others were resting, I can still recall some of the men laying or sitting on the ground in the shade with their horses tied or grazing on the grass. I watched as some were smoking their pipes and I am sure they were speaking of loved ones, home, and sweethearts. I noticed one comrade in particular sitting on a rock along the riverbank. He found the time to drop a few lines in a correspondence. Without warning, a Yankee cavalry regiment surprised us and attacked from the wooded area with their Spencer rifles."

Pete paused and without looking at Hayward, he continued to focus on the river area. He spoke in a broken voice as he described the events of that horrible day. "Very rarely were Mosby's men taken by surprise, but this day it was different. We were totally taken by surprise from an enemy that was hidden among the trees. There was great confusion among our men because of the rapid sound of gunfire, but no one panicked. When I heard the firing, I grabbed my carbine and raced toward the sound of the gunfire. When I got there, I witnessed the Yankees deliberately shooting down our men from the wooded area. Many of our boys didn't know what hit them. The air was full of bullets whizzing around. For about a half an hour, we fought vigorously in the open, taking many losses. Suddenly, some of the Yankees came boldly charging at us. I witnessed one Yankee nearby trying to beat a friend to death, but I shot him and he fell to the ground dead. The next thing I know, I was struck with the handle of a pistol and I lost consciousness."

Hayward gazed at Pete as he paused. Hayward noticed some tears flowing down Pete's cheeks. His features appeared troubled and gaunt. He heard his friend sniffle, but Pete's pride wouldn't allow him to turn and face his friend.

Suddenly, Pete started speaking again in the same broken voice. "When I regained my senses sometime later, I thought to myself, I could have lost my life just as I came close to at Funkstown in July of '63. Then remembering the words of the lady that took care of me for many months after being shot, Hannah Graceham, they once more resurfaced within my mind. She had spoken a truth to me that I was given a second chance in life and to go home and use it wisely and get out of this thing while I could. After recalling those words that day after the fight at Myers's Ford, I decided then that someway, somehow, I had to get out of this war. I had already witnessed too much killing and maiming to want to continue the effort. As I walked around the field after this engagement, I witnessed men tossing and turning, screaming in pain and gripping the grass in anguish. Then there were some whose eyes were open and lay lifeless because death had rescued them from this terrible conflict. They didn't have the second and third chance such as myself. In my heart, I wonder at times why the good Lord had spared me from such a destiny. But after this last fight, I knew with His help that my decision to get out of this conflict was the right one."

"Yose been through a lot. It's gonna take time to git over it all. Misse Katie was a helpin' ya, I'se knows, cause she'd sometimes talk with me. Misse Katie was the best thing to happenin' to you. I'se can't see ya throwin' all's that away."

Even though Pete knew that Hayward was right in his observations, he repressed the guilt and his friend's words. He remained quiet ignoring Hayward's wisdom.

Pete and Hayward proceeded along a rugged mountain road in the direction of the Pomeroy Farm. Hayward knew Pete still had one thing in mind, revenge. Hayward and Pete arrived at the homestead and like many in Jefferson County was tarnished from neglect. The property appeared shabby and untidy, and a few of the outbuildings were about to crumble to the ground from the need of repair. Weeds and underbrush appeared to overtake the premise. One could tell that any hope had vanished to rebuild the small farm and make it profitable.

As Pete continued to look around, he was met by an elderly gentleman, who appeared to be well into his eighty's. Pausing and continuing to look around, Pete turned his attention to the old gentleman holding onto a pitchfork. "Old timer, does Milford Pomeroy live here?"

Lifting his gray brim hat and scratching his baldhead, the old gentleman answered. "Yeah, he's still here for what good he's worth." Pete gestured for Hayward to look around the house and farm. The elderly gentleman became defensive. "Hey what's goin' on? What's that darkie lookin' for?"

Pete pulled his pistol, cocking the hammer. "Well, where is Pomeroy?"

As the old man glanced occasionally at Hayward searching the property, he replied. "That no good bum has gone into town with that other no good scallywag Ben Watson. Neither one is worth the time to shoot. All's they do is git drunk and talk 'bout that dang blasted war!"

Shortly, Hayward returned. "This old man is the only one here."

Pete looked at the frightened old gentleman and tipped his hat in a friendly gesture to calm his fears. "We'll leave you alone. Have a good day sir."

* * * *

Without hesitation, Pete and Hayward proceeded hastily in the direction of Charlestown. After maneuvering around a cavalry patrol on the outskirts of town, they entered along Washington Street from the western end of the village so that they could avoid the provost detail near the old jailhouse at the corner of George and Washington Street. As they rode slowly along the street and as inconspicuous as possible, Pete and Hayward's eyes searched the citizens walking around looking for Ben. It was Pete's intentions to search out the few bars that remained in town when Hayward suddenly paused and pointed in the direction of the four-story hotel, adjacent to the old Market House. "I'se see that horse the day that Miz Elizabeth was shot. That Watson man was on it. I knows I'se will never forgit that day. "

"How do you know?"

Again Hayward pointed. "That animal has a diamond over his tail and if I'se right, as we's gits closer, it's gonna have a bloody bald spot at the tip of its tail from some kind-a mange."

As Pete and Hayward rode alongside the horse in question, they noticed the animal was surely the one that Hayward had described. Pete and Hayward dismounted. As they looked in the direction of the hotel's entrance, Pete heard a chuckle and deep sounding voice calling. "Barker!"

Pete turned around and stared at Ben Watson and Milford Pomeroy standing behind Hayward and him. Pete nodded his head. "Ben, Milford."

"What brings ya to Charlestown this late in the afternoon?" Ben asked. "I know ya didn't come all this way to look at my horse."

"You might say I have some unfinished business to take care of."

"Oh, I see. And ya needed to bring along ya darkie I see to take care of matters also?"

"He's not my property. He's a free man to do what he wants, when he wants, and yes, I brought him along to take care of matters also."

Milford Pomeroy stepped forward boldly. "Ya know Barker, just before the war I always did have my doubts about ya and the darkies. I thinkin' that maybe ya were too good to them, more then they deserves." With his piercing dark-brown eyes, Milford continued to make the attempt to threaten Pete. "See, Ben and I don't like having them around. We don't see them savages as good as us and we feels that they should still be serving the master. We don't like the idea of them havin' their freedom and rights and this talk and nonsense of allowing them the chance to maybe run for office to tell the white man what he can do and can't do." Milford pointed at Hayward. "This country can never be run by his kind!"

Seeing that matters were beginning to race out of control, Pete kept his hands close to his hips where his weapon was concealed by his coat.

"Well the Yankees won the war and there is nothing that you can do about it," Pete answered.

"No Barker, the war ain't over with yet. It can never be over with until we have ridded the area and the South of the darkies and their kind."

Pete could tell by Milford's breath that he'd been drinking his liquor heavily and this was why he was so aggressive. Pete glanced at Hayward and then again at the two men. In an angry tone, Pete asked, "Were you at my home several days ago?"

Ben took up the conversation at this point. "Yeah Barker, ya might say that we had some unfinished business to take care of in your part of the county."

Milford laughingly added, "Yeah Barker, we wanted to stir up a little fun ya might say and string up that there darkie."

"Why? What has he done that is so wrong?"

Ben quickly replied in a tone of anger pointing in an intimidating fashion at Hayward. "Six years before the war, ya darkie was helpin' his kind to escape. They was our property that he stole from us. And you know what makes it worst, ya Barkers knew nothin' about it, or ya jist didn't care. Several times Milford and me almost caught up to him and if we would have, we'd strung him up then. The last time he made good his escape."

"What he did is all past now. Besides neither one of you own slaves so it wasn't your concern what he did. But there is a greater problem for all of us. In your little raid on my home the other day, my mother was seriously wounded and may not live because of you two trying to kill Hayward."

"Well Barker, we didn't know. She should have stayed in the cabin," Milford remorsefully replied.

"Milford shut up!" Ben shouted.

"Hayward, are these the men?" Pete asked as he glanced at his friend. Hayward nodded in agreement. Pete continued angrily, "Well Milford, as I see it, you only have one of two choices. You can walk over to the jailhouse and confess what you've done to the Provost Marshall and live or you're going to die here on the streets of Charlestown."

Ben chuckled as he spoke to Milford. "He's a foolin'. Why hell, he doesn't even have a gun."

Pete unbuttoned his coat where Milford and Ben could see the weapon. "Gentlemen, what's it going to be? Are we going to walk across the street and see the Provost Marshall or are we going to settle it here and now?"

Milford didn't have a weapon and lost his nerve after seeing Pete's pistol. He fearfully pleaded. "Look Barker, we didn't mean to do any harm to ya momma. We only wanted the darkie. Only a little fun."

Pete slowly and patiently pulled the weapon from his trousers, placing it to his side and cocking the hammer.

Again, Milford pleaded. "Don't shoot, I will do as ya asked."

"Then go now while you can."

As Milford walked slowly away in the direction of the jailhouse, which was at the end of the street on the opposite corner, Pete looked at Ben and asked, "Well, are you going to join him?"

"Barker, you're bluffing."

Pete looked coldly into Ben's gray eyes and quietly raised the weapon and aimed.

A stunned and fearful expression covered Hayward's face. He raised his arms in the air. "Boy, what's ya doin'! He's not armed. Ya jist can't kill him."

Pete remained quiet and ignored his friend's plea. Without giving any thought to Ben's wife and three children, Pete fired three times hitting him in the chest. Ben fell backwards, staggered and then tumbled to his knees and then on the ground. Without hesitation, Hayward grabbed Pete by the arm. Pete paused to make sure that Ben was dead.

Hayward grabbed Pete as he glanced in the direction of several Yankee guards approaching. "Come on boy before we's git shot."

This time without hesitation, Pete dashed for the horses with Hayward knowing that jail awaited them. As Pete was mounting, he heard several Yankee guards shout for them to surrender. Again, he ignored the request. Suddenly, there was the popping of musketry. Pete heard the whistling noise of the musket balls whizzing by his body as he had many times in the past during the heat of battle. Racing westward on their horses, Pete and Hayward made good their escape from town leaving Ben Watson dead on the street.

Chapter 37

The bright harvest moon was rising over the mountains giving Pete and Hayward plenty of light as they reined their horses to a halt along Barker's Ridge. For the latter part of the afternoon, Pete and Hayward had retraced their route, re-crossing the river using the mountain trail. Both were hungry as they crested Barker's Ridge, which overlooked the cabin, but they were cautious in proceeding still not knowing if there was a guard present.

Pete was still quiet as he looked around the area surrounding the cabin. He noticed a candlelight beaming from his mother's bedroom. This was a good sign that she was still living. As for the incident today in Charlestown, his heart was still callous and his mind was insensitive toward his actions. He believed that he was justified in his punishment of the trespasser.

Hayward was still stunned and shocked at Pete's actions of gunning down Ben Watson. He knew it wasn't like the young Barker to do something so drastic and unlawful, especially since he had studied law at the University of Virginia. But again he thought, these were extraordinary times and a person could only endure so much before they crumbled under pressure. It appeared from Pete's actions today that he had surrendered to his breaking point.

For the first time since leaving Charlestown, Pete broke his silence. "It appears the Yankee guard is gone. For now, I feel that it's safe to return home."

"What's we gonna do after that?"

"I don't know."

As Pete and Hayward proceeded in the direction of the cabin, they still remained cautious. After dismounting, Pete said, "If you'll take the horses to the rear of the cabin and then keep watch along the lane, I would greatly appreciate it."

Hayward nodded and complied knowing that Pete was greatly troubled. In his heart he knew if Miss Katie had been here to speak with him, all of the troubles that had transpired today wouldn't have happened. Hayward decided to speak to Pete as soon as possible to prevent any further bloodshed.

Pete didn't know if there was a guard or two within the dwelling. He calmly and cautiously entered the cabin with his pistol drawn prepared for such a confrontation. Once inside the dwelling, he noticed the living area was vacant. As he concealed the weapon once more under his coat, he walked slowly in the direction of his mother's bedroom. Pete entered the room to find Caroline asleep in the chair next to his mother's bed. Ann was slumped over the side of the bed with her head resting on its side and holding onto her grandmother's hand. As Pete looked on them, he was gratified by their faithfulness and commitment in this endeavor to nurse his mother back to health.

Pete walked over and touched Caroline on the shoulder. She awakened and was startled, but when she recognized Pete, she relaxed. Immediately, Caroline gestured and rose from her seat and followed Pete from the bedroom.

"How is she?" Pete asked once in the living area.

Caroline walked from one side of the table to the other where Pete was standing. "Well, Doctor Marmion was here again today, but there's still no improvement. At least now she's not losing any more blood." Caroline glanced in the direction of the room and again at Pete continuing, "Since you have been gone, Mother Elizabeth has only been lying there unconscious."

Pete walked over to the fireplace and poured a cup of coffee. His eyes were looking at the smoldering embers. "I can recall when I was wounded after Gettysburg and fortunate enough to make it to Hannah's home. For a week, she told me that I was unconscious and wouldn't respond to her voice. It took me months to recover from that gunshot wound."

It was dark outside and beginning to cool down in the cabin. Pete knelt near the fireplace and tossed some wood on the burning embers. After stoking the fire, Pete turned and glanced at Caroline with a glimmer of a smile covering his face. As Pete turned and walked quietly to the far end of the table, Hayward came walking through the door with a concerned expression covering his face.

Caroline turned around and recognized Hayward's facial features. Immediately, she became worried. "Hayward." When Hayward didn't answer, but instead ignored her, she turned and looked at Pete and asked, "What's going on that you're not telling me about?" Pete's expression changed to somberness as Caroline was persistent for an answer. "Pete, what happened today after you left?"

Unable to look Caroline in the eyes, Pete slowly answered, "I found Ben Watson, the man that shot mother and I killed him."

"It was in self-defense wasn't it?" Caroline quickly asked.

Pete remained silent, shaking his head in frustration as he turned toward the fireplace.

Caroline remained silent, placing her hands over her mouth in shocked and disbelief. She slowly walked over to where Pete was standing. "How could you just shoot him down?"

Pete turned, pointed toward his mother's bedroom and snapped with anger. "Did he think twice before pointing a gun at her! No! He shot an innocent woman who was trying to defend her home. What Ben Watson got he deserved and it was right to do so! Yankee justice would have rewarded him for killing the mother of Charles Barker."

Caroline grabbed Pete's arm and cried. "It still doesn't give you the right to play God, does it? Your mother is lying in that room seriously injured and she may never recover. And you take off and do something so irresponsible that's going to have an influence on your life and maybe your freedom. Didn't you think for a moment that we might need you here instead of getting into more trouble?"

"I did what I had to do. With Ben and his friends there wouldn't be any peace. They never would have left us alone! Never!"

Hayward was silent. He continued to watch as Caroline fired back. "When I agreed to help you I thought that you were going to just find out who was responsible for shooting Mother Elizabeth and allow Captain Brackett to take care of matters. But not with that hotheaded temper of yours, you let it get away from you. Now what are you going to do with the probability that every Yankee in Jefferson County is looking for you?"

"Hayward and I are going to hide out at a cave for several weeks..."

"What cave? Where?"

"It's a cave somewhere along the river that Hayward used to hide runaway slaves in before the war began."

"It's not going to work. It's only going to be a matter of time before they catch you or you get yourself killed."

Ann came walking from the bedroom. "What's all of the loud talking about?"

Caroline frustrated and angry about the conversation decided not to continue the argument. Instead, she walked over to her daughter. "Come along Ann, we must change Mother Elizabeth's dressing."

"Misse Caroline has a point. We's needs to give up whiles we can," Hayward said to Pete.

"I need time to think things out. Maybe both of you are right. God only knows I've caused this family enough grief over the last five years."

"Ya knows, things can change."

Pete paused and walked around the table reflecting on all that was said between Caroline and him. He turned. "Hayward, can you feed the horses? After I look in on my mother and Caroline, we'll leave."

Hayward began to open the door and he turned. "Ya knows, the sooner we's gives up, the sooner its gonna be all right for all of us."

Hayward quietly departed as Pete gazed without an answer.

Pete pondered on his friend's words, but he wasn't sure that it would be the right course of action. After all, he could receive death for his actions and breaking his parole. Finally, he walked over to the bedroom doorway and watched Caroline and Ann taking care of his mother. As Pete gazed at the ladies, Caroline would occasionally glance in his direction. Pete's heart and mind was progressively beginning to convict him. The actions that he had taken against Ben Watson and the consequences that his family might bear could cause them tremendous harm. Pete turned. "I'll see you when I can."

As Ann looked on, Caroline remained silent and nodded, continuing to dress Elizabeth's wound.

Pete walked into the living area and grabbed his hat, still thinking on what took place today. Once he opened the door and stepped out onto the porch, he heard in the distance. "Barker, this is Captain Brackett. Raise your hands above your head and surrender now or we'll fire on you!"

By instinct, Pete retreated through the doorway, closing it behind him and bolting it. Pulling his weapon from underneath his coat, he walked to the rear entrance and opened the door. As he did, he heard the same command to surrender. Again, he went to the front of the cabin and glanced out the window. His heart was racing as he quickly thought of his choices. After hearing a sound, Pete turned with the weapon's hammer cocked to fire and aim. There, he saw Caroline standing near his mother's bedroom doorway with a terrified expression covering her face. Once again, he turned his attention in the direction of the outside door and window. Pete knew he was surrounded on all sides and most likely the Yankees had captured Hayward. Again, he quietly turned around and glanced at Caroline and Ann, both sobbing from fear and uncertainty. Again, the question surfaced in his mind as to what his options would be, to surrender or make the attempt to escape.

Chapter 38

As Pete continued to gaze out the window into the darkness of night, he noticed the Yankees had lit torches to provide light. It appeared from those many lights that he was completely surrounded without any way of escape or could it be a deception. Pete remembered during the war, many times the Confederates would attempt to deceive the Yankees by performing something similar in order to disguise the size of their force. But still, he was one person against many. Besides, he had his family's welfare to be concerned about and this was his main concern now.

Again, Pete heard the command from outside. "Barker, this is Captain Brackett, you have one minute to surrender or we'll fire."

Caroline was still standing by the doorway to Elizabeth's bedroom with a terrified expression covering her face. She cried out, "Pete, don't you understand, there's been enough killing. Please listen to me and surrender before you get yourself killed."

For a brief moment, Pete was quiet as he stared at her. Then looking down at the floor, he walked over to the table and laid down his gun. With his head down, he walked slowly to where he unbolted the door and placed his hand on the door latch to open it. Pete turned and looked at Caroline. "Everything that I did as far as fighting during the war and now killing Ben Watson was to protect this family, our way of life, and Shenandoah. If no one else will, then I hope that you'll believe that."

A steady stream of tears began to flow down Caroline's cheeks as she nodded in agreement. "I know, you've tried, and I am gratified by all that you've attempted for this family and accomplished. And for that, I love you."

Pete slowly stepped onto the porch feeling a sense of failure and discouragement. There, three Yankee soldiers with carbines pointed in his direction swiftly approached. Immediately one of the soldiers searched him for a weapon and then they escorted him to where Captain Brackett was standing near the foundation of the old mansion. Pete remained quiet as he looked at the middle-aged officer.

Captain Brackett shook his head in frustration, staring intently at Pete. "Barker, this time you're in a lot of trouble. For killing an unarmed man you could get the death sentence, which unfortunately I'd have to carry out. And I must admit whether you believe it or not, I hate that thought."

"Watson deserved to die for what he did to my family. He was the one several weeks ago who tried to kill Hayward and me along the river. If the situation would have been reversed what would you have done?"

"I would have arrested him such as I am doing to you. I am no respecter when it comes to you troublesome rebels."

Pete heard the sound of several horses coming from the direction of the rear of the cabin. He turned and glanced, seeing Hayward's hands bounded by rope and accompanied by a Yankee guard on each side. He turned his attention once more to the officer. "Why do you have him bound? He didn't do anything to harm Ben Watson. It was me who shot him. Matter of fact, Hayward tried to talk me out of killing Ben, but I wouldn't listen."

Captain Brackett pointed in Hayward's direction. "As I see it, he should have informed us. If he would have, then maybe you would have only gotten off with 30 days in the guard house to cool down, but no Barker, you like many want to continue the war in some way or another. It's my duty to protect the innocent people of this county against scoundrels like you and him, and to re-establish law and order. And if I have to hang you as an example, then I'll do so. Understood!"

"Understood!" Pete answered defiantly.

As a Yankee soldier bound Pete's hands with rope, he glanced at Caroline and Ann standing on the porch. He felt unbearable guilt and condemnation. Not so much for shooting Ben Watson, but for the tribulation that he was putting Caroline and his family through.

Once the Yankee soldier helped Pete mount his horse, Captain Brackett ordered the command toward Harpers Ferry. Again, Pete glanced at Caroline and Ann quietly standing and watching.

* * * *

At 8 o'clock the next morning, the passenger train from Washington arrived at the depot. An unexpected passenger to Harpers Ferry stepped off one of the coaches. As Seamus McBride looked around, the town appeared in a greater desolated condition than his first visitation with his sister Katie here in the spring of 1863. He still wondered with amazement how Katie's profession of love compelled her to live and endure such conditions for as long as she did and ignore the prosperous life offered to her in Boston. But knowing his sister's qualities, she loved a challenge, and her persistence compelled her to refuse failure as a way of life. Looking around, Seamus wasn't familiar with this area and didn't know where the Barker's estate was located. The thought that surfaced in his mind was to visit the Provost Marshall's office. After asking the stationmaster for directions, Seamus proceeded toward High Street.

It was only a short walk for Seamus. As he approached the entrance, Seamus looked at the appearance of the building, nodded a friendly gesture to the guard at the outside entrance and entered the dwelling. Once inside, the clerk's eyes followed Seamus in a suspicious manner knowing that he was new in town. Again, Seamus looked around the office and then approached the clerk sitting behind the small desk. "Corporal, could you give me a bit of information?"

"It depends on its nature."

"I want to know where the Barkers live in this area."

A smirk rose on the clerk's face. "Over at Brown's old fort at the armory yard. He'll be there until we can ship him to the jailhouse in Charlestown. But Barker can't have any visitors, now, or until further notice."

Thinking maybe that Charles had been captured, Seamus fired back. "Which Barker?"

"James Barker."

"Why is he imprisoned?"

Pointing toward the board hanging on the wall behind him with all of the arrests for the last several days, the clerk replied, "Yesterday in Charlestown, he shot and killed an innocent, unarmed family man."

As Seamus looked in the direction of the board on the wall, he was amazed and surprised. He became concerned. "Where's the Provost Marshall?"

Captain Brackett answered as he stepped from the back room, "I am here." Approaching to where the clerk was seated, his gray eyes suspiciously examining Seamus. "Do you have some business with me about the Barkers?"

"Yes, matter of fact I do."

"Then get to it. I don't have all day to fool around with you."

Seamus' fiery eyes were fixed on the officer. "Very well then, I am Seamus McBride of Boston and I would like to see Mr. James Barker?"

"I don't think that your request is possible."

"Why not?"

Captain Brackett became angry. "Because I said so! I have been given the authority and law in this town and that's final."

"What about my sister; was she involved in all of this? Do you have her imprisoned also?"

"We just have Barker and his darkie in the guard house. They were arrested as the clerk informed you for killing an unarmed man. Several days ago, Barker's mother was wounded when some intruders raided his homestead. Barker claims that a man named Ben Watson and his friends carried out the assault. Later, out of revenge he took the law into his own hands and shot the man, claiming that his actions were justified."

"What about my sister?"

"The only women at the homestead were Barker's mother and sister-in-law. No one else, so I don't know about your sister."

"Then I must speak with Barker; maybe he knows of her whereabouts." The Captain remained silent as he gazed at Seamus. Again, Seamus pleaded. "From one comrade to another in arms against the rebellion, Captain, please, I must speak with Barker, it's urgent. My younger sister is missing."

"I see, and you think that Barker has some information that might help you."

"Possibly, yes, he may be of some help.

Pausing and thinking, the officer conceded. "All right McBride, but only if I am with you."

Seamus nodded his head in agreement. Even though in his heart he was doubtful of finding her at Harpers Ferry, there had been hope he could have been mistaken. Of what use Barker could be to him at this point was uncertain, but still, Seamus believed that he needed to speak with Pete and maybe he could shed some light on Katie's mysterious behavior.

Chapter 39

As Pete and Hayward sat quietly in the dimly lit, damp, old brick engine house that was used by John Brown as a fortress against Colonel Robert E. Lee and his company of Marines in 1859, many thoughts surfaced in Pete's mind. He was greatly troubled. Looking at Hayward pacing around the dwelling, Pete gave thought to Katie's life and the happiness he hoped that she might be pursuing since he left Boston and returned to Shenandoah. In spite of all his troubles, Pete knew he still missed her companionship, the relationship they shared, and most of all, the abundant love that she so richly gave. His mind returned to the day when Katie and he spoke after she returned to Shenandoah at the conclusion of the war. He had promised his love to her and that they would never separate and always be together. Now in the short span of five months so much had changed their lives and affected their relationship.

As Pete looked at the beams of light that glimmered through the boarding where round windows once appeared on the upper portion of the structure, tears filled his eyes. With everything that had so rapidly transpired over the last several days, he had found little time to reflect on his life let alone hers. Now in fellowship with only his thoughts of Katie, he was beginning to experience the anguish and void of separation for which he alone was responsible.

Pete turned his attention toward his friend, Hayward. Hayward stopped his pacing. "It stinks in here, and that food no old hound would wonna eat." When Pete said nothing in return to his friend, Hayward asked, "What's we'd gonna do now? Dey's can't leave us here forever."

Pete rose from the wooden floor and approached Hayward. Looking into Hayward's troubled eyes, Pete replied, "I don't feel that they'll leave us here permanently but in all probability they'll move us somewhere else. Before that happens we'll make the attempt to escape."

"How's we gonna do that? Deys gonna be a lot of dem Yankees. Yose know's dey's jist not gonna let us walk out of here. Dey's will have us bounded. Yose must have some plan as to what we's gonna do."

Hayward noticed the defiant glare in Pete's eyes, and in the sound of Pete's voice. "I have an idea."

Pete remained silent without expounding on his plan of escape.

"Well, are yose gonna tell me?"

Pete quietly gestured with his hand for Hayward to approach, to be silent, and sit near him. " Sometime after dark, I am going to call for a guard. And when he asks what the problem is, I am going to tell him that you're having some kind of a spell. When they open the door to investigate, I will jump him and hopefully take his gun. If there is another guard with him, then you'll have to deal with him." Pete pointed toward the doorway. "With what little I've been able to notice through the cracks in the boarding there are only several guards here at a time. If we are lucky this evening, one of those will be that small kid that helped in escorting us here after we left the provost office. He should be easy to overpower." Sighing and shaking his head in frustration, pointing toward the ceiling of the engine house Pete added, "It would have been better if we'd been able to escape through that trap door to the dome but we have no way, it's too high up."

"And then what? Where's will we go?"

"Once out of here, we'll split up with you going south along the Shenandoah, and I'll go west along the Potomac. Somehow, we'll meet up at the cave along the Shenandoah that you spoke of."

"You's don't know's where its at. How's will ya find it?"

"I know in or about the location. Besides, we'll be more difficult to track in the wooded area with all of the thickets and underbrush. Remember, the only thing is we'll have to separate once we make good our escape from here. But, until it's our time there isn't much we can do but wait."

Again, Hayward began to pace, chuckling as he rubbed his hand across his perspiring forehead, "Boy, yose always git ya self in trouble doin' something. I'se remember the first time that I'se came to Shenandoah. Ya pappy was gittin' after ya that day for fightin' with Mr. Charles. As I'se recall, yose was gittin' the best of him." Hayward continued to laugh as he turned toward Pete and continued to reminisce in a jovial way. "Miz. Elizabeth was a shoutin', runnin 'bout and tryin' to break the fight up but nothin' happin' until ya pappy jumped down from that buggy, shook his head in anger, throws away the cigar and then gits between ya two. I could tell then, that yose was a scrapper. I'se took a likin' to ya from that first time."

Pete looked at Hayward and laughed. "Yeah, I still remember all too well. Charles and I were fighting over who was going to clean out the stable and who was going to ride out to the western pastureland and summon Henry Larkensmith, the better of the two overseers that worked for us."

In a very serious manner, Hayward confidently replied, "Yeah, that Mr. Daniel was a evil man."

"Again Hayward, thank you. Daniel was an evil man and he would have killed Katie and me in Frederick City if you'd never intervened. But I guess what puzzles me the most is how you spent all those years at Shenandoah and kept us in the dark about helping runaways."

"It was a risky thing. When Mr. Cooper give me my freedom, he's asked me too use it wisely and in some way I'se was to help my people. He didn't have to say, I'se knows what he meant. So when ya pappy come to Philadelphia City, I'se was hired out to him by Mr. Cooper who ya pappy knew already. This was my chance. Fore leavin' that city, Mr. Cooper give me names and places who to speak to in the freedom route close to ya area. It took me months to git the thing up and runnin' but I'se had some help." Pausing and waiting for an answer, Hayward asked, "Does ya feel bad towards me for what I'se did?"

"No Hayward, you did what you thought was right and you lived by your convictions. I guess I will always respect that, but come to think of it, you must have been very good at what you did to fool old Daniel. You know that he would have killed you in a moment if he had any idea of what you were doing."

"He's never did have a likin' for me. I'se should of killed him long the river when I'se had the chance that day as I 'se was makin' my own escape."

"At times in life we all stop and think of certain matters if we would have done this or that differently. And we always wonder what if? But as it is, life is full of mistakes and regrets and I must admit that I have quite a few to deal with myself."

After speaking with his friend, Pete laid back on the engine house floor and turned away from Hayward laden with guilt. As he lay motionlessly watching the guard through the cracks in the wooden doorway, his condemnation increased. He quietly gave thought over all that he had put his friend through in the last several days but more so the tribulations that he had brought on Caroline and Ann for his actions.

Chapter 40

Once Pete had finished speaking, the door of the dwelling opened. Immediately, a guard stepped through the entrance followed by Captain Brackett and Seamus. Without hesitation, Pete rose to his feet, shielding his eyes from the bright sunlight. He failed to recognize Seamus. As Pete swiftly approached, the guard raised his weapon and placed the bayonet against his chest. As the soldier did so, Pete paused, and recognizing Seamus, knew that something of great importance had taken place in order to bring him back to Harpers Ferry.

"What happened to Katie?" Pete anxiously asked.

"She is missing."

"Missing! What's happened?"

"Well Barker, we are trying to determine this. That's why Mr. McBride is here to see you," Captain Brackett replied.

"Have you seen or heard from her?" Seamus asked.

"I haven't seen Katie since leaving Boston. After escaping..."

"Escaping!" Captain Brackett interrupted shouting and continuing angrily as he turned toward Seamus, "What's going on here McBride?"

Seamus sighed and rolled his eyes around at the officer. "Not long ago, I was mugged by two men in Boston while Barker was visiting with my sister and family. Naturally at first, we thought that Barker might have been responsible since he and I can't stand the sight of each other. But as I found out shortly thereafter, it turned out; a couple of acquaintances of mine were guilty of the violent act. After my father tried to implicate Barker, he took off and returned here only I see to get into greater trouble."

"Well McBride, let's get down to matters."

Seamus turned his attention to Pete. "Katie has been missing for the last three days. My father and she had traveled to Washington City where she had hoped to enlist Secretary Stanton's help in saving your property from confiscation, which she failed to do. The next day after her meeting with the Secretary, she disappeared and vanished into thin air, not leaving a trace or a clue as to what happened. I really didn't think that she might be here with you because whatever happened, happened suddenly."

"What led you to that conclusion?"

"All of her clothing and belongings were still hanging and her toiletries remained in their place, except for her brush. It was lying on the floor next to her seat in front of the vanity."

"Why did your father let her go to Washington City of all places? She was abducted! Why! Was it because maybe she was really spying?"

"I don't bloody know. Quite frankly Johnnie, it doesn't make a world of difference if she was. She is my sister and I'll turn the bloody world upside down with every bloody person in it to find her if I must."

Hayward angrily spoke up. "Misse Katie is in a lot of trouble and needs our help. Yose need to stop fightin'."

"You better listen to the John Henry, he has a point," replied Captain Brackett.

Pete nodded in agreement as he looked at Captain Brackett and Seamus.

"Yeah, I guess firing off tempers won't help Katie now. I guess I am so bloody frustrated because I don't know where to start looking or why someone would want to do this," Seamus calmly said.

"I agree," Pete admitted as he rubbed his hand through his long hair. Turning around and walking toward the back of the engine house, he paused for what seem like an eternity. Turning around once more, he made a fist and gripped it in frustration and anger. As Captain Brackett spoke with Seamus, Pete thought of who might want to take vengeance on Katie or what the motive would be for such an aggressive act. Surely if Katie had been spying for Federal authorities during the war that could possibly be a motive but with the conflict ended, the only reason for retribution would be something of a personal nature. If she would have been taken and held hostage for money, the abductors would have made their demands by now or left behind a message. As he walked back over to where the conversation was continuing, he heard Captain Brackett. "Well McBride I know we'll be more than willing to inform you if anything comes up that will help you find your sister."

"Well, Johnnie," Seamus said, "it's apparent you have enough trouble of your own to deal with and don't know anything that's going to help me about my sister. So I guess I'll leave you to face your punishment."

"Captain." The officer and Seamus turned and looked coldly at Pete. "Have there been any strangers in Harpers Ferry lately?" Pete asked.

"There have been a few."

Pete approached the officer and Seamus. "They possibly could have been Confederate agents."

Captain Brackett answered sharply, "Well Barker for some of us, the war is over with."

Seamus had a surprised expression on his face. "No, no, Barker might have a point. Didn't you at one time ride with Mosby?"

Quickly glancing at Captain Brackett's tense features, Pete answered. "Yes, for a short period of time."

All was quiet in the engine house as Seamus stared coldly at Pete thinking of Mosby's raids and guerrilla activity throughout northern Virginia in 1864 and 1865. Finally after what seemed an eternity of silence, he asked, "Did you, like many of Mosby's men, often live with civilians using false pretenses to hide your identity?"

Pete again looked at Captain Brackett knowing that he would scrutinize every word that proceeded from his mouth now that it was revealed that he had been one of Mosby's men. Methodically thinking of his words, Pete answered. "Yes, that's how we conducted warfare. When word was passed, we assembled at an agreed meeting place and was only informed of what the mission was going to be when Colonel Mosby was ready."

"But you were one of his scouts, most trusted, you should have known?"

"Not always. John Russell headed up the scouting duties and I shared in them occasionally. He would have been more privileged to information than me."

From the little information that he had received from Pete, Seamus was sure that Pete wasn't telling him everything but only bits and pieces. He believed that Pete was trying to keep Captain Brackett off balance. Whether he wanted to admit it or not, Seamus realized that Pete might be useful to him. Time was wasting and he knew that he had to secure Pete's release. He turned around and faced Captain Brackett. "Sir, I would like to have this man released into my custody immediately."

Captain Brackett laughed and shook his head in disagreement. "Now McBride, you know that I can't do as you requested. This man is a cold-blooded killer. He must stand trial for his crimes and in all probability if found guilty, he'll hang for it."

"I understand that, but for now he'll be of great use to me."

"In what way?"

Seamus didn't want to reveal what he suspected of Pete's activities and knowledge while riding with Mosby. "Not now Captain. Once all of this is over with, then I'll explain."

"That's not good enough McBride. He stays put," Captain Brackett insisted.

As Captain Brackett turned to leave the building, Seamus called out. "Wait Captain."

Once the officer turned around facing Seamus with his full attention, Seamus pulled from his coat pocket a piece of paper. With his eyes on the officer, Seamus said, "Captain Brackett, I have here in my hand a letter from Secretary Stanton giving me the authority to obtain any and all assistance from you or any other military official."

Captain Brackett quickly grabbed the letter from Seamus' hand. As the officer quickly glanced over its contents, Seamus continued to explain. "As you see, it instructs me to employ the use of any civilian or civilians having information and or any means to find my sister's whereabouts and her safe return." Seamus pointed to the signature. "And you see that it's signed by Secretary Stanton."

With a smirk covering his face, Captain Brackett replied. "And you feel that Barker can help you?"

"By all means. As I understand, he knows the northern Virginia area and is very skilled at tracking. So, therefore, in many ways his abilities could help in the safe return of my sister. Now Captain, I want him released to me."

"I can't do this until I can confirm the authenticity of this letter."

"Sir, I can respect that, but time is wasting and Katie could be in great danger." Seamus removed the letter from Captain Brackett's hand. "Barker goes with me now."

After Seamus gestured to Pete with his hand to follow, Pete grabbed his coat. "What about Hayward?"

Seamus turned, "He stays."

"He can be of great service."

"I don't need the darkie. Now let's go."

"If he stays behind, then you can go alone."

Seamus paused, realizing that time was wasting and not wanting to argue, he submitted to Pete's request. "Well, then bring him along."

As the trio started for the door, Captain Brackett said, "Now wait a moment."

Seamus paused and turned his attention to Captain Brackett. "Sir, we don't have anything further to discuss."

At Captain Brackett's gesture, two guards at the entranceway of the building raised their muskets at Pete, Seamus, and Hayward. Seamus turned. "What are you doing?"

"I just can't let you men walk out of here."

Seamus angrily approached the officer. "Sir, if you don't comply with the Secretary's order, then I'll personally see to it that your busted down to a private or driven out of the army! One or the other, I don't care!" When Captain Brackett remained silent, Seamus continued in a tone of anger, "Now Captain, what is it going to be?"

Captain Brackett chuckled. "McBride, I am not afraid of your temper or threats."

Pulling his watch from his pocket and noticing that it was a little past noon, Seamus replied as he looked at the officer with a stern expression, "You better be. Because if I don't return to Washington in the next six hours, which is when I am expected to dine with my father and Senator Wade, then they'll know that something is wrong. I am sure Secretary Stanton will be called on." Pausing and angrily looking the officer in the eye, Seamus added, "All right Brackett, what's it going to be?"

Captain Brackett gestured for the two guards to put their weapons down and nodded in agreement that the three men were free to leave.

Pete breathed a sigh of relief as they departed. He was anxious to find Katie as soon as possible, but first he wanted to see his mother.

Chapter 41

After leaving the old engine house, Pete and Seamus had a brief verbal confrontation concerning the time it would require to return to Shenandoah to see how his mother was doing before departing for Washington City. With Pete's stubbornness, Seamus grudgingly conceded.

As Pete, Seamus, and Hayward rode along the lane to the cabin, Seamus quietly attempted to visualize the appearance of Shenandoah during the antebellum era. All that he had witnessed thus far on their route to the estate was nothing short of complete devastation. Seamus knew that his family had been fortunate and spared the traumatic, emotional events that many in this area must have experienced during the war, especially his adversary, Pete Barker. Seamus knew as he looked around the property that prior to the war, the Barker family had been very wealthy just as Katie had led his family to believe. He was impressed with all that he had witnessed thus far. In spite of its desolation, Shenandoah was still as beautiful and majestic as Katie had described. He could only attempt to imagine the rest. Somewhere within his heart he knew that given the opportunity, Shenandoah could be just as prosperous as it had been before the war, though he attempted to repress the thought.

On their arrival at the cabin, Pete jumped from his horse and anxiously raced into the cabin. Seamus and Hayward both dismounted and followed. Pete entered the dwelling and everything appeared quiet. He headed for his mother's bedchamber. At the doorway, his face glowed with joy and thanksgiving. His mother was eating some of the meal that Caroline had prepared. As he entered, Ann rose from her seat and hugged him. "Uncle Pete, thank God you are home."

Caroline placed the bowl on the wooden stand next to the bed, rose and embraced Pete. "I have prayed constantly for your freedom. What happened?"

Breaking the embrace, Pete pointed to Seamus standing in the doorway. "This is Katie's older brother, Seamus. He was able to secure my release because he has come for my help."

Fearing the worst, astonishment covered Caroline's features. The sound of anticipation was revealed in her pitched voice. "Help. What's wrong? My God, what has happened to Katie?"

"Mrs. Barker, my sister is missing," Seamus sadly replied.

Elizabeth had been quietly listening to the conversation. Her heart was touched with compassion after witnessing the despair covering her family's face and that of Seamus.

Pete noticed his mother was slowly gesturing with her hand. Without hesitation, he approached and knelt alongside her bed to listen. "You need to find Katie and return her safely home to her family," Elizabeth said in a whisper. "Never let it be said that a Barker refused to help someone when they were in need. Now go, don't worry about me, I'll be here when you return. I promise."

Pete was amazed at his mother's sudden change of heart. He nodded his head in agreement. As he looked at her with compassion, his heart and mind was relieved after witnessing her recovery from the gunshot wound and the emotional agony that the family had been experiencing since the incident. His expression was filled with peace as he continued to gaze at her. His eyes filled with tears as his mother added, "The war is over for this family. When you return home, there is something that I must speak to you about. Much has happen in this family over the last four years and there are matters that you and I must come to terms with. I guess if we don't, there will always be that wall between us."

Within his heart, Seamus was impressed with the warmth and affection that he was witnessing between Pete and his family. He wondered for a moment if the roles had been reversed how his family would have endured such loss and tragedy in their lives. Again, he felt fortunate.

Once Pete rose, he heard the sound of horses approaching. He turned and looked at the door where Hayward had just entered. "That man from the county that says yose owe him is a comin'. This time he's alone."

Pete quickly departed from the cabin with Seamus and Hayward following. Once the horses and buggy were brought to a halt, Pete approached Mr. Smith grudgingly. "What do you want?"

Under the tense circumstances, Mr. Smith smiled and answered. "Well Mr. Barker, your time is up. Unless the tax burden can be satisfied today, then you and your family will have to vacate the property immediately."

"We can't do that, my mother is recovering from an injury. Captain Brackett had promised us an extension. We need time."

"Your time has expired. Now you must pack up and go."

Pete lost his temper and grabbed the county treasurer by his coat collar to pull him from the wagon. Hayward and Seamus raced toward Pete.

As they pulled him away from Mr. Smith, Hayward shouted, "Boy, yose has cause 'nough trouble. Yose need to calm down."

Pete turned, looking defiantly at Hayward. "He can't throw my family off of their land. I'm not going to stand for it!"

"Now Barker, get off of the property now or I'll be forced to return with the soldiers from town and have you thrown off by force if necessary."

Seamus pulled from his possession his purse. He looked to see how much money he was carrying. "Now sir you won't need to do that. How much will it take for you to just leave?"

"What kind of a person do you think that I am? I don't take bribes."

"You'll be the first bloody politician that hasn't. Now come on, how much will it bloody take to get rid of you?"

Seamus knew the county official wasn't going to negotiate. "Alright, how much do the Barkers owe the county?"

Mr. Smith snapped as he straightened his coat collar. "$2,500 dollars."

"Well, I don't have that kind of money on me at the moment, but once I return to Harpers Ferry, I'll telegraph my bank in Boston and you'll have the money in the morning."

Mr. Smith just stared coldly at Seamus. After a moment, he shook his head. "That will not be satisfactory."

Pete's patience was exhausted. Again, he lunged forth at Mr. Smith. "Let me get my hands on him and teach him a thing or two, then he'll change his mind."

Hayward grabbed Pete by the arm.

"Sir, it's quite apparent that you don't know who I am," Seamus angrily said.

"No, I don't," Mr. Smith nervously answered.

"I am the son of Thaddeus McBride, My name is Seamus McBride. If you know anything about the abolitionist movement then you know who he is and you know that I can make good on the note." As Seamus spoke, Mr. Smith shook his head in acknowledgement as Seamus continued to speak. "Now, I feel that it would be prudent of you to accept my word and promise. You'll have your money tomorrow. If you don't, then by all means foreclose on the property. What's one more day?"

Mr. Smith rubbed his chin, his beady eyes ablaze, silent in thought on the proposition that Seamus offered. "All right, but just for one more day. If I don't have the money in my possession by 3 o'clock tomorrow afternoon, then I'll return with soldiers and have these people thrown off the property. Understood!"

"I dare you..."

Seamus interrupted Pete. "You have my bloody word. Now get the bloody heck out of here and don't come back. If you do I'll personally pull your butt off of that bloody buggy myself. Now do you bloody understand?"

Quietly, Mr. Smith nodded in agreement and departed. Seamus looked at Pete. "Time is wasting, we have to go."

Pete returned one more time to the cabin. Once they entered, Caroline and Ann were anxiously standing by the door in anticipation of the meaning of Mr. Smith's visit. As Pete smiled, Caroline was relieved from the stress and pressure she was experiencing knowing that something positive had occurred. Pete looked at Ann and Caroline. "Seamus paid off the debt against Shenandoah."

Caroline was speechless as she placed her hands against her mouth in amazement. Ann rejoiced saying as she raised her hands towards heaven, "Oh thank God, this is an answer to prayers."

Once Seamus entered the cabin, Caroline dashed and embraced him with tears flowing down her cheeks. "I want to personally thank you for your help. You don't know how much this means to us."

Seamus backed away and held his hands on Caroline's shoulders. "It's only a down payment. Your brother-in-law is going to earn every bloody dollar of it, trust me."

As Caroline and Seamus were speaking, Pete entered his mother's bedchamber and was seated.

"What's all the excitement about?" Elizabeth whispered.

With a smile radiating from his face, Pete answered as he brushed the hair from his mother's face, "Mr. Smith came with the intentions of driving us from the property, by force if necessary. I was ready to pitch into him to avoid it from happening, but Katie's brother intervened and is going to loan us the money in order to halt the foreclosure of Shenandoah."

There was a peaceful expression covering Elizabeth's face. She smiled, nodded her head in acknowledgement, and closed her eyes and fell back to sleep. As Pete stood, he knew the issues surrounding Shenandoah for now were resolved. Now of greater importance, he wanted to find Katie as soon as possible. In his mind, he began to follow his suspicions and concentrate on the Confederate undergound that operated in Washington City during the war. It was obvious to him that some agents that were affiliated with the organization might have been responsible for her abduction or at least have knowledge of who the guilty party's identity might be.

Chapter 42

During the evening hours, Margaret McBride was standing and looking out the window in the direction of the gaslight lamp that stood along the cobblestone street cresting her Beacon Hill residence. The crackling sound of wood burning in the fireplace to warm the parlor was the only semblance of life within the house. It was quieter than usual. All of the servants, who were generally busy with duties, had been excused for the evening with the exception of the butler.

Within the past hour, Margaret had received news from her husband Thaddeus in Washington City that Seamus' trip to Harpers Ferry did not produce positive results of Katie's whereabouts. What made matters more distressing was the fact there wasn't a clue or witness that could add to the investigation that had been launched by the Washington authorities into Katie's disappearance. As Margaret stood by the window, she wiped away the tears that filled her eyes. She thought of the wall of division that had separated Katie and her for the past year. The friction had come upon Katie's insistence to be independent and make her own decisions, such as returning to Harpers Ferry at the conclusion of the war.

Margaret suffered not only from the guilt and condemnation over her recent harsh treatment of Katie but also over an incident that occurred many years ago when she was young, and before she had made Thaddeus' acquaintance. For the past thirty-two years she had carried within her heart a secret, known only to her. Often, it had manifested a merciless guilt. She knew the thought of committing an act against the standards of society would have brought rebuke and shame upon her. Even her husband Thaddeus was oblivious to her actions and in all probability wouldn't have taken her hand in marriage had he known of her former life.

In her heart, Margaret believed that she was receiving her overdue punishment for her sins against society. She was discovering that it was becoming more than she could bear. As Margaret turned around and walked to the sofa, she heard the sound of a loud knock at the front door. It was close to 9 o'clock in the evening and she wondered who could be coming this late unless it was a courier with news from her husband regarding

Katie. Her heart beat rapidly as she anxiously watched Robert approach the entranceway. As he opened the door, Margaret was amazed to see her good Irish friend, Gwendolyn Darby standing at the entrance.

Once Gwendolyn stepped through the doorway, she handed Robert her gray shawl and green bonnet that covered her dark brown hair. Immediately turning her attention to her friend, Gwendolyn took notice of Margaret's troubled features. Already having knowledge that Thaddeus and Katie were in Washington City, she knew that Margaret had received some kind of distressing news. Without hesitation, Gwendolyn asked, "Margaret, have you received news from Thaddeus?"

Margaret quietly held her hand against her mouth and burst forth sobbing and nodding her head in acknowledgement.

Gwendolyn began to feel her friend's pain and anguish. Tears filled her eyes. She embraced Margaret and allowed her time to release her emotions. Afterward Gwendolyn helped Margaret to regain control of her emotions, she asked Robert to bring some hot tea. As the butler complied with the request, Gwendolyn sat her friend on the sofa. "What has happened that troubles you?"

Margaret wiped her eyes with a handkerchief and answered. "Katherine is still missing and we don't have any idea what has happened to her." Gwendolyn gazed at Margaret with her compassionate gray eyes. She listened to her friend continue in a broken tone. "We had hoped that Katherine would have returned to Harpers Ferry with the Barkers but earlier this afternoon, Thaddeus received a message from Seamus that she had not shown up there either. She has just vanished from the face of the earth."

"Why didn't you call for me sooner? You should know by now that I would have come."

Still trying to control her emotions, Margaret answered in an angry frustrating tone. "Oh, I thought that maybe Katherine had quarreled with her father and needed time alone. Thaddeus and I haven't seen eye to eye with her over her relationship with that James Barker she is supposedly so fond of."

"Why didn't you talk to me about all this? Maybe I could have spoken with Katherine."

"I couldn't because I was just too embarrassed. We all had our differences with her while she was here over this Mr. Barker. But, you know Katherine, she won't listen, she has a mind of her own. And when it's made up, there is no changing it."

"Well maybe something will turn up tomorrow. For now, you should think about getting some rest."

As Margaret stared at the flickering fire, she didn't think and chose her words inappropriately before speaking. She blurted out in a burst of emotion. "Oh, who can rest? I guess I am paying for my sins." Shaking her head in frustration, she continued to speak while attempting to control her tears and frantic emotions. "Somewhere I always thought that my sins would catch up with me and when they did, I'd pay a terrible price for what I did."

Gwendolyn had an astonish expression covering her face as she attempted to sort out all that Margaret was revealing. "What sins, Margaret, what in the world are you talking about?"

"Back several years before I made Thaddeus's acquaintance," Margaret sniffled, "I was a young woman struggling to make ends meet in a new world and a new life such as yourself. When I came to this country, I didn't have anything but the clothes on my back. I was penniless and frustrated but most of all scared and desperate for survival. As ambitious as I was, I was naive and careless, and quite frankly, I didn't always make the right decisions. The only opportunity that was given to me was a few jobs washing laundry for the riffs down at the waterfront. I felt that this was really below me, so I passed up those kinds of jobs. Finally after some other undesirable positions and after having nothing to show for my efforts, I turned to a woman who earned her living by undesirable and questionable means..."

Gwendolyn was greatly troubled. She interrupted and said slowly as she held her hand to her mouth in disbelief. "You were a prostitute?"

Looking into Gwendolyn's tearful eyes and quietly shaking her head in acknowledgement, Margaret felt the guilt. Quickly jumping to her feet and walking toward the fireplace, Margaret paused and turned.

"But why? Why would you do something such as that? All of us who came over from the old country found it difficult, but what you did was unacceptable."

"When one has a low feeling and impression of themselves because of continuous failure and they can't control matters in their life, they become angry, frustrated and finally depressed.

When that happens, you allow yourself to become vulnerable and run the risk such as I did of being used in an unappreciated way. At that time in my life, I associated myself with individuals who today I consider nothing more than white trash. But during that time and because of my beauty, they easily persuaded me that I could make a lot of money very quickly. I turned to liquor in order to deal with my feelings of guilt knowing within my heart that what I was doing was wrong. As it turned out, I was with child, scared and all alone in the world. I had no place to turn for help. So with the help of a friend and through the secret efforts of a priest, I found a family who agreed to take my baby girl."

Gwendolyn was quiet, gazing with unbelief at Margaret as she returned to her seat on the sofa. Margaret continued. "That was many years ago, but I can still see my baby as if it all happened yesterday. I can still recall what she looked like when I gave her up. She was long in length and had very beautiful blue eyes. And even then, her countenance had such a graceful manner. It's difficult for me today to describe but I'd know the expression if I saw her."

"Why didn't you tell Thaddeus? Didn't you think that he'd understand?"

Margaret sighed as she continued to look at Gwendolyn. "When I met Thaddeus and was sure that he loved me, I wanted to tell him about my past, but I couldn't."

"Oh Margaret, why? Why couldn't you tell him? He would have understood."

Margaret shook her head in disagreement as she took Gwendolyn by the hand. "No I couldn't bear to do that to him. Already he was quickly working his way up at the bank with a promising future. I wanted him to have that opportunity and not do anything that would tarnish or jeopardize this for him, either with the board of trustees, or his popular standing within the community. So, I constantly over the years continued to cover up my past, lie when needed and attempted to repress the matter. But as life would have it, I only found out that it continued to get worse over the years. Oh, I tried to make up matters and tell myself that I was a good mother and loved my family after I gave birth to Seamus and Katherine. But still, there was always that little secret from the past that continued to haunt me and torture me. Where was my baby girl and what happened to her?"

"Are you ever going to tell Thaddeus and the children?"

Margaret paused and looked in Gwendolyn's eyes for along time. "To be honest with you, I really don't know if I can. I have lived with the lies this long; I would be afraid of what might happen if I did confront them with the truth."

After her reply, Margaret was silent as she stared at Gwendolyn. Margaret wondered how Gwendolyn would judge her, but after all of these years of silence and guilt, she had to share her previous life with someone that she knew and loved. As she finally looked away from Gwendolyn and again in the direction of the fireplace, she gave thought to Katie and her welfare. Like her first born, she feared she'd never see Katie again and that something dreadful had happened to her.

Chapter 43

Early the next morning, Pete, Seamus, and Hayward arrived by train in Washington City. The first place they went to was the Willard Hotel to see if Seamus' father had been able to turn up any information concerning Katie and to speak again with Robert Bateman, the last person to be with her. As they rode in a covered coach through the city toward their destination, the drizzle intensified into a drenching downpour, driving what few people left on the street for shelter. Once the threesome hastily entered the hotel, Seamus shook the water from his coat and headed in the direction of Thaddeus' hotel suite while Pete and Hayward waited in the main lobby. Once at his father's room, Seamus knocked several times, calling before his father finally answered the door.

"I received your telegram and forwarded it to your mother. I can tell by your expression you were not able to turn up anything else of benefit," Thaddeus anxiously said.

Seamus entered the room shaking his head in frustration. He had a gloomy expression on his face. As Thaddeus closed the door, Seamus silently turned and faced his father. "No, I couldn't turn up a bloody thing."

"So what do we do now? We just can't sit and wait. God only knows what will happen to her if we don't find her soon."

Seamus took off his wet coat and laid it on a chair. He turned. "That's why I brought Barker and his John Henry with me."

Thaddeus swiftly approached Seamus angrily pointing. "Why did you bring that bloody troublesome rebel with you here after all that he has put this family through. If it wouldn't have been for him, this family wouldn't be in the bloody fix that it is in."

Seamus lost control of his composure and fired back. "I did so because I had no choice. Barker rode with Mosby during the latter part of the war and he is I am sure, familiar with how the Johnnies carried out underground activity."

Thaddeus slammed his fist down on a small stand next to the bed and shouted. "The war is bloody over with! Why would the bloody rebels want Katherine? She knows nothing; she's no spy."

"Apparently, someone has a grudge against her or us and they want to get even. I feel it must have something to do with the war.

Even now that Lee and Johnston have surrendered, there are those that still want to wage conflict and harm against us in some way."

Thaddeus held up his hands for Seamus to stop speaking. "Seamus, Seamus, I don't want to hear it. You know as well as I do that Katherine wasn't passing information or spying for anyone. That's all a bunch of bloody hogwash. We both know that it was all some made up notion."

"Even though I accused Katie in order to cause division between Barker and her when they were in Boston, anymore I am not too sure that it wasn't the truth."

"Lad, you better have a bloody good basis to draw your bloody accusations of her."

Seamus knew he had greatly angered his father. He brushed his long red hair to the side and replied as he poured some water into a glass. "For one thing you know as well as I that the church doesn't appoint women to teach in their schools. When I think back on it, it was sort of strange that Katherine had been offered a position that was traditionally for men only and in a place so far away from home in the South. Furthermore, when it appeared that the Southern states might withdraw from the Union the Federal government placed agents working through the War Department in various locations to keep them informed of any strange events or happenings that they should know of that might cause the country harm or further division."

Pausing and taking a sip, Seamus placed the glass on the stand and approached his father continuing in a suspicious tone. "Now you know as well as I that Harpers Ferry was a major transportation area of military importance to the Union cause before the war. Not to mention that it was the place of one of two armories for manufacturing weapons in this country. I'd say that it was very important to have someone there to keep an eye on things, wouldn't you?"

"But she was just going to help teach temporarily! For crying out loud Boy, that doesn't make her an agent for the bloody government!"

"Katherine was not only very well educated but she was a woman. If a man would have shown up in Harpers Ferry in 1860 from Boston amidst the tension-taking place in that area after the Brown raid, he would have easily been a suspect of impropriety, but a woman would not. No. Women before the war were not considered a threat for passing information. And even after the conflict was well under way, women got away with passing information and spying with little or no penalty extracted against them." Thaddeus remained silent in disbelief. Seamus continued, "For now, all this must be kept quiet between us so that I can continue to have Barker's cooperation. But at the moment, I want to speak with Robert before he returns to Harrisburg."

"Robert Bateman wouldn't do anything that would cause Katherine any harm. In the short period of time that he knew her, I believe he had become quite fond of her."

"No, no, I know Robert wouldn't harm her, but maybe he saw something or someone hanging around." Pausing and thinking, Seamus walked over to the window and glanced out at the people walking along the busy Pennsylvania Avenue. He turned toward his father. "Father, get dressed. I'll meet you in the lobby with Barker."

* * * *

Once Thaddeus was dressed, he met Seamus in the lobby. Upon entering, he noticed Pete with Hayward. It was all Thaddeus could do to control and withhold his anger and contempt for all that he believed that Pete was responsible for. As he walked up to them, he said in a tense tone, "Well, gentlemen." Staring intensely at Pete, Thaddeus continued, "Mr. Barker, we meet again."

Hayward nodded but was silent as Pete answered calmly and frankly, "Sir, I feel as uncomfortable about this meeting as you do. And believe me, once this is all over with, I hope that we don't see each other again as I am sure that you feel the same."

Seamus intruded angrily. "If we are going to act like this we are not going to find Katie. We must maintain some unity and then we can go our separate ways. But for now, let's try to cooperate with each other."

Seamus walked over to the front desk to speak to the hotel clerk. Impatiently clanging the bell, the clerk gave his full attention to the four men. The clerk asked as he approached, "What may I do for you?"

"Mr. Bateman, what room is he in?" Seamus impatiently asked.

As the clerk positioned the spectacles on his face, he replied after glancing at the register, "Parlor #6 in the corner, on the second floor overlooking Pennsylvania Avenue."

As the men were turning away from the desk, an assistant clerk was standing within listening distance. The assistant clerk said to the other clerk, "Let me look and see, he was checking out early this morning."

Pete looked at Seamus. "We don't have time to wait while he goes through his records."

The four men scurried off to Robert's suite; they didn't converse in any manner. As they approached the room, Thaddeus looked at his timepiece. It was 8:00 o'clock and he hoped that Robert hadn't departed.

Once they arrived at the room, Seamus belted out several loud knocks at the door. At first no one answered. As Pete tried to open the door, a voice came from inside. "Wait a minute, wait a minute, I'm coming."

Once Robert opened the door, he was stunned to see Thaddeus and Seamus gazing at him. "Mr. McBride." Recognizing his old war friend, he continued, "Seamus, it's been some time."

"Yes Robert it has. We spent a lot of time together fighting the Johnnies, but I'll never forget the personal chats that we shared around the campfires while campaigning around Richmond."

Robert looked around at Pete and Hayward. "What's going on? Who are these other men?"

"If we may come in," Seamus asked, "you'll know."

Robert stood to the side with his one hand on the doorknob and the other gesturing for the men to enter the room. "Do you have news of Katherine?"

"No, nothing at all," Seamus replied as he walked over to the chair. "And to make things worse, we don't have a clue. That is why Mr. Barker and his friend are with me. Instead of waiting on the Washington authorities, we have decided to take matters into our own hands and make the attempt to find Katie before anything else happens to her."

Robert quietly walked over to a table and lit a cigar. After taking a puff, he turned. "How may I be of assistance?"

"You can start by telling us everything that transpired after you left me in the dining room," Thaddeus answered in a stern tone.

Robert took a deep sigh. He sat down in the chair next to the table. Taking another puff of the cigar, he contemplated how he'd express in words what he was thinking. After placing the cigar in a tray, he looked at Seamus. "As your father probably told you, we had dinner in the dining area after your father and sister returned from the War Department. We discussed briefly the issue over her concerns for a family that lived in Harpers Ferry who had lost everything during the rebellion and her attempts to help them recover their loss. Other than that, it was an enjoyable time together. After dinner Katherine decided to depart for her room, suffering from a headache and exhaustion from the day's activity. Of course I wanted to see her safely to her room, which she consented."

Pete was surprised at what occurred between Katie and Robert. He struggled with his feelings so that they wouldn't be visible to everyone, especially the apprehension that he was experiencing as to what Robert would say next. He turned his attention once more to the conversation.

Robert paused to take another puff of his cigar. Returning it to the tray he glanced at Pete and Hayward standing near the sofa with eyes on him. Thaddeus and Seamus appeared more relaxed standing in the middle of the floor.

Finally losing his patience, Thaddeus asked, "Well, come on lad, what happened next?"

"Once we arrived at her room, we spoke."

"About what?" Seamus asked.

Robert looked up and smiled. "About us. Then I asked her if I could come into her room and she said that it wouldn't be right. I asked if I could return later, and somewhere within I believed that she would have consented if I would have pressed the matter, but I didn't. After that, I kissed her and then after a moment of silence, she kissed me. She said that she'd see me in the morning before departing for Harpers Ferry. I left and rejoined you in the dining area."

Inwardly, Pete felt betrayed and forsaken. He found it difficult to accept what he had heard. Was Katie a different person then she professed? If she really loved him as she alleged, then somehow their differences concerning their issues would they all work out? He thought that maybe somewhere in time that Katie and he might have been able to reconcile their differences, but he didn't think that she would be so quick to entertain another gentleman. But for now, it didn't make any difference; he had to find her and was determined to do so. He attempted to shrug off his anger at Robert and his feelings of betrayal from Katie. Once she was found, then she would be free to do or be with whomever she desired.

Pete's mind returned to the conversation as Seamus asked Robert, "Was there anyone hanging out in the hallway or that appeared suspicious to you?"

"No. We passed some couples or individuals on the way to her room, but to answer your question, no there wasn't anyone near her room or watching us or following that I know of." Robert silently paused and an expression of thought surfaced across his features. He looked at Seamus. "I do remember something."

"Even the littlest detail could be important," Pete said.

Robert stood and walked toward Seamus ignoring Pete. "At times, Katherine appeared troubled, her mind was elsewhere. A couple of times I watched her out of the corner of my eye looking at an officer sitting at another table near ours. I figured that she knew him. She seemed to be uncomfortable with his presence."

Seamus turned. "Father, do you remember who he might have been or what he looked like?"

"No, I didn't take notice, but I do know that earlier that afternoon at the War Department, Katherine had spoken with an officer, a Colonel Langsten I believe. She was very troubled with him. Matter of fact, she didn't even speak to me on the way back to the hotel. She was very withdrawn for the rest of the afternoon. It wasn't like her to be so quiet."

"Let's speak with the hotel clerk and see if he remembers anyone asking for her or if someone was trying to find out the location of her room," Pete replied.

"Yes," Seamus nodded in agreement, "by all means we'll do that. At this point, any information can help."

As he walked with the gentleman to the door, Robert said, "I have a friend by the name of Maxwell Leonard who works on special projects with Mr. Pinkerton. I will speak to him this afternoon and see if we can't render his assistance. It's of the greatest importance to me to locate Katherine and know that she is safe. And I'll use any and all of my connections to do so. I care for her in a great way."

After Pete, Hayward, and Thaddeus departed the room, Seamus nodded in agreement. "We'll stay in contact."

Again, Pete struggled with his emotions over all that he heard in the conversation. He was somewhat disappointed, but he knew there was an answer for her actions. For now, he must work with anyone or anybody that had information and would cooperate with them in finding Katie and bring her home safely.

Chapter 44

Pete left the room and immediately moved patiently through the crowded hotel lobby and approached the same clerk that Seamus had confronted. Pete looked around the area as the clerk assisted an elderly gentleman and lady as they discussed some issues concerning their bill for their room. Once the elderly couple finished transacting their business and stepped to the side gazing disapprovingly at Pete's plain appearance, he stepped quietly forward. The clerk had turned his back to the desk and was scribbling something on a blank piece of paper and handed it to a young boy of color.

After receiving the clerk's attention, Pete asked, "Sir, you know that Miss McBride is missing? Right?"

"Yes sir, by now everyone in Washington City knows that. What a shame, what a shame. She is such a nice girl."

"I see. Then let me ask you, by chance were you working last Wednesday evening?"

"No, but I believe that Geoffrey was here. Let me ask him."

After the clerk walked away, Pete looked around the busy establishment. He thought of the reasons that Katie might have been abducted. It was quite obvious from the information he received from Seamus that she didn't put up a struggle so therefore Katie probably knew her abductors. Apparently in agreement with Seamus, money wasn't a motive for the action or any type of blackmail to discourage her father's desire to run for national office. There were no demands left behind in the form of a correspondence to discourage such an attempt. That only left the Confederate underground, leaving Pete with the thought that Katie might have been involved with secretive activities or there was some other personal reason unknown to him. Although, it did appear that she knew more than what she led him to believe concerning her attempts at spying against the Confederacy. As Pete continued to wait on the clerk's return, he realized spying could be a greater probability for her apparent abduction.

Finally Pete's thoughts were broken and once again his attention returned to the skinny clerk approaching from the back room. He smiled and rubbed his baldhead. "Geoffrey isn't here at the moment. I was told that he was asked to run an errand by the hotel manager. If you would like to wait, I am sure that he'll return before too long."

"No, no, I'll return later." Pete paused and turned to the clerk, "What is your name?"

"Arnold. Arnold Crumbly."

The clerk smiled and nodded in acknowledgement and walked away. As Pete turned to rejoin the others, he paused and glanced at the clerk. The nervous tone in the clerk's voice caused him to be suspicious. The thought surfaced in his mind that the clerk knew more then what he had said. Not only did Pete have these suspicions but also Hayward was standing within listening distance and heard every word that transpired. By his cold expression, Pete knew he was also suspicious.

* * * *

After traveling to the War Department, Pete and the others found out from the clerk that Colonel Bradley Langsten wasn't on duty. The same clerk that had spoken with Thaddeus and Katie informed them that Bradley resided at a boarding establishment on 6th Street across from the National Hotel.

As the men departed from the War Department, the rain had ceased leaving a chill in the air. Pete turned around and looked at Hayward. "Will you return to the hotel and keep an eye on the clerk that I was speaking to? For some reason, I don't trust him."

An expression of astonishment covered Thaddeus's expression. "Well if I may ask Lad, what does he have to do with all this?" Thaddeus asked.

"Aye, Barker. Why are you suspicious of him?" Seamus added.

"I think that he knows more than what he is letting on. He just appeared too nervous. Not comfortable when I wanted to speak with the other clerk. Maybe it was the tone of voice that tipped me off."

With cane in one hand Thaddeus gestured with the other as he replied, "It's really only a suspicion and nothing firm. Barker, you're not going to lead us on a wild goose chase."

Seamus anxiously interrupted. "Father, Father, it may not hurt to do as Barker has asked. Besides, his John Henry wouldn't be suspected."

For the first time in over an hour, Hayward spoke. "I'se have a idea to git what yose want." As Hayward walked away, he turned and pointed at Seamus. "And for ya kid, I'se is no John Henry. My name is Hayward and don't yose forgit it."

Seamus didn't answer Hayward, but instead, turned. "If you will Father, can you find out if anything has turned up with the police?"

"Yes Son, I'll meet you back at the hotel."

* * * *

Within the next thirty minutes, Pete and Seamus were standing in front of the well-kept brick boardinghouse where Bradley Langsten resided. After making inquiry from an elderly lady that resided at the home, Pete and Seamus headed for the second floor front room where they were informed that the Colonel lived.

After arriving, Pete knocked once on the front door.

Bradley opened and rudely asked, "Yes, what is it?"

With a cold expression covering his features, Pete answered firmly. "I would like to ask you a few questions about Katie McBride."

Bradley turned away from Pete ignoring his request. As he took his hand to shut the door, Pete charged in knocking Bradley to the floor. Turning him around, Pete again demanded as Seamus rushed through the door closing it behind him. "Now let's start over. What do you know about Katie McBride?"

"If you get off of me, I'll talk to you," Bradley angrily pleaded

As Pete stood, Seamus reached out and helped Bradley to his feet. Impatiently, Pete said, "Well, answer the question."

Looking defiantly at Pete, Bradley replied with tenseness in his voice. "Just casually, though I tried on some occasions to get better acquainted."

"What do you mean by that?" Seamus asked.

"I met Katie in the early summer of '61 just before Bull Run when she was visiting Washington City. Immediately after introductions and spending the afternoon and evening in her company, I wanted to see more of her, but unfortunately, it was two more years before I saw her again."

"And when did that occur?"

"In July of '64 at Harpers Ferry. Katie met me at the train station and escorted me to General Howe's headquarters with the dispatches that I was carrying."

While Seamus and Bradley were speaking, Pete remained silent, though listening to every word spoken. As he gazed out the window at some of the couples walking along the street, he thought of what Katie and his life would have been like if they hadn't gone to Boston and their disagreement wouldn't have transpired. But he pondered; he wouldn't have known about the apparent mysterious side of a lady that he once thought he truly knew.

Once Bradley had finished answering Seamus' question, Pete turned. "Why did she meet you there?" Pete asked.

"I don't know. When Katie was visiting Washington in '61, she said that she had just come to the city to visit Mrs. Greenhow after the death of her child. Knowing Rose Greenhow's vocation of spying and later her arrest for passing information to the enemy, I suspected that Katie was looking for evidence implicating Mrs. Greenhow of involvement with the Captain; later Colonel Jordan of the Confederate army."

Seamus interrupted. "I don't understand how all of this comes together with my sister?"

Bradley rubbed his hand across his stubbled face, looked at Pete, and then again at Seamus. "Before the war, Thomas Jordan and I were good friends as well as serving together in the army. I knew his strong sentiment for the Southern cause, but I didn't think before he resigned his commission in the army that he was already attempting to establish a group of Southern sympathizers within the city to pass information to Confederate authorities. When I look back, I feel that she might have thought that Jordan was inadvertently using me through Mrs. Greenhow for information since at that time I was an aide to General Scott and we were preparing to march on Richmond." Pausing and pouring a drink of liquor, Bradley turned and smiled. "For sometime, your sister really fooled me."

"In what way?"

"She led me to believe that there was really an attraction there, but all she was doing was leading me in order to get out of me all that she thought that I might know about Jordan and his ring of spies."

"You still haven't told us why she met you at Harpers Ferry?" Pete impatiently asked.

"I don't know! I didn't ask. I was just glad to see her. Although she was a different person than the one I had met and became interested in two years before."

Pete was already greatly troubled by the information that he heard earlier from Robert Bateman about Katie and his involvement with her. Now with Bradley's revelation, Pete had lost all trust in Katie. The words that he had heard today were tearing him down inwardly. Though it was his belief that Katie and he were finished with their relationship, he would still remain committed in helping the McBride's to find their daughter in return for Seamus' financial help in securing relief for Shenandoah and his release from prison.

Seamus asked as he approached Bradley, "What about the papers you were carrying? What information did they contain and what did my sister know about them?"

Bradley quietly walked to the nearest chair and had a seat. He stared at the smoldering embers in the fireplace and thought of what he would say to satisfy Seamus' request. He turned his attention once more to Seamus and Pete. "We had learned from reliable information that some of the residents in the area had been hiding and supplying Mosby and his men shelter and provisions for their raids on the B & O railroad. With the information that we had, the decision was made by General Hunter to deprive the enemy of any and all substances that could be of use. The documents that I carried contained the names of individuals whom we knew were helping Mosby. We thought it would be too easy to arrest them and place them in prison but instead it would inflict greater punishment to destroy their homes and farms using this method to intimidate any others in the area from assisting the enemy in anyway."

Inwardly, Pete burned with anger as he listened to Bradley speak. From his boot, he pulled a derringer and pointed it at Bradley thinking that he was one of the individuals responsible for the destruction of Shenandoah. Seamus turned around. "No, Barker, that's not going to help us find Katie."

Pete put the gun to his side. "No, it won't, but it will give me great satisfaction for what he did to my family."

Seamus turned his attention once more to a frightened Bradley. "What did Katie know?"

Bradley held his hands in the air. "I don't know, she didn't ask my business in our conversations on the way to General Howe's headquarters nor was she present when I spoke with him. I do know, if it can be of any assistance to you, we believed there was an individual who was playing both sides of the game."

Pete interrupted. "Someone was employed by the Federals as well as the Confederacy?"

Bradley looked at Pete. "Yes, but at the time we didn't know it. Anyway, it was through a courier, a Negro, that we received the information. He refused to give the identity of the person who supplied the information to him. But that person knew which families were supplying Mosby and had the means to do so. As you know by now, some of those families had political ties to the Confederacy and others were very sympathetic which made them as guilty as anyone."

"Yeah, it sure did, and in return it got the good citizens' homes of Chambersburg torched in return. Us rebels never waged warfare on innocent civilians when we invaded Pennsylvania in '63 but Hunter changed all that," Pete blurted out.

Bradley jumped from his seat angrily. "Shut up!" Turning angrily at Seamus, Bradley continued in a rage. "McBride, why did you bring that Johnnie here?"

"Because he can bloody help, that's why. Now both of you settle down now and stop the arguing." Pausing and quietly waiting for tempers to calm, Seamus continued. "So you're saying that Katie didn't know anything?"

"I didn't say that. I said that we didn't discuss my business and that she wasn't present when the General and I spoke." Again Bradley tossed his hands into the air. "I don't know gentlemen, I don't know."

Pete turned and noticed some of Bradley's personal possessions lying on the small table next to the bed. An envelope attracted his attention in particular. Without a word, Pete walked over and picked it up. Immediately, Bradley noticed what Pete was doing and raced in his direction.

As Pete began to open the envelope, Seamus intercepted Bradley and grabbed him by the coat. "Why were you at the Willard on the evening that my sister disappeared?"

Bradley struggled to get away, but Seamus tossed him on the bed. "Well Lad, I'm bloody waiting? Why were you there?"

Bradley breathing heavily glanced at Pete. "I was trying to revive her interest in me, that's all, nothing more than that." Continuing to glance at Pete, Bradley pleaded, "Please tell him to stop going through my things."

Pete smiled and tossed the envelope in Bradley's direction while Seamus stood and pulled Bradley from the bed.

Pete and Seamus turned to leave. For some reason, Pete believed that Bradley wasn't responsible for Katie's disappearance. During the war when Pete rode with the 1st Virginia Cavalry and later with Mosby's men, the Yankees they captured were always interrogated for any useful information that would help them gain the advantage over their adversaries. Pete had learned such methods as the use of physical force and intimidation when needed. This would apply psychological pressure such as Seamus and he used on Bradley. Many times their enemies responded to these actions, and the tone of their voice. This gave them the indication whether or not they were telling the truth or withholding something of value. When pressed, Bradley had that angry and sometimes fearful tone in his voice that goes along with innocence. Not only that but Pete had learned something else of value during the war. He learned from experience when soldiers were afraid of physical danger a fearful glare would radiate from their eyes even though they wouldn't shed a tear. When they wanted to be intentionally captured for the purpose of deception and planting misleading information, there appeared that cold confidence beaming from their eyes no matter what force of intimation was used. If Bradley had the intentions of deceiving them, there would have appeared that certain cold confidence in his eyes no matter what method had been initiated but instead he was fearful. Pete was taught this wisdom from Hayward. The eyes never lie. For now he would eliminate Bradley from his list of suspicious characters. Unless Hayward came up with something, it appeared that they were at a dead end in suspects and clues.

Chapter 45

As Hayward stood across the street from the Willard Hotel at 14th and Pennsylvania, he was thinking of a way to get into the hotel without raising suspicion. He observed several ladies of color walking in his direction. It appeared from their dress that they were most likely married to husbands that had made a successful living from the war and maybe were fortunate that they didn't suffer the horrors of slavery.

Hayward's thoughts turned to David and his family whom he helped escape in the spring of '62. After they had remained hidden for several days in a cave concealed by heavy forest and underbrush along the Shenandoah River, Hayward and the family finally managed late at night to cross the Potomac River below Harpers Ferry near Sandy Hook. There they sought help from the Carper family and received needed supplies. Afterwards, they crossed over Elk Ridge Mountain and across Pleasant Valley and then ascended South Mountain and headed north into Pennsylvania. Hayward, David, and his family stayed near Chambersburg until June of '63 where they were all nearly captured by some of Brigadier General Albert Jenkins' Confederate cavalry during Lee's invasion of Pennsylvania. Had the rebels captured them, they would have all been returned to the South and once more into slavery. After this close call, David moved to Harrisburg and settled his family into the community where he knew they would be safe. David then enlisted and fought with the 30th United States Colored Troop Infantry. The last Hayward heard of David's welfare was from his wife during the winter of 1865. She informed him that David had fought valiantly and had given his life willingly on the field of glory in the fighting around Petersburg, Virginia in July of 1864.

Hayward then considered returning to Mechanicsville, Maryland. During his stay at that location with the Jones family, he fulfilled a dream of learning to read and write. While there, he made several more trips into Loudoun County, Virginia to help several families escape the bondage of slavery. On one occasion in the summer of '63, he had a close call with death by being shot in the arm by the Confederate Home Guard near Noland's Ferry along the Potomac. Again, during the winter months of '64, a

Confederate cavalry patrol came close to trapping him and an elderly Negro couple near Bloomfield, but once more he escaped by using the Short Hill Mountains under the cover of darkness to escape.

The sound of creaking wheels stirred Hayward's attention as he watched the wagon with several men of color riding slowly near the Willard Hotel. Hayward thought this might be the opportunity that he'd been looking for most of the day to enter the hotel and do some investigating under a pretense. As he observed intently, the wagon came to a halt and the two men jumped from the seat. Hayward moved slowly and inconspicuously across the cobblestone street and continued to watch as one of the men knocked on a door. It appeared to Hayward that the wagon was loaded with granny-sacks of grain used for baking. If they unloaded the goods, then this could be his best opportunity and maybe the only chance of accomplishing his mission.

Within a few moments, another man opened the door and spoke briefly with the two deliverymen. He gestured with his hand for the two deliverymen to enter. Hayward waited until the two men each took a sack and placed the goods on their shoulders before he approached the wagon. Once the agent of the Willard had disappeared, Hayward took a sack of grain and did likewise, entering the hotel storeroom. Once on the inside, he was approached by one of the deliverymen. "Hey old man, what yose think ya doin'?"

"I'se was sent here to help you boys."

"We needin' no help from an old man like you. Now be gone."

"Like I'se said, I'se jist doin' what the boss man told me to." The young man laughed after he had aroused Hayward's temper. Hayward continued in a low tone as he approached the boy grabbing him by the collar of his homespun coat. "Yose look here, if ya's think that yose can mess with dis old man then yose need to come on and do so. Otherwise ya needs to shut up, fore's ya gits hurt by dis old man."

After noticing some of the disagreement taking place with Hayward and his partner, the other deliveryman approached with a surprised expression on his face. "What's goin' on?"

Hayward released the one man. "Nothin'….. nothin' at all."

Hayward was quiet as he pushed the young boy to the side. With a serious expression, he quietly watched as the two men returned to pick up some more goods from the wagon. Once they had disappeared from sight, he turned and noticed a door off to his left. Hayward tried the latch and opened the door. After looking around to make sure no one was watching, he entered into a dimly lit hallway. Moving quietly and cautiously, Hayward made his way to the first door on his left. After trying the latch to open it, he found that it was locked. Cautiously he continued until he found the next door. It was unlocked. This might have been, Hayward thought, the office that was used by the man that allowed the two deliverymen entrance into the hotel.

Hayward cracked the door open far enough to peer through to see if there was anyone on the other side before entering. The room appeared to be some kind of office. It was well-lighted, messy, and appeared disorganized with papers out of order. A small desk in the far corner appeared cluttered with books and more papers. A cigar was still smoldering indicating that it was used. Whoever occupied this area of the hotel would soon return. Hayward didn't want to be confronted while standing in the office and have to give an explanation that probably wouldn't be accepted.

Hayward stepped away from the office and noticed there was a turn at the far end of the hallway. After advancing to the end, Hayward paused and glanced around the corner. There was some banging noise about thirty feet away coming from a large opening to his left. From all sounds, it must be the kitchen area. Hayward noticed another door before reaching the kitchen. As he continued, he opened the door and entered what appeared to be another storage room. He thought of the direction where the main lobby would be. It was important for him to find out what Arnold was up to and if he really did know of anything of interest concerning Katie's disappearance. To continue toward that particular area of the hotel, he needed another disguise. As he looked around the dimly lit room, he noticed some tools in a wooden hand-held box. Immediately, Hayward picked them up knowing he had his cover and most likely wouldn't be suspected of any improprieties from any of the hotel staff.

As Hayward departed from the room, he looked in both directions and moved confidently toward the lobby area. Finally, after going through another short hallway, he came upon the hotel registration desk. Looking around the area, he noticed that Arnold was on duty and checking in some guests. Keeping an eye on the hotel desk clerk, Hayward knelt on his knees and made out like he was examining some creaking floorboards around the entrance to the hotel lobby area and hallway.

Suddenly, Hayward heard a voice.

"What may I ask are you doing?"

Hayward was accustomed to risk. He looked up at the heavy set individual, retaining his composure and coolness. "I'se was told to look at these lose boards and fix dem. That's all."

"It's about time. Well hurry up, I don't want any of the guests to see you!"

As the gentleman proceeded down the hallway toward the kitchen area, Hayward watched. "Yes'um. I'se will do that."

Hayward turned around and noticed that Arnold had disappeared and was apparently finished with the guests. Hayward stood, looked around and made his way to the registration area, kneeling and moving along unnoticed behind the huge desk. Slowly, he stood and once more looked around. Before him was the hotel registry with all of the information on its guests. He kept his ears open for any sound of Arnold's return and began to flip as inconspicuously as possible through the pages. He turned the pages, noticing by the dates of registration that he had gone back too far in the book. He quickly flipped the pages until he came to Tuesday, October 5th. Moving his fingers along the guest names, he came to Katie and her father's registration. Quickly turning to the next page for Wednesday, the day in question of Katie's disappearance, Hayward moved his fingers rapidly down the page and noticed that from 3:00 o'clock in the afternoon on, Arnold was on duty at the desk and was the clerk signing in each guest until sometime around midnight. From that point on, it didn't appear that anyone registered until the next day. Out of all the names registered, Hayward didn't recognize anyone of interest or importance. Now he was sure that Arnold had been untruthful and was surely trying to cover up something for someone. As for Geoffrey, his name didn't appear on any pages for that day, meaning that he had intentionally lied to Pete.

As Hayward continued to look at the pages, he heard the sound of footsteps heading in his direction. He quickly looked around for a place to hide.

Arnold walked behind the desk and immediately noticed that the registration book wasn't on the current page for today's dates. He was bewildered and frightened when he noticed that the page with the entries were dated for the evening that Katie disappeared. He suspected someone had been looking through the registry and was attempting to gain information for this purpose. As he looked around, he didn't see any of the hotel employees nearby but only many of the guests mingling as they do everyday in the lobby area.

As Arnold stepped from the desk to another smaller one behind him, Hayward pulled back the covering that concealed his cramped hideaway under the registry desk. He noticed Arnold jotting down a few lines on some paper. Hayward quickly ducked into his hideaway as Arnold began to turn around.

Arnold stepped back over to the registry desk and called for a porter. "This letter is from a guest and is very important. It must go to the War Department and make sure that Mr. Winesmith gets it. Now hurry along and stop for no one!"

Hayward stayed in his hideaway until Arnold once more disappeared. Looking around, Hayward quickly left from his hideaway, grabbing his tools and calmly retracing his footsteps through the hallway. He knew that he had gained some valuable information and must find Pete as soon as possible.

Chapter 46

For about an hour, Hayward stood near the corner of 14th and Pennsylvania Avenue waiting for Pete and Seamus to return from speaking to Colonel Langsten. Anxiously looking up and down the street of crowded citizens for any signs of the two men, Hayward wanted Pete to have the opportunity to confront Arnold again while he was still on duty at the hotel. Moving across the street to the main entrance, Hayward noticed a carriage approaching close to the curve as if to stop. Once the team of horses was brought to a halt, he immediately noticed Pete and Seamus stepping from the carriage. Quickly he stepped forward. He noticed both men had troubled expressions covering their faces.

Immediately, Pete noticed the anxiety on Hayward's face. "Did you find out something?"

Hayward smiled and shook his head in acknowledgement. "That Mr. Arnold knows more than what's he's a tellin' ya."

"In what way?" Seamus curiously asked.

"He's was a workin' the night that Misse Katie was missin'."

"Then he was lying just as I suspected," Pete replied.

Turning around and glancing at the hotel entrance and then again at Pete, Hayward answered. "'Bout a hour ago, he was still in there."

"How do you know he was working the night that my sister disappeared?" Seamus impatiently asked.

"I'se saw the book with all the names and dates. His name is beside all of dem."

"You mean the registry book?"

"Yes'um," Hayward continued with confidence and calmness about the details of his adventure, "And dere's more. He's had the porter take a message to Mr. Winesmith at the War Department. I'se hear all, I'se was listinin'."

Pete looked at Seamus. "He has some questions to answer. Let's go and see him before he gets away."

Seamus nodded his head in agreement as the two men dashed through the front entrance to the hotel. Once they arrived at the registry desk, a different clerk politely asked, "May I help you gentlemen?"

As Seamus looked around the lobby area for signs of Arnold among the many gentlemen, Pete said, "Yes, I would like to speak with Arnold Crumbly."

"Sorry sir, something unexpectedly came up and he is gone for the day."

"How long ago did he leave?"

"Oh, I guess about thirty minutes."

Impatiently, Seamus interrupted, "Where does he bloody live?"

Knowing Seamus and Pete were angry; the clerk hesitated until Pete leaned forward discreetly, grabbing the clerk forcefully by the arm. "With his mother on 6th Street next to St John's Church," the clerk cried.

Within minutes, Seamus and Pete arrived at the residence in question. After several knocks on the front door and no answer, Pete and Seamus tried to open the door. It was unlocked. Pete and Seamus cautiously entered the well-kept dwelling, looking around as they walked through the entrance. To the left was the dining area, which they entered and then went through a pocket door to the drawing room. It appeared that no one was home. Continuing to look around the house, Pete walked back toward the front of the house and into the parlor where he noticed the many photographs on the mantel of the fireplace. He approached the photographs out of curiosity. One in particular caught his attention. It was an image of Arnold and a Confederate soldier standing near a fence with a brick house and large porch in the background. The structure possessed some familiarities that reminded him of Shenandoah before the war. The scene looked recognizable to Pete because when he rode with Mosby it was the plan for them to stay with civilians throughout Loudoun and Fauquier County Virginia. Although Pete was unfamiliar with the soldier's identity who was standing with Arnold in the photograph, he recognized the homestead by the line of dogwood trees that stood on each side of the path that led to the stairs of the house. He also recognized the huge web-like fan shaped window over the door and side light panels surrounding the entrance. This was the same place where he had stayed after he had returned to the army after being wounded at Funkstown, Maryland. He knew the area to be somewhere near Ball's Mill along Goose Creek in Loudoun County.

Suddenly, Seamus calling from the upstairs area of the house broke Pete's thoughts. Pete turned and raced up the narrow stairway to the second level of the dwelling knowing that he had discovered something important. Once he entered the doorway to his right, he immediately noticed Seamus standing over Arnold's lifeless, bloody body lying across the bed face down.

As he leaned over Arnold's body to examine his wounds, Seamus said, "Well Barker, it appears the bloody lad died from a number of wounds. Several wounds at least to the neck and one to the upper chest. From what I can tell, Arnold might have been taken by surprise when he walked into the room because it appears that a struggle didn't take place. And everything is neat and tidy so therefore it wasn't robbery."

Pete added as he walked around the room looking at some of the personal items, "Someone wanted to keep his mouth shut because he knew too much." Turning around and facing Seamus, Pete continued confidently, "They were afraid that he would give in under pressure and might reveal too much, or someone's identity."

"I agree."

"Come with me; I have something else that you should see," Pete said as he gestured.

Seamus and Pete walked to the main level of the plain well-kept three-story dwelling and back into the parlor. Quietly, Pete walked over to the mantel where he picked up the photograph that he was looking at when Seamus called him. He turned around and approached Seamus, pointing to Arnold and the soldier in the picture. "I would be willing to bet you that Arnold was passing information during the war to agents working within the city concerning things he overheard or knew from congressmen or other prominent individuals that patronized the Willard. Undoubtedly, he knew who came into the hotel on the evening that Katie disappeared and was involved in a planned scheme. I am convinced of that. The war still goes on for some, it didn't end at Appomattox."

Seamus rubbed the side of his cheek as if deep in thought looking in the direction of the large front window. He turned around and took the photograph from Pete's hand and quietly gazed at it.

"You rode with Mosby; what do you know about the Confederate Secret Service?" Seamus asked.

"Only, at times, I would pose as a preacher to gain information on troop strength, design, and position."

Seamus interrupted. "You Barker, a preacher, speaking of the good book? Oh, the Johnnies must have been desperate." When he noticed by Pete's expression that he was getting angry, Seamus held up his hands. "I apologize, go on."

"Ever since I joined up with Mosby's command, I was always assigned to duty such as that because I knew the area quite well. And I was a skilled tracker and possessed a good memory for details. One evening in particular as I was visiting a Chaplin and some soldiers on Bolivar Heights, I overheard several officers speaking of someone who had been playing both sides of the game at passing information. Apparently this person was very skilled at deception. I assumed that this person, whoever it might be, was very knowledgeable and also wouldn't be scrutinized by soldiers either Yankee or Rebel. Certainly, that person must have had connections in high places of government and was well trusted by those people. I knew whoever it was had caused a lot of trouble for our forces in the Shenandoah Valley by revealing our intentions and designs. So for them, money must have been the reason instead of principal. After overhearing this revelation, Shenandoah was torched by Yankee cavalry and without hesitation I left for home before I could discover the identity of the individual. That same night, Daniel told me Katie was with a Union officer, apparently Langsten at General Howe's headquarters, just as he said earlier. Shortly thereafter, the burnings began. Like my brother, Daniel accused her of spying because he had been watching her for William Pierce. Daniel informed me that Katie had been missing off and on for quite sometime. Naturally with this information my curiosity was aroused. I wanted to find out the truth of her possible involvement and why, but Katie wasn't in Harpers Ferry at the time."

"Do you feel that she would have told you the truth if confronted?"

"Anymore, I really don't know. But I have always held the belief that regardless of any involvement on her part for your cause during the war, it wouldn't have made any difference."

"You mean to tell me Barker that if my sister was responsible for the raid on Shenandoah, it wouldn't make any difference to you?" Shaking his head in amazement and grinning, Seamus continued in a serious tone. "How could anybody in their right mind take that attitude?"

"My brother Charles was convinced beyond a doubt that Katie was an agent working for the War Department and sent to Harpers Ferry before the war. Harpers Ferry was very important you know because of the weapons manufacturing and the transportation that it offered. Charles thought it strange that a woman would be sent to be a schoolmaster of the Catholic school instead of a man, which you know yourself, is customary." Pete paused and continued, "Besides, I guess the question was answered in Boston several weeks ago when you indicated that she had been spying and was just using me like some naive fool to gain information."

Seamus turned cold in his attitude toward Pete and replied in an angry tone, "When we find Katie, then I guess you should let her tell you the truth about her double life. It's not my bloody responsibility. But as for what I said in Boston about you, I have no regrets whatsoever. Even now! My words that evening accomplished all that I could have hoped for and more because it caused the division that I had hoped for you two." Seamus glanced at Pete's angry expression and fiery eyes. He continued his verbal assault as he gazed boldly at Pete. "The last thing that I would have my sister do now or in the future is marry you and have your bloody children."

Pete pointed and answered loudly with boldness and contempt in his voice. "Have you ever thought McBride that maybe if you had kept your blame mouth shut and your nose out of our business then maybe we wouldn't be looking for your sister, and finding people dead here in this as you Irishmen would say, 'bloody' no good forsaken city?"

"Barker, I am telling you once and for all…"

Seamus was interrupted when he surprisingly noticed a man departing from the dining area. As the mysterious individual gazed at the two men, Seamus yelled. "Hey you!"

The individual was quiet and then suddenly raced for the door. Without wasting a moment, Pete turned around to catch him as Seamus shouted once more. "Hey you… wait, wait a minute!" As the young man ignored their request, he opened the front door and raced from the house with Seamus and Pete chasing.

Once outside on the porch, Pete and Seamus noticed Hayward knocking the intruder onto the cobblestone street. As they began to scuffle on the ground, the mysterious man got the upper hand and unleashed several quick blows to Hayward's face. Witnessing the event, without hesitation, Pete and Seamus moved rapidly to capture the individual, but unfortunately Hayward wasn't a match for the much younger man and he began to flee. As Pete paused to assist an injured Hayward, Seamus gave chase down the street after the speedy mysterious individual but was unable to catch him.

Hayward began to rub his hand across his bloody face as Pete examined the wounds. Other than some abrasions and a nasty cut over his left eye, Hayward appeared uninjured elsewhere.

Seamus was out of breath as he returned and looked at Hayward lying on the ground. He looked at Pete. "How is he?"

Instead of Pete answering, Hayward forced a chuckle. "I'se will be all right. It will take more than that young man to keep me's down. I'se will catch up with him and when I'se do, he's a gonna pay for what he's has done."

Seamus shook his head in disagreement as Pete glanced at him. "If he says that he's going to do something, then you best believe that he'll do it."

"We'll see Barker. We'll see," Seamus sarcastically said as he looked around the area.

Pete helped Hayward to his feet.

"Now what Barker?" Seamus frustratingly asked. "We have one dead man to contend with and another that escaped."

"Hayward, did you get a good look at that guy?" Pete asked.

"Yes'um."

"Go and get the photograph that I was showing you before all this happened," Pete said to Seamus.

Within minutes, Seamus returned from the dwelling with the photograph in hand and showed it to Hayward. Immediately, Hayward nodded in agreement that this was his assailant.

"Is there anything important in his description that we should know about that has changed?" Seamus impatiently asked.

"Yes'um, I'se think that I'se broke his nose when I'se knock him to the ground. He hit the stone walkway face down."

"Anything else?"

"His dark brown eyes were cold and strange. I'se will never forget dem."

Pete removed the photograph from the frame to place it under his shirt. He noticed what appeared to be a ciphered message neatly placed behind the cover of the frame. As he unrolled the paper, he recognized that the code was written unreadable cipher which Confederate agents used during the war for passing secret messages. Pete gestured for Seamus and Hayward to follow him to the house. There he found a pencil on a stand at the entranceway next to the door. With the cipher's familiarity, Pete next used the clear text to set forth on the paper using the Vegenere alphabet square for deciphering the message. It took several minutes to match the numbers and letters of the alphabet.

"What does it say?" Seamus anxiously asked.

"Will come tonight for the package, signed Colonel L. That's it."

"Who is Colonel L?"

As Pete rolled up the paper, he placed it under his shirt. "I don't know, but it confirms our suspicions about Arnold's involvement in Katie's disappearance."

"I'm not familiar with code."

Pete placed his hand on Seamus's shoulder. "For now, we must go to the War Department and speak with Mr. Winesmith. Maybe he can shed some light on who Colonel L is."

"What about Arnold?"

"He's dead; there's not much that we can do for him."

"But we can't leave him there like that; we must summon the police."

"And what, have them ask us a bunch of questions about his death and then suspect us of his murder? No Seamus, we don't have the time. Whoever that intruder is working for knows by now that we are on their trail and looking for them. Katie could possibly be in greater danger now."

"You know Barker, you're starting to make sense."

As Pete departed with Hayward and Seamus, his thoughts were consumed with the identity of Colonel L. It was either the beginning of the first, middle, or last name of the person who now he was sure abducted Katie from her hotel suite. Many names of individuals he knew surfaced within his mind but none with the initials of L.

Chapter 47

It was nearing sunset as the red glow of the sun began to hide slowly behind the western horizon. Before anyone returned to the Crumbly residence and discovered their presence, Pete placed the photograph in his shirt with the ciphered message and departed with Seamus for the War Department.

Seamus had given some money to Hayward and asked him to rent a team of horses and a buggy and bring them to the corner of 17th and G Street to await a hand signal from Pete. If things proceeded according to plan, then by the time that Mr. Winesmith left the War Department, Seamus and Pete would be in a very favorable position to abduct the clerk.

On their arrival at the War Department, Seamus left Pete outside while he went alone into the building to identify Mr. Winesmith. Once he entered the dwelling, he took immediate notice of a heavyset individual wearing spectacles stacking papers behind a desk. Seamus approached the desk but was ignored. Looking at the guard posted by the Secretary's door, Seamus knocked several times loudly on the wooden railing. The clerk looked up from his work angrily at Seamus, but the young Irishman wasn't intimated by the clerk's expression.

"What is it?" the clerk rudely asked.

Knowing the impossibilities of seeing the Secretary of War at this particular hour of the day, Seamus requested in a calm tone, "I would like an audience with Secretary Stanton on the most urgent business."

"No, it's too late in the afternoon. Secretary Stanton only sees the public that must transact business during the morning hours."

"I didn't know that. I just arrived from New Bedford, Massachusetts about an hour ago. I had hoped to conduct my business as soon as I arrived. It won't take too long."

"No sir. Rules are rules, and no one sees the Secretary of War this late in the day." The clerk continued speaking as he straightened a stack of papers. "Do you understand?"

"Yes, I guess I have to."

Turning and walking toward the door and opening it, Seamus turned around. "Oh, by the way, who am I speaking to?"

The clerk once more looked angrily up from his work. "Thomas Winesmith."

Seamus smiled and turned around and pulled the door shut behind him. He noticed Pete standing along the walkway looking his way. Smiling as he approached, he paused and spoke to Pete who was working out the details for Winesmith's abduction. Once everything was coordinated with Pete, he walked to an area across from the War Department near the five-story Winder building.

An hour had passed since Seamus first confronted Thomas Winesmith. He was very apprehensive and impatient as the sunlight continued to fade behind the buildings. From his waistcoat pocket, he pulled his timepiece noticing that it was a little after 7 o'clock. Glancing across the street, Seamus noticed Pete slowly and inconspicuously walking in the direction of the government dwelling after speaking with Hayward about their plans. Again, Seamus turned his gaze in the direction of the War Department entrance. He noticed an officer departing quickly with an orderly walking in the opposite direction of where Pete was approaching.

Within a few minutes, Seamus anxiously noticed a lone individual leaving the entrance to the War Department and walking across the street in his direction. He placed his left hand on the brim of his black hat as a pre-agreed signal to Pete. Seamus intently observed Pete step from the walkway behind the individual to be abducted.

Once Mr. Winesmith stepped onto the street in front of the Winder building, Seamus approached, smiling. "Sir, do you remember me?"

Displaying a cold expression as he stared at Seamus, Mr. Winesmith answered. "Yes sir, I do." Staring quietly for a moment at Seamus' appearance, he continued in a sarcastic tone. "Who wouldn't fail to recognize you with all of that red hair hanging from your head? Now if you'll excuse me, I must go."

Seamus gently grabbed Mr. Winesmith by the arm. "Not so fast. You have a few questions to answer."

"About what?"

"The disappearance of my sister, that's what," Seamus replied with an intimidating tone.

By the time Seamus finished answering, Pete was standing behind Mr. Winesmith giving the hand signal to Hayward to bring the carriage.

Mr. Winesmith turned around and gazed defiantly at Pete with his beady blue eyes. There was a surprised expression covering his face. "Do we know each other?"

"Would it make any difference?" Pete responded.

Mr. Winesmith looked at both Pete and Seamus. "No, I don't guess it would."

An astonished expression appeared on Seamus' face at Mr. Winesmith's question and Pete's answer.

Hayward brought the horses to a halt and kept looking around the area. Pete quietly gestured for Mr. Winesmith to get into the carriage. Again, Mr. Winesmith quietly paused gazing at Pete and said to him before he stepped into the carriage. "We have met."

Pete didn't answer. Instead, he gently nudged the middle-aged man into the back seat of the open carriage. Once Mr. Winesmith was seated next to Pete, he glared defiantly at Pete as if betrayed.

Seamus climbed alongside Hayward in the front and said in a commanding tone, "To the Southside area."

Hayward knew the area to be dangerous in nature. It was located in the area of the city between the canal and the marshy banks of the Potomac River. Many thieves, thugs, and all sort of lawless, unruly individuals could be found roaming freely among the saloons, gambling houses, cheap theaters, and brothels. Hayward didn't agree with the chosen area. He was quiet as he complied with the demand and headed the team of horses in the direction of the Irish settlement in the vicinity of North Capitol Street.

The sun had set below the horizon and darkness filled the ill-lighted streets of the Capitol. As the sound of horse hooves echoed, Pete began to think of how all this was going to play out. It was apparent with Arnold's death that one less link with possible information to solving the abduction to Katie had been broken. Other than Winesmith's cooperation, they would be back at the beginning having accomplished nothing, but a photograph of an unidentifiable individual, a ciphered message, and an obstinate gentleman that might reveal some information if prodded.

Pete gave thought of Katie's welfare and how she might be holding up with such a traumatic experience in her life. It could be possible, he thought, that she still might be in the city or her abductor had already moved her to a safer and more secluded area. Often during the war, many agents or individuals of clandestine activity were smuggled through the enemy lines by regular upstanding citizens of the community who were never suspected of improprieties. Pete recalled one in particular that he had connections with on one occasion in late '63. His name was Robert Archibald. Before the war began, Robert had acquired a respectable reputation and was found to be an upstanding citizen of the eastern Fairfax County community. Once the conflict began, he became an outspoken Unionist suffering great persecution from Southern loyalists who lived in the county. Little did anyone know in reality, he was an active member of the Confederate underground and became very useful on many occasions. Often he was used to pass information, and on many occasions agents with a pretense would be smuggled in and out of Washington with his assistance since it was easy for him to obtain a pass from the Union Provost Marshall at Fairfax Court House.

The more Pete thought about the situation he was convinced that Katie's abduction was linked in someway to her possible involvement during the war. If instincts were serving him well, then he had just cause to be concerned over her sincerity with their relationship. Her integrity was questionable. Did she just use him for the purpose of obtaining information during the war? The question arose within his heart concerning the reason she returned to Shenandoah after the war and suffered the hardships that they faced over the last six months. Maybe it was out of guilt since she at one time had been close to the family or inadvertently fell in love with him. Once she was found, there would be time to answer all the questions.

Pete turned his thoughts to the more complicated issue. Who was responsible for her abduction and who was Colonel L? He knew from his limited knowledge involving underground activity that many agents wouldn't use the initials of their own name. Often they assumed an alias and always a disguise of some type. All the time they covered up their true intention by misleading, lying, and deceiving in every way to achieve their goal. Maybe someone blessed with the gift such as Robert Archibald was one of the conspirators that assisted with Katie's abduction.

Pete turned once more and glanced at Thomas Winesmith. For the first time since his abduction, Thomas opened his mouth. "It has been a long time." When Pete didn't answer, Thomas continued in a confident tone. "I didn't know that you were helping the other side."

"I have a personal interest in this."

Thomas chuckled as he continued to gaze at Pete. "We have met."

"Maybe." Pete replied.

As Thomas pulled a cigar from his pocket and lit it, he said as he flicked the match into the street. "Yes, yes, now I recall. You were a preacher of the gospel in the spring of '64 when I was at Harpers Ferry." Pete remained quiet knowing that he was there. Thomas continued to examine Pete's facial appearance for some answer. He continued with assurance. "Yes, I am sure. I had arrived from Washington earlier in the day and was speaking with an officer in his tent about an informer that was playing both sides of the game. Afterward when I stepped from the tent, I noticed you sitting around with Chaplin Barnes under his fly. What were you doing there? I'm sure that you weren't preaching the Good Word."

Pete turned his eyes away from Thomas. "No, I wasn't but at least I wasn't playing both sides of the game." Pete paused and turned to look at Thomas. "Does Secretary Stanton know that he has a traitor in his office?"

"What do you mean? I am a person of respectable means."

"I'll tell you what I mean. Arnold Crumbly earlier today sent you a message from the Willard Hotel after he became afraid that his involvement in the abduction of Katie McBride was revealed. That's why Arnold is dead. He knew too much, and he knew who her abductors were and he had to be silenced."

"And you must be insane. I don't know who Katie McBride is or who Arnold Crumbly is."

Pete continued angrily as he pulled the contents from his shirt. "Well then let me refresh your memory."

Pete held the photograph before Thomas' face, and then the ciphered message. Thomas suddenly was quiet. His face turned pale with shock as he tossed the cigar into the street.

Pete knew that Thomas was guilty by his troubled expression and sudden silence. A short moment ago he was boastful and full of pride and ridicule, but now he was lost for words.

Seamus had been listening to the whole conversation. He turned to glance at Pete. Once he caught Pete's attention, he winked with a smile of agreement. He knew they were slowly gaining ground and he was confident in the means he would use to bring Thomas to a more talkative manner.

Chapter 48

Shortly, Hayward neared the Market Place along 7th Street. Turning the carriage in a southerly direction, they crossed the steel girder bridge over the Washington Canal. As Pete looked around, loud singing and shouting noises were coming from some of the taverns where many of its occupants were becoming merry from too much whisky. In many ways, it reminded him of the area in Boston where several weeks ago he had rescued Seamus from a couple of rowdies. From the appearance of this area of Washington City, it gave one the impression that the city was less civil than Boston.

As they proceeded along the street, Pete heard some of the men milling around, shouting out some of the worst language since his days in combat with the 1st Virginia Cavalry. It was an oppressed area made up of the common laborers who worked long hours for little money. As Pete gazed at the men, he noticed some appeared to be like the soldiers that he fought with during the war. Their trousers were worn and ripped in some places, faces dirty, and gaunt in appearance. Pete noticed some of the women apparently couldn't afford shoes for their feet. Their clothing, like the men, was dirty and worn and hair needed grooming.

As the carriage creaked along, Pete looked up at a second story porch where even at this hour of the evening, laundry was still hanging from clothes lines stretching from one porch column to the other. It wasn't a community where the well-respected lady or gentleman would live; instead the area appeared forsaken by the rest of the city. Many of the buildings appeared dilapidated and poverty ruled with an iron fist over this area of Washington City.

Once Hayward slowed the pace of the horses, Pete noticed a young man speaking with another individual, pointing, gesturing obscenely, and laughing as he kept his attention focused on them. Without warning, Hayward brought the horses to a halt because several kids playing ran in front of the horses. Pete noticed out of the corner of his eye that the young man was approaching the carriage. By impulse, he placed his hand on his pistol but not pulling the weapon from concealment. The carriage began to move once more. As it did, the young man ran alongside.

"Stop, stop ya bloody fools. Come back here now!" The young man shouted.

Pete knew in all probability that he had too much to drink. The young man attempted to climb into the carriage, but Pete took his foot and shoved it against his chest ejecting him from the carriage and onto the ground.

Seamus laughed at the incident as he observed the encounter between Pete and the young man. "I do believe Barker you could survive us rowdy Irishmen," Seamus laughingly said.

"Why did you bring us here?" Pete asked.

As Hayward brought the carriage to a halt in front of a saloon, Seamus jumped from the seat. "Shortly Barker, you'll see."

Once Pete stepped from the carriage, he gestured to Thomas to do the same. By the inscription on the front window, they had arrived at a place called Murphy's. Following Seamus' lead toward the tavern entrance, Pete noticed several ladies of questionable motives. One of the ladies called out to Pete and his party only to have her request ignored.

After entering the gloomy establishment, Seamus paused and looked around and then gestured for everyone to follow. He found a table where there was little light and everyone sat down. Without a word, Seamus pulled some money from his pocket.

"Barker, go and get us several beers and a bottle of the establishment's best whisky." Seamus said..

Pete quietly took the money and proceeded to the bar.

Seamus turned his attention toward Thomas Winesmith and grinned. From Thomas' expression, Seamus knew that he was frightened. Seamus next glanced at Hayward. He knew Hayward felt uneasy and that he was hoping they would be able to accomplish their objective in little time.

A few minutes seemed like eternity to Hayward as Pete returned with the liquor and sat next to him. Hayward tapped Pete on the forearm. "Why are we's here?"

Pete turned around after taking a sip of his beer. "Hayward, let's just say that we have to get this weasel relaxed so he'll answer a few questions."

"Doesn't yose think that there would be a better way then dis?"

Pete took another sip of his beer as he watched Seamus pour some whisky for Thomas, "No, this is the best way."

"Praise God. I'se glad that Romans 10:13 says that I'se can call on the name of the Lord and be saved."

"You may need His help before we get out of here," Pete replied.

Thomas looked at the glass of whisky. His face was pale and his eyes teary.

Seamus poured himself a glass of whisky and said to Thomas as he held it high, "Bottoms up Lad."

Thomas watched as Seamus downed the drink with ease. Seamus placed the glass on the table. "Come on chap, drink now. We haven't much time."

Thomas hesitated until Pete quietly laid his pistol on the table. One look at Pete's angry expression caused Thomas to take the glass and drink its contents. After he finished, he removed a handkerchief and wiped his mouth. Again, Seamus filled the glass to the brim and demanded, "Have another friend."

After about twenty minutes had passed, Thomas was beginning to feel the effects of the liquor. His speech was slurred and he was a little unbalanced sitting in the chair.

Feeling confident, Seamus wanted to anger Thomas in a way that he would speak freely. "You know Thomas, the war was a trying experience for all of us. It really didn't make any difference who you fought for." Pausing and pointing at Pete, Seamus continued in a friendly tone. "Now for example, you take Barker sitting over there. His whole family was sympathetic to the Confederacy and Barker himself fought with the Johnnies. In return, my Yankee friends burned his home and destroyed everything of use. You know Thomas they got everything they deserved. Really it wasn't punishment enough." Pausing with his eyes on Thomas, he continued his assault. "We didn't have time to finish the South off right. If given a few more months, we could have burned every blasted city and town, totally devastating everything in the South." Pausing and taking another sip from his glass, he continued, "No, no the job wasn't finished and I guess that's why there are some still on the Southern side that want to wage the continuation of the war."

Thomas felt less inhibited, and more freely with his tongue as he angrily answered, "Destroy the South. Young man you'll never destroy the South. If it hadn't been for Lincoln's re-election in '64, then McClellan would have won the presidency and made peace. But no, Lincoln wanted to continue to wage war and force the will of the abolitionist and his own personal selfishness on the good people of the South."

"Why Mr. Winesmith, I thought that you were a Unionist?" Seamus replied.

"No, I've always been loyal to the Southern cause. I am from Baltimore." Pausing as Seamus forced him to take another drink of whisky, Thomas continued after wiping his mouth. "My three brothers fought for the Confederacy. Two fought with the 2nd Maryland Infantry while the other was a gunnery corporal with the Baltimore Light Artillery."

"Did they survive the war?" Pete asked.

Thomas quietly shook his head with tears flowing down his cheeks. After composing himself, he said, "My brother Jim of the Baltimore Battery was mortally wounded I am told from a comrade. He passed on several days later after his battery was overrun somewhere near Moorefield. I also lost another brother, Ben, in that same fight. A Yankee cavalryman slashed him with a saber blow as he was trying to surrender. My last brother was captured and never returned from Point Lookout, Maryland."

"Well that would make anybody mad as hell and want to gain revenge, now wouldn't it? And revenge I feel that you are still seeking," Seamus said as he patted Thomas on the shoulder and poured another drink.

Pete asked as he took Hayward's untouched beer and began drinking, "You mean to tell me that all these years that you've been at the War Department, no one ever expected you of spying and passing information?"

"No, I always appeared to be nothing but loyal."

"But you said that you were from Baltimore. That city was known to be filled with Secessionists. Didn't that arouse suspicion within the War Department and the Provost Marshall or did you change your name and area to conceal your true identity?" Pete asked.

Thomas paused knowing that the liquor helped trap him in his words and that it wasn't any use to continue to lie. He took a deep sigh. "I guess you'll find out sooner or later. My real name is not Winesmith, I am Phillip Reynolds from Warrenton, Virginia."

"How did you gain a position at the War Department?" Seamus eagerly asked.

Thomas gazed at Seamus, pausing in thought before answering. Finally, he softly answered. "In 1853, my father gained a position as a clerk under Jefferson Davis. At the time, he was serving as the Secretary of War under Franklin Pierce. In order to have any future and a fresh chance at life, my father changed his name from Reynolds to Winesmith. The reason was because his brother had been hung for a string of murders in nearby Stafford County. The murders had almost ruined the family's life. Therefore, in order for him to start over again in life, he knew that he would have to change his name and identity."

Pete interrupted. "It seems to me that anyone serving under Davis would have been suspected of Southern loyalties. This would have disqualified you for the position, especially with Edwin Stanton as the Secretary of War." Pete paused briefly in thought and continued in a curious tone. "Winesmith, how did you do it?"

Thomas chuckled as if winning a victory. He became suddenly solemn and erect in posture. "No one could question my father's loyalties to the Union and its preservation. Even today my father doesn't know that I was frequently passing information across the river to Colonel Jordan or Mr. Bowie. My father was such an ardent Unionist that he was quite upset with my brothers even to the point of disowning them and swearing upon their death. As for me, he has always believed that I was loyal to the Union and that I stood for its preservation such as he did. I never gave my father or Mr. Stanton any reason to suspect otherwise or anyone else associated with the War Department."

"Not even with knowing that your brothers were fighting with the Confederates?" Pete asked.

"Not with my name changed. At the outbreak of the war, everyone was under some type of scrutiny. I never gave them any reason not to trust me."

Seamus urged Thomas to take another drink. He willingly complied. Seamus took the candle and lit his cigar. Blowing the smoke into the air and looking around, he turned his attention to Thomas once more. "Who is Colonel L?"

Thomas shook his head in a gesture that he didn't know. Seamus took him by the coat sleeve and became more forceful. "Come on, who are you fooling, you know the identity of Colonel L."

"I don't know. And take your hands off me!"

Pete sighed and began to become impatient with the progress of their interrogation of Thomas. "Why did Arnold Crumbly send you a message?" Pete asked loudly.

"I don't know who you are talking about."

Pete turned and looked at Hayward. "Did you recognize the porter that Crumbly gave the message to?"

"No, I'se couldn't see him. I'se jist hear them talkin'."

Seamus pulled the revolver from his coat and cocked the hammer. He said in an angry tone. "Winesmith, it would be in your bloody interest to tell us what we want to know. If you don't, then you may not see the bloody sun come up another bloody day."

Without a word, Seamus pressed the barrel of the revolver against the left side of Thomas' body. Seamus anxiously asked, "Well, what's it going to be, huh?"

"I was to warn Colonel L to be on the alert that someone might be looking for him."

Pete fired back. "Just a minute ago you said that you didn't know who Colonel L was. Who is L?"

Thomas answered in a slurring and loud voice. "Truly, I don't know. Messages are passed through a courier."

Thomas passed out face down on the table. Immediately, Seamus grabbed him by the collar of his shirt and commanded in an authoritative tone. "Who is the bloody courier? His name!"

Thomas looked at Seamus. "Jacob Lyles from Loudoun County."

Pete noticed that Thomas' head began to tilt forward and his eyes rolled. He wanted to probe for more information before Thomas lost consciousness. "Where in Loudoun County?"

"A homestead with his family somewhere along Goose Creek. That's all that I know."

Again Thomas' head fell forward. Pete was sure Thomas knew a great deal more information concerning the Confederate underground. He placed his hand under Thomas' chin. "What do you know about Charles Barker?"

"We haven't time for him now," Seamus fired back.

Thomas struggled to hold his head up as he replied, "The last I heard, he was somewhere in Virginia. In hiding. Where I don't know."

Finally as Pete attempted to find out more information concerning Katie and his brother Charles, Thomas unfortunately passed out on the table.

Pete glanced at Seamus. "I think that you gave him one too many to drink."

Without hesitation, Pete stood and headed in the direction of the bar. Amidst all the turmoil from Katie's disappearance, inwardly, he was very happy to know that Charles was alive and couldn't wait to share the news with Caroline and his mother. He thought about sending a telegram to his family. Realizing the potential danger of it being intercepted by the Provost Marshall's office in Harpers Ferry, he knew he would have to devise another scheme to get the message through to his family. Charles' safety and welfare was one less burden for him to carry. Pete thought of Robert Archibald. Maybe he knew something of where Charles or even Katie might be located. Hopefully, once they made contact with him, he might be able to shed some light on these problems.

Chapter 49

Once Pete arrived at the bar, he looked around for the bartender who was standing and speaking with several individuals at the opposite end of the bar. Pete impatiently waited. Looking back in the direction of his table, he watched as Seamus attempted without success to revive Thomas. Turning once more to look at the bartender still standing at the far end of the bar, an attractive woman walked up to him.

"You must beware. Your life is in danger," she warned.

"Who are you?"

"It doesn't matter."

The bartender arrived while Pete had his back turned. "What do you want?" the bartender asked.

Pete turned to give him his attention. "I want a pitcher of cold water."

As the bartender turned his back on Pete to comply with the request, Pete turned around again to speak to the young lady, only to find that she had vanished. Puzzled and taking to heart all that she said, Pete turned and watched the bartender drawing the water. A young man in his mid twenties caught Pete's attention as he approached from the far end of the long bar. Pete watched the individual, as he appeared to intensely watch Seamus, Hayward, and Thomas. Pete pulled the photograph of Arnold and the young man from his shirt and glanced at it. He looked at the man standing near the end of the bar and again at the photograph. Recognizing the individual at the end of the bar as one and the same in the photograph, he returned the item to his shirt. As he began to approach the young man, the individual turned and noticed Pete approaching. Without hesitation, he pulled his gun and fired at Pete. A wooden splinter from the bar hit Pete in the side of the face as he ducked. Pulling his pistol from concealment under his coat, Pete returned the fire as the young man again fired one round at Seamus. Pete missed his target. Pete jumped to his feet as some of the customers of the establishment were yelling and ducking for cover. Looking toward the table, Pete noticed Seamus and Hayward were not hurt.

Quickly, Pete proceeded toward the corner of the bar where the young man had stood. Rapidly glancing around, Pete noticed a back door to the tavern was still open. Joined by Seamus, Pete quickly approached the door and cautiously glanced out into the alley. To his right, the alley came to a dead end. To his left it led to the street. He dashed to the left hoping to catch a glimpse of the young man. At the end of the alley, Pete noticed the mysterious man racing into what appeared to be a boarding house directly across the street from where he was standing. The mysterious individual turned and fired once more. The bullet's whizzing sound came close to hitting Pete and Seamus as they ducked behind the brick wall of another building along the street.

Pete watched as the mysterious young man raced through the front door to the dwelling. In quick pursuit, Pete and Seamus dashed across the street. Pete gestured for Seamus to use the alleyway in hopes of capturing their prey if he attempted to escape from the building using a rear entrance. Pete approached the front door of the boarding house. He cautiously opened the door and entered. It was dark and quiet as he stepped into the entrance hallway. He glanced around, listening for any signs of life. He looked into the parlor and then the dining room. Then he paused and heard a creak coming from a loose floorboard on the second floor. His suspicions were aroused. He quietly cocked the hammer of the pistol.

Slowly and cautiously taking one step at a time, Pete was shortly on the second floor suspecting to find his attacker. Looking around, there appeared to be three doorways to various rooms on each side of the hallway. He tried to open the door to one room on his left. It was locked. Then there was another room to his right that was open. He walked through the doorway and looked around the vacant room for any signs of his enemy. He began to walk through the doorway into the hallway to investigate the next room. Several shots in succession rang out. Pete ducked back into the doorway firing in the direction of a room on the right at the far end of the hallway. Pete felt a funny sensation along his face. He placed his hand against the side of his face and discovered that he was bleeding from a flesh wound to his left cheek. Immediately, he became angry but maintained his composure. Pete thought that Seamus must have heard the sound of gunshots by now and was closing in on their prey from the rear.

Pete noticed each doorway was recessed. He quickly moved to the doorway to his right across the hallway. It was empty. Again, he moved forward to the open doorway where the shots came from. As he entered, Pete looked around finding no signs of his attacker. The room gave the appearance that someone had occupied it. Pete walked over to the window and looked into the alleyway for Seamus. He noticed Seamus walking and trying several doors to enter but to no avail. Pete looked across the roofs of several buildings, especially the one at the end of the alleyway. Noticing an individual emerge and take aim at Seamus, Pete fired his pistol multiple times at the individual. The attacker started to run across the flat roof of the building apparently unharmed.

Convinced that any further pursuit would be useless, he shouted to Seamus. "Are you all right?"

Seamus stepped out into the alleyway and looked up. "That bloody fool is going to get it when I catch up with him. I'll pitch in to him like nothing he has experienced before!"

"Meet me down in the front!" Pete yelled.

Thinking this particular room might have been the residence of the attacker, Pete looked around for some clue or indication as to his identity. After a brief investigation that turned up nothing, he departed to meet with Seamus.

By Seamus' expression, Pete could tell when he met him in front of the boardinghouse that he was still fuming over the attack.

"It was bloody close," Seamus angrily said. "At least most of the time during the war, I could see you Johnnies face to face. I am not use to someone trying to ambush me."

"For some reason, I don't believe that Katie is still in the city."

"What makes you say that? We must be close for them to try and put up such an effort to bloody kill us."

"I agree that our attacker was trying to kill us if he could but he was unsuccessful. I believe he was attempting to delay us."

As they walked across the street to the tavern, Seamus added confidently, "Well then Barker, if you're correct, then it appears that we are getting close."

"I believe our attacker is probably the courier Thomas spoke of. He might have had more instructions for him or maybe was just sent to kill him."

Both men returned to the tavern where Hayward was sitting with Thomas Winesmith. Pete and Seamus entered through the back door. No one paid any attention to them. After thirty minutes of excitement, all appeared to have returned to normal to the establishment with its occupants merry with drink.

Seamus noticed that Thomas was still passed out from all the whisky. He immediately went to the bar and summoned the bartender, asking for water. The bartender quietly complied with the request. Seamus walked to the table and quietly poured the cold water over Thomas' head. It quickly aroused him. He surprisingly shook his head and sighed. With his patience exhausted, Seamus grabbed Thomas by his hair, pulling his head from the table. "Who else do you keep in contact with other than Crumbly?"

Feeling somewhat sober, Thomas began once more to harden his attitude against Seamus' questions. "I have no other contacts than Crumbly and Lyles," he replied in a calm tone.

Pete looked around the area where Thomas was sitting knowing the attempted assassination was meant for Thomas. He noticed a bullet lodged in the wooden wall near Thomas' lower body. Angrily, Pete grabbed Thomas' coat collar and pointed to the bullet hole. "Do you see the bullet lodged in here?"

"Yes, I do."

"That was meant for you. Someone wanted to shut you up. They wanted you dead."

Pete pulled the photograph from his shirt and placed it before Thomas.

"Now Winesmith, answer our question and we'll let you go," Seamus impatiently said.

Thomas held his hands in the air and shouted. "All right! All right! Yes, this is Jacob Lyles. That's all I know. Please!"

Content that Thomas was telling them the truth, Pete, Seamus, and Hayward stood to depart the establishment.

Thomas looked up and pleaded, "Please, you are not going to leave me here are you?"

With an angry expression still covering his features, Seamus replied. "We are finished with you. As far as I am concerned, the buzzards can have your carcass."

Once they boarded the carriage, Pete knew they must leave for Loudoun County without delay. Maybe, Katie's abductors were unable to gain much of a head start on them. Quite possibly, whoever abducted her was caught by surprise and didn't have any plans of departing from the city, but rashly changed them at the last moment. Pete pondered as they departed for the hotel whether to inform Thaddeus of all that had taken place or not.

Chapter 50

It was late in the evening as Seamus, Pete, and Hayward arrived at the entrance of the Willard Hotel. Even at this hour, the hotel was still doing a bustling business with people coming and going from the Washington establishment. Immediately, Pete noticed a young attractive lady that resembled Katie departing with a gentleman from the entranceway. Her appearance in dress and demeanor reminded him of Katie and caused thoughts to surface within his heart as he gazed at her for the longest time. Time was passing rapidly and there was queasiness in his stomach. He was concerned that Katie's abductors might harm her or even kill her before Seamus and he found where they were keeping her.

Seamus was standing on the walkway. He curiously looked up at Pete watching the young lady. "Barker!" he shouted.

Pete didn't answer and Seamus called out again. "Barker, come on, let's go!"

Pete quietly looked at Seamus and stepped from the carriage. Walking toward the direction of the front entrance to the hotel, he noticed some of the patrons looking over his unfavorable appearance. Emotions of unworthiness began to surface much as they did before the fighting at Crampton's Gap in September of 1862. During that time, he had felt as though he had accomplished little in his life and had little to show for his efforts. In many aspects, he was no better off then or now. Only at that time, he perceived Katie's feelings for him. Now with her disappearance and the alarming revelations he heard from the mouth of Bradley Langsten and the sword-stabbing words of Robert Bateman, his heart continued to be pierced with distrust. Thus far this evening, he thought, the only thing that kept him going was his Southern pride much as it did during the war and discovering the truth from Katie's lips. Or was his quest now to renew her love for him?

Pete's thoughts returned to reality as he listened to Seamus ask Hayward to return the carriage and horses to the stable from where he rented them.

Seamus looked at Pete's troubled expression. "Barker, are you all right?"

"Sure… sure, everything is fine."

"I want you to come with me while I speak with my father. And then afterwards, we will have to figure out what we're going to do next."

"I'll tell you what we must do next. As soon as we can acquire some horses, we have to leave for Loudoun County. During the war there were many sympathizers that were active in the Confederate underground. I know a few. Hopefully they'll be helpful."

Seamus nodded in agreement as the two turned and walked through the hotel entranceway. Once Pete walked into the lobby, he observed the most distinguished in Washington society mingling, laughing, and enjoying intelligent conversation over a drink of mint julep or brandy. They carried on their life as if they didn't have a care in the world. It wasn't until he walked over to a blue sofa and overheard several middle-aged businessmen speaking and gloating about the money that they had made off of the civil war, manufacturing cannon tubes for the Union army, that Pete's wrath began to surface. He thought of the thousands of Confederate soldiers that had been wounded and killed by such instruments of death. He paused and continued to listen.

Seamus looked around and noticed Pete standing near the sofa with the two men. He returned and noticed the angry expression covering Pete's features. Listening to the two men speak of their success, Seamus grabbed Pete by the coat sleeve. "Come on Barker, it's not worth it. Besides, I don't know how I would get you out of any more trouble.

"It just angers me how anyone can boast over how they have profit from this war when it cost so many men their lives. They speak as though a rebel life was of no value. Money isn't everything in this world."

"Well Barker, you people did start the whole rebellion. What were we suppose to do? Just allow you good Southerners to do anything that you wanted?"

"You Yankees should have kept your nose out of Southern affairs and allowed us to determine what was best for us."

Pete was ready to continue the verbal confrontation. Seamus held his hands up. "Barker, this isn't the time nor place to discuss this."

The altercation had attracted the attention of the two businessmen as well as several gentlemen and ladies standing nearby. One of the gentlemen placed a brandy to his mouth with an expression of profound disagreement. Pete coldly stared at him. Seamus grabbed Pete gently by the coat sleeve and nodded for him to follow. Pete quietly complied.

Once at Thaddeus' room, Seamus knocked once. Almost immediately, Thaddeus opened the door. Seamus noticed the worried, tired expression that covered his father's face as he entered the room.

"Is there any word?" Thaddeus asked. "Have you uncovered anything that would help us to locate Katherine?"

Seamus sat on the sofa and raised his hands. "There are some things to go on but not much."

Impatiently Thaddeus raced across the room. "Well Lad, come on. What did you bloody find out?"

"After we left you, Barker's John Henry informed us that the hotel clerk, Arnold Crumbly, had sent a message to Mr. Winesmith; the same clerk that you and I both had the pleasure of confronting. Barker and I went to Crumbly's house only to find him dead."

"Dead! What in the world happened?"

Pete approached. "Apparently he was murdered."

Thaddeus turned and looked surprisingly at Pete. "How do you bloody know that?"

"You assume it when someone has had their throat slashed."

Seamus took a deep sigh and continued with patience. "While Barker and I were there, we found a ciphered message and a photograph of Crumbly and another unidentifiable young man." Seamus continued with confidence, "These two are apparently left over from the Greenhow spy ring that operated here in the city during the war. Although we do have one stroke of luck with us and that is, there might be the possibility that Barker knows the location."

"I believe that it's in Loudoun County. The homestead looks like a place where I hid at times during the war when I rode with Colonel Mosby," Pete added.

"I see," Thaddeus interrupted. "Then there has been some progress made?"

"Just some," Seamus replied as he lit his cigar. "After we left Crumbly's residence, we went to the War Department and abducted Mr. Winesmith and took him to the Southside of town."

Thaddeus threw his hands into the air. "I don't believe what I am bloody hearing. You mean to tell me that Barker and you bloody kidnapped an official of the United States Government? And on top of it from my friend Edwin Stanton's office." Thaddeus began to pace rapidly in front of the sofa screaming. "How in the bloody name! How could you two do this to me? "

"Yes, that is exactly what we did after Winesmith left the building. But you must as you say, bloody understand that it was most profitable for us. There wasn't any other choice, and he's not going to remember a whole lot tomorrow anyway," Pete answered.

Thaddeus looked angrily at Pete and then at Seamus. "How in the world will I explain all this to Edwin? How does all this play into Katie's disappearance?"

Finally losing his patience, Seamus angrily replied, "We have discovered after a serious confrontation that almost cost me my bloody life that Winesmith relayed messages through a courier to a Colonel L."

Thaddeus was puzzled. "Who in the bloody world is L?'

Pete answered. "During the war nobody working secretly usually used their real name. So, if we find out who L is, then in all probability we'll find Katie."

Thaddeus paused and then with a somber expression, he quietly nodded his head in agreement. "Then she was kidnapped by rogue agents of the former Confederacy."

Pete answered as he handed Thaddeus his water. "Most likely."

"Then everything that Katherine said in Boston in front of Chief Connor and myself must have been true."

"What did she say?" Pete swiftly asked.

Seamus took a puff of the cigar, blowing the smoke into the air. He stood and interrupted Pete. "Apparently the police know nothing."

"No, they are at a dead end in their investigation. It is as though Katie has disappeared from the face of the earth. None of the police over there bloody impresses me as to what they're doing. I was thinking about asking Colonel Baker for help," Thaddeus said.

Seamus rubbed his hand across his mouth. He looked at Pete. "What do you think Barker?"

Pete pondered before answering. He believed that the least amount of people looking for Katie the better. His reasoning was if the scoundrels who abducted her were cornered or rushed then they might become desperate and kill her out of spite. He cautiously replied using a good and reasonable conclusion though deceiving Seamus and Thaddeus to protect his own fears. "I disagree because Baker's face was all over the newspaper after Lincoln was assassinated and he headed the pursuit of Booth. I don't believe the person that we are dealing with necessarily knows us. Though I could be wrong."

"Tomorrow, I feel that you should return home and comfort mother. She must be terribly worried with all this," Seamus said.

"No, I can't until we find Katherine."

"Father, tomorrow at dawn, Barker and I are going to leave for Loudoun County."

"Yes, once Winesmith discovers where he is at and what he may have said, he may attempt to make things unpleasant for us by lying and deceiving Colonel Langsten and the Provost Marshall's office. In other words, he'll try to get even either by stalling us or to see us taken completely out of the picture by having us tossed in jail. If that happens, then we'll never find Katie. We must act quickly and stay ahead of the authorities," Pete added.

Thaddeus turned away from Seamus and Pete and walked over to the window, glancing out into the street. He turned and took a deep sigh. "I see. I guess you leave me no other choice."

"You have to get out of danger. They may come after you." Pete paused waiting for an answer that didn't come. He lost patience and continued in a whispering voice as he picked his hat up from the chair. "Well, I must leave.

"Where will you stay tonight?" Seamus asked Pete as he approached.

Pete shrugged his shoulders. "I don't know. I don't have the money that's required for accommodations."

"I'll see that you have a room. Besides, it's pouring out there."

* * * *

As the two men departed the room and were walking through the hallway to the lobby on the first floor, Seamus cleared his throat. He set aside his pride. "I want to thank you for saving my life tonight. If you hadn't fired when you did then that assassin would have had a clear shot at me. I might not have been walking down this hallway with you or had the chance to see my father again."

"I assume that you would have done the same for me."

"That's not the point."

"Then what is?"

Seamus paused, opened his heart and did something that he rarely did and that was revealing his true emotions. "For the last several weeks, I've given Katie and you a very difficult time. I have accused you and degraded you in every attempt to inflame feelings of animosity, and I've wanted to destroy your relationship with my sister; though more so to personally devastate you beyond measure. And to be honest, I don't know why... other than you were a rebel, costing many of my friends their lives and their families much sorrow. Your views I am sure, even today, are still the same as they were before this rebellion began and will probably never change."

Pete was quiet as Seamus continued to speak earnestly. "In all honesty, I have found very little that I can say that I like about you or that we have in common. Should I continue this war of animosity? The answer is no. I have failed in all my attempts and find it useless. It won't change how Katie feels. I guess I have attempted to pour out my frustrations and anger over the war and the pain and anguish that it's caused me. It's not an easy thing you know, to see a comrade caught between the lines with you, mortally wounded and in pain. Suddenly, without warning, he pulls his jack-knife from his pocket and cuts his throat and dies to relieve his anguish." Shaking his head with a tear dropping from his cheeks, he continued in a quivering tone. "True... you fought for what you believed in and so did I. But it's going to take sometime to heal the wounds between us."

Seamus turned around and put out the cigar he was holding, and returned his attention to Pete. He continued. "Over these last couple of days I have learned by being with you that in many ways you are no different than me. And you're not the evil person that I envisioned you to be. It's just that our social views are not the same and probably never will be in spite of Negro independence. After this is all over, I'll promote vigorously their equality as a people and will do everything in my power to promote their success." Seamus was hesitant, pondering as if to continue expressing his emotions. After fighting with his pride and digging deep within his heart, he said in a tone of humbleness, "What you did for me this evening says a lot for your character and style of person. I am grateful to you for saving my life and I guess having a second chance at it. And again for your intervention, I am grateful. As a token of my appreciation, I will not require you to pay off your debt on Shenandoah to me." He continued in a more serious and hardened tone, "As for Katie, I still hope that she doesn't want to marry you and have your children. They can never succeed living in the South. It's my desire that she'll return home to Boston once we find her."

"As Katie use to tell me, she is a big girl. If she wants to marry me and live in Harpers Ferry and raise our children then that's up to her. You can't stand there with an open conscious and tell me that you would have nothing to do with her nor her children. And besides Seamus, you might be worrying over something that might not happen anyway. Remember, Katie and I didn't depart on the best terms." Pete placed his old brown hat from the war on his head and continued in an audacious manner. "I am only here to help you find her. That's all. And on behalf of my family, I would like to thank you for your financial generosity concerning Shenandoah. Once we are on our feet again, I will still repay you with interest."

"We'll speak of it later. For now, let's get you a room."

Silently Pete walked with Seamus down the stairway toward the lobby area. His mind was on Katie and the thought that they might not be able to reconcile their differences. There were too many questions that needed to be answered concerning the mysterious life that she may have led, and her actions toward Robert Bateman. Pete's mind was troubled with despair and perplexity over these issues. For now though, he knew they must get out of the city at first light or possibly face arrest from the Washington authorities. Now more then before, Pete was sure they would have to move with speed since they possessed important information that might close the gap in Katie's disappearance.

Chapter 51

Over seven hours had passed since Pete, Seamus, and Hayward trotted down Maryland Avenue and crossed the Long Bridge into Alexandria, Virginia. The three men had covered 25-miles, traveling slowly through a heavy fog and in damp, dreary, and cool conditions. Most of the time, the three-men remained silent in thoughts and tried to stay warm with the drizzle falling steadily upon them.

Often during the journey, Pete gave thought to Katie. He didn't know what the outcome would be concerning their relationship or what the future if any would hold for them. Regardless of what Katie might or might not have been involved in during the war, he knew he still had feelings for her. Over the last five years, she had made a remarkable impression on him. She was far from being conservative like most Virginia women. On more than one occasion, her aggressiveness had gotten her into trouble with his family. Her love for a challenge was unquestionable. Teaching at the Catholic School and coming from the North caused her to be solid in her voice of equality for all. Yet, she was a lady that possessed deep emotions, and openly showed her affections. Even if they didn't reunite in their relationship, he knew he had learned many lessons of life from her.

Pete's anger began to build within as he pondered on the conditions and emotional hardship that she might be placed in. He knew Katie all too well. With the hardships of the war and living at Shenandoah over the last five months, if she was still alive, could she endure? He had to find her before it was too late.

Again, Pete thought about the identity of Colonel L. Over the quiet hours in the saddle, his mind shuffled over many names of possible individuals that he knew were involved in underground activity during the war. Who out of those names might be responsible or have some knowledge. Everything that surfaced in his mind over this issue led back to Robert Archibald. The reason was because of his many contacts, unchallenged trust, and competency within the Confederate underground. Pete and Robert had developed great respect and trust for each other while he rode with Mosby's battalion. Pete was confident this would be a beginning. The only question was how would he deceive Robert to gain information of Katie's possible presence.

Pete's thoughts were interrupted at the sound of horse hooves. He held up his right hand and gestured for the threesome to pause. Quietly, Pete listened and attempted to determine which direction the horses were taking. Pete turned and witnessed the troubled expression covering Hayward's face and the fire glowing in Seamus' eyes. Pete pointed to some brush near his left and they led their horses into a small ravine. The visibility from the thick fog behind some pine trees gave the three men ample cover.

Once the two riders galloped by, Pete turned to Seamus. "We must stay off the main roads and cross over fields."

"Why's should we's do that?" Hayward asked in a troubled tone.

"What difference does it make?" Seamus added abruptly.

Pete answered confidently. "The authorities could be after us. Maybe Winesmith blew his temper after revealing to us what we wanted to know."

Seamus shook his head in agreement. "You have a point."

For another ten minutes, the three horsemen headed in a southwesterly direction along what appeared to be a rugged, stony farmer's road. The sunken lane appeared to be unused. It was beginning to get dark. They continued on until they came to a thick pine forest. After proceeding slowly among the trees, they finally noticed an opening. Pete turned to Seamus. "Wait here."

Pete rode his horse several hundred yards and paused. Looking ahead, he noticed the cupola and chimneys on the roof of the brick structure called Fairfax Court House. The town had been of strategic importance during the war because of its road connections with Washington City and northern Virginia.

Cautiously, Pete proceeded at a slow pace until he came to the square. He looked around. The village of a few homes appeared lifeless. From the chimneys of several dwellings he noticed the smoke rising toward the sky and the flickering candlelight in the windows. He rode along the street passed a church until he found the stable area. Before dismounting, he looked around and still no one appeared to challenge him. He dismounted and pulled his pistol from its holster and forced open the stable door. Pete knew they needed fresh horses. If they had to attempt to outrun any of their potential pursuers, then jaded horses would be as good as having nothing.

Pete forced the stable door. Again, he cautiously looked around to see if anyone had detected him. After entering the structure, he lit a lantern hanging from one of the stable stalls. Pete noticed seven healthy looking mares and geldings. He removed his saddle and quickly placed it on the back of one of the younger mares. Once the straps were secure, he placed bridles with rope on two of the other mares and led them slowly from the barn. Departing the village by a different route, Pete found Hayward and Seamus within a short distance of the courthouse near some trees.

Seamus looked surprisingly at Pete. "Barker, what do you have here?"

"Fresh mounts." Pete glanced at Seamus as he adjusted the bridle. He continued in a calm tone. "These horses of ours are too lame. If by chance we are chased by the authorities, then we may not get away."

Hayward nodded his head in agreement. "I'se agree. Dey's might jist be too hard on dis old black man. And I'se is too old to stay in jail."

Once everyone exchanged horses and was ready, the threesome rode into the town square by the courthouse building and headed in a westerly direction toward the Archibald homestead.

* * * *

The fog continued to cover the area impairing the party's progress. The area looked somewhat familiar to Pete from riding with Mosby's battalion. He guessed they were in the vicinity of Germantown. The Archibald homestead would be the first farm along the road before entering the village. When they were close to the Archibald homestead, Pete paused. "I feel that I must go alone from here."

Seamus was cautious, distrustful, and answered in a suspicious voice, "No you don't Barker. At this point, you're not going anywhere without me. You made a promise. Remember?"

"No McBride, I don't think you understand," Pete angrily answered as he turned to look. "If we all go riding in there, Archibald will become suspicious. And if that happens and he knows something, then don't you think it might be difficult trying to get information out of him? I really don't want to take the course that we did in Washington City with Winesmith. Archibald is smart and like I said earlier, he knows me. It can only be this way."

Seamus deeply sighed. Pete noticed the disturbing expression covering his face. Gesturing for one of Seamus' cigars, Pete said, "Give me one of those."

"But you don't smoke."

"I do tonight."

Seamus reached into his pocket and handed Pete a cigar. Pete took a match and struck it against his boot. "You and Hayward need to stay out of sight. Once I am satisfied with the information I obtain then I'll meet you here but not until then. And I said wait, do you hear me!"

A displeased expression covered Seamus' features as he steadied his nervous horse. "Don't make it too long Barker or we're coming to get you. You have an hour."

"Look McBride, we have to exercise some patience in this ordeal. Whatever I am fortunate enough to find out will benefit us. I don't need you to come busting into this man's house and destroying any chance of finding Katie. Remember, this is not about you and me. This is about her!"

"I'se will keep him quiet," Hayward calmly added.

"I don't need some John Henry telling me what to do," Seamus angrily fired back.

It was beginning to drizzle again. Pete threw his arm into the air in frustration. He snapped at Seamus, "And you Yankees call yourself the great emancipator. That John Henry as you call him is my best friend. I trust him more then I do any white man...even my brother. And by the way, his name is Hayward."

Both men stared at each other. Finally, Pete turned his horse around and slowly headed for the Archibald homestead.

*　*　*　*

It was a short ride of about a mile to the Archibald homestead. As Pete found their farm, he rode along the long dirt lane still smoking the cigar. The surroundings of what he could see reminded him of Shenandoah. The tall oak trees crowning both sides of the lane and the stone wall barn to his right appeared to be almost a copy of the one the family owned that was destroyed.

A few whitewashed buildings stood near a fence in the barnyard. The only difference was some trenches had been constructed by either blue or gray during the war.

Pete gave thought to the explanation for his appearance at the Archibald home this late in the evening. He knew that it must be something to do with his brother Charles. If Robert still had any connections with the existing Confederate underground, he would have some knowledge of Charles' whereabouts.

After putting his horse into a trot, he noticed to his front the dim light glowing from the front window. As Pete brought his horse to a halt, an old spotted hound ran up to him from the front porch barking loudly. Once Pete dismounted, he rubbed the animal's back and then walked toward the house.

Pete stepped onto the porch and knocked several times on the door before anyone answered. The door was opened far enough that Pete could see a shotgun pointed in his direction. A low-solemn male voice spoke. "Who are you and what do you want?"

Pete held his hand away from his coat where his pistol was concealed. He slowly answered, "It's me... Pete Barker from Jefferson County. You know me from the war. I rode with Colonel Mosby."

The light from the lantern was shined up close in Pete's face for identification. "Enter."

It felt good to Pete to walk into a home with a warm fireplace blazing. As the wood crackled in the background, Robert again looked closely at Pete's shambled appearance. "It is you Pete. It's been a long time. I heard that you were captured just before the fight around Winchester in the autumn of 1864."

Pete didn't know if Robert really knew of his defection from the army or if he was trying to entrap him. Pete decided to give him half-truth and half-lie. "The truth is, I actually deserted to see if my mother and family were all right. I previously told you, the Yankees burned our home and everything of value. I was worried... concerned for my family's welfare... so after delivering a dispatch to General Early in Winchester, I returned home to Harpers Ferry. While there, the Yankees captured and arrested me where I served a short duration on the Island Prison and then was shipped to Point Lookout, Maryland where I stayed until the end of the war."

Robert beckoned Pete to enter the parlor. Pete didn't sit on the old worn sofa; he walked to the fireplace where it was warm. Robert was quiet as he followed. As Pete rubbed his cold hands together, Robert picked some wood from the box beside the fireplace and stoked the fire with an iron. After the fire was blazing, Robert lit his pipe. "Well Pete, what brings you to these parts this late on a freezing night?"

Pete blew against his hands and continued to rub them looking at the dancing flames. Again, he replied confidently. "I am looking for my brother Charles."

"And you think he is here?"

Pete answered in an innocent tone as he looked into Robert's piercing blue eyes. "No, not really. I was hoping since I stayed with you various times when I rode with Colonel Mosby that maybe you might have heard or had some idea were he might be. With a worried wife and a troubled daughter, it is important for the family to find him"

"I see." Robert turned away, rubbing his clean-shaven face. He placed his hand on the wooden mantel and looked down at the fire and quietly shook his head in the negative. Pete was disappointed. He felt maybe Robert had some word or clue as to Charles' whereabouts.

Robert looked up from the fire. He turned his attention to Pete. "Quite honestly Pete, I haven't had part in anything since the end of the war. As it was, I darn nearly got caught several times in April just before Lincoln got shot. I knew that Mosby had some kind of secret thing going on when they brought a fella by the name of Harney here to stay for a short spell. He told me, he was an expert with explosives. They were tryin' to smuggle him into Washington City. The Yankees came here one night on patrol. Before I could put him under cover in the barn like I use to do you, they entered the house just as Edna took him through the back door. It was close, but we hid him." Robert walked to the center of the room and turned. "After he left, we didn't do anything like that again. Of course we didn't know that Lee had already surrendered. But I don't think that would have made things any easier on us if the Yankees caught him here. When I think back on that time, the Yankees were probably lookin' for him."

"I see."

Robert scratched his baldhead. "I heard through the underground that your brother had escaped and wasn't captured with Jeff Davis. I heard rumor that he's here somewhere in these parts, but I don't know where or I'd tell you."

Pete didn't know whether to believe Robert or not. He always knew the man to be solid and firm with his word. Tonight he appeared to be nervous and unsure of himself. Something was wrong. He walked across the floor and removed his coat placing it on a wooden chair in the corner. He turned and noticed that Robert was watching his every move.

Robert's wife, Edna walked into the room. " Pete, Pete Barker."

"Miss Edna," Pete said as he embraced her, "you are just as nice to me as when I stayed here with you. I've never forgotten your smile that would fill any room once you entered."

"I always thought of you as my own," she said compassionately. Edna turned and said to her husband in a scolding tone, "Robert, why didn't you tell me he was here?" Pete noticed the appearance of a fire glowing from her gray eyes as she angrily continued, "Shame on you."

Robert attempted to answer, but his wife ignored him. "My poor boy, when was the last time that you had something hot to eat?"

"It's been some time."

"Well, we'll take care of that right now. Come here and sit down."

Edna turned and walked from the room toward the back door to the kitchen house attached to the main structure. Robert walked over to the table in the small dining area. Pete was seated and poured the coffee that had been prepared and setting on the table. He took a sip. It tasted good. He looked at Robert and noticed his eyes appeared troubled. Within a few minutes, Edna carried in a plate of eggs and country ham and placed it before Pete. He thanked her and turned his attention again to Robert. "You appear to be troubled this evening. Is everything all right?"

"Nothin' is the matter."

"We know each other well enough that there is some trust between us." Pete continued in a compassionate voice. "Is it money?"

Robert didn't answer or even look at Pete as he spoke. Pete wondered if it was some kind of guilt or embarrassment. He continued to investigate. "If it is, I have a little that you can have."

Robert held up his hands pleading. "No, nothin' is the matter. My mind is pressin' on some things. Nothin' to do with you."

Pete didn't press the issue although his suspicions were still aroused. He quickly second guessed his decision of making the inquiry and hoped that it wouldn't be costly. He decided he would ask Robert if he had heard of any information that might help him in finding Katie and the possible identity of who might be behind this whole abduction scheme.

"There is another reason why I am here."

"What's that?"

"I am looking for a young girl with auburn or red hair. She is medium height with green eyes, and most attractive. She is in all probability traveling with one, maybe two men. I am not sure. But I must find her as soon as possible."

"Why? Were you married to her and she run away?"

"No, quite honestly, her life might be in trouble."

"No, there hasn't been anyone fittin' that description. Matter of fact, no one has been through here in days that I'd say is a stranger."

Pete didn't believe what Robert was saying to him. For one thing, he answered too quickly. This was uncharacteristic of the Robert Archibald that he knew during the war. Robert never answered any questions without giving thought to it first and maybe asking a question in return. His excuse was that this was a lesson of the Good Book. The real reason was that he was afraid of being judged by others.

After overhearing the conversation, Edna walked into the room. She curiously asked Pete, "Did I hear you say something about a young girl with red hair?"

"Yes, I did."

A troubled expression appeared on Edna's face as she answered in a confident tone. "Late yesterday evening about this time…"

Robert jumped from his seat and loudly interrupted. "Woman, now shut up before you get us into trouble."

Edna began to weep as Pete slowly stood. "What is going on here?"

He noticed a teary and frightful expression on Edna's features as the clicking of a pistol's hammer was cocked to fire. Pete froze as he felt the barrel against the back of his head. "Barker," a graveled voice demanded, "sit down."

Pete didn't attempt to turn his head and identify his assailant. Instead, he cautiously complied with the command. Noticing the terrified look in Robert's eyes, Pete knew he'd have to look for an opportunity to overcome his adversary, at least to acquire Robert and Edna's freedom. He suspected the scoundrel was Jacob Lyles. Many thoughts raced through his mind. Hayward and Seamus, almost a mile away, wouldn't be able to lend assistance. Lyles wouldn't be someone that Pete could bargain with. His first thoughts, apparently Lyles followed him from Washington with the intentions of killing him. But as Pete quickly summed up the opportunities that Lyles had throughout the day with the cover of fog, he knew the villain could have ambushed them on more then one occasion when they rode through some of the wooded areas along the way to Fairfax Court House.

Pete was ordered to place his hands on the table by the intruder. "What do you want Lyles?"

"So you know my name?"

"Yes, I know who you are." Pete began to turn his head to look at Jacob.

"Keep your eyes forward, I want you to see something," Jacob commanded.

Pete turned and a single shot was fired. Edna screamed and held her hands to her mouth crying. Blood poured rapidly from Robert's head as he fell from the chair to the floor. Something had to be done. Compulsively, Pete quickly jumped to his feet to intervene knowing that Jacob would commit the same act toward Edna. As he did, he felt severe pain from the metal barrel of the weapon striking the side of his head. He fell on the floor losing consciousness with the last sound being another gunshot.

Chapter 52

Several hours had gone by. There wasn't any word from Pete nor had he returned. Seamus was concerned. He quietly rose from the log that Hayward and he had been sharing in a pine forest. Without the advantage of a fire to keep warm, the temperature was plummeting, causing difficulty from the cold. Seamus rubbed his hands together. He looked at Hayward staring aimlessly at the ground. He appeared not to be concerned about the coldness that filled the nighttime air.

After walking over and checking on the horses, Seamus returned to find Hayward still looking at the ground. Seamus softly said in a troubled tone, "Hey... Hayward... I feel that something has gone wrong."

At first Hayward didn't appear as if he heard Seamus. Finally, Hayward looked up slowly. "I'se know. That boy has a gonna and gotten himself in trouble."

"Or he has run off."

Fire filled Hayward's eyes. "Mr. Pete is a man of his word. Something has happen!" Hayward rose from the log and continued, "I'se knows, I'se feels it in my soul. We must find him."

Seamus stared at Hayward. In a rapid manner, they mounted their horses and headed down the road at a gallop in the direction of the Archibald homestead.

Once they arrived, Seamus noticed the candlelight was barely burning. Seamus looked around and noticed no horses. "Hayward, can you go and see if Barker's horse is in the barn?"

Hayward nodded in agreement and proceeded to the area. Seamus dismounted and quietly climbed the steps with his hand on his pistol. He knocked several times on the door. There wasn't an answer. He placed his hand on the doorknob and pushed gently against the door with the weight of his body. As he slightly jarred it open, he looked around. There wasn't a sound with the exception of the crackling fire. He pulled the pistol from his belt and cocked the hammer. Next, Seamus proceeded into the parlor. He noticed Pete's coat still on the chair. This aroused his suspicion that something had happened. Who would be foolish enough to go out on an evening such as this without any covering unless they were in a hurry? He feared the worst.

Seamus glanced around the room for any additional evidence of Pete's presence. There was nothing. He walked to the dining area where he was shaken. On the floor dead was Edna Archibald with one hand touching her gray hair, the other gave one the impression that she was attempting to reach for her husband who also was lying dead nearby. She had suffered a single bullet to the chest. Seamus thought the husband might have been the first to die.

Seamus heard a sound coming from the back door. He pointed his pistol in the direction of the kitchen. He patiently waited. Hayward walked into the room and paused. Seamus noticed the anguish that covered Hayward's facial features when he saw the two dead bodies. He watched as Hayward knelt and touched Edna's lifeless body. Hayward stayed in the same position mumbling what sounded like a prayer.

Hayward looked up with tears in his eyes. "Who's is coward enough to kill a woman?"

"I don't know. Is Barker capable of this?"

Hayward jumped to his feet and shouted. "No! No, he's not!"

"Was his horse in the barn?"

"No."

Hayward paced around, still angry with Seamus and at the same time, concerned over Pete's welfare. His intuition directing him, Hayward turned around and looked at the floor where the dead bodies were lying. There, Hayward noticed another small pool of blood not far from where Robert Archibald was lying. He walked over and again knelt down looking around. With careful examination, he noticed some bloodstains on the leg of the table, opposite where Robert must have been seated. Hayward beckoned to Seamus. Seamus knelt beside Hayward who pointed to the table leg.

"Dis is where Mr. Pete was sittin'. Mr. Robert was a sittin' there across the table from him. Some kind of fight happened."

"How do you know that happened?"

Hayward pointed at the chair lying on its side. "The force of the bullet caused dis man to fall backwards. With Mr. Pete, he must have tried to stand. I'se believe that Mr. Pete was hit with something and hit his head fallin' to the floor." Hayward pointed to the bloodstains five feet away, near Robert Archibald's bloody body. "If that was his blood, and he's was dead, he'd been layin' here too. Mr. Pete is a prisoner. He's still alive."

Both men rose from the floor. Seamus lifted his black hat and rubbed his hand through his hair still trying to digest all that happened. He shook his head in agreement with Hayward's observations. Seamus sighed. "Let me get a blanket and we'll bury these people. And then we'll move on."

* * * *

Pete awakened. He was lying against his horse's neck. He had been placed on the mount while still unconscious. He was groggy. His head ached and his vision was blurred. As he attempted to move his hands, they were tied behind his back. He looked around the landscape. He was apparently moving along another rugged and deserted road and was being held captive. There were no familiar landmarks to indicate any difference in his observations. Pete attempted to raise himself up in the saddle. He felt the pain from behind as someone pulled his hair to assist him. Looking to his side, he noticed Jacob Lyles.

"Where are we going?" Pete asked.

Jacob laughed. He struck Pete in his side with the barrel of his pistol and replied sarcastically. "Some place where you're gonna meet your end."

Inconspicuously, Pete attempted to work his hands free but to no avail. The rope was too tight. For now, he would have to play along and see where they were going. "Why did you have to kill the Archibalds?"

"The old man wasn't any use to me any longer."

"So Katie McBride was there with her abductor? And he was helping in this plot?"

"The old man knew nothing until she appeared. He was forced to help."

"By gunpoint and threats I'm sure."

"Yeah Barker, you're right, by gunpoint and threats." Jacob answered as he taunted Pete by laughing. "It makes no difference at this point in the game. I really don't mind telling you. We kept Miss McBride there for the evening while we ate and rested. Then Mr. Pierce and her moved on. Archibald's wife just seen us as innocent comrades of the war that didn't surrender and receive our paroles. She truly believed we were on the run from the Yankees. She played into the whole thing. When Mr. Pierce and Miss McBride left, I returned on the suspicion that you would come after her. And you did. I hid out in the barn and when you arrived, I entered the house from an upstairs window. Archibald was nervous; he knew how the game worked. He knew that I'd be close by to protect our lady. Only his wife was surprised when I entered the room."

"How could you kill unarmed civilians?"

Jacob shook his head in disagreement as he spit some tobacco juice on the ground. He wiped his mouth with his hand and replied in a strong tone. "Come on Barker, who are you foolin'? You know from the war, it's how you get things done. When I rode with Mosby…"

Pete angrily interrupted. "I didn't know something as low as the scum of the earth could have rode with Mosby. I never saw you once."

"Like many, only when I was needed."

Pete rose again and snapped. "Or when it was to your benefit, you scoundrel."

Looking into Jacob's brown eyes, Pete noticed a cold and terrified glare. It reminded him of the appearance of Daniel's eyes the afternoon he arrived in Frederick City to kill Katie and him at the National Hotel. Pete thought of Jacob as a person that possessed a passion to hurt and destroy. The act of violence gave him self-gratitude and pride. Jacob laughed as he cocked the hammer of the pistol.

"Shut up or I'll kill you now!" Jacob screamed.

"If you were going to kill me you piece of scum, you would have done it back there."

"Your day is coming to meet your Maker, and I am going to be the one who will help bring about the event."

"Don't count on it."

Pete laid his head once more against the horse's mane and closed his eyes.

It seemed like time had quickly passed when the horses came to a halt. Without thinking, Pete sat erect in the saddle and attempted to shake the cobwebs from his head. His vision was greatly improved, but his head still ached. He noticed Jacob dismounting. Jacob helped Pete dismount because his hands were still bound behind his back. Jacob cut the binding. Pete's hands were numb from being in the same position for too long. He immediately flexed his wrist and hands to get the blood circulating. He staggered and then touched the side of his face. Pain radiated throughout. After feeling an abnormal sensation, he placed his hand on the side of his cheek. Something felt crusty. Pulling his hand away from his cheek, he noticed the crimson residue from dried blood.

Pete and Jacob had arrived at an antebellum mansion surrounded by trees. Pete gazed around in an attempt to identify the area. After riding with Mosby's battalion during the war, he thought there might be something recognizable of the landscape in this area. But with the foggy conditions, there was little that was identifiable.

Jacob nudged Pete with the barrel of his pistol. "Move Barker."

Pete slowly walked along the pathway to the three-story mansion.

"What are we doing here?" Pete asked.

"Shut up and do as you are told. Understand!"

Pete stumbled as he attempted to ascend the steps of the mansion. Again, Jacob nudged him with his hand and this began to anger Pete. Once at the doorway, Jacob knocked on the wooden door in a type of code of three quick raps, pausing, and then two more. A Negro servant soon opened the door and allowed Pete and Jacob to enter. Pete fell to his knees, semi-conscious.

Pete heard a familiar voice. "You blasted fool, why did you bring him here!"

As Jacob was answering, Pete glanced up and was stunned at the male figure he recognized towering over him. As Pete attempted to stand on his feet, he felt a thrust against his face and once more he lost consciousness.

Chapter 53

The strong southern wind blew against Pete's face. The loud clattering sound of the back door to the barn and the coolness of the early morning hours caused him to awaken for the first time in hours. The brightness of the morning sun shining through the open door caused him to squint and struggle with fully opening his eyes. Pete's arms were tied. His hands were numb. He looked toward the roof of the barn where an iron hoist and heavy rope attached to a wooden beam supported by two wooden columns held him prisoner. It reminded him of someone being hanged by the neck. It was impossible for him to touch the ground because his limbs were hanging at least two foot off the surface. He struggled to break free. The more he attempted, the more the rope cut his skin. He was bound too tight. There was nothing he could do at the moment but wait and hopefully have an opportunity later to fight his way out of the situation.

Pete began to wonder if this event would be the one that would lead to the end of his life. After all, Jacob had sworn the previous evening the act would be fulfilled. It would surely be a miserable and torturous way to die. Pete thought of Hayward and Seamus. Where could they be? Pete knew that Hayward was a skilled tracker but he feared the rain might have washed out his horse's tracks making it difficult for Hayward to follow.

Pete gritted his teeth with anger as he remembered the last recognizable figure before losing consciousness. The identity of the person was William Pierce from Richmond. William had once been a close and trusted friend of the family, especially his brother Charles. It was William who sparked the flames of interest in Charles' heart for the game of politics and political office before the war. He enlisted Charles' help in the campaign for governorship of Virginia in 1856 on behalf of Henry Wise. Then again in 1860, William sought Charles' help for Vice President John Breckinridge's candidacy for President of the United States. William had been like a brother to Charles. Pete had noticed the mutual relationship they enjoyed before the war had slowly deteriorated. Pete recalled one instance when he received a correspondence from Charles before the great invasion of the North in 1863. In that particular letter, Charles had informed Pete of the change in William's demeanor. Charles recalled in the letter that he knew William had felt betrayed and ignored. He always appeared angry and critical of the administration's policies on solving issues with the other Southern governors. One occasion in particular was when Captain Moss, an aide to Confederate President Jefferson Davis, called on Charles at his residence in Richmond. William had naturally attempted to self impose, but the military officer rebuked him and his request was denied. After the incident, William continued to play a role in the Davis government but didn't enjoy the President's favor such as Charles. Quite often, his counsel to the President was limited on many affairs of state. William was not one to follow. He was very obstinate, strongly believing he was a leader. Still, when Davis and his government in April evacuated Richmond, William left the city with them while Charles escaped later with Secretary of War Breckinridge.

Pete struggled to grip the rope in the attempt to relieve the pressure from his exhausted arms and wrist. This was torture he thought. He quickly looked around for something; anything to place his feet on to relieve his body from the physical exertion. Whoever placed him in this situation, left nothing within his reach.

Pete began to ponder on his family in Harpers Ferry. By now, he hoped his mother was recovering without any complications from the bullet wound. Maybe, Caroline and Ann had heard something to give them hope and brighten their life concerning Charles. As he hung by the rope, Pete could identify with Caroline's void in her heart and life. Whether he was willing to admit it or not, life had been difficult without Katie. He wondered if Katie had really been spying during the war. All evidence pointed to the indication that she must have played some part in the game of espionage. He had heard enough spoken on the issue from Seamus and Bradley Longsten. It was now his convictions that she was passing information to the Federals and some Confederate agents wanted to avenge their anger on her.

For Pete, the whole mysterious picture was all coming together. He recalled when Jonathan and he had helped Katie to escape the clutches of prison in Winchester last year. William Pierce had been there and now he believed was in many ways involved with the Confederate Secret Service. Up until now, it never occurred who the identity of Colonel L might be. Now, undoubtedly in his mind, it must be William Pierce. Until last night, Pete had always thought that William had escaped the country and was hiding in the Northern British region. He thought that he was west in Mexico like other soldiers who refused to surrender and politicians who feared imprisonment.

From the very outset of the war, it was William and Charles that made the accusations of Katie's complicity in spying. They believed she only came to Harpers Ferry and acted out the role of a schoolteacher to cover up her true intentions. Two things did make sense to Pete. One was the fact that she was a female and wouldn't be suspected of such impropriety as spying. It was known that many civilians passed information to both Federal and Confederate armies, especially women. The renowned Belle Boyd of Martinsburg was an example in this type of participation. Secondly, it was known that the Federal government placed agents in various strategic areas of the South when the threat of war loomed over the nation. When Katie was confronted about the question of spying by him, she never declared her innocence. Instead, she would answer, "Would it make any difference?" Where was she? He didn't know.

* * * *

In the dimly lit cellar of the mansion, Katie McBride anxiously paced. It was cool, musty, and the smell was offensive to her. The only light was a candle barely flickering. Katie was exhausted after spending the day and night in such a horrendous atmosphere and sitting with little sleep. She was thirsty and hungry but in a greater way, she was angry. The side of her face was sore from the continuous abuse of her captors. In her heart and mind, she wondered if she would ever be free from captivity. The only thing that kept her going was the hope that Pete was searching for her.

Katie recalled last year when she was imprisoned. Pete had come under the disguise of a Confederate officer to escort her back to Richmond. Up until that time for over a year, she was under the impression that Pete was dead. Over and over in her mind during this captivity, Katie relived the evening when she was to be sent to Richmond. A guard appeared and escorted her to Captain Massey's office. Once she entered, there stood Pete waiting. When she first noticed it was Pete, it was all that she could do to withhold her emotions and affections. Would it happen again? For most of the journey to this place, Katie had battled within her heart the terrible guilt of allowing Robert Bateman to kiss her and for giving him the impression that she possessed strong emotions for him. These actions happened more than once she thought. Several occasions occurred at various times during the war with other men. She knew now her reasons behind all that she did.

Katie had her arms crossed trying to stay warm. She paused and looked toward the top of the stairway when the noise of an opening door interrupted her thoughts. She noticed it was Jacob Lyles. He walked part of the way down the stairs and looked coldly at Katie. "Come on little lady, the boss wants to see you."

"You can tell the bloody boss for me that he can freeze in bloody hell. I don't want to see his bloody face. Do you bloody understand?"

Jacob walked down several more steps. "Will I have to beat some sense into your head again, or are you going to listen?"

Katie walked toward the stairway and paused to give Jacob an angry look. He didn't respond. Katie walked around him and he followed. At the top of the stairway, Jacob grabbed her by the arm and quietly pointed her in the direction of the dining area. Katie complied. When she walked into the room, there was seated and glaring at her the most contemptuous and evil individual.

William Pierce stood and smiled as Katie entered. He quietly gestured for her to have a seat next to him. She paused standing by a chair. William walked near her and pulled the chair from the table. Katie looked into his piercing gray eyes. All she could see was an evil aggressiveness, uncanny deception, and hatred. He was far from the individual that she met on the train from Baltimore. At that time, William appeared to be reserved in demeanor, gentlemanly in his behavior, and humble in his actions. She knew over the duration of the war that William was romantically interested in her. What puzzled her was that something drastically changed him. He gave her the impression that he was always angry and deprived from what he was entitled. When she was imprisoned at Winchester, William surprised her when he viciously and physically attacked her, striking her to the floor. She never forgave him for that act.

Katie noticed William was no longer pudgy as he was when she first met him on the train from Baltimore to Harpers Ferry in August of 1860. He had lost considerable weight and was in proportion to his short height.

William took his seat. He rang a bell and a servant entered the room. The servant placed before Katie a plate with over easy eggs and potatoes. He placed the same before William. Once the servant turned, he walked to the server and poured coffee into two cups.

William took a sip of his coffee as Katie sat quietly watching. He placed the cup on the saucer. "Are you not hungry?" When Katie continued to gaze defiantly at him, he chuckled. "I really can appreciate a woman that has a lot of fire about her. And you know what? You beat them all."

"I've never in my 25 years on this earth known such bloody scum and trash of the earth such as you." Katie turned her attention and pointed in the direction of Jacob standing at the doorway. "And that bloody fool too."

William abruptly laid down his fork, wiped his mouth and sat back in the chair. He paused as if in thought gazing the whole time at Katie. "I see that after spending the last 12 hours in the cellar, it hasn't calm you down one bit. You're just as uncooperative as you have been since you left the Willard Hotel."

Katie answered with contempt. "How in the bloody world can you say that I bloody left there on my own free will? You kidnapped me."

Shaking his head in frustration, William quietly ran his hand through his long sandy hair. William looked at Jacob and finally gestured for him to leave their presence knowing his sight inflamed Katie all the more.

"You still haven't told me why you abducted me and why we are here in the middle of nowhere," Katie loudly snapped.

William pushed the plate aside and quietly pulled a cigar from his coat pocket. He stood and lit the tobacco from a candle burning on the table. Again he was seated. "Katie, the time has come to be candid with you. Do you remember last year in Winchester?"

"How could I forget the miserable experience?"

A grin covered William's features. "When I saw you in prison, I told you that I came to see my cousin, Colonel Moore. That was all a lie. The colonel isn't any relation to me whatsoever."

"That doesn't surprise me at all."

William took a puff of his cigar and continued. "I came there because my brother was murdered."

Katie's features were one of astonishment. "I didn't know that you had a brother. When you were at Harpers Ferry, you never spoke once of him."

"No one knew. Not even the Barkers."

"Charles too?"

"Not even Charles."

"Why? Why would you keep something like this a secret unless there was something in his life or yours that you are ashamed of? Or maybe this is all made up like everything else."

"No, I'm not lying. My brother was such an embarrassment to the Pierce family name. He was, let's say a good swindler, one of the best rogues that I know, and a womanizer." William paused and puffed on the cigar again. He continued to speak in a casual manner, all the time gazing coldly at Katie. "He didn't have our class or prestige, but he was a flamboyant, handsome type of lad. Still, you might say he was the black sheep of the family. So, I won't beat around the bush anymore." William paused and looked at Katie for a reaction. Her features appeared mystified. He continued, "My brother was an agent with the Confederate underground."

"He was spying?"

"Yeah, just like you."

Katie shook her head in denial as William continued. "I received word from Colonel Moore that my brother had returned from Washington City after receiving valuable information from one of our associates, a clerk in the War Department by the name of Mr. Winesmith."

Katie remained silent. She knew Thomas Winesmith, only she didn't know that he had been associated with the Confederate underground. Katie had met him through Bradley Langsten while at Washington's Fourth of July celebrations at Lafayette Square in 1861. She listened as William continued.

"See, my brother had kept in contact periodically over the late spring months of 1864 with Mr. Winesmith. And it was because of the information he received from Winesmith that he knew the identity of the person who was keeping Federal authorities abreast of information pertaining to Confederate sympathizers and the families that were helping to shelter and supply our men with information in their attempts to disrupt the B & O Railroad. Once he returned to Winchester, he shared the identity of the individual with Colonel Moore."

"And you came to the conclusion that it was me?"

William looked away from Katie and sighed. He turned once more and continued. "My brother was in Harpers Ferry for two reasons. The first was to gain all of the valuable information that he could garnish concerning General Sheridan's intentions for moving against General Early's forces. And yes, my brother was watching you and posing as a sutler under an assumed identity who had traveled to the Ferry to sell his goods to soldiers. After gaining information on you, he was evicted from the Provost Marshall's district for selling whiskey to the troops." William began to chuckle as he took another puff of his cigar. He became quickly composed and continued. "My brother was always blessed with a good memory for details. He gave a vivid description of you to Colonel Moore. That's why he was murdered in his hotel room at the Taylor Hotel on Loudoun Street the night before your arrest. Once Colonel Moore informed me of his death, he brought to my attention the conversation that my brother and him had shared earlier that same evening. Once he gave your description, I knew that it was you."

"That doesn't mean a thing."

Answering with swiftness, William pointed and answered in a loud and forceful tone, "Oh yes it does. The colonel recalled the description of you on your pass. Forged of course. He knew you were in the city." William paused waiting for a reaction from Katie. She remained composed and silent. "With Harpers Ferry in the hands of the Federals at this time, I want you to tell me how you got out of the place. And I want to know how you were able to cross enemy lines."

Katie remained silent.

"Or did you use Mrs. McDonald's sister's sickness as an excuse to secure the passes for you all?"

Katie's expression turned to fear. She was defensive in her tone. "Polly McDonald had been ill. Our journey to Winchester was permissible. I had nothing to do with your brother's death."

"His death might have been for the best," he said in a whisper.

"William, what do you mean?"

William raised his head and looked at Katie. "My brother was all too fond of money and I guess so was I. When it appeared to me that Charles had the promise of a brighter and more prosperous political future with a new Confederate nation, then I must admit that I became envious. I felt I was being pushed to the side and rejected. My first thoughts were that someone had found out about my brother Arlen. Arlen had already been greatly involved in underground activity. But he was too greedy. A female agent working for the Pinkerton Agency somehow found out about my brother's position with the Confederate spy network. She was young and attractive such as you. She used her deceptive ways...played innocent...and used seductive words to persuade him to spy for the Federals."

Katie quickly interrupted. "He was playing both sides of the war?" When William didn't answer, then Katie challenged him. "And you knew what he was doing?"

Reluctantly, William shook his head in agreement. "Yes, you are correct. I knew and I tried to convince him otherwise but he'd laugh and say now was the time to make his money. Whoever had the money for his services, those would be the ones he'd work for." In a regretful manner, William murmured. "And I received my share to keep quiet."

"That doesn't surprise me at all. But, if I may ask, how does this all involve me?"

"Like I said earlier, Arlen knew you were the one who had supplied the names of certain individuals who were supplying and sheltering our raiders in the area. To further back up my accusations, Daniel had seen you at General Howe's headquarters in Harpers Ferry earlier in the evening before the Barker estate was destroyed."

"It is all an accusation. It was just a strange coincidence that I was there."

"My brother was able to do in a short period of time what no other Confederate agent had been able to accomplish."

"And?"

"And that was to discover the identity of Miss Lucy Williams. We tried using all means and contacts at our disposal, but we always came up empty because your trail suddenly ended. My hat is off to you because you were the master spy." He continued in a calm manner. "Somehow once you found out about my brother knowing your identity, you plotted to kill him."

Katie jumped from her seat. "Oh William. That's nonsense. You know I am not a spy. Besides, do I look like someone who would take another life?"

A wild glare appeared in William's eyes as he spoke in a pitched tone. "My brother knew you were the enemy on the evening that you killed him. You allowed him to have his way with you. When he didn't talk, then you maliciously killed him while he was sleeping."

Unable to control her composure, Katie angrily fire back. "Yes William you are bloody right. I was there in his bloody hotel room with him, but I didn't allow him to have his bloody way with me nor did I kill him."

Katie walked over to the window and glanced in the direction of the dirt lane trying to compose her temper. She knew William had psychologically trapped her by causing her to burst in anger.

With a deep sigh and her emotions repressed, she turned and continued in a calm tone. "What's the use?" Katie paused. Tears flowed down her cheeks. She continued in a calm tone. "Fortunately, I eluded capture quite often. To this day, I don't know how I managed it. And yes, your brother knew I was the one responsible for the destruction of Shenandoah, and the other homes that were destroyed by fire in the area. You were correct. It was me, who supplied the information just like I did over the last four years. With the knowledge that Arlen was in Winchester, and him knowing that I was an agent, I went to his room, hoping to convince him and even pay him money to remain silent about my involvement in these affairs. He wouldn't have anything to do with it. He was drinking too heavily and he laughed at me. When I couldn't reason with him, I angrily left his room. He was still alive. I swear."

"Katie McBride, you're the scum of the earth, not I."

Katie walked over to her chair and placed both hands on it. Her feelings were greatly bruised. She bowed her head and then raised and looked at William. "When I came to Harpers Ferry, I didn't plan for things to happen as they did, especially with Pete and his family. Like everyone else, I hoped that war would pass and there would be some kind of a compromise. But it didn't happen. For Katie McBride didn't plan on falling in love with someone that would eventually be her enemy and having a friend in Caroline who was just like a sister. What I did, I did with the hopes that the war would come to an end quickly and that Pete and Seamus would be spared the destiny with death. Overall that was my main goal for doing what I did. To me life is more important than anything else, not the material things that we tend to hold to and allow to control us."

Katie approached William and continued to speak. "Do I regret everything? Yes. Every time I look at Pete and see how he suffers and struggles with trying to build something that I helped to destroy in the first place. I get sick to my stomach. Do I enjoy living a lie about my part in this war? The answer is no. Afterward, I attempted to gain the favor of my father in helping the Barkers in their quest of holding onto their property. He as well as Secretary Stanton denied me. Maybe, I should have admitted to my father my wrongs. Maybe it would have been different and Pete and I wouldn't be in this situation we are now facing."

Katie walked back toward the window and paused. Once more she turned around. "If Pete finds out, there will never be anything between us again."

William chuckled. "You regret nothing. Maybe I should let Jacob go ahead and shoot you now so that he will have the opportunity and not Pete."

"Enough with your bloody sarcasm. Haven't we all paid the bloody price for our convictions?"

Katie waited for an answer from William. He didn't respond. She knew that she would probably never see her family again. At least her conscience was clear. She knew William was going to kill her. Now it was only a matter of time.

Chapter 54

William gazed at Jacob leaving the dining room with Katie, escorting her once more to the cellar. William was frustrated. He walked toward the window and paused, tossing his cigar furiously at the server. The pressure of losing his financial assets, including his estate, the tension of alluding Federal authorities, and most importantly, the thought of Katie taking his brother's life were causing his anger to greatly fester. She must be dealt with once and for all, he thought. William decided to kill Katie and Pete at the same time this evening after sunset. Jacob would be the one who would carry out the execution. It would be Pete first. William knew that the act and witness would cause Katie great emotional harm and pain. Then lastly, he would allow Jacob to kill her and then they would depart for the hill country of western Virginia.

No matter what words Katie spoke, William still believed she was responsible for Arlen's death. Her actions were premeditated, deliberate, and skillfully carried out. William couldn't find it in his heart to forgive her nor would he listen to her cries for mercy when the time of death arrived. He had given up his quest for her love. Now, it was only a burning anger that dominated his thinking and vengeance on his mind.

As William began to turn away from the window, he heard the rushing sound of horses approaching. Without hesitation, he glanced out the window and noticed in the distance a wagon with a lone black man hastening the team. He was curious and apprehensive, especially if it came to questions concerning Mr. Hammond the owner. John and Emma Hammond were not only informants with the Confederate underground during the war but also had been close friends of William's before and during the conflict. When William arrived at their home seeking refuge, he was vigorously questioned by the Hammonds which ended in a heated argument. Some of the questions were sensitive in nature to William because they had uncovered Arlen's relationship to him and his double-agent spying activities. Arlen had caused the Hammonds to suffer imprisonment after disclosing their underground activities to Federal authorities. William became uncontrollably angry. At his command, Jacob killed and buried the Hammonds on the premise.

William placed on his black day coat and hat and walked out the front door and stood on the veranda waiting. He cautioned Jacob to stay out of sight and to make certain that Katie didn't begin to scream for help knowing that someone was arriving.

Once the wagon pulled into the front entrance of the heavily hedged circle of the mansion, William inconspicuously placed his hand on a small derringer concealed under his unbuttoned coat. When the wagon and horses came to a halt in front of the step, William stepped off the veranda and came down to the wagon.

The black man raised his old gray hat and quietly looked at William. Immediately, William recognized him as one of the slaves that had previously worked at Norfolk, his plantation along the James River in Chesterfield County. "Darby, where in the world did you come from?"

"Mr. William, I'se tell ya later. I'se brought yose something important."

Darby quietly stepped down from the wagon seat and again glanced coldly at his former master. He walked to the back of the wagon, which was filled with hay. William quietly followed. Darby again turned and glanced at William and then turned and quickly began to unravel the hay.

"What's going on?" William impatiently asked.

Darby remained silent until he was near the bottom of the pile of hay. "Be patient."

Again, William turned his attention toward the hay and noticed another pair of hands rapidly moving beneath the pile. His first instinct was to pull the derringer from concealment and place it to Darby's side. He eagerly continued to gaze. He was astonished when the individual began to cough and crawl free of the hay. Who could it be, he thought?

William was surprised when the male individual turned and looked at him. It was Charles Barker, whom he had last seen at the 14th Street train depot on April 2nd, the evening that Jefferson Davis and his cabinet members escaped from Richmond. Like many, William had departed with the presidential party. After quickly concealing the weapon, William assisted Charles from the wagon. Once Charles' feet touched the ground, he stretched his body and began to wipe the hay from his ragged, tattered clothing. To William, Charles appeared slimmer than six months ago. His face was hollow, and in the sunlight, his black hair revealed streaks of gray. At 36, Charles' appearance was untidy and shabby. Charles appeared tired; his face showed signs of strain and emotional pressure.

After Charles finished cleaning the hay from his trousers, he stretched forth his hand. "William, I am glad that you were able to escape capture."

"It's been a long six months for all of us. For me personally, it hasn't been an easy experience trying to escape from one place to the other eluding Federal authorities. Lets go into the house where you can clean up and we'll catch up on matters. I am interested in knowing how you made out."

Charles agreed. The two men turned around and ascended the steps and entered the house while Darby remained by the wagon.

* * * *

Pete was still hanging by the rope and hoist in the barn. His prospects of deliverance from this dilemma were appearing gloomier. He had earlier noticed a wagon moving along the lane but couldn't identify the individual guiding the team of horses. From Pete's position in the barn, he was several hundred yards behind the house. He could only observe the wagon until it disappeared among the heavy tree line. His thirst was increasing. He was sweating from the unusual autumn heat. His body was numb, feeling little pain. It was a slow and agonizing way to death he thought. Something of interest caught his attention near the chicken coop. There was the appearance of fresh dug dirt, like the ground had been disturbed in some way. Straining his vision, Pete knew it was a fresh gravesite. He looked around the property grounds again. With a second look, the area appeared more familiar to him. It was the Hammond's estate. The Hammond's had been friends of the family for sometime before the war. On more than one occasion when he needed shelter when riding with Mosby, the family was always quick to provide their assistance. He was touched by the thought of their demises.

Suddenly, Pete heard a faint sound coming from the area of some outbuildings behind the barn area. He attempted to kick at a lantern hanging on a wooden column. Pete succeeded in his attempt. It caused greater pain to his arms and wrist. His attention was directed to the front entrance of the barn. Pete noticed Jacob had entered with the noise that he created and was quickly approaching.

Jacob had a devilish smile covering his features. He took the handle of a pitchfork and thrust it against Pete's ribs. Pete sighed in pain. Jacob looked up at Pete hanging. "Trying to make some noise, huh, Barker? But that's all right. It will all be over with soon. Maybe as early as tonight."

Pete looked down. "I really wouldn't count on it."

"Barker, at this moment, it appears that I hold the upper hand. And you're not going anywhere anytime soon." Jacob paused and walked around Pete, laughing as he occasionally thrust him with the handle. When Pete murmured with pain, Jacob laughed more.

Jacob continued in an angry tone. "Barker, I am really going to take pleasure in killing you and that lady friend of yours. She has a feisty temper and can be a real headache to handle." Jacob laughed and continued, "A couple blows across her unruly mouth took some of the fight out of her though."

Pete became enraged with anger as he listened to Jacob describe the abuse that Katie endured. He became wild with attempting to break free, but Jacob jabbed him more with the handle. Finally seeing the uselessness of his effort, Pete, exhausted, diminished his attempts. For a brief moment, he was relieved to know that Katie was still alive and near.

Jacob turned around and placed the pitchfork along the railing to one of the stalls. He turned to leave and then paused. He turned around again. "Barker, I will promise you one thing. When I am given the privilege by Mr. Pierce of killing the both of you, I will bury you and her together."

Pete was infuriated as Jacob departed. Again, he mustered the last of his strength to break free but failed. He could only imagine the agonizing torment that Katie must be experiencing. Did she know he was nearby?

Pete's attention was concentrated again on a sound near the back of the barn. Pete quietly gazed at the back door to the structure. He recognized Hayward cautiously entering.

"Hayward, Hayward," Pete called in a loud whisper.

Hayward turned his attention upward in Pete's direction and was astonished at what his eyes were seeing. He gestured with his left hand and immediately Seamus appeared. Hayward pointed to

Pete. While Seamus moved toward the front of the barn to keep watch, Hayward quickly cut Pete down from the hoist.

For a moment, Pete didn't move. He just laid there with his eyes closed. Hayward shook Pete on the shoulder. "Pete, Pete, is ya all right?"

At first Pete didn't answer and Hayward called again. This time, Pete opened his eyes. "My arms and wrists are numb. I have no feeling in them."

Hayward began to take both of Pete's hands and rubbed them in order to promote the circulation of blood through the limbs. After several minutes of this procedure, he held Pete's head in his hand and gave him some water to drink from a canteen. Pete began to move his hands around on his own, making a fist and exercising them.

Once it appeared secure, Seamus returned to where Pete and Hayward were now sitting. "How are you Barker?"

"I'll be all right," Pete said as he continued to massage his wrist.

"Is this where the bloody fools are keeping Katie?"

Hayward helped Pete to his feet. "She is in that house somewhere with William Pierce."

"Is he Colonel L?"

Pete nodded in agreement. He continued as he walked to the edge of the stable area looking in the direction of the house. "Yeah, he is the one. I should have figured this out long time ago, but I really thought since William was one of Jeff Davis' advisors during the war that he had escaped and had been fortunate enough to leave the country."

"Well Barker, what are we waiting for? Let's go and free my sister."

Pete grabbed Seamus by the arm as he began to charge by. "We can't all go rushing in there. If we do, then William or Jacob will kill her. We have to come up with a plan."

"But we outnumber them and with the element of surprise, we will catch them off guard."

Pete pointed in the direction of the chicken coop. "Look out there. This is what happens to friends of William Pierce that have betrayed him. If my suspicions are true, then that grave out there is where the Hammonds are buried."

"Who are they?"

"They were friends of my family but also they were close friends to William. About an hour ago, a wagon arrived and hasn't left. We must proceed with caution. We can't go charging in there like we did during the war."

Pete noticed the troubled features on Seamus' face. He was understandably anxious and wanted to free his sister of her captors. Pete began to lay out a plan in detail drawing the layout of the estate with a stick on the dirt floor. Hayward and Seamus listened knowing that someone might have to give their life in return for Katie's freedom.

Chapter 55

Charles was in a spacious room, in the back, on the second floor of the mansion. He quietly sat alongside the bed. Charles pondered on the wealth and power that he enjoyed before the war as his mother's representative over Shenandoah.

The influence Charles enjoyed as one of the leaders of Jefferson County after assisting John Letcher's elevation to the governorship of Virginia elevated him in the public domain and political circle. All these opportunities had given him great hope and confidence of pursuing his own political future. After actively participating in John Breckinridge's candidacy for the presidency in 1860, he assisted President Davis as an aide on issues concerning differences between the new Confederate government and the rights of the sovereign Southern states. Charles possessed ability for negotiations. This was why he walked in the President's favor. Charles knew this would have been an advantage for his own future. If there would have been a new Confederate nation, then Charles had possessed hope of running for a Senate seat. Now, all his dreams had vanished.

As far as Shenandoah, Charles was financially devastated. There was little to return to, and maybe if captured, time in prison. He stood and sighed. The opportunity to see his family and to be alive was grace in itself. Charles stood and walked over to the window. This was certainly the Hammond's estate between Leesburg and Ball's Mill, but the family wasn't anywhere to be found.

Glancing out the window in the direction of the barn, the estate appeared lifeless to Charles. The slaves that one time of day were working around the property were gone. Their huts vacated and in shambles. They, like many, fled north and to freedom. Some of the outbuildings, such as the carpentry shop, appeared to have collapsed from neglect or were dismantled by soldiers for firewood. The barn's roof was partially gone. The stable was the only building that appeared undamaged by nature or the war. One time of day, the flower gardens were full of various plants, full of blossom, and multiple colors. All of the marvelous wonders of nature had vanished. Like all else in Virginia, death had taken its toll and the once vibrant garden appeared full of weeds and undergrowth. The stately four white columns, three-story stucco mansion from the opportunity that he could see, appeared in great need of repairs on its exterior more than its interior. Apparently, there had been some fighting that had taken place on the property. The bullet holes in the walls of the dwelling gave evidence to this.

Charles recalled one time of day before the war the experience of visiting the Hammond family on more than one occasion. They were always hospitable, religious in nature, and hosted some of the largest and most enthusiastic socials in Loudoun County. Some events continued through a second day. The Hammonds held some of the most popular foxhunts and equestrian tournaments in Northern Virginia. As he walked toward the mirror in the corner to trim his long black beard, he was still bewildered over the absence of the family. Something was terribly wrong, but what?

Charles turned his thoughts toward his family. How were Caroline and Ann? How was his mother? Surely they were like everyone else in the old Confederacy: penniless, being harassed by a Unionist local government, and maybe had threats of confiscation of Shenandoah. Charles knew the cries echoing from the North for retribution. He read their newspapers. It had been six months to the day of the evacuation of Richmond since he had last seen the family. The ability to communicate with Caroline had been severed. The reason was because of the fear of reprisal against her and the family if Federal authorities discovered their exchange of messages. For all Caroline knew, he might be dead. The pain and anguish of separation had been unbearable. There was a void in his heart. Night and day, he envisioned holding her in his arms, kissing her lips, and looking into her glowing eyes. At various times, he thought out of desperation of risking the attempt even to the point of death in order to see his family again. Patience had been his virtue during this time of separation. It would prevail a little longer.

Often after Caroline's departure from Richmond and even now, Charles could still vividly recall the great turmoil, the out-of-control lawlessness, and panic that had erupted over Richmond on that day. But through it all, he especially remembered the last words that he spoke to his wife. "I love you so much that if anything happens to you, it will destroy me." He then assisted her into the carriage. She gently touched his hand. Her last words of promise, love and commitment to him were, "I will be waiting for you." Over the past months, those words of Caroline's continued to echo through his mind and give him strength, compelling him to return. All that he could do amidst the adversity of his world collapsing and the upheaval of the Confederacy was think of her, hoping they would be united once more. The sorrow and despair that filled his heart today is just as alive and fresh as it was in Richmond six months ago. He knew from traveling secretly through Virginia that Caroline and his family had returned to Shenandoah. They were less then thirty miles from here and he was determined to see them.

Charles' greatest guilt and the issue that depressed him the most was his inability to remain awake and vigilant on the night that Richmond was evacuated. After meeting with President Davis, Charles had returned and assisted his family with their departure from the beleaguered city. Rebecca had refused to forsake her Aunt Daisy, who was ill. He did all that he could to persuade his younger sister Rebecca to leave but with his mother's intercession, he gave way to her wishes just as he always did in life.

Once performing a last minute errand for President Davis before his departure and after returning home, Charles was so exhausted from all that had been taking place over the last week with the demise of the Confederacy that he fell asleep. While sleeping in the downstairs, a Confederate straggler had entered the mansion and killed his aunt and mortally wounded Rebecca. After killing the Rebel, Charles laid Rebecca on a bed where she apologized for arguing with him earlier and not leaving with her mother when given the opportunity. But it wasn't only the issue of leaving the city; it was repentance for all the years of differences they shared. On few issues in life had they agreed. Still, amends with Rebecca didn't relieve his conscious. He was responsible and had failed to protect them. Maybe exhaustion, maybe confusion but at the time Charles couldn't understand why she refused to leave with such anarchy in the city. Some months afterward, Charles finally understood Rebecca's loyalty and commitment to their aunt. She was the one who gave Rebecca a home and formal education during a period of continuous strife and division within the family at Shenandoah. It was only natural that Rebecca wouldn't want to forsake her incapacitated aunt. Maybe it was the love and attention that she drew from her aunt. Still with the passing of time, the wound was still fresh. Even after many months, Charles still awakened after experiencing nightmares of her death.

Charles stepped away from the mirror and put on a clean white shirt. Again, he turned toward the mirror and began to arrange the tails of a black tie. He heard a muffled noise and glanced at the door. For some unknown reason, his eyes briefly scanned the wooden floor, as if the sound came from a room below. In his discernment, he perceived something was greatly wrong. This feeling had been part of him for several days. Again, he glanced back at the mirror and finished tying his tie. Once satisfied, Charles picked out a multi-colored vest and put it on. As he was buttoning the black buttons, a soft knock was heard at the door. He cautiously opened the door and saw a servant standing there.

"My name is Milton, may I come in?"

Charles' first impression of Milton was favorable because his diction was that of an educated individual. He was greatly surprised knowing a servant would only enter the room upon an invitation. He was amazed by this young man's aggressiveness. "Uh, yes you may."

Charles' suspicions were aroused again when he watched Milton quickly glance down the hallway. "What is going on?" Charles asked.

"You need to take care and watch. Mr. Pierce is an angry man."

"All of us are since we lost the war. Our lives have changed because of people like you."

Placing his finger to his mouth in a gesture for Charles to lower the sound of his voice, Milton came quickly to the point out of fear of being exposed. "Yes sir, our lives have greatly changed and will especially change if we are not careful."

"Just get to the point and tell me what you mean."

The servant's dark-piercing eyes were blazing. "Mr. William had my master killed! He didn't have a chance." Milton walked to the far end of the room and continued. "He pleaded for mercy for the Misses, but there was none to be found. The man is cold and contemptible, and I've risked my life to tell you that you must watch your back and not anger him."

The servant could tell by the tense features covering Charles' face that he was troubled. Charles gazed at Milton as he sat in a chair by the bed.

Charles looked up at Milton. "It's impossible. Totally impossible that William would kill a trusted friend. We've known the Hammonds for years. We have visited this house on many occasions and spoke of the day when the South would be free of Northern tyranny. We spoke of our dreams of a new Confederacy, a new nation and the role that we might play in such a new government." Charles quietly stood and approached the servant. He shook his head from one side to the other in perplexity. He paused in front of the servant. "Are you sure? Because your accusations have had a strong effect upon me. I am deeply troubled."

Quietly shaking his head in acknowledgement, Milton spoke. "And that's not all. He is holding a woman against her will in the cellar. I know because I served Mr. William and her breakfast about an hour before you arrived. They started to argue after I left the room."

"About what?"

Suddenly, the conversation was interrupted by the sound of boots walking through the hallway. Charles and the servant froze. The sound stopped and there were several quick knocks on the door. Charles gestured for the servant to hide which he swiftly accomplished behind the small sofa. Charles regained his composure and slowly opened the door. It was Darby.

"Mr. William would like for ya to meet him in da dining room."

"All right, I am on my way."

Darby nodded in acknowledgement as Charles closed the door.

Milton glanced with fear in his eyes at Charles. He quietly stood and made his way to the door with Charles watching. He cautiously opened the door to make sure that neither Darby nor anyone else would see him leave. Milton turned and looked at Charles. "Watch your back. Mr. William has another man here with him. He did all the killing."

"Thank you, thank you for the information."

Once the servant disappeared, Charles shut the door and pondered on all that the servant had said to him. He took his words seriously. Now he knew his instinct had served him well.

He was still in disbelief, attempting to absorb the shock and revelation concerning William's behavior. His thoughts turned toward the woman. Who could she be?

* * * *

Many thoughts about William's honesty and their friendship raced through Charles' mind as he approached and prepared to descend the stairway to the first floor. It was strange and still quite unbelievable to Charles all the information that he had just received from an individual, whom he knew little about, let alone trusting his credibility. One question lingered in his mind. Why would William murder close friends and associates in the great cause that they had believed and endured so long? What secrecy was he protecting? Did they accidentally stumble onto information William was trying to protect? Was the lady that he was holding captive in the cellar knowledgeable of William's secrecy?

Charles took a deep sigh as he descended the stairway and repressed his concerns. He didn't want to give William the impression that he knew anything of the mystery.

Once at the bottom of the stairway, Charles turned and walked to the second room on his left. He noticed William sitting alone smoking a cigar and gazing at him, as he entered. Charles took a seat at the opposite end of the table. William's smile was smug and not genuine. It gave Charles the impression that he was hiding something. Charles thought he might ask where the Hammonds might be and determine on what course to take from there. As Milton, the servant, placed before him a breakfast of buckwheat cakes, Charles asked, "William, I've noticed that John or Emma are not around. I wanted to thank them for taking me in and asking for their assistance in helping me return home to see Caroline and the family."

William cleared his throat and replied. "John isn't here. As I understand from Milton, he is still in prison for helping Mosby and some of his men continue the fight after Lee's surrender. Whether you know it or not, Mosby carried on the war in these parts, refusing to surrender our cause. So… the Hammonds were followed by Yankees agents and they were captured for sheltering the colonel during that time."

William glanced at Milton. "Isn't that correct?"

"Yes sir, that is correct."

The servant next approached Charles and poured him coffee. When Charles glanced up at Milton, the servant's eyes glanced at him. Charles noticed a sadness radiating from them. Somewhere, inwardly, Charles refused to question Milton's sincerity any longer.

Turning his attention away from the servant, Charles took a sip of the coffee. He shook his head in frustration. "That's a shame."

William coldly stared at Charles. "This war has had a horrible effect on everyone. And I am afraid that it's going to be a long time before the South will ever be able to recover. As I was traveling across Culpepper County, you wouldn't believe the destruction and devastation the Yankees caused. Anything of use was totally destroyed. Even some homes were burned to the ground just like what you experienced with Shenandoah. In reality, there is no way these homesteads will ever be productive again." William took a puff from his cigar as Charles remained silent. William continued in a broken tone. "The most heart wrenching thing I witnessed was a small child crying, partially clad, and suffering because he was hungry and was abandoned. My heart ached when I noticed several along the way and knew they didn't have any family and no one to care for them. I would have, but I have been afraid of capture ever since we left Richmond." William's mood changed. "I have never witnessed such atrocities against civilians and it still angers me to the point that I would still kill anyone of those scoundrels if I was given the chance!"

"Virginia isn't the only place suffering. In one way or another, all of the Confederacy has paid the price for the rebellion. And I agree it will be many years before we will recover from the effects of the war. The war was so wrong for all of us. And, I was so wrong in believing we could actually pull off the rebellion. I didn't realize the actions would have serious consequences."

"Such as?"

"We Barkers have lost everything. A beautiful home that my father spent long days and years building. One of the most prosperous businesses in the Shenandoah Valley has been lost, and probably ruined for the rest of our lives. And there is no money to start over again and the separation from the ones that we love is unbearable. But my heart aches most of all for my sister

Rebecca who was murdered during an attempted robbery on that miserable night in Richmond."

An expression of anguish covered William's face. He shook his head in grief. "Oh no, not little Rebecca." He looked at Charles and said in a sympathetic tone, "I am so sorry to hear this. I suspect that it was a Yankee of course."

"No. It was one of our own who apparently stayed behind."

"I see. Well Charles, the boys were desperate. And you know when matters are in a state of mayhem like they were in Richmond, then confusion takes place and people act otherwise irrational."

Charles jumped from the chair in a heat of anger. He struck his fist against the table's surface. "Not at the cost of my sister's life!"

William noticed a wild glare in Charles' large blue eyes. He didn't continue the subject. It was too heated an issue and still carried fresh wounds. Instead, William gestured for Jacob who was standing in the doorway to enter the room. Jacob walked over to where the men were seated.

"Charles, I'd like for you to meet Jacob Lyles. Jacob has been of the greatest assistance to me in my endeavor to elude Federal authorities as with yourself. Jacob has been of the greatest use in acting as a courier and scouting ahead for us and finding friendly citizens who will take us in."

Charles' eyes looked at Jacob. His thoughts returned to the revelation that Milton had shared. He believed they were words of truth and Jacob was in his opinion, a cold-blooded killer. As Charles paced around his curiosity was aroused. He turned and faced William. "After our last meeting, did you desert the President and his cabinet?"

"Yes. Matter of fact that same day. Several elderly sisters near Greensboro temporarily gave me shelter until it was safe from Yankee raiders. Eventually, I was smuggled north by agents working with the underground and given shelter near Charlottesville by Jacob's family. Like everyone, including you, I knew the war was all but over. Staying with the President and his party would have meant certain capture, maybe life imprisonment, or having to fight the Yankees and getting myself killed. Actually Charles, I didn't have the stomach for either."

Charles placed his hands on a chair and gazed at William asking, "What are you going to do now?"

"I hope soon to be in the mountains of western Virginia," William said as he put out the cigar he was smoking. "There are many good folks there that Jacob knows that may indefinitely extend their hospitality to us. Maybe you should think of going along."

Charles quietly nodded his head in disagreement.

William continued in a confident tone as he looked at Charles. "You know you're not going to be able to stay with Caroline and the family. Sooner or later, the Yankees are going to find out about you returning home. And when they do, you'll end up like President Davis in some God forsaken dungeon somewhere. Maybe even hung for treason. Who knows?"

"No, no William. I have to take my chances. I'm tired of running and living like some kind of a fugitive. It's worth any gamble at this point to see Caroline and Ann. I don't even know if they still believe that I am alive. Over these past months, I haven't been able to communicate with them because I was afraid of being captured, or maybe reprisal against them. God only knows how much anguish and pain I have caused them to suffer for a dream and belief that wasn't worth following. No, William, they must know that I am alive."

William stood and approached Charles. "Then you won't accept my offer?" He asked in a sharp tone.

Shaking his head in disagreement, Charles stood. "No. No, I must see my family."

William turned and nodded to Jacob. From concealment under his coat, Jacob pulled a pistol and pointed it at Charles.

Charles was surprised as he glanced at Jacob. "What's going on here?" When there wasn't an answer, Charles turned to William. "William, what has happened to you? We were the best of friends and fought for the same beliefs. We confided in each other about things." Charles waited for an answer. He noticed William's cold gaze. "Have you gone insane over the defeat of the Confederacy?"

"That was then, and this is now. Today is a different world that we live in. I hope you will try to understand why I am doing this, but quite frankly, my friend, I am fighting to survive. If the

Federals happen to capture you then I am afraid that in order to save yourself by swinging some deal, you'll reveal my plans."

"That's nonsense!"

Jacob walked over and gestured for Charles to be seated.

"My friend, I wasn't expecting you to show up. But now that you have, I must decide what to do with you," William answered as he continued to pace.

William swiftly departed the room as Charles looked on in amazement and distress.

As Jacob held his pistol in hand, Charles thought of how he was being betrayed by a friend that had been invited on many occasions to his home. He had trusted William's confidentiality on family matters and was the one who was respected and looked upon in the same degree as a brother. Charles was mystified by William's behavior. He was positive that William had begun to distance himself from him during the middle of the war. As President Davis requested his advice on important government issues on a frequent basis, he now knew the animosity had grown and this was probably the manifestation of it. It wasn't until the autumn of 1864, that William's irrational behavior had accelerated and had become unpredictable. Now, he thought, he was a prisoner. His freedom had disappeared. Somewhere in his heart, Charles didn't know if he would walk out of this situation alive. Somehow he must either look for a way of escape or attempt to reason with William for his release.

Chapter 56

After Pete and Seamus finished discussing different ideas and the details of a possible plan to rescue Katie, they stood and walked to the front entrance to the barn. The sun had disappeared and the sky had turned dark. From all appearances, a severe storm was developing. Staying concealed, they looked in the distance beyond the tree line where the mansion crested a slight elevation.

Pete pointed in the direction and turned his attention to Seamus. "Katie could be anywhere in the house, even the wet cellar. That seems more logical because it doesn't offer her a way of escape. I am sure they placed boards or some barrier over the doorway to prevent her from doing just that. So…we will go out the back of the barn and use the apple orchard for shelter. Then we should be able to come into that grove of trees near the rear of the small brick structure where the overseer once lived. From there we will have to proceed across open ground. It will be risky but there is no other choice. You'll have to use your own discretion when to act. Hopefully, they will not see either of us. Once there, the back porch will shelter you. While you are doing this, I'll proceed to the entrance on the northern side of the house. But wait until the thunder begins so they don't hear you trying to break down the door. Once you are in, and if she is there, leave immediately and signal Hayward. After you find Katie, get away as fast as you can."

"What about you?"

"Well, this Johnnie has done this several times during the war. So…don't worry about me. Just get Katie out of here. Understood?"

Next Pete turned to Hayward. "I want you to search the stable area and run off any extra horses so that once we escape with Katie, they can't follow. After you accomplish that, we will need four horses. Use the far end of the orchard and wait in the grove of trees near the front of the house on the northern side. Once we have Katie, Seamus will signal you."

After Pete and Seamus checked the bullet magazine of their weapons, they proceeded out the back door of the barn and toward the apple orchard. Once there, they started to feel a few drops of rain. They moved through the tree-covered area.

At the edge of the orchard, Pete glanced at the sky and noticed that the lightning was intensifying. Just as planned, he gestured to Seamus and they both dashed for the grove of trees about 100 yards from the mansion. Then quickly over to the rear of the overseer's home. Unexpectedly and fortunately for them, there was a back entrance. Pete entered first and then Seamus. For sometime, it appeared the dwelling had been deserted. Pausing and resting, Pete looked out the window. By his guess, they were less then 75 yards from the mansion. Pete took notice of the mansion.

"There is a light burning in the back room closest to us."

"Yes, I see. The porch covers the whole back. On the opposite side of the house where the porch appears to set back under the window might be the area where the door to the cellar is located. That is where I'll head for. Hopefully, no one will see me."

"We must hurry while we have the storm to hide our intentions," Pete replied.

Lightning flashes streaked across the sky and the crashing sound of thunder rapidly began to echo across the landscape. Without another word, Pete raced out the back door, around the side of the house and in plain view toward another grove of trees, directly opposite and within 30 yards of the mansion. Still partly concealed, Seamus dashed to another tree line. Now, he would have to cross the grounds where gardens once occupied, which was directly in back of the mansion. It would be more tedious crossing the unpredictable little ravines and landscape where plants and hedges once were. In doing so, he would be totally exposed if William or Jacob were glancing out the window. More than Pete, he took the risk of being fired on. He was closer to the house.

With the longer route and also the possibility of being exposed, Pete made it safely to the grove of trees. He worked his way to the edge of the small forest, stayed out of sight, and glanced around for Seamus.

Seamus raced over the broken ground to a pathway that was in the center of the garden. He moved swiftly toward a hedgerow just off the back porch. Once there, he caught his breath and glanced around. The light was still beaming from the room at the far end of the mansion. It might be, he thought, where everyone was congregated. Hopefully, he hadn't been exposed because it would mean William and Jacob had laid a trap for him once he entered the house. Just as he suspected, there was a small wooden door with several heavy boards nailed across it. He moved cautiously from the hedgerow and down several steps to the cellar door. Seamus looked around for any tools to help him pry it open, but there were none to be found.

Pete believed that Seamus had enough time to be in place. He swiftly moved along the grass to the side entrance. With pistol in hand, he laid his body against the exterior wall. The lightning flashes had increased. Looking up at the sky, the rain beat against his face. Again turning his attention to the task at hand, he gently tried the door with his left hand. It opened with no difficulty. Pete cocked the hammer of his pistol cautiously entering the wing of the house.

There was an increase in the intensity of the storm. It was getting closer. Seamus' first observation of the door revealed it was damaged in some areas and appeared to be in poor condition. As the loud sound of thunder filled the air and shook the ground, Seamus kicked and pulled at the barricade. Finally after several attempts, he was able to break down the barricade and slam his full weight against the door. It only took a single effort to smash through. Inside was faintly lighted. Katie wasn't there. The only evidence of her presence was a white handkerchief lying on the dirt floor and the appearance of a makeshift bed made from straw. Seamus was horrified and angry that his sister had been treated this way.

As Pete stood, he noticed there were stairs that led to the bottom floor and another that led to the upper floor. Pete knew this was to the dining area where the light was shining. One time of day it gave the appearance it could have been a kitchen area. Pete continued to move with caution toward an entranceway. Once in the hallway, he noticed a narrow stairway to the main floor. On his left, was another door.

He opened the door with his pistol held before him. He noticed Seamus quickly turned and was about to fire on him. He held his hand up in a friendly gesture. "Seamus, it's me, Pete."

After recognizing Pete, Seamus put his arm down. "We just bloody missed them. What now Johnnie?"

"I am going to the top of the stairway. Once I open the door and the area is…"

Pete was interrupted by the sound of someone opening the door to the cellar area. He quickly gestured to Seamus. Pete stepped back behind the doorway to the kitchen with pistol ready and Seamus ducked under the stairway.

The creaking sound of feet descending the stairs and the unexpected event was an experience that Pete was use to from fighting during the war. He knew they had the element of surprise and the capture of one of the villains would make their work much easier. Pete waited until he could hear over the thunder the muffled sounds indicating that the individual was at the bottom of the stairs moving on the dirt floor. At that time, he would step forward and challenge them. With hammer cocked on the weapon, it was time.

Simultaneously, Seamus and Pete stepped forward, ready to fire. Pete placed the weapon in the individuals face. "Who are you?"

"My name is Milton. I was Mr. Hammond's personal servant until those men up there arrived. Then they killed the Master and the Misses."

The cold glow from Pete's eyes revealed his anger. He gazed at the sadden expression covering Milton's face. "That's all going to end today," Pete replied.

Swiftly, Seamus changed the subject. "Who else is up there?"

"They are holding captive another man and girl. And there is also one other servant. I don't know if he can be trusted."

"But a woman you did say?"

Milton nodded in agreement. "Yes."

Pete looked at Seamus and again at Milton. "What does she look like?"

"Auburn hair, medium like…"

Seamus looked at Pete and smiled as Milton described Katie. There was a sigh of relief in his voice. "It must be my sister."

Pete continued the interrogation. "Why did you come down here?"

Milton pointed to the corner. "I came to get some sugar for coffee. But if I don't return, they'll know something is wrong."

"He's bloody right you know," Seamus said.

"We are here to free the girl you just described," Pete said.

"I want to help," Milton said. "To be honest with you, I watched you cross the yard from the trees out there and knew what you were up to." Turning his attention once more to Pete, he continued, "At the time I was in the dining room bringing some water to one of the rebels. When I turned and knew your intentions, I waited until I was told to leave so that I could block their view of what you were up to for as long as possible. Finally, by the time that I was ask to leave, you were already out of sight. So, I presumed that you might have found this back door and I made the excuse to get sugar."

"How many weapons do they have?" Seamus anxiously asked.

"The one that is called Jacob has several pistols strapped to him."

"How is the house laid out upstairs?" Pete asked as he looked around.

"Up there is the library," Milton answered as he pointed, "and then directly across the large hallway is the dining room. This is where they can be found. When you come up the steps, you will be in a room off the library. That's for us servants."

"Is my sister in the dining room?" Seamus asked.

"I don't believe. She might have been taken to the upper floor where she can clean up. This has been the habit each day."

Testing the servant's intentions, Pete hoped that he would comply. "All that we want from you is to open that door up there and see if the area is free."

Milton nodded and filled a tin cup with some of the little sugar that was left. He turned and slowly made his way up the stairway. Opening the door, he looked around and quietly gestured for Pete that the area was safe.

Pete looked at Seamus. "Remember, you proceed to the upper floors. I will distract William in the dining room and give you cover to get Katie out of the house."

Seamus quietly nodded in agreement as he followed closely behind Pete. Once Pete peered through the door, he moved into a narrow hallway. With Milton watching, Pete led, moving along the wall with his weapons ready.   Seamus was about 10 feet behind Pete covering the rear.

Shortly, they came to a rear doorway that entered the library. Less than another 10 feet there was another doorway that led into the drawing room.

Pete turned and whispered. "Give me several minutes to get into position and then move out."

Seamus nodded in agreement as Pete glanced through the doorway to the drawing room. Once the sound of thunder was heard, he moved undetected to the opposite doorway that led into the hallway and was directly across from the dining area where they saw the light.

Once he felt comfortable that Pete was in a secure position, Seamus proceeded to the next opening where the library was located. He quickly looked around, but the area, as well as the parlor directly across the wide entranceway appeared vacant.

Cautiously glancing into the hallway, Pete noticed Seamus moving toward the direction of the stairway. Pete gestured that he would proceed to the dining area. Moving slowly in that direction, he leaned his body against the wall. He heard William speaking in a loud tone. "The problem with our government was that the states were never in complete unity with the each other. If there is division, then nothing much gets accomplished." Pete heard a moment of silence and then the sound of footsteps. Again he heard William. "If that crazy old man would have listened to me, then things might have been different."

A surprised expression covered Pete's face as he recognized the next mellow voice as Charles. "No William, you're wrong. I realized after Lincoln was re-elected that we wouldn't have any chance of negotiating an end to the war. Lincoln was a leader that would settle for nothing less than total subjugation of the South. Our boys were tired. I could see in their faces over the months leading up to the fall of Richmond. But I couldn't say any of my thoughts to President Davis."

"I disagree. As leaders, we let them down."

"No, I whole-heartily disagree. We were defeated. Demoralized. I later heard General Early talking to Colonel Robertson. He explained General Lee's perception of the war."

"What did the General say?"

"If Grant was allowed to cross the James and a siege began, then it would only be a matter of time. He was speaking of the evacuation of Richmond and the total collapse of the Confederacy."

In a burst of anger, Pete heard William. "I don't believe it for a moment! Not a moment!"

By Charles tone, Pete had the impression he was somewhat frustrated in his answer, "And you probably won't. But the truth is that the outcome or continuation of the war didn't make any difference politically. Militarily, we were defeated. The only thing politically of any significant benefit would have been the total agreement among the state governors and leaders. That would have caused the Confederate government to run more efficiently. But that is all."

"If it wouldn't had been for you, then President Davis would have listened to me. You gave him too much bad advice."

It sounded to Pete as if William had lost his temper and slammed something on the table. He became fearful of William's unpredictable behavior. He wasn't ready to act until Seamus had Katie out of harm's way. He felt compelled to confront William, especially with the element of surprise.

Pete looked cautiously through the doorway and noticed William standing at the far end of the table and his brother Charles seated at the opposite end. Near the center of the table, he noticed Jacob standing over Katie. She wasn't on the upper level as Seamus and he were led to believe by Milton. This could be a trap, he thought. Suddenly, above his head there was a creaking sound, probably from a loose floorboard that Seamus had accidentally stepped on. The noise also attracted William's attention. He anxiously broke off the conversation. "Who is upstairs?"

"Nobody," Jacob swiftly answered.

"Go and see what's going on!"

As Jacob approached the doorway, Pete disappeared into the library. Once Jacob ascended the stairway, Pete proceeded to the doorway to the dining room. He took a deep sigh, cocked the hammer and entered.

When Pete entered the room, he noticed William was sitting and a startled expression was on his face. Fear covered Katie's expression. She remained seated. Charles cautiously turned with an expression of astonishment.

"William put your hands on the table where I can see them," Pete demanded.

William complied, but he was holding a revolver, and instead, he pointed it at Katie. As Charles stood to protest, William fired the weapon and hit Charles. William again pointed the weapon at Katie before Pete could get off a shot.

Pete glanced at Charles to examine his injury. He was holding his right arm. "I am all right, it's just a flesh wound."

"Put the weapon down now or she is dead!" William screamed.

Pete tossed the pistol on the floor.

"Kick it this way," William commanded in a sharp tone.

Pete complied as he looked coldly at William. He then turned and noticed Katie sobbing. He started toward her but William pointed the weapon at him.

"William you won't get away with this," Pete calmly said.

"You would be surprised if you knew what I could get away with."

Charles answered as he held pressure to his wound. "I am sure that we would."

Unprepared for events, Milton hastily entered the room. Surprised to see all that was now transpiring, he was uncertain what to do. "Mr. William, do you want me to fetch some rope to tie them?"

"Yes Milton, a very good idea. Now hurry along!"

Seamus was conscious of the fact that he had just accidentally blundered by stepping on a loose board. He knew someone would be investigating so he looked for a place to ambush his advisory. He heard a faint noise making its way up to the second floor so he darted into an unlocked bedroom. He didn't know who it might be other than possibly Jacob. Jacob was much larger than him in statue, but he believed he had the advantage. Anxious and uncertain, he opened the door and hid behind it. He was troubled because he still didn't have the opportunity to search the remaining four rooms to see if Katie was a prisoner in any of them.

Seamus could hear doors opening and closing. With pistol, he took the risk and cracked open the door to glance into the long and wide hallway. It was Jacob just as he thought. It seemed like an eternity. Jacob arrived at the room opposite the narrow stairway and directly across the hall from Seamus. Seamus stepped from his hideaway and placed the gun barrel behind Jacob's neck.

"Drop it or I'll bloody drop you," Seamus commanded.

Jacob was quiet as he reluctantly complied with the order. Seamus knew Katie wasn't in any of the other four rooms which told him that she must be in the dining room where Pete was going to enter. Quickly, he pushed Jacob into the empty room and closed and locked the door.

Suddenly, he froze at the sound of a single gunshot. This caused him to be apprehensive for fear that something happened to Katie. He realized he had to remain calm. He knew he couldn't charge into the dining room and maybe cause greater injury to all or to himself. He would rely on the instincts that he had been taught to use by experiences during the war.

With little time wasted, Milton returned with the rope. He took notice that everyone was silent with various uncertain expressions covering their faces.

William pointed at Pete. "Tie Barker."

Milton walked over to Pete and began to strap him with the rope. He looked into Pete's cold eyes and knew his dissatisfaction with him, as if he had been betrayed. Milton was close to William and watching his every move out of the side of his eye. Inconspicuously as possible, he noticed Charles was gazing defiantly at William and holding his arm in an attempt to stop the bleeding. Tears were flowing down Katie's cheeks. She appeared very nervous. The anger over John and Emma Hammond's vicious death began to swiftly rise in Milton's heart. Without warning, Milton turned around and yelled, lunging at William. As the gun fired, Milton fell face down on the floor. In Milton's effort, he had dislodged the weapon from William's hand. The gun fell near, and was where Katie was seated.

Noticing where the weapon was, Pete hurriedly untied the rope as Charles jumped from his chair and raced for the weapon.

William quickly shook his head in an attempt to regain his senses from the blow that he received from Milton. William pulled a tiny pistol from under his coat and aimed it at Katie.

Katie quickly fell to the floor and grabbed the weapon. She coldly raised the revolver and fired twice in succession, hitting William in the chest. The action was carried out as if she had done this many times in the past.

William gasped for air. He dropped his weapon and fell face first to the floor.

Katie jumped to her feet crying uncontrollably. She embraced Pete and began to stroke his hair and kiss his cheeks.

Charles walked over and examined Milton. He was dead. Charles walked over to where William was lying and turned him over for examination. He too, was dead.

With the noise of gunfire, Seamus came running into the room. He was surprised to see the dead bodies lying around but was relieved to see his sister unharmed. He rushed to her.

"Let's get Katie out of here as soon as possible," Pete suggested.

Seamus headed for the front door to signal Hayward with the horses. Pete and Charles escorted Katie, who was between them. They walked by a closet. Jacob lunged from the area and pushed Charles out of the way, grabbing Katie. Pete quickly reacted but Jacob was too quick. Immediately, Jacob commanded Pete to drop his weapon. With his pistol drawn, Jacob ordered Seamus to toss his gun out the front door and then he ordered everyone into the library.

As everyone proceeded to that area, Jacob held his arm around Katie's neck, using her body as shelter. He held his pistol pointed at her head. Charles was the last to enter the library. Without a word, Jacob closed the back door and locked it and then he did likewise to the hallway entrance. Gathering the gun that Pete dropped on the floor, Jacob stepped back toward the front door, still with his arm around Katie's neck and gun in hand against the side of her head.

"Open it," Jacob anxiously commanded.

Katie nervously complied knowing he would kill her if she didn't. She was afraid and uncertain of Jacob's intentions. At least the ones she loved were safe and it was apparent that she was just being used as a hostage for his escape. Katie was sure that once Jacob's purpose had been accomplished that he would probably kill her just like he had with everyone else. The only thing that puzzled her was why didn't he kill everyone else when he had the opportunity.

Once Jacob stepped out the door with Katie, he noticed Hayward. Without warning, he fired once. Hayward fell from the saddle and lay motionless on the ground.

Katie began to scream. "You bloody beast! You bloody deserve hell fire from the devil himself!"

Jacob cocked the hammer once more on the weapon. "Shut up! Shut up now or I'll kill you."

Jacob forced Katie onto the horse and then he mounted. They raced off together around the house toward the direction of the old farmer's lane. As they rode near the rear porch of the house, Pete escaped out the window. He lunged from the porch railing and onto Jacob's horse, knocking Jacob from his mount.

Both Pete and Jacob struggled viciously, striking at one another. When it appeared that Jacob had the upper hand, believing that his foe couldn't continue, he jumped to his feet and grabbed a huge rock to crush Pete's skull. Katie tried to intervene but was shoved to the side. Just as Jacob picked up the rock above his head to strike Pete, there was the sound of several gunshots. Pete had grabbed the weapon that had fallen from Jacob's possession and fired it but it was Seamus' pistol that made the difference.

Katie came rushing to Pete's side and placed her arms around him. "Are you all right?" she anxiously asked.

Pete rubbed the side of his face. He sighed. "Yes. I'm all right."

Pete waved with his hand in appreciation. Seamus laughed and yelled back. "Now Johnnie, we're bloody even."

As they walked into the house, they noticed that Charles was gone. The front door was open. Pete, Katie, and Seamus walked to the front and noticed that Charles was leaning over Hayward. Without hesitation, Pete raced from the doorway, down the steps and over to where Hayward was lying. Once he arrived, he noticed Charles was beginning to help Hayward to his feet.

Hayward had some blood running from a left shoulder wound. He laughed. "Now yose shou've known that nothin' is gonna git old Hayward down."

Pete smiled and was glad that his friend was not seriously wounded. He turned and looked at Katie, who was approaching. Her life had been spared, but he knew their future was still uncertain. There were too many questions that needed to be answered and their trust had been shattered, maybe even beyond reconciliation. He wanted to accept her gestures of affection and love, but he was cautious. For now at least, he took joy that she was alive and had the opportunity to return home with Seamus and begin a normal life.

Turning around, Pete glanced at Charles and hugged him. They were both silent as they gazed at each other. Now with Charles home, Shenandoah would be his property once more. The reunion with Caroline and Ann would mean everything to him, even if it meant imprisonment. There was much that had happened. Emotional feelings and differences needed to be resolved. They needed to catch up on all that had happened. There would be time to do that, but for now, they must return to Shenandoah, their home.

Chapter 57

It was late in the afternoon when the rain ceased. The sun was peering through the clouds. With the weather change, Pete and Charles wrapped William and Jacob's dead bodies in blankets and removed them from the house and garden area. They had placed the two corpses in the wagon that Charles had arrived in and Pete took them to the western side of the orchard where he planned to bury them in a single grave. Then he returned and buried Milton near the Hammonds. As for Darby, he had fled once the firing began. Hayward was resting on a sofa near a burning fire in the parlor after Katie removed the bullet from his shoulder and packed it with tree moss. This was an old Cheyenne remedy that Seamus had learned during the war from a surgeon from Kansas that had ridden with his cavalry brigade. The surgeon had informed him that the tree moss had some kind of an agent that prevented infection from setting into wounds. Katie took his advice and it worked effectively.

Seamus was stacking logs on the grate in the fireplace in the drawing room as Katie quietly watched, but her mind was deep in thought. Once Seamus lit some paper and placed it between the logs, the fire began to spread and the air near the fireplace began to feel warm and become comfortable. He quietly stood and walked over to the front window. Seamus glanced out to see if Pete and Charles had returned.

Katie approached Seamus and broke her silence. "I guess you are quite upset with me. And, rightfully so."

Seamus turned and just stared at Katie as her eyes were on him, waiting for a response. "In a bloody way, you might say, yes I am bloody angry with you. If you had listened to me and stayed in Boston, then all of this bloody mess that we've been in wouldn't have happened. I wouldn't have been shot at and people wouldn't have been killed." Seamus pointed toward the other room across the hallway. "Maybe the servant would still be alive and Barker's John Henry over there wouldn't have been wounded." Seamus walked over to the fire and placed his arm on the mantel and looked around at Katie. He continued in a calm manner. "Katie, you could have been well on your way to beginning a new life with everything at your fingertips. But no, as usual, you never heed to good advice, but instead, you're just as stubborn as a bloody mule."

Katie walked over to the fireplace with a faint smile. She gestured with her hands. "I felt that I had to make every effort to help Pete and his family from losing Shenandoah."

"Out of guilt, I am sure."

"No, Seamus, you're wrong. I have nothing to feel guilty about."

Even though Seamus didn't pursue the subject, Katie could tell by the still expression covering his face and the sadness in his eyes that he didn't believe her. She didn't continue the subject, but instead she returned to continue her former explanation.

Katie took a hard swallow from the guilt she was experiencing. "You don't know what it's like to be without. But Pete does. He knows what it's like to have prosperity and wealth and then lose it all, and then have to start all over again." Katie paused and then said in a whisper, "And maybe this time I am the biggest loser. Maybe, I have lost him for good."

Seamus rubbed his hand across his stubble face. "The Barkers are not going to lose their property.

"What makes you so sure. For all I know, maybe they have by now. The deadline has come and gone. It's past the first of the month you know."

Seamus moved away from the fireplace with his back turned from Katie. He swiftly held up his hands in a gesture for silence, and swiftly turned around. "Because I was bloody desperate and bloody foolish enough to pay off the bloody debt."

"Why did you of all people have a change of heart toward someone that you considered the dirt of the earth? I still remember and hurt from all that you said to Pete and me in Boston on the evening you were mugged by those thugs."

"I did it so that the bloody rebel would help me find you." Seamus turned once more facing Katie. "Now, you can return to Boston with me."

Katie's expression turned from amazement to seriousness. She knew whatever she said wouldn't please him because she dreamed of different intentions. Katie refused to take her eyes off him. She quietly approached Seamus until she stood directly before him.

"I know there is no way of saying this," Katie said in a serious tone, "so that you'll accept my feelings, but I plan to return tomorrow to Shenandoah with Pete and Charles. I can never expect you to understand, but this is where I belong. It's my home."

"I am not too sure of that, or that he'll want you to."

"Why?"

"Because Barker knows everything."

A dismal expression covered Katie's features. "I was afraid of that. How much does he know about me?"

"As much as I know. Your friend, Bradley Langsten had spoken freely of his time with you in Washington City in the summer of '61 and later at Harpers Ferry. What was more damaging was the fact that Barker listened to the details as Robert Bateman openly expressed his feelings for you. And to throw more fuel on the fire, he spoke of spending the evening with you…"

"And Father?" Katie hastily asked.

"And yes, Father. Robert spoke freely of how he had dinner with both of you, and apparently, your interest in him. For some reason, I feel he wanted Barker to hear him say everything, especially when he kissed you, and his interest in you. He even offered to help but Barker wouldn't have anything to do with it."

Katie was silent as Seamus gazed at her. He continued in a raised voice. "Now, how in the bloody world do you expect that he'd still want anything to do with you?"

"I am sure after hearing all that you have said, he probably will never trust me again. Still, I must speak to him and explain because he must be very hurt."

"I don't know that it will do you any bloody good to speak to him. He won't listen."

Katie wasn't getting anywhere with this discussion. She knew it was useless in any further attempts to try and deceive her brother. After a trail of confusion and deception, it was time for her to tell him the truth about all of her activities. Her fear was how he would judge her. She took no pleasure in some of the activity that she participated in during the war. Always loving a challenge, now Katie's greatest task would be how she would be able to pick up the pieces of her life and continue.

Tears began to flow rapidly down Katie's cheeks as she opened her heart and slowly expressed her earnest emotions. "I know, I agree. Seamus, I've made more mistakes than you could even begin to comprehend or that you have knowledge of. There are events in my life, occasions where I have betrayed someone's trust, and things that I have been part of, and lives lost that I will always regret. And I have to live with these memories and events for the rest of my life bearing the guilt of my actions. There have been those such as Pete that I've hurt and been the cause of their loss in ways that have changed their lives." Katie paused and held her face in her hands crying. She continued in a whisper, "But it was only in the belief that I was saving his and your life by hopefully an early end to the war." Katie looked once more into his eyes. "You must believe me. I did what I had to do."

"What are you saying?" Seamus asked. When Katie remained silent, then it dawned on him what she was trying to tell him in her own way. "Then I wasn't making up a lie about your spying involvement that evening in Boston, was I?"

Wiping her eyes with a handkerchief, she sniffled. "No, to a great degree it was the truth. Only I didn't expect to meet Pete and fall in love with him." Now fairly composed, Katie walked over and sat on a small chair. Seamus quietly followed though still wanting information on this revelation of his sister's mysterious life. Again wiping her eyes with a handkerchief, Katie looked up at him. "Going to Harpers Ferry against everyone's wishes was just a pretense. In reality, it was for another reason."

"I see. I remember, you were very excited about going to that hell hole of a place to teach school."

"You knew Harpers Ferry's military importance's before the war?"

"Yes, other than Springfield, Massachusetts, it was the only armory in the South."

Katie nodded in agreement and continued to speak in a soft tone, "When I traveled to Harpers Ferry, my only intention was to teach school. That all changed while traveling to the Ferry. Once I arrived in Baltimore, and was settled in for the evening at the Barnum's City Hotel, a gentleman approached me by the name of E. L. Todd. He shared a seat with me on my trip from Philadelphia. Mr. Todd was a detective with the Pinkerton Agency of Chicago but was traveling to Washington City to be assigned to a new secret service organization. Everyone knew the great possibility of war looming between the states and the government property at Harpers Ferry was of major concern to the War

Department. Arrangements were made and I began to gather information for that newly forming War Department organization on the activities of the secessionists in and around Harpers Ferry. It was believed that there was the strong possibility that Virginia was going to secede from the Union if there was war. And they would attempt to capture the armory and arsenal with its weapons and machinery. With the information that I was able to acquire on my visits to Shenandoah, and knowing this possibility, the War Department still did nothing. To this day, I still don't know why Harpers Ferry wasn't reinforced with more troops."

Katie continued as she gestured with her hands. "Anyway, when I returned to Washington City and saw Bradley Langsten in July after the war began, I didn't think I would be going back to the Ferry. But he asked me to on behalf of General Scott. As time went by, I got deeper into the whole thing until I was under the supervision of General Sharpe."

Seamus was shocked. His features revealed his astonishment at the revelation pouring from Katie's mouth. He never suspected her of any involvement with spying for the Union. He turned away, as if in thought and rubbed his hand through his hair. Once more he turned around angrily. "Didn't you for one moment consider the danger? You could have been shot or thrown into prison."

"Yes, I did. But being a woman had its advantages."

"Why all you had to do was open your mouth and anyone could tell with your accent that you were from the North."

"Probably. But I am sure it was because the secessionists and Confederate army were not really suspecting me, a woman, of any improprieties. And being friends with the influential Barker family…no one ever suspected me. Meeting William Pierce on the train from Baltimore, and having knowledge of his esteemed position in Virginia politics, and meeting Charles Barker, the leading secessionist in the lower Valley caused my work to be so natural. The only downfall was, I didn't know how personally involved I would become with the Barker family…especially Caroline and Pete."

"But you know Katie, I still don't understand why months after the war ended why William Pierce would still want to abduct you and eventually, I am sure, had the intentions of killing you."

Walking over by the fire, Katie again looked down at the flames and then again at her brother. With a heavy heart, she replied. "I am not too sure about that. Actually William confessed his love for me even though I suspected that he knew that I had his brother killed at Winchester in late August of '64."

"Well, did you?"

Katie felt that Seamus with his inquisitive questions was cornering her. As her habit had been in the past, she remained silent, returning an expression of exasperation.

Impatient for her answer, Seamus quickly added, "You were very calm and deliberate when you shot William. Where did you learn to use a weapon so efficiently?"

Katie abruptly answered. "Seamus forget it. It doesn't matter, it's all over with." Katie paused as if in thought looking aimlessly at the fire burning. She looked up. "The only thing that does concern me is that Pete is to never know that I was his enemy during the war! And I'll do whatever I must do to protect that secret!"

Seamus answered with a tone of doubt, "Why Katie? If you feel that he really loves you…"

Katie replied in a forceful demand. "You don't understand. I am not so sure how he feels anymore. Or if he has his own suspicions about me. Whether I return to Boston or not, you are the only one who has any knowledge of all that I've done over the last five years. And I told you the truth because I needed to tell someone. To clear my conscious." Katie stood and slowly paced around the area in front of the fireplace. "You are the one I have trusted the most in my life. Please if you respect me and love me as your sister, please drop this matter and forget anything that I've told you."

The only sound in the room was the huge wooden clock chiming four times. Seamus looked at the troubled expression and the fear that filled his sister's eyes. He approached and embraced her in his arms. He kissed her forehead. "Sure. I'll never betray your trust in me. This day, your words will go with me to my grave."

* * * *

Charles arrived from the carpentry shop where he had found an extra shovel. He paused and gazed around the property. He glanced back at the house and considered all that had happened today. In his heart, Charles felt betrayed and angry for the accusations and anguish that William had put him through. It had concerned him from the beginning as to why William pursued such an evil path to follow. The only conclusion he could derive was that William's expectations of power and greed had eluded him because, as he suspected, William had lost favor with President Davis. William couldn't deal with failure. The principle of states' rights and values of its sovereignty that he once stood for had been corrupted by his false delusions of esteem and glory.

Charles turned his attention and glanced at Pete who was taking the first turn at digging the grave. They had said little other than Pete had given him the good news that Caroline and Ann were safe. Although, Pete said nothing of their mother, Charles' heart condemned him with guilt over the way he had misled his younger brother and had deprived and schemed him out of his rightful part in ownership of Shenandoah. To some degree, he had manipulated their mother into believing that he was the most qualified to own and operate the estate. He used Pete's weaknesses against him on every occasion. Ultimately, the decision was hers, but Charles promoted the business disagreements with his brother to his advantage. It was their father's wish that the two brothers would equally own the farm and share the responsibility. He remembered before the war how Pete would labor long hours with the slaves and was certainly a major factor in the business' success. This is why Pete had their respect and admiration, and he didn't.

The wind began to blow intensely. Pete paused and glanced up at the sky. It was beginning to darken. He picked up the pace, wanting to accomplish the task as rapidly as possible. As long as the rain held off, it was his intentions to leave immediately after the task was finished for Shenandoah.

"Take a breather. I'll pick up where you left off," Charles cried out.

Pete paused and tossed the shovel from the grave onto the dirt embankment. He glanced at Charles and hoisted himself from the pit. He brushed off the Virginia red clay from his trousers and again looked at Charles.

"I see that you are still angry with me," Charles said.

"Not angry, Charles. My feelings about anything are deadened. Not only with you, but Katie, and life in general. I am just like everyone else, I've had so much happen over the last four years that I've become insensitive when it comes to showing any kind of emotions."

"Well, I can't speak for Katie but I apologize to you for everything that I've said or done."

Pete questioned his brother's sincerity. He half-chuckled to disguise his hurt. "Charles, you always got everything in life that you desired. You didn't have to work for anything. You didn't play by the rules; it was just expected that all things would be there for you. Yes, I have faults. Many of them. But, I have always tried to do and treat others accordingly, even if they disagreed with me. And look. It got me nowhere." Pete paused, removed his hat, and wiped the perspiration from his forehead. He glanced off into the wooded area nearby and looked once more at his brother. "I have learned a lot about life. If one good thing came from the war, it would be the challenges that I faced and endured. I learned to benefit from the hardship of doing without, such as the simple things that are taken for granted in life, food and water. But mostly, I have learned to respect life. Even though life may never deal me a good hand, no matter what situation that I am in, I will always attempt to make the best of it. There are many that I served with and I am sure that I've killed that will never have the opportunities that I still have, even though it appears that I have nothing. But I do. I have my life and the chance to start over again once we leave from here."

The grave was as deep as needed to be for the two bodies. Charles lifted himself from the six-foot hole and looked at Pete. "The war has changed me also. Toward the end of the conflict when I left Richmond, the separation from Caroline and Ann frightened me beyond the thought of dying while trying to escape the city or fighting the Yankees in an effort of eluding them. I didn't know how long it would be or if I'd see them again. I am sure you know what I am speaking of with your experiences and feelings for Katie. It leaves an unspeakable void in your heart, especially if you don't know if you'll ever see them again. Even before Caroline departed, I felt that heaviness of spirit over the uncertainty that was going to take place. As I stood in the street and watched until Caroline's carriage disappeared, I really believed I had said my final goodbyes. The next morning as I sat on my horse across the James watching the city burn, I knew that my life and dreams had changed forever. I really didn't expect to see the end of the war. With Shenandoah's destruction, my family on the run, and more so, Rebecca's death, it was more then I could bear. Still at night, I have horrible dreams of the events that took place that night in Richmond."

Tears filled Charles' eyes as he continued in a quivering voice. "In Rebecca's final moments, I did something that I never did before. I held her in my arms; I brushed her long chestnut brown hair from her face. I can still see her peaceful brown eyes looking at me on her deathbed. She asked for forgiveness for all that she had said that was unworthy and her rebellious action toward the family. Rebecca knew she was dying and so she attempted to comfort me with her words. She poured out her heart to me in those final moments by saying that she wished we could have been closer in our relationship and that she really and truly loved me in spite of all our differences. Those words pricked and pierced my heart in a way that is beyond words. Often I still hear them in the quiet of the night. She really wanted to live but I was negligent. So exhausted from everything that had been taking place within the government on those final days, I fell asleep. Of all people, it was a Confederate straggler and not a Yankee that committed the atrocity. The guilt of her murder is something that I'll live with the rest of my life." Charles paused and looked at the grave. He continued in a somber tone, "Once I see Caroline and Ann I never want to be apart from them again even though I know that jail time might await me."

Pete nodded in agreement. "I know what you mean. After all these months, the pain is still there from her death. But it may be nothing compared to what mother bears for her."

After placing both bodies into the grave, Pete and Charles began to rapidly shovel dirt into the hole. The rain was once again beginning to intensify. Once they were finished, they tossed the shovels onto the wagon and boarded it for the ride to the mansion.

"For over an hour you haven't asked about Mother. Why?" Pete curiously asked.

"I missed her, but not like Caroline and Ann."

The horses moved steadily around the rear of the barn and in the direction of the lane leading to the mansion. Pete knew that

Charles should know what happened in the event, upon their arrival at Shenandoah, their mother was deceased.

Pete took a deep swallow. "I have hesitated to tell you but much has happened since the war ended."

"Do you have bad news to tell me about Mother?"

"I'm afraid so."

Tears began flowing freely from Charles' eyes. "Oh God no! What happened?"

"As I am sure that you know, once the war was over, the Unionists moved to legally attempt to confiscate property belonging to those who supported the cause, even soldiers."

Charles was wiping his bloodshot eyes. "They tried to collect, I am sure, on back taxes."

"That's right. I tried to get the money from old man Larson at the bank, but he said they were short on funds. I am sure he was because there were limitations on who they could loan to."

"How much do we owe?"

"$2,500."

"We can't raise that kind of money. We lost everything during the war. We have nothing, nothing at all."

"Katie, had this hair-brain scheme of traveling to Boston and making a serious request of a loan from her father. Of course, that miserably failed. After Katie and I had a serious disagreement, I returned without her. On the day that I did, Mother was wounded by a stray shot by some raiders that wanted to harm Hayward."

"Tell me, who did this?"

"Benjamin Watson."

There was an astonished expression covering Charles' features. "He worked for us on many occasions. Daniel and him were very fond of sharing spirits. They were the best of friends."

"I've thought about it often since it all happened, but somehow, Ben found out about Hayward being the one who shot and killed Daniel at the National Hotel in Frederick and he was probably looking to avenge his death."

"I'll deal with him, first thing when we get back into the area."

"I already have."

"What do you mean?"

"I shot and killed him over a week ago in Charlestown." Pete brought the horses to a halt in front of the mansion. "Mother's wounds were severe. She was still living when I left."

"Shenandoah doesn't matter at this point, only her welfare."

Pete continued as he looked at Charles still sitting in the wagon. "After the shooting, I was captured and jailed in all places, the old Brown fort. The next day after shooting Ben, Seamus arrived in Harpers Ferry. Katie was missing and he needed my help. So he prodded the Provost Marshall with documents from Secretary Stanton to let me go so that I could help find her. The Provost was resistant to the idea until Seamus threatened to use his influence. Then the Provost conceded. Not only that, but Seamus generously paid the back taxes. We owe him."

As Charles stepped from the wagon, he looked at Pete. "Then we must leave at once for Shenandoah."

"No, we can't leave until this weather lets up. Besides, the river might be flooded and we will be unable to cross."

Charles was anxious to get home before they were discovered by a Federal patrol and apprehended. If this occurred, then he wouldn't have the opportunity to see his family. He held his head low in disappointment and nodded reluctantly in agreement. As he turned to ascend the steps of the front entrance to the mansion, he thought of his hopes and dreams that laid across the river at Shenandoah. He knew it would never be the same as before the war. He knew there wasn't much to return to. The Unionist would surely make the attempt once more to find a reason to confiscate the property and deprive him and his family of an income and home. He reasoned that as long as Caroline and the family were safe, for now that would be the fulfillment of his greatest hopes.

Chapter 58

The food supplies were exhausted. Everyone had quietly eaten a skimpy dinner of hard biscuits and a few pieces of cold country ham, chased by water from the well. Katie rose and began to clean the dishes from the table. "I'll check on Hayward," Pete said.

Katie took a long look at Pete as he disappeared through the entranceway to the hall. She frustratingly departed for the kitchen area.

Seamus looked at his sister and then turned toward Charles and took a sip of water. "So your Charles Barker, huh?" Seamus casually asked.

Charles also turned his attention from following his brother's departure and answered defensively. "Yes... I am he, and I assume that you are Seamus McBride."

"You assume bloody correct."

"I see. As I understand, I owe you a debt of gratitude. Just a while ago, my brother informed me of your generosity toward my family. I would like to personally thank you."

"It was earned."

In many ways, he was grateful for Seamus' act of kindness but in many ways Charles didn't believe behind the smile that he could be trusted. Maybe it was from the effects of over caution during the war. Charles leaned back in his chair and coldly stared at him. He was apprehensive and his emotions were genuine. He firmly believed Seamus was still his enemy and only satisfied the debt on Shenandoah enough to benefit from the skills of his brother. In someway, Charles believed Seamus would come back on them and attempt to legally confiscate the property for his own business interest just like carpetbaggers were doing.

"Now you know who I am. What's next?" Charles curiously asked.

Seamus chuckled and answered in his usual sarcastic tone. "I am sure the Provost Marshall in every district must be keeping a watch out for you. I'd be willing to bloody bet you that the servant that took off earlier when the fighting erupted headed toward Leesburg to notify the Yankees of your whereabouts. And, when my Yankee friends catch up with you, then your fate might hang in the balance the same as old Jeff Davis."

Charles angrily jumped from his chair. "Well if you're going to have any part in it, then you'll have to kill me because I have every intention of returning home to see my wife and daughter. I will not be hindered by you or anyone else! Do I make myself understood?"

As Katie was about to re-enter the dining room, she heard everything that was spoken. It sounded as if tempers were beginning to kindle with the embers of animosity and hatred still fuming from the war. She didn't believe after all that had transpired this afternoon that Charles and Seamus would still have the energy to continue the struggle by battling in a war of words. Her face turned red as her anger surfaced. She felt compelled to act swiftly.

"Haven't you two had enough of the bloody bickering?" Katie shouted, "When will this bloody war end? When will everyone try to pick up the pieces and move on?" Several times in anger and frustration she hit the table with her hand. She dropped to a chair and broke down and began to uncontrollably weep. "Isn't all that we've been through enough? Or does there have to be more bloodshed to quench your thirst for vengeance."

In his usual style of aggressiveness and stubbornness, Seamus wanted to continue the argument. "Should we let the bloody Johnnies go free after our boys paid a dear price of sacrificing their lives to save this land of ours?"

Charles looked defiantly at Seamus as Katie continued to sob. Seamus pointed at Charles and continued his verbal assault. "Should this man who helped propagate the duration of the war by his so called wisdom be allowed to live freely among us without due punishment?"

Charles turned his attention to Seamus. "To answer your question, Sir, no. But once I return home and know that my mother is still living after being wounded..."

Quickly, Katie looked up with a confused expression covering her features. "Oh no, no." She shook her head in frustration. "Who did this to Miss Elizabeth?"

"As I understand from Pete, it was some renegade raiders." Charles pointed toward Seamus and continued to answer Katie's question. "Of course, it was men such as your brother who can't put the war behind them! My family has suffered enough!"

Seamus stood and returned the gesture. "It was you Johnnies that started the whole thing. We just finished the job."

Anger dominated Charles' expression. Once more, he began to lose his composure. He began to approach Seamus and suddenly paused. "Once I know that my wife and daughter are safe and taken care of, I have the utmost honorable intentions of surrendering myself to the Provost Marshall at Harpers Ferry. But until then, as I said earlier in our debate, I'll kill anyone that stands in my way." Charles paused and gazed sternly at Seamus. "And McBride, that means you also. Now do I make myself understood?"

As Katie's bloodshot eyes were looking at them, Seamus quietly nodded in acknowledgement.

* * * *

Pete was sitting in the parlor by the sofa where Hayward was resting. He was a safe distance from hearing the heated discussion that was transpiring in the dining room. He quietly watched as his friend struggled to chew on one of the biscuits. Pete took the bread from him and soaked it in some cold water to soften the hardness and then returned it and placed the food to Hayward's mouth. He partook of it and slowly chewed. The whole time his eyes followed Pete's every move. His friend was unusually quiet. Hayward noticed by his friend's grave expression that his emotions were somewhat distressed.

He took the piece of bread that he was eating from his mouth. He handed it to Pete. "I'se finished."

"No Hayward, you have to eat more than that. If you're too weak, we might have trouble getting you back to Shenandoah."

Hayward gazed defiantly at Pete and quietly snatched the bread from his hand. "I'se see that I'se not the only one 'round here that's havin' troubles."

"What do you mean by that?"

"Yose's knows what I'se mean. Yose and Misse Katie." Hayward paused and waited for an answer from Pete. There was no reply. Hayward's good perception of people had surfaced. He knew Pete was sure of where he was going with the conversation but was too stubborn to continue. When Pete ignored him, Hayward continued in an angry, forceful tone. "Are yose gonna jist sit dere, or is ya gonna say something?" Again, Hayward gave

Pete the opportunity to speak. Exasperated and exhausted, Hayward continued to speak louder. "Den be that way. Darn stubborn fool boy."

Pete noticed the sorrow in Hayward's eyes. He quietly rose from the chair. It wasn't that he was trying to be rude, there just wasn't an easy answer or way to deal with all that had happened between Katie and him. He felt uncomfortable being around Katie. He was uncertain how to approach her with all that had happened since leaving Boston, and more importantly, his deepest feelings for her. Could he ever trust her again? With all that he heard from Robert Bateman and Bradley Langsten, he was unsure of the identity of the real Katie McBride. For him, it was too late for a new beginning. The trust they shared had vanished like the vapor on a cold wintry night. He felt betrayed and manipulated by someone who professed to love and constantly shower him with her affection and words of commitment.

Pete felt tense. Finally, he subdued his pride. "I don't know what will happen between Katie and me. There was so much revealed about her in Washington that I must admit I've found it hard to believe. Maybe, with Katie, I am just too blind to see the truth. But what saddens me the most is the reality that I had been involved in a relationship with someone that I really don't know. How do you live with someone that you don't know? How can there ever be anything between us? No Hayward, it's over with!"

Hayward groaned with pain as he struggled to sit up on the sofa. Once comfortable, he confidently, calmly answered. "Dis war has changed everyone. I'se see the sufferin' that's gone on around me. The changes that have takin' place. You, Mr. Charles, and me. But also, Misse Katie. We's all change in sum way, and done things wrong. I'se sure she's made mistakes jist like the rest of us people, but yose must forgive and move on with ya life. Yose still young yet. Don't waste what the Good Lord has given ya."

Out of anger, Pete looked for a fault in Hayward's statement against Katie. When he found one, he swiftly turned around and snapped. "Then you are saying that you believe all the accusations made against her in Washington City?'

"No, no, I'se didn't say that. Yose not a listin', but only what yose want to hear."

"Well, it sounds that way to me," Pete hastily replied.

"If yose gonna be hard headed, and let ya pride rule ya, den she is a gonna leave ya and dis time, she isn't gonna come back. Does ya understand?"

"I don't want to speak about this with you any longer," Pete angrily shouted as he rushed from the room.

Hayward had known Pete for many years. He knew from the past when he had spoken words that had pierced Pete's heart that he would hastily look for a way of escape. Just as now, such as rushing from the room, his friend was troubled. He had to learn to lay aside his differences and move on with life or he would always be hindered by the blindness of his pride. Regardless of all that may have taken place during the war, everyone for sometime would suffer from its effects. Katie and Pete were no exception.

As Hayward pondered on this matter, Katie was racing through the hallway toward the front door just as Pete had done several minutes earlier. There might be a chance, Hayward thought.

* * * *

As Pete leaned against one of the white columns on the veranda, he gazed across the field and watched in the distance a husky black bear casually making its way toward a wooded area. The thoughts Hayward spoke of continued to trouble him, causing him to feel restless in his heart. Maybe Hayward was right. Maybe he was too prideful, but it was the only defense he had to protect himself from any kind of hurt and pain. Katie allowing another man to kiss and become emotionally involved with her wasn't something that he could easily forget let alone forgive. To him, this showed an unfaithfulness, and concerned him that in the future, she would run to another man's arms when their world seemed to be in disarray. Another question that concerned him was if this was someone he wanted to share the rest of his life with and to be the mother of his children.

Katie was startled and surprised as she stepped from the front entranceway onto the veranda. She quickly paused. She wasn't prepared to face Pete and speak with him regarding what was left of their relationship. Inwardly, she was anxious and afraid. Knowing she couldn't show her true emotions to Pete, she repressed her fears. Her heart raced as Pete turned around and glanced at her. Katie wiped the perspiration from her hands onto her apron. Her eyes were staring, waiting for him to speak. When he turned around and didn't address her, she swiftly scrambled for words to say. As difficult as it was for her, she remained composed and spoke with a calmness, and softness.

"I notice that you're watching the animals as you always did frequently when you're at Shenandoah?"

Pete didn't turn. His eyes continued to look toward the direction of the wooded area.

Katie waited anxiously for him to speak. When he didn't, she took several more steps in his direction. She stood patiently, continuing to gaze at him.

Finally, Pete took his finger and scratched the tip of his nose. "Do you ever feel like you need to get away from everything that is happening in your life? And even those who are close to you?"

Hesitating for words, Katie slowly replied. "Yes, I guess sometimes. That is why I would take long walks along the ocean when I lived in Boston. As much as I loved my family, we didn't always agree."

"When I was growing up at Shenandoah, my father use to always go to the area along the river that I've shared with you. It was a time for him to think and work out his business issues, but more often, his family problems. Unfortunately, my mother and he didn't always see eye to eye on matters. From all I observed, they never had much of a marriage. They were too distant. When he had had enough of all the bickering and arguing, he would just drop what he was doing and go to that area for several hours along the river, and sometimes even longer. He thought of us kids and the possibility of a broken home life, I am sure. When I look back on everything, I believe that's why Rebecca and my mother never got along. She was angry. She was just as close to Father as I was. Sometimes, I think this is what he felt that he had to do to keep Mother and him together and a home for his children. Going off to himself."

Taking a deep swallow, Katie walked near Pete and gently placed her hand on his shoulder. "I know that I've put you through a lot lately. After siding with my father on the evening that Seamus was injured, I had serious reservations about whether I did the right thing or not, by backing him…even though I felt that you were out of place. And then afterward, I thought of the determined effort my family was trying to accomplish in separating us. I was so afraid that everything had ended for us. You wanted the best for me, I know, and were looking for something like this to happen, so that you could have an excuse to set me free. But I didn't want to stay in Boston and forget about all that we had shared and said to each other. I really didn't believe for a moment that this was what you wanted either. Truthfully, I don't care what my family thinks or how they feel about us. All that matters to me is that I can win back your love and trust. I don't care where we live or if we never have anything of wealth. All that matters to me is you, and your love for me. That's all."

Pete shook his head in disagreement as he looked away in the direction of the mountains. "We can't look over the fact that a lot has happened between us. Both of us have changed. The war changed us. Our circumstances in life have changed us. All that's recently happened has changed us." He looked up and gazed into her sad eyes. "I don't know if there is a future for us. How many lies have we lived and hid to protect one another? I want time. Time to think about whether I will stay at Shenandoah with Charles' return and time to think about my life."

"What about us?"

"I don't know. There are a lot of questions to be asked and answered. Such as why were you in Washington City in the first place?"

"I wanted to continue the effort of trying to do something to save Shenandoah before you lost it." Katie saw the sorrow on his face. She pleaded in a frightened tone, "You must believe me; that's the only reason I went to Washington City."

"What about Robert Bateman? You couldn't have been too concerned about what was going to happen to Shenandoah or even me while you were kissing him. Now were you?"

Katie was silent. Tears filled her eyes and flowed rapidly down her cheeks. She looked up at him. "You wouldn't understand the loneliness and emptiness that I was feeling at the time. No one could. After all that I'd been through, I just wanted everything in my life to return to normal and for all the troubles to go away. Even if it was just for a short time before reality returned and the same issues continued to trouble me. For a short moment in time, Robert provided that for me. I guess I allowed myself to be too vulnerable with him and wasn't in control of my actions."

Katie paused and looked down at the floor of the veranda. Shame and guilt filled her heart. She took a deep sigh and once more looked at Pete. Tears still flowed as she continued in a broken tone. "Let me explain fully because you must hear it from me. After you left with General Johnston's Confederate army in June of '61, I traveled to Washington City to meet my father. While there, a friend of the family, General Scott, introduced me to Colonel Bradley Langsten of his staff. It was the fourth of July and the city was celebrating even though many were preparing to march out and eventually fight your army at Manassas. I must admit Bradley took an interest in me. I didn't respond to him in any form because my heart was with you, and only you. Early the next morning, I returned to Harpers Ferry as planned."

Katie turned away from Pete and glanced at the once beautiful grounds that covered the front of the mansion. She continued to speak in a soft tone, "When I was in Washington City last week at Secretary Stanton's office, Bradley walked in and made various attempts to rekindle something that never existed in the first place. He even had the bloody audacity to show his face at the Willard that evening. I was with Robert and my father having dinner. When I left, Robert walked me to my room, and yes, I allowed him to kiss me. How did I feel afterwards? Whether you want to believe me or not, my heart condemned me and I've had hell to pay for it ever since. I betrayed not only your trust in me but my own trust in my commitment to you."

"I appreciate all that you tried to do for us. On more than one occasion, you've been an inspiration to me and you've lived in a way that you're not accustomed. And as for the money that Seamus loaned the family, I have the fullest intentions of seeing that he gets it back. Again as I said earlier, I just don't know what will happen to us. Too much has taken place between us that I can't get out of my mind. I feel so confused from all that I have heard from others about you. I am exhausted trying to figure everything out with retaining Shenandoah and avoiding its confiscation by the Unionist. Anymore, I just don't know who you are, and I can't believe anything that you say to me."

Katie quietly turned and looked at Pete. She felt frantic inwardly, but quickly repressed these emotions, struggling vigorously to control them. Katie continued looking around the landscape in front of the mansion.

"By chance, did you know the Hammonds?" Katie asked.

"Yes. They were good people. On some social occasions, we would visit them."

"From all appearances, I would assume that this estate was probably just as majestic as Shenandoah."

"The Hammonds were very wealthy and of the highest esteem in Loudoun County's social and political circles. It was John Hammond, who not only supported, but used his own money to help provide uniforms and supplies for the 8th Virginia Infantry regiment, which was from this county."

"Well look at all of this now," Katie said as she gazed around the property. "Just as with Shenandoah, this place is dead. Its vibrancies have disappeared. Look around. There are no more slaves working to keep the place beautiful and productive. There are no more laughing people at barbecues and socials, sharing their lives with one another. The life that it once possessed has vanished. There is nothing that remains to bring back the existence and vitality that it once enjoyed. Division between people and the effects of war destroyed it all." Katie paused as she waited for Pete to answer. When he remained silent, just gazing at her, she cried in a more forceful tone. "Can't you see that our misunderstandings are doing the same thing to us? They are destroying anything that we had between us. That we shared. Most of all, it's destroying our love for each other. Are you going to allow that to happen?" Pete still didn't respond. Katie continued in a calmer tone. "After everything had happened in that house and I kissed you, I really thought that you would be happy to see me. I thought that you cared. But I guess I was wrong,"

"Katie, I do care. I wouldn't have gone through and taken the risk that I did if I didn't care what happened to you. When Seamus leaves, you should also go with him. Start your life over again and learn from all that you've experienced from the war, our relationship, and the mistakes that we've made in our relationship. Just maybe, this will help and prosper both of us some day when we start over."

Realizing that Pete was still unmovable in his convictions and that it was useless to continue this conversation, Katie just looked at him, nodded in agreement, and quietly walked to the door.

Feeling somber and taking a deep breath, Pete continued to gaze and look across the landscape, still pondering on all that had happened over the last three weeks and where his life would go from here.

Chapter 59

The next morning, the sun was slowly rising over the wooded slopes on the ridge to the east. All was quiet with the exception of a lone rooster crowing in the distance near the barn. With little sleep the evening before, Pete was up early. He was busy at the front of the mansion hitching the team of horses to the wagon for the journey to Shenandoah. His thoughts were on the conversation that transpired the previous evening with Katie. He was still uncertain concerning her trustworthiness. There were many questions about her life that were unanswered. Much damage had been done to their relationship by all the events that transpired since leaving Shenandoah for Boston. Another issue concerning him was the reality that he knew with Charles' return that possibly his stay at Shenandoah would be of short duration. It all depended on how much, if any time, Charles would possibly be imprisoned for his role in the Confederate government. If so, then he would stay and help until his release from confinement.

Once everything was ready, Pete ascended the steps of the mansion to inform his brother that he was ready to return home. Before he could enter, the door opened and Charles appeared, assisting Hayward. "Are we ready?" Charles asked.

"Yes, I found an old canvas in the barn that we can tie over the top of the wagon to hide Hayward."

"That might not be enough if a Yankee patrol stops us on the road and wants to search the wagon. If they discover we are hiding Hayward and he has been wounded by gunfire, then they'll detain us and ask us questions."

There was a troubled expression covering Pete's face as he sighed. "I had thought of that happening. But it's a chance we will have to take. I believe if we travel the farmers' lanes and back roads toward Snickersville, then we can cross the mountain. I know a place where we can ford the Shenandoah and head eastward along the riverbank."

Seamus and Katie departed the mansion and quietly approached Pete, Charles, and Hayward. Ignorant of their presence, Charles hastily asked Pete, "And what do we do once a Yankee patrol spots us?"

"What is this about a Yankee patrol?" Seamus inquisitively asked.

Pete quietly looked at Charles. Turning his attention toward Seamus, Pete decided to disclose little of their intentions. "We are apprehensive over how we will be able to get home without Yankee interference. If they see Hayward is wounded, then there will be too many questions and maybe one of them will be able to identify my brother."

"Aye, I'm sure they have Charles' bloody photograph in every Provost office in these parts," Seamus answered sarcastically. "He deserves to be caught."

Charles' anger was aroused as he looked at Seamus. "Now look here McBride, as I told you yesterday, if you attempt in anyway of interfering with me returning home, then, as I said before, I would kill you, or you will have to kill me. Now what is it going to be?"

Seamus refused to take his eyes off Charles. He slowly backed away. "Come on Katie, let's get out of here."

Turning and looking at Pete's troubled features, and then again at Seamus anxious expression, Katie replied, "No Seamus, I am returning to Shenandoah with Pete."

At first Seamus was quiet. His features were tense with anger and displeasure. "What?" When Katie continued to gaze at him and didn't answer, he asked again in a more forceful tone. "After all that I've gone through over these past days to find you and free you, you're bloody telling me that you're not going to return to Boston with me? You must be crazy."

"Crazy or not, I am needed at Shenandoah."

"I agree with Seamus. You should return to Boston. We are far from being out of trouble," Pete said.

"No. I have thought this through. If I am riding with Charles on the wagon and under the pretense of being his wife, then maybe we can pull it off and safely return to Shenandoah." Katie turned her attention to her brother and continued. "Once we have returned to Shenandoah, I'll board the train at Harpers Ferry and immediately come home."

Charles looked at Pete and agreed. "You know, she has a point. There would be less suspicion."

With a deep sigh and a concerned expression, Seamus reluctantly answered in a tone of displeasure. "All right. For now,

I am returning to Washington City. But if I don't hear from you within the next couple of days, then I will bloody return. And when I do, I'll bloody put you over my shoulders and force you to return to Boston with me."

Quietly, Katie approached and kissed him on the cheek. She smiled. "I promise."

Seamus tipped his hat in a farewell gesture, turned and descended the steps. As Katie watched, she was saddened by his departure. Seamus mounted his horse and looked at her once more. With a wave, he turned his horse around and galloped down the lane.

Pete helped Hayward into the wagon and covered him with a blanket. He securely tied the canvas over the top of the wagon while Charles assisted Katie onto the wagon seat. Once all was ready, Charles climbed aboard and sat next to Katie, taking the reins of the team of horses and moving them forward. Pete mounted and closely followed. At the end of the lane, Charles turned the wagon along the Old Carolina Road toward Leesburg. They only traveled on this road for a short distance before turning onto a farmer's lane that led to a heavily wooded ridge in the distance.

Pete rode along side the wagon. "Quickly! Keep going until you get into the woods. I'll stay behind until I know you are safe."

Charles nodded in agreement as Katie quietly looked on. Pete stayed and closely watched Seamus riding slowly toward Leesburg. He continued to observe until he felt that Charles and Katie were at a safe distance. Pete noticed a small sapling tree and removed a branch. Rapidly, he brushed the leaves of the branch along the surface of the area where the wagon had traveled to disguise the wheel prints. His mind was racing as to what action to take next. It was difficult for him to maintain a clear mind with Katie traveling along with them. More determined than ever, he vowed he would force her to return to Boston just as she had promised Seamus.

After Charles entered the tree line, Pete galloped off in the same direction, occasionally pausing and destroying their tracks. Once he entered the first tree line and out of sight from any one that traveled the road, he again paused and followed Seamus' progress with a spyglass. He had confiscated the item from the library of the Hammond's home knowing its importance.

For several minutes, all appeared normal. Suddenly, Yankees, numbering ten in the cavalry patrol appeared on the road from Leesburg. Pete became quite anxious. His first thought was that Darby had arrived at Leesburg and informed the Provost Marshall of Charles' presence at the estate. The patrol was slowing down. They paused in front of Seamus and appeared to be questioning him. Pete feared that Seamus may disclose the plans and then it would be nearly impossible to escape their grasp. He knew Charles didn't have enough safe distance to avoid the patrol and possible capture. Pete quickly looked around for a place he could fire from and attempt to lead them in a different direction if needed away from Charles and Katie.

After several minutes had past, the Yankee patrol proceeded rapidly toward the estate. Pete continued to observe, especially when they came to the area, which led toward his direction. When the patrol passed and entered the lane leading to the estate, Pete continued to observe, determining to discover their intentions. For almost thirty minutes, he continued to follow the Yankees' progress with the spyglass, as they covered the estate searching.

Pete remained calm, knowing every minute the Yankee cavalry spent at the estate searching the property, Charles was increasing his chances of escaping. He watched as several soldiers walked to the rear of the barn near the location of the gravesite and several more to the area of the orchard where William and Jacob were buried. Maybe, this would keep them occupied for sometime. Minutes slowly past as the soldiers continued to investigate the area. It looked like an officer was speaking to someone else under his command that had authority. The officer pointed to five soldiers that were still mounted and again spoke with the officer of lesser rank. Immediately, the officer of less rank gestured to the others that were mounted, and after mounting himself, headed rapidly toward the end of the lane that intersects with the road to Leesburg. Once there, they turned south, apparently looking for Pete's trail or some evidence indicating the direction that Pete and his party might have traveled. When it appeared there wasn't any indication that they traveled in that direction, the patrol turned around and headed again in the direction of Leesburg. Beyond the lane to the estate, one of the soldiers dismounted and walked slowly, constantly looking on the ground. At the area where Pete and Charles left the road, the cavalrymen paused.

A scout, Pete thought, dismounted and searched the ground for tracks. Pete continued to look through the spyglass as the scout began to speak with a sergeant. Pete noticed the scout was pointing in his direction. As he pulled his revolver from under his coat, he heard a voice from behind. "Still up to the same old bloody tricks, huh Johnnie?" When Pete didn't answer, Seamus added. "As I bloody recall, during the war you people like to ambush us whenever given the chance."

With a surprised expression covering his features, Pete swiftly turned around and looked. Much to his surprise, there appeared Seamus gazing at him, grinning. Seamus moved his horse forward until he was beside Pete.

Both looked at the Yankee cavalry patrol. "You know Johnnie, the war is over. It would be foolish to try and harm anyone of them. This time you would hang."

Pete did not take his eyes off of the cavalry patrol. "I will do whatever it takes for Charles to get away," he snapped.

"Even at the expense of your life?"

Pete coldly replied as he turned and looked at Seamus. "Even at the expense of my life."

Seamus was in disbelief over Pete's willingness to sacrifice his life. "That is some blame, bloody sacrifice for someone who beat you out of your bloody share of the estate." When Pete didn't answer, Seamus continued, "Or is it my sister that you're really trying to protect?"

"No, it's not because of Katie."

Removing the hat from his head and wiping his forehead, Seamus looked at the soldiers, turned and smiled at Pete. "Well Barker, I am not like you. I am not blinded by pride and bloody arrogance concerning issues in my life. I can be honest with myself." Seamus' expression revealed the seriousness of his heart. "I am here to protect Katie. Other than that, there is no bloody reason for my return. If it wouldn't have been for her traveling with you rebels, then I would have wasted no time in helping my Yankee comrades in capturing your brother. But because of my sister's stubbornness, I have no choice in this matter."

Pete put down the spyglass and turned. "Did you ever stop and think that this may have been the reason for her doing it? She didn't trust you?" Seamus nodded his head in agreement as Pete continued. "Besides, as you say, I don't need your bloody help."

"Well you're going to get it any bloody way whether you like it or not!"

Pete turned around and noticed the Yankee patrol was about a thousand yards away and slowly heading in their direction. Wiping his mouth with his hand, Pete remained calm. He refused to take his eyes off the patrol. "Since your demanding to help out, I believe we need to distract their attention from following this trail and lead them off in a different direction. This will give Charles and Katie some borrowed time. Perhaps an hour."

"That's not much."

Pete pointed toward the mansion where the Yankee soldiers were still looking around and replied with unease. "I know but it's the best that we can do. Hopefully, the others will follow."

"Barker, no matter what takes place. Don't even think about shooting any of them. If you do, then I'll be forced to shoot you. Do you understand?"

Pete refused to answer. He looked defiantly at Seamus and smacked the hindquarter of his horse. "What, to save your own skin. Come on," Pete shouted.

From the cover of the wooded area, Pete and Seamus charged in the direction of the Yankee patrol. They fired their weapons at the ground in an attempt to cause the Yankees' horses to become nervous and throw some of them from their saddles. This scheme didn't work. Immediately, Pete pointed toward some steep heavily wooded ridgeline in the distance. Both headed in that direction at a full gallop. Pete looked back and noticed that all five of the cavalrymen were in full pursuit. Several of them fired their weapons, but missed hitting Pete and Seamus. Pete and Seamus smacked their horses on the hindquarter to increase their speed. Across the field and jumping over a small stream, Pete and Seamus' horses raced side-by-side at a fast pace. Noticing a gap in the distance between the wooded ridgeline, Pete pointed and turned his horse in that direction. As Pete turned and looked once more at the Yankees' progress, he determined they had failed to close the gap on them. It appeared now there were only four of them. Apparently, one had fallen off his horse when he attempted to jump the stream of water.

Again, Pete turned his attention toward the heavily wooded ridgeline. "Over there, we can take cover and try to scare them off," Pete shouted.

Shortly, they discovered a path and entered the tree line. They continued until they noticed a line of huge boulders on both sides of the trail. Once sheltered by the mountain of rocks, Pete knew it was a well-fortified area and would give Charles additional time to escape. They dismounted and tied their horses to a tree.

Immediately, Pete and Seamus spread out over the area. The Yankee patrol cautiously entered the tree line expecting an ambush. Pete and Seamus quietly waited. When the Yankees were near, Pete fired over their heads. Quickly, the Yankees dismounted and took what cover they could find behind rock outcroppings or trees, and returned fire. As Pete glanced over the rocks, a piece of stone clipped the side of his face from a bullet fragment. Again, he fired twice with the intentions of missing his target and then paused. He noticed Seamus was hesitant to raise his weapon in defense. Pete could understand. After about a fifteen-minute stand off, Seamus noticed there was movement by several of the Yankee cavalrymen. "They are going to try and get in behind us. Now is the time to get out of here."

Pete nodded in agreement. Both of the men cautiously and as inconspicuously as possible moved away from the shelter of the rocks and to where their horses were tied. Keeping the horses calm as they untied them, Pete and Seamus mounted and slowly departed from the area. After following the trail for a short distance, they took a different direction off the mountain. By all indications, the Yankee patrol had given up the pursuit.

At the bottom of the mountain, Pete and Seamus paused. Seamus quietly gazed at Pete rubbing the neck of his horse.

"I want to thank you for your help," Pete said to Seamus.

The glimmer of a smile covered Seamus' features. He quietly stretched forth his hand in a friendly gesture. Pete smiled and did likewise. "I guess this time will be it. Over the last week, we have had too much excitement and too many close calls. But I must admit, it's been a once in a lifetime bloody experience for me. For the first time, I realize how fortunate I have been to have survived the war and its horrors and now this experience in life." Seamus chuckled. "I guess the Good Man above has been with me, and it's just not my time to go."

Pete smiled and replied jokingly, "I guess we both can say that." Pete paused and continued in a more serious tone. "Again

Seamus, thank you for loaning us the money. I will see that you are paid in full."

Seamus held his hand up in a hesitant gesture. "No hurry Johnnie."

Seamus turned his horse and started to leave. Suddenly, he brought his horse to a pause and turned around, looking once more at Pete, who was watching. Seamus pointed at Pete. "Whatever my sister decides to do, please Barker, take care of her. Do you bloody understand?"

Pete nodded as Seamus turned his horse around and departed.

Pete took a deep sigh as he glanced off in the direction of the Shenandoah Valley. Somewhere out there, he thought, was Katie and his brother. Hopefully, they were still on the road to the estate and had eluded capture by the other Yankees at the Hammond estate. He was anxious to return with haste to Shenandoah. The uncertainty of his mother's health concerned him, but also, he knew he had important decisions to consider that would impact his life. With these matters constantly on his mind, he galloped off in the direction of the little hamlet of Snickersville.

Chapter 60

As Pete casually rode through the small hamlet of Snickersville, which was located near the summit of Snicker's Gap, he didn't see any evidence of Charles' presence or that of any Yankees. He paused along the street and allowed his horse to drink water. He looked around and noticed a blacksmith examining the hoof of a horse in front of his stable. The gentleman glanced at him and continued his labor. Continuing his observation, he saw a wagon with a lone man heading in his direction. He looked like he was hauling granny-sacks of feed. Several gentlemen walked across the dirt road to the church that was nestled among some trees. Charles and Katie couldn't be too far ahead of him. Once he departed the hamlet, he paused and looked back toward the village. He turned, only to notice that a detachment of Yankee cavalry had just entered the village from the direction of Lincoln.

Pete was concerned and troubled. Like many occasions during the war when he was scouting for General Stuart, he remained calm and focused. He quickly evaluated the situation and his options. Most likely these Yankee soldiers were looking for Katie and Charles. He didn't know the extent of their distance from the village. It wasn't an option to pull the same scheme that Seamus and he had successfully accomplished. Pete noticed this area of the road had a steep grade to the summit of the mountain. Hopefully by this time, Charles and Katie had at least reached that point.

As Pete began to wheel his horse around, he noticed the soldiers pausing and dismounting. Some watered their horses while others were lighting pipes and engaging in conversation. With these non-aggressive actions by the soldiers, Pete wasted little time and moved on with haste.

Nearing the crest of the summit, Pete noticed Charles and Katie standing near the back wheel of the wagon. Pete immediately glanced and recognized the problem. The back axle of the wagon was severely damaged. Pete knew this was caused by the heavy rain from yesterday that created deep ruts in the mountain road.

Without hesitation, Pete jumped from his horse. Kneeling and closely examining the wagon axle to see if it could be temporarily repaired, he looked up at Charles with an expression of frustration. "I don't think that we can fix this. Even if we could, it would take too long."

"We have to do something," Charles demanded in a forceful tone.

Quickly, Pete jumped to his feet. "We don't have time, the Yankees are less then a mile behind me at Snickersville.

"What's all the shoutin' 'bout?" Hayward anxiously asked.

"Hayward, just stay put and be quiet until I tell you to come out," Pete replied.

"We have to find cover for Charles and Hayward until we can determine what were going to do," Katie said in an anxious tone.

"I recall that I was here in this same area on my way to Winchester carrying a dispatch from Colonel Mosby to General Early. As I remember, there is a stone farmhouse not too far from here. Maybe, we can get a horse from the old gentleman that lives there. We will unhitch the two horses pulling the wagon and Charles and Hayward can use them. You'll have to ride with Charles so I can return to the village and see what the Yankees are up to."

"Let's get started, it's our only choice," Charles added.

Quickly, Pete and Katie pulled the canvas cover back so Hayward could freely get out of the wagon while Charles began to unhitch the horses. Once finished with helping Hayward, Pete assisted Charles. Carefully Katie pulled off the bandages she had made and examined Hayward's wound. After the horses were freed from the wagon, Pete and Charles rapidly began to make several makeshift bridles from some rope in the back of the wagon. Katie replaced the dirty bandages with clean ones.

Pete informed Charles of the most direct way to proceed to the old gentleman's homestead near the river. Once everyone was mounted, Pete watched as Katie, Charles, and Hayward proceeded down the western face of the mountain along a trail off the Snicker's Gap Turnpike. Still, he wasn't sure that they would make it safely home. Their biggest challenge would be crossing the Shenandoah. By now the waters had risen from the heavy rains. He also knew that if Darby had really informed the Yankees of their presence at the Hammond's estate, then the warning had been sent to Captain Brackett's Provost office at Harpers Ferry. He knew they were watching Shenandoah for Charles' return.

Once Charles and the others were out of sight, Pete returned to the village. He arrived at the western entrance to the hamlet. Moving off the road among the trees to shelter himself from view, he noticed the Yankee patrol mounting their horses. He watched as the blacksmith spoke to an officer and confidently pointed in his direction.

As the Yankees moved along at a gallop, Pete wheeled his horse around and headed toward the crest of the mountain. As he left the area, he wasn't noticed by the Yankee patrol. Once at the summit, he could hear the muffled sound of the horses not far behind. He scrambled for ideas. How could he delay and disrupt the patrol from its route. After pulling his pistol from under his coat, he suddenly heard the sound of gunfire coming from the direction of the cavalry patrol. Were the Yankees ambushed? He decided he wouldn't waste precious time investigating but use the time wisely to hasten Charles and the others across the river.

Turning his horse around and beginning down the western slope, he heard several more gunshots in the distance.

Shortly, he arrived at the old gentleman's homestead. Katie and Hayward were still mounted in front of the stone house. As Pete approached, he could still see the old man standing on the front porch. He remembered the man from a year ago when he had passed through here on the way to Winchester. The suspicions that Pete possessed concerning the old man's loyalty to the Confederate cause had alarmed him. Pete still could visualize the cold look in his eyes and the distrust in his demeanor.

Bringing his horse to a halt next to Katie, Pete watched as Charles was knocking loudly on the front door. The old man was either too afraid to answer the door or he was out working somewhere around the property. Pete quickly looked around. A barn not far from the house caught his attention. He wheeled his horse around and galloped to the area. Quickly dismounting, he entered the barn with his pistol. It appeared the homestead was vacated and had been for sometime. Maybe the old man was deceased.

Again, Pete returned to where Charles was standing. "There isn't anyone here."

"I know."

"We must move on," Katie anxiously said.

When everyone was mounted, Pete gave Charles specific instructions concerning the fording area of the river. Once there, he instructed Charles to proceed upstream for about one hundred yards to a sycamore tree near a group of rocks. Directly in front is where he should cross the Shenandoah.

After Charles and the others departed, again, Pete covered their horse tracks in the direction of the river. He glanced and listened for horses coming from the lane in the distance knowing the Yankees would be coming.

The old man's homestead wasn't far from the Shenandoah River. Pete found Charles and the others in the vicinity that he had directed them to earlier. He couldn't understand why they had dismounted and delayed crossing the river. Something was terribly wrong and unexpected. Maybe the river waters had risen too high for them to cross.

As quickly as possible with the rugged terrain, Pete approached and noticed that Hayward was lying on the ground with Katie ministering to his wound.

Pete was alarmed not only at the delay in their progress, but the frightening scene surrounding his best friend. Leaping quickly from the saddle, he raced to where Hayward was lying, believing that he was dying. He glanced at Katie and started asking questions. "What's going on? Is he all right?"

Katie sighed as she looked at the wound. "He didn't say anything; he just fell forward in his saddle trying to regain consciousness."

Charles returned with a piece of Katie's undergarment. The garment had been moistened in the murky waters of the Shenandoah.

As Katie placed the wet garment on the wound, she glanced at Pete. "He has lost a lot of blood."

"Are we being followed?" Charles asked as he stood over Pete.

"I believe so. But before I met up with you back at the farm, I heard multiple gunshots. I believe that someone was trying to buy us time by ambushing the Yankee patrol. But I am not sure."

"Then they might be close behind."

Pete removed his hat and wiped his forehead looking toward the area of the farm. "Why don't you take one of the horses and cross the river and head for home?"

"No, I can't do that. I've run for too long," Charles replied. He gazed at Pete. "Give me your pistol and I'll cover our rear."

Pausing, Pete glanced at Katie and then again at Charles. "I can't do that," he softly answered.

"Why? Why can't you do that?"

"Remember, I am the one who is use to fighting. Not you."

"I want to do my part," Charles said as he stretched forth his hand for the gun. He continued in a composed tone. "I know why you are doing this. You're trying to protect me so that I will see Caroline and Ann. And don't think that after all of the pain, deception, and anguish I've put you through that I don't appreciate all that you're doing for me," Charles paused, waiting for the weapon. "Now please give me the gun."

Continuing to look at his brother, Pete quietly pulled the gun from under his coat and handed the weapon to his brother. Turning and watching as Charles walked away to mount his horse, Pete's mind raced with concern.

"Once I know their position, I'll return," Charles confidently said.

Pete nodded in acknowledgement as Charles rode away. He prayed he wouldn't be ambushed by some of the Yankees. He knew Charles wasn't use to fighting such as he was, and Charles didn't know some of the tricks of soldiering that he had learned the difficult way. Still, he had to consent, knowing it was important for his brother to partake in his share of the burden.

Chapter 61

After watching his brother ride off, Pete returned to where Katie was still tending to Hayward. At first glance, it appeared to Pete the bleeding had ceased. Hayward was still lying on the ground, groggy from the loss of blood. Pete looked at Katie for some visual sign that his friend would survive. No indication was given because she wouldn't take her eyes off Hayward, and he was too prideful to be the first to speak.

Pete rose and walked over to the riverbank. He noticed a few stones and knelt and picked them up. A faint grin covered his features as he began to skip them one by one across the river.

Katie joined Pete. She quietly stood with arms crossed watching as the stones skimmed the water's surface. Memories began to surface in her mind from the previous year during the war.

"As I remember, this is the same place where we crossed the river the night that you helped me escape from Winchester," Katie softly said.

Continuing to gaze at the water, Pete replied. "Yes, it's the place. I noticed it hasn't changed any since we were here." He turned and pointed to the rocks and trees covering the hillside. With a somber tone, he continued to reminisce. "Up there is where you and I hid when the Rebel cavalry was approaching."

Katie turned and observed the setting. "It was beginning to storm. The thunder, lightning, the downpour, oh, how could I forget. But that was nothing compared to the fear that filled my heart. I was frightened, knowing if we were caught that in all probability I could have been shot or hung over the silly accusations against me for spying. And the same fate might have awaited you for helping me."

"For the most part, you're probably right. Especially knowing now after Daniel's revelation in Frederick, that it was that rogue William Pierce who was behind it all. I really don't feel bad for him at all. First he had you imprisoned and then once you were there, he beats you when you were defenseless. Then to inflame matters, he sends that worthless overseer, Daniel, to kill us. And to make matters worse, then he pulls this stunt of kidnapping you and wounding Charles. Thank God it wasn't serious. No, I don't have any guilt or remorse for William's fate." Pete shook his head. "William got everything that was coming to him. I didn't believe it until he tried to have us killed, but William was a deceptive, wicked man that would have killed his own mother if she would have stood in his way."

"Do you remember what else happened that night?"

"Yes, I do. I began to wipe the dried blood from your lips, and I wanted to know who was responsible for such a cowardly act of aggression. You didn't want to tell me, but finally as you began to weep, you revealed that it was William. I was angry. I wanted revenge for all that he did to you and put you through. I felt whoever was hurting you was also hurting me, and it was my place to defend you."

"Do you remember what else happened that night?"

"As I remember, I scolded you for prowling through the camp of the 1st Virginia looking for information about me," Pete said and then paused.

When Pete hesitated, Katie finished the memories. "You said I was the only one that you had thought about and you had risked your life for me. And I asked you why. And you said you couldn't run from your feelings for me any longer."

"Yes, that is correct."

"Then why are you running again?"

Before Pete could answer, his attention was interrupted. He heard the sound of a horse rapidly approaching. Quickly, he looked and noticed Charles riding rapidly from the tree line near the farmer's lane. Perceiving the Yankee patrol was close behind, he glanced at Katie. "There's trouble! Come on, let's stir Hayward so that we can get started."

Still lying on the ground, Hayward could hear everything that was taking place. As Katie came near, Hayward demanded painfully, "Ya all go on and leave me. I'se is too weak. I'se gonna slow ya down."

"No, we won't do that. Now try," Katie forcefully replied.

Pete arrived and took Hayward by one arm and Katie took the other. They hoisted him to his feet. Once they had him balanced, Pete hastily grabbed the reins of his horse. "Come on Hayward, let's go."

Pete tossed Hayward onto the saddle while Katie held the reins of the animal. Once he felt that Hayward was secured, Katie mounted the same animal behind Hayward. She would support him from falling while they were crossing the river. Charles reined his horse to a halt.

"How far behind are they?" Pete shouted.

"Not far. They are at the old farmer's house looking around."

Just as Pete had perceived, the river had risen with the rains the previous evening. Pete's attention was concentrated on the water swiftly moving over some fallen tree limbs along the riverbank. At this particular area, the river was about one hundred yards wide. As his eyes examined the opposite riverbank, the area was heavily populated with trees. This would provide shelter, and they would have the advantage of noticing the Yankees first. But was it worth the risk, he thought. There was no way of traveling north or south on this side of the river. It was infested with undergrowth, trees and thickets. The only way of escape was across the river or it would only be a matter of time before they were captured or have to fight. This is something he wanted to avoid at all cost. He determined, escaping should be their first priority, even if it meant taking the risk of crossing the troubled Shenandoah.

"Follow me," Pete commanded after mounting his horse.

Pete guided his horse into the water with Katie and Hayward following and Charles bringing up the rear. At first, Pete's horse acted nervous, but like many times during the war, he spoke calmly to the animal, rubbing its neck. He glanced back and noticed Katie and Charles were using the same tactic with their horses. With every step, it seemed to Pete the force of the water was becoming more treacherous. The water was over his knees and near his hips. Their horses were moving sideward with the flowing force of the water. Everyone was fighting to keep their horses under control. It was too late to turn back.

When they were several hundred feet from the opposite shore, Hayward began to fall from the horse. He was still unconscious. Frightened, Katie screamed. Charles reacted quickly. When Pete turned and looked, he noticed that Charles was moving to her side to assist in the effort of keeping Hayward from falling into the water. Pete also turned his horse around when he noticed Charles was struggling to keep his horse under control and Hayward's head out of the water.

With Katie screaming, Pete hoped the Yankees didn't hear the noise. In the river, they would make easy and quick targets for the Yankees' carbines. Finally, with Hayward clutching to the horse's mane, Pete took the reins from Katie and with Charles again in the rear, they proceeded cautiously in the direction of the opposite shore. The distance was slowly being accomplished.

After what seemed like an eternity, they all made it safely to the opposite riverbank. Everyone was exhausted from the endeavor. Quickly before being noticed by the Yankees, Pete told everyone to hurry to the trees. Here they would be out of sight from anyone on the opposite riverbank from where they first began.

Charles returned to the edge of the tree line and watched for the Yankee patrol. Both Pete and Katie rode a short distance to a dirt road that ran parallel along the river but well out of sight of the Yankees. Quickly, Pete dismounted and rushed to help Katie, who by now was uncontrollably coughing.

"I am all right," Katie cried.

Pete turned around and examined Hayward's shoulder wound. It was slightly oozing.

"I'se will be all right," Hayward assured as he forced his eyes open.

With the constant coughing coming from Katie, Pete was concerned as he turned around and looked. She was kneeling and attempting to control the problem but was unsuccessful. "How much of the river water did you swallow?" Pete asked.

"Some," Katie replied as she held her hands over her mouth.

"I am sorry. It's just that I didn't feel that we had a chance unless we made the attempt to cross the river."

"I know, and I agree. We did the right thing. It was the only course of action to take."

Pete wanted to build a fire so Katie would be warm and not chilled from the cold river water, but he knew they would have to continue if there was any chance of eluding the Yankees. Time was precious in any escape from danger. Both Pete and Katie knew this from narrowly escaping capture last year at Winchester when William Pierce showed up at the jail to take Katie back to Richmond.

Pete's attention was interrupted as he heard the sound of Charles' horse. He stood and quietly watched as his brother appeared from the cover of the trees.

"Are they crossing?" Pete asked.

"Not yet. They are looking around near the place we were at."

"How many of them?"

"From what I could tell, maybe seven or eight."

Pete turned away from Charles for a moment in thought and walked several steps. He glanced at Katie. She had heard everything and her troubled expression revealed her anxiety. Pete sighed, turned, and approached Charles.

"We have to watch them to determine their intentions," Pete said. "If they cross the river, then you must make haste with Katie and Hayward north along this road."

"What about you?" Katie asked as she jumped to her feet and approached.

"As before, I will attempt to distract them and lead them off in the direction of Berryville."

With his answer, Pete hurriedly mounted his horse and returned to the riverbank among the trees. Katie and Charles removed Hayward from his horse and waited along the road for word from Pete.

Looking through the spyglass, Pete immediately took notice of the Yankees across the river scouring the area. Quickly, he counted seven soldiers. He calmly observed their every move just as he use to when scouting with the 1st Virginia. After sometime had passed, he noticed four of the Yankees mounting their horses and entering the water in single file. The other three also mounted but headed north through the underbrush in the direction of Castleman's Ferry, located one mile north of their present location. Pete believed these three would circle back on the road where Charles and the others were waiting, and with the four soldiers now crossing the river in the most direct route, possibly attempt to catch them in a trap.

Returning to meet up with Charles and Katie, Pete quickly thought of a plan of escape. Their enemy would be coming by two different routes. The road leading south was unknown to him, but he knew in all probability that it would lead them to Millwood. The Yankees that would be circling around would cut them off from traveling north. He was sure of what laid west. Berryville was less then five miles from the river.

As he departed from the tree area, Pete noticed Charles had already helped Hayward onto the horse anticipating their quick escape.

He approached Charles. "There are four of the Yankees crossing the river behind me while the other three are crossing about a mile up at the Ferry. We have to move quickly over this ridge and to the west. Just like us, it will take sometime for them to cross the river and should give you a lead. Once you are about a mile from here, turn north and head in that direction, using ridges for shelter from sight of any Yankee patrol coming from Berryville. Be sure to stay off any of the busy roads. If all goes well, I'll meet up with you at Myers's Ford."

After Charles mounted, he turned and handed Pete the pistol. "Now don't take any risk. My life isn't worth any more bloodshed."

"Please hurry along," Katie added in a troubled tone.

Pete watched Katie and Charles disappear into a wooded area and then he covered their tracks the best that he could. The area was still muddy in places from the rain the previous evening. He knew it would take them more time with Hayward being injured before they had traveled the mile. Returning to determine the Yankee's progress with crossing the river, Pete hoped this time they could finally elude them.

When Pete arrived at the tree line and peered across the water, he noticed the soldiers were making good progress and were more than halfway across. He turned around and headed back to the road and headed into the wooded area after Charles and Katie. Once he ascended the ridge, he paused to determine the Yankees intentions once they were finished crossing the river. He planned to stay between Charles and the soldiers.

Soon the Yankees that crossed the river appeared from the wooded area along the river. They looked around with one of them dismounting and looking for horse tracks. Within minutes, the other three appeared but stayed mounted. It appeared that several in authority were speaking, most probably, Pete thought, of what direction to pursue. One of the soldiers in the ranks moved his horse to the side of the road near the tree line. It appeared he noticed something of interest. Maybe some tracks discovered in the mud, Pete thought. The Yankee shouted and gestured to one of the others that were speaking. They took notice and approached. Apparently, Pete thought, they had found something that would give them the impression they had traveled into the woods rather than use the road south.

The cavalry patrol slowly entered the wooded area. Pete turned his horse around and swiftly ascended the ridge to its summit and then down the opposite side.

Once he broke into the open, he noticed in the far distance, Charles and Katie ascending another high ridge with a heavily wooded summit. They were near where he estimated that they should turn north. Now he would follow their trail distorting their tracks to deceive the Yankee patrol into following him to Berryville.

Pete proceeded to follow until he came to what appeared to be at one time of day a wealthy estate. It was desolated like most homesteads in the Valley. The barn and outbuildings looked like they had been destroyed by fire, and the house was tarnished. As he glanced down at the ground, he noticed the tracks of several horses. It might be Charles and Katie's because the prints of one of the horses was deeper in the muddy surface of the road than the other. This told him there was more weight on one horse than the other. Still, he wasn't sure. Approaching slowly toward the mansion, the tracks suddenly broke off in another direction.

Pete proceeded to destroy the tracks, especially in the muddy area. He quickly mounted and headed the short distance to the mansion. It appeared lifeless.

"Is there anybody here?" Pete called out.

At first no one answered his call. He cried out a second time. At the front door appeared an elderly lady of color. When Pete approached, he noticed the fear covering her features.

"Is there anyone else here?" Pete asked.

"Yes'um. Me and da lady of da house."

The servant followed shouting as Pete quietly walked by. "Ya's jist can't come in here!" Pete ignored her as he looked around. She continued to follow shouting. "Does ya hear me?"

When it appeared that no one was on the first floor, Pete ascended the stairway to the second floor. He quickly glanced into all the rooms, ignoring the servant's pleas until he came to a bedroom in the rear of the mansion. There he noticed a middle-aged lady lying in a bed. She was frail, breathing heavily when she wasn't uncontrollably coughing. She quietly looked up at Pete but didn't speak. There was a somber expression covering her face. Pete knew that death was near.

Pete turned and asked the servant, "What's wrong with her?"

The servant looked tearfully at Pete and frantically replied in a gravel tone. "I'se don't know. She's been like dis for a couple of days. I'se mix her sum honey and whiskey for da cough, but all day, she's worsen." The servant paused and knelt down beside the lady's bed and began to weep. "I'se pray to da Good Lord, I'se jist feel I'se done all that I'se can."

"Did you send for a Doctor?"

"Yes'um." The servant answered in a frustrating tone. She continued speaking as she slowly stood to her feet. "But he jist shook his head and give me dis stuff dat's no good. It don't help Misse any. I'se don't wanna lose her, cause she's da only family I'se has."

"I am sorry."

Pete turned around and slowly departed from the bedroom. The servant quietly followed. When he entered the hallway, the lady made a noise. The servant rushed back into the room. Walking over to a large window in the hallway overlooking the lane that led to the house, Pete noticed cavalry rapidly approaching in the distance. Immediately, he raced down the stairway and onto the front porch. Quickly, he mounted his horse and dashed around the side of the house in a full gallop.

Glancing over his shoulder, Pete noticed that only four of the seven soldiers were in pursuit of him. As they followed, he noticed that his horse was increasing its lead.

After racing over another ridge, Pete glanced around and lost sight of his pursuers. He believed that the soldiers had given up the chase so he slowed his horse to a trot.

Within minutes, Pete arrived at the eastern outskirts of Berryville, Virginia. The town was busy with farmers who were selling what few agriculture goods they possessed to other citizens of the community. A few ladies milling about the general store glanced at him as he passed along the street. He discreetly glanced around for Yankees.

Suddenly, a few soldiers appeared after departing a local establishment and were walking leisurely along the street toward him. He maintained his composure and acted as natural as possible not wanting to draw their attention. Finally, he came to the road that led to Charlestown and turned his horse north. Charlestown was roughly fourteen miles away, but he had to circle around and meet Charles and the others at Myers Town.

Now that he had safely made it through the town without suspicion, Pete came to Buck Marsh Church where he turned northeast and traveled across farm fields and deserted lanes. He hoped that everyone had evaded capture by Yankee cavalry roaming over the area. He would soon know once he arrived at Myers Town.

Chapter 62

The journey for Charles, Hayward, and Katie was slow and tedious, traveling over many farmers' lanes, treacherous ravines, and rugged terrain. From all indications, Pete's scheme had worked. The Yankee cavalry had followed him toward Berryville. The sky was beginning to darken as the sun was sinking slowly behind the Allegheny Mountains, giving them only a short duration of daylight. As Charles and the others were slowly riding, they were sheltered on one side by the river and on the other side by a steep ridge. Occasionally, Charles rode to the crest and looked around for any advancing Yankees and then returned to Katie and Hayward.

At times since leaving the river, Katie still battled intervals of uncontrollable coughing. She was holding onto Hayward and following Charles, who was about thirty yards in the lead. Hayward was fully conscious and sitting upright and looking around. Katie noticed that his bleeding had subsided and he was more alert than several hours ago when they were along the river near Castleman's Ferry. She was frightened and uncertain if Yankees would cross the ridge and surprise them. She depended on Charles for guidance to Myers's Ford.

Many troubling thoughts plagued Katie's mind over the different issues that divided Pete and her. It was her hope with the additional time helping to transport Hayward home that by some miracle it would provide her the opportunity to speak to Pete concerning all that happened over the last three weeks. She understood his dissatisfaction. Could she possibly salvage anything between them? The effort had to be made. She had to know before she left for Boston.

Katie's thoughts were interrupted as Hayward groaned with pain. Their horse had just begun to trot, causing Hayward distress. Hearing Hayward's discomfort, Katie slowed the horse's pace. "Are you all right?" Katie asked in an apprehensive tone.

"Misse Katie, jist keep a goin'. Don't yose worry 'bout me, I'se gonna make it."

"I don't want to do anything that is going to cause you to start bleeding again."

Hayward laughed and coughed several times. "My pappy raised me to be a tough old crow. And if I'se lives my life, I'se doesn't regret a thing that I'se done for Mr. Pete and yose. He's been good to me and I'se won't ever forgit that. Yes sir, I'se think the world of that boy jist as my pappy did with me."

"I know. If it weren't for you, Pete and I wouldn't be here today. I'll never forget when I thought Daniel was going to shoot us. I was frightened. I really thought I was going to die. And there you were. And you shot him, saving our lives. Until then, we didn't know where you were, just that you had escaped."

"I'se can tell ya now with everything over with. After I'se left Shenandoah in the spring of '62, I'se 'scape into Pennsylvania. After a bit, I'se return and I'se helped my people. On all of my trips, I'se brought back news I had learn along the way 'bout the Rebels. And I'se started givin' it to a Yankee captain in Frederick City. Then he started askin' dis of me. He's praised me for bein' faithful in doin' dis. He says that I was one of the best black fellas that give him dis kind of news. I'se was..." Hayward paused thinking of a descriptive word to use.

Katie finished the sentence, "reliable."

"Yeah, that's the one."

"Well Hayward, I must admit, you did your part in helping to serve the Union cause. And if I were you, I'd say nothing to anyone, not even Pete about your secret activities."

Hayward quietly nodded in agreement as Katie continued to follow Charles.

Many thoughts were racing through Charles' mind. He was less than an hour away from Shenandoah, and after the last six months of constantly fleeing the pursuit of government authorities and detectives, he was quite anxious to see his wife and daughter. In the past, he was never good at expressing his feelings and emotions to Caroline. In verbal communication with his wife, he would always attempt to rehearse his words, but this time he determined within his heart that it would be different. The words spoken to her would be from deep in his heart. He knew their time together would be limited. In desperation, he desired to look on Caroline's peaceful expression. He wanted to hold her in his arms, to softly kiss her lips, and to share words of reassurance.

As for Ann, Charles knew she was worried and concerned. She was always sensitive toward troubling issues. He hoped to ride with her along the river as in times past. He hoped that if imprisoned, it would be for only a short duration. The most meaningful desire in his heart concerning his daughter was to continue to play a role in her life and be an inspiration. Most important, he wanted to speak to her about her future and the hopes of a new beginning in life.

With his mother, it would be another matter. In Charles' heart, he strongly believed he needed to express his apologies and further relieve the condemnation and guilt of Rebecca's death. Within his heart, once his mother heard the truth of all that happened in Richmond on that fateful night after their departure from the beleaguered city, it was his hope that she wouldn't hold his negligence against him. As for Shenandoah, there were many questions that concerned him since he was the legal and binding owner. What would he do with the estate?

The time seemed to be slowly passing, and the anticipation of being reunited with his family and mother was all that he could bear. Charles attempted to hasten their speed, but he knew Katie and Hayward were lagging behind because of Hayward.

Bringing his horse to a halt, Charles waited until Katie and Hayward were along side. "We have been riding for sometime. I feel it's best that Hayward and you rest for a moment while I go up to the top of the ridge and try to determine where we are."

"I agree," Katie replied as she swept the hair from her face.

The wind began to blow intensely as Katie quietly watched Charles turn his horse around and galloped toward the crest of the ridge.

As Charles paused on the ridge, he could see in the distance the little hamlet of Myers Town. He was too far off to be able to determine if Yankees were present but instead he rapidly descended the ridge.

Once Charles arrived, Katie curiously asked, "Well Charles, what did you see?"

"We are too far off. I couldn't tell."

"Then I assume you were not noticed by anyone?"

"Fortunately we are at a safe distance," Charles replied with a tone of confidence. He quickly continued, "I think we should press on."

"No Charles. We agreed with Pete that we would meet him here. And I won't go back on my word and have him wondering what happened to us."

"I disagree Katie, we should press on," Charles demanded in a forceful tone.

Hayward said as he pointed, "I'se don't knows 'bout that Mr. Charles. The river's ford is not far from here. Dey's might be someone in that area, or the Yanks could be a watchin'." Hayward added, "We's come dis far now we's can't be slack and git in some trouble."

* * * *

In an attempt to rendezvous with Charles and the others before dark, Pete pushed his horse to the limits. Finally, he came to an area where the road passed through a wooded area. He assumed he was close to Myers Town and the river. He brought his horse to a pause and looked around. The question was where would he find Katie and Charles. Maybe since he was close to the Shenandoah, it might be in his best interest to observe the activity taking place in the village before setting out to look for them.

Cautiously, Pete proceeded down the road until he was about to emerge from the cover of the wooded area. He directed his horse from off the road and among the shelter of the trees. Off in the distance, he could see the village. He pulled the spyglass from his saddlebags and carefully observed the activity in the village. To his surprise, there were three Yankee soldiers dismounted and speaking to a gentleman and lady. Did they know about Charles? He was cautious and had to assume that anything was possible with the capabilities of the telegraph. Swiftly, he returned the spyglasses to his saddlebags and headed directly toward the river.

Returning by the way that he had come from Berryville, Pete veered off the road as soon as he cleared the tree line and pushed his horse at a full gallop in the direction of the river. In the distance, he noticed a long ridge that extended as far as his eye could see both north and south. It wasn't far in front of him. After ascending to the crest, again he paused and quickly looked around for Charles and Katie. The darkness had increased and the lack of light was making it difficult for visibility. Thoughts raced swiftly through his mind. Something may have happened to Hayward. If all went accordingly, they had to be ahead of him because they traveled the most direct route, but where? As Pete continued to look around, he remembered the area from the fighting that took place near here during the final days of 1864 when he rode with Colonel Mosby. Surely Yankees might be watching the fording area if they had received word that Charles was in the area. He took the gamble and headed toward the fording area.

Pete didn't travel far before he noticed Charles and Katie in front of him. He pushed his horse to the limits to catch them. Shortly, he overtook them.

He reined his horse to a halt. "You have to wait, you can't go any further."

"Yankees?" Charles asked.

Pete pointed toward the village. "There are three of them at the village. I don't know if they are part of a squadron that's guarding the river ford or if they are just several scouts out looking for some scoundrels."

"But we are close to Shenandoah, I must press on," Charles frustratingly demanded.

"I understand your feelings that you are this close, but we can't afford to make any mistakes."

"No, I am pressing on," Charles demanded in a disputed tone.

"No," Pete authoritatively answered. "For once, we are going to do this my way. Do you understand? I'll not have you compromising our safety because of your impatience."

"Listen to him Charles," Katie pleaded as she placed her hand on his arm. "He is only thinking of what is best for all of us. And I know that his intentions are to get you home so that you can see Caroline and the rest of the family."

Charles looked defiantly at Katie and then at Pete. His anticipation and anxiety was beginning to control his reasoning.

When Charles refused to answer, Pete quietly galloped toward the ridge shielding them from view of the Yankees at Myers Town. He went riding along the crest, observing intently in the direction of the village from a grove of trees. All appeared quiet in that direction. He turned and glanced toward the river and noticed Charles and the others waiting. Again, his attention was focused on the village where he noticed sixteen additional soldiers arriving from the direction of Berryville to join the other Yankees. Calmly, he waited to determine their intentions. Several minutes passed and then the other soldiers mounted their horses. All of the cavalrymen assembled in formations of two and began at a trot in his direction. He wheeled his horse around and surprisingly noticed that Charles and the others were heading toward the fording area and would cross the road with the Yankee patrol unless he intervened.

Striking his horse into a full gallop, Pete vigorously pushed the animal in Charles' direction to intercept them. As he reined his horse in, Charles and Katie halted and looked.

"Come on, the Yankees are close behind," Pete commanded.

Without a word spoken, Pete took the lead and they rapidly headed in the direction of the fording area. To their advantage, the area on both sides of the road was heavily shrouded with trees. Pete knew they couldn't continue toward the ford. About several hundred yards from the area, he noticed there was little undergrowth and thickets to hinder them should they take this direction. Without speaking, he gestured with his hand and everyone quietly followed. They crossed the rugged terrain and battled the undergrowth. The process was slow. Off in the distance, Pete heard the sound of horses rapidly approaching. Quietly, he held his hand in the air for all to pause. They were less then fifty feet from the road as the Yankee cavalrymen passed. Fortunately for Pete and the others, their horses remained silent and didn't become nervous with the excitement, and the Yankees passed without incident.

Once the Yankees were out of sight, Pete quietly gestured for the others to follow him. After struggling with the entanglements of the landscape they came to a clearing. Pete knew they were in the vicinity of Kabletown, and there wasn't any sign of Yankees.

Immediately, Katie wanted to examine Hayward's wounded shoulder. Several times during the escape, Hayward had groaned with pain. Pete called a halt and jumped from his saddle. Staying mounted, Charles kept watch for anything suspicious.

After Hayward removed his shirt and slightly turned toward Katie, she glanced at the injury. Katie was satisfied. It wasn't bleeding as she thought.

"We are fortunate. Now if we can just make it the rest of the way without any problems or delays," Katie said.

"I know. Let's get started before they return," Pete softly replied as he turned and walked away.

Katie was troubled as she watched Pete mount his horse. He was cold and continued to be distant. One way or the other, she determined, this matter would be settled as soon as they arrived at Shenandoah.

As they continued toward the estate, Charles knew they would be on the property in less than an hour. Would soldiers be nearby or on the property watching for his return? If by chance they were not, then how long would he have with Caroline and the rest of the family? These were questions that tormented his mind. With Shenandoah and his family only a short distance, he wouldn't be deprived of maybe his only opportunity to see them. He determined the risk would still be worth it.

Chapter 63

Darkness had fallen as Pete and the others rode along the family's property that bordered the Shenandoah River. Pete's thoughts were concentrated on what may have happened since leaving the estate over a week ago. Hopefully, all was well with the family and especially his mother, who he was sure, was still recovering without any complications. When it came to Charles, he knew his time was limited and it must be spent with the family. It would only be a matter of time before the Yankees arrived and arrested him for his involvement as an aide to President Jefferson Davis and the failed Confederate government. When it came to Katie, he wasn't certain of his feelings. Still, he felt betrayed by her actions with Robert Bateman and all that Bradley Langsten had revealed concerning her involvement during the war.

As she rode behind Pete, the uncertainty still troubled Katie over her future with him. So much had happened in such a short space of time to jeopardize and tarnish their relationship. She knew Pete deserved answers to the questions he asked. How much should she tell him? If he knew the whole truth of her intentions when she arrived at Harpers Ferry in the late summer of 1860, then surely, he would completely forsake her. She feared he would only believe she had actually used him for information on Confederate activity in the surrounding area, and most of all, her feelings and emotions would be no more than a pretense. All that had happened between them before and during the war was real. The trust she shared, the words she spoke, and the depths of her unfailing love and commitment were sincere.

Hayward was still suffering from his gunshot wound but slowly improving. He didn't know what kind of future he had at Shenandoah. His first intention was to complete the task of rebuilding Shenandoah just as he had promised Pete. Then once he finished, he wasn't sure. Maybe he would stay or maybe he would leave the area and begin a new life elsewhere. So much had happened and he feared he'd still be frowned upon because of his race. There was one hope. He was always amazed and infatuated with the idea of moving west to California or Oregon. It had been a dream that he had and an adventure he desired to undertake before he died.

Charles was greatly anxious to see Caroline and Ann. Before the war, he had the world at his fingertips. He was one of the most powerful men in the Shenandoah Valley and was greatly admired for his leadership in Virginia politics. All the glory and honor bestowed upon him was now but a mere vapor that continued to vanish. The only matter of any substance now was his reunion with his family. He had much to redeem in the amount of time away from home. He had words to say, and emotions to express, which were never previously revealed to Caroline or Ann. Showing his true emotions was something he always considered a weakness because his mother had taught him that in life you had to be extremely strong when failure prevailed. Further, it was impressed on him that you should demonize those who opposed your views and to always be shrewd in business transactions, especially taking advantage of those who were less fortunate. Since the conclusion of the war, he questioned these actions. Was he wrong?

Shortly, Pete and the others arrived along Barker's Ridge. They paused and gazed in the direction of the cabin. On this chilly evening, there was a candlelight beaming from the front windows and smoke ascending toward the sky from the chimney. Every indication gave the appearance of solitude and quiet.

Charles gazed steadfastly at the cabin with anticipation. His long awaited reunion with his family was near. The extreme difficulties, the unimaginable sacrifices, constant hardships, and the loneliness had been unbearable. He had learned to prevail through life's unfair circumstances to achieve his goal. Anxiously, he began to advance his horse.

"Wait, we just can't go riding in like nothing has happened," Pete cautioned.

"I am not just going to wait here," Charles snapped as he turned and glanced at Pete.

"Allow me to scout the area near the cabin and make sure that it is safe."

"All right, but hurry."

Pete rode slowly in the direction of the cabin. "Charles, you'll be with your family soon," Katie said. "Since Caroline returned last month, I know with your absence she has felt the void in her heart. It's been difficult for her not knowing if you had escaped with your life. Once, she had said that maybe you had traveled somewhere abroad or maybe you were imprisoned by Federal authorities."

Charles shook his head in frustration and softly replied. "Katie, you don't know how many times I wanted to contact Caroline and let her know I was alive. I feel extremely guilty for allowing this to happen to my family, but I didn't have any choice. If the Yankees found me then I wouldn't have had the opportunity I do now. It was worth the sacrifice and risk even if it is only for a night."

Katie began to uncontrollably cough. She composed herself the best she could. "I know. I understand. It was difficult when I believed that I had lost Pete at Gettysburg. The pain and anguish was unbearable. I didn't know how my life would continue without him. The expectations of a life, family, and future without him made life intolerable for me. I, too, wanted to die. I didn't want to live a life that didn't include him and still despite everything that has happened, I feel that way."

"Den yose better do something that gonna cause him to listen to ya," Hayward added in a whispering tone.

"But what?"

"As I'se told him many times, ya need to follow ya heart. The words will come."

Charles wanted to add to the conversation, but out of guilt, he remained silent. Before the firing on Fort Sumter and Virginia's secession from the Union, he was the first to invite Katie to Shenandoah after her arrival in Harpers Ferry. He was the one who promoted the relationship with Caroline only to initiate its termination during the conflict for fear that his own covert activities would be discovered. Along with William, he had vigorously accused Katie of spying, and condemned her for the activity, although they could never prove it.

Time passed and finally Pete returned. He rode over to Charles. "From what I can tell, it appears to be safe."

Without a spoken word, Charles proceeded slowly toward the cabin with the others following. Once they arrived Charles dismounted as Pete assisted Katie and Hayward from their horse. Charles stepped onto the porch and paused at the front door. Bowing his head as if to say a small prayer, he slowly lifted the latch and entered. As he walked through the entrance, he first noticed Caroline leaning over the fireplace stirring dinner in a black kettle. When she looked up, he noticed the dazed and surprised expression covering her features. He knew by her relieved appearance that for now, her worries had ended. He raced toward her. She cried out his name, dropping the wooden spoon and rushing into his arms crying. Charles passionately kissed Caroline. Tears began to fill his eyes.

"For six long, long months I have dreamed and struggled for this day to happen. So many times at night I could see your face and hear your soft voice." Above all the tears he shed, Charles began to smile with joy. "The war made me realize how much I love you, and how much I've missed you."

"My love," Caroline sobbed, caressing his face with her hand. "I have been through pure hell without you. Night after night I have allowed sleep to escape me because I have worried and wondered what had happened to you. As the weeks and months passed by and you didn't come home, I thought that you were dead and I'd never know. But somewhere within my heart, I couldn't give up hope."

In the loft area of the cabin, Ann was reading the "Phoenix and Turtledove" by Shakespeare that Katie had given her as a birthday present in 1862. It was a work of literature that she had read many times. After hearing the emotional weeping on the lower level, Ann became concerned. She quickly glanced from the loft and noticed her mother embracing her father. With haste, she climbed down the ladder and dashed for his open arms. She was just as emotional as her mother. Ann struggled to speak over her crying.

"Father, Father, oh thank God you're alive." In the attempt to control her sobbing, Ann attempted to speak as she tightly clutched her father. "Oh, I was so afraid I would never see you again. I thought I had lost you for good."

Charles began to wipe away Ann's tears on her cheeks with his fingers. "Do you remember what I said to you in Richmond when you left with your mother and grandmother?" he softly asked.

Ann nodded. "Yes Father. You said you'd pray for me and you would see me again." Again the tears began to flow rapidly down Ann's cheeks as she continued in a broken whisper. "And those were the last precious words you spoke to me. I struggled with my own doubts but I held to your promise"

"And I went through hell to keep my word to you," Charles replied.

A glimmering smile began to cover Ann's face. "You've always kept your word to me."

The door opened again, as Charles, Caroline, and Ann paused and looked. Pete and Katie were assisting Hayward.

Immediately, Caroline responded by pulling a chair from the table for Hayward to be seated. She glanced at Katie with a terrified expression. "What happened?"

"He was shot while helping Charles and me."

"Shot!" Ignoring the implications of Katie's answer, Caroline raced to retrieve some hot water that was simmering over the open fireplace. Again Caroline screamed, "Oh my God!"

Pete glanced at Charles as Katie with Caroline's assistance finished cutting the shirt from Hayward's body.

Charles turned and looked in the direction of the bedroom. He walked toward the doorway with Pete following. As Charles paused and quietly gazed into the room, he could barely make out his mother's features in the dim light.

"My Son, please come in," Elizabeth joyfully said as she turned her head in his direction.

Charles was amazed. His mother was greatly diminished in appearance from her former days. With his heart full of anguish at the scene he was witnessing, Charles entered the room and Pete did likewise. Once by the bedside, Charles embraced and kissed her forehead. Afterward, he knelt as Pete stood behind him.

Charles took his mother by her hand. "Mother, how are you?"

"I believe I've improved. But I still feel so weak."

"Is there anything that I can get you?"

"No, my Son," Elizabeth replied as she glanced in his direction. "At the moment, I have everything that I could hope for."

"And what's that?"

Elizabeth's eyes brighten as she looked upon her two sons and answered in a whisper. "I have both of you home with me." She began to smile as she continued. "I can ask the Good Lord for no more than that. Now can I?"

"No Mother, I guess we are fortunate."

Elizabeth looked at Pete and softly asked, "Is Katie safe?"

"Yes Mother, she is in the other room with Caroline tending to Hayward."

"What happened?"

"He was wounded in the shoulder but I am confident he'll recover."

Over the past few days, Elizabeth had given great thought to the words she would choose to say if she ever saw Charles and Pete again. Now that they were home, and she was alone with them, the opportunity was perfect. She remained calm and composed. She began to speak confidently to Charles. "Our lives have changed so much over these past four years that I know within my heart our way of life here at Shenandoah will never be the same. I can't rebuild all that we had and I don't expect you to either. I am so grateful to God that both of you are alive and here in this room with me and alive to share this moment. But although I am glad to see you, my heart weighs heavy on the evil that I've brought upon you two."

"Mother, you don't have to do this. Everything is forgiven," Pete said in a tone of humility.

"Yes Mother, I agree with Pete," Charles added in a soft tone.

Elizabeth raised her hand in a gesture for silence and continued in a soft tone. "But I must." She turned sadly and looked at Charles. "I have always favored you above Rebecca and Pete. And it was so selfish of me because I robbed them of the best of my love that I could have given them. You are so much like me. Strong-minded, prideful to the point that you can't admit when you're wrong, and persistent when it suits your own selfish interest. Shenandoah became yours when war tore the country apart. At the time I believed that it was the right thing to do. At least then I did but I was so wrong." She turned and looked at Pete.

Taking a deep breath, Elizabeth said as she again looked at Charles and took his hand in hers. "I have always loved you so much. You would have done anything for me. But I allowed myself to use you in the most grievous ways to achieve my own selfish goals." Her tone was angry. "It didn't matter who was hurt, or who paid the price, just as long as I got what I wanted. Even to the point that I lied to Caroline. Oh, yes as much as I love her and thought of her as my own, I lied to her. It happened when Katie and Caroline spoke one afternoon along the river about my real intentions of turning over ownership of Shenandoah to you. Caroline raced home and angrily and tearfully confronted me. At first my defense was that I had acted correctly in order to save a life's worth of hard labor and effort in building an estate. Although deceptively, I used words to try and cover up my sin and shame because I knew I was hurting her and had lost her trust in me."

Tears began to flow from Elizabeth's cheeks as she continued, "All along, Caroline was right about me. And for once, someone didn't believe me. It made no difference who I stepped on. She wanted to know how this would affect us once you knew the truth. At the time, I was so angry and depressed over losing everything we had worked so hard to achieve, and our way of life changing, that I really didn't care what anyone thought. Not even Caroline. Ever since I came close to losing my life, I have laid here in this bed day after day thinking of why I was so angry at the world. I was wrong. I led you to believe one thing when my intentions were elsewhere. Caroline said I abused your trust and confidence for my own personal gain. For this my Son, I am sorry."

Elizabeth beckoned with her hand for Pete to step forward where she could see him. Quietly, he complied with his mother's wishes. Charles stood and gave his brother the opportunity to kneel so he could hear her faint words.

"Out of all of my children, I have committed the greatest sin against you." With a faint smile, Elizabeth confessed, "I will always stand by my belief that you were a rebel. Because you reminded me of one."

"I did Mother, who?" Pete asked, smiling as he gazed at her.

"I married him over thirty some years ago, your father," Elizabeth answered in a humble tone. She paused and struggled with her emotions. Pete remained silent as he gazed into her teary eyes. She continued to speak. "When I look at you, I see his heart being manifested. Just like him, you are so humble, taking nothing for granted, and fair in all situations that life deals you. When I listen to your words that you speak, I hear his wisdom, and in extreme difficulties, you use it in your ability to compromise. Oh, he use to make me so mad when he wanted to play fair with another in a business transaction. I know I always took the credit for Shenandoah's success, robbing him of the glory that was due him. He never said anything in his defense, nor would he admonish me for my inconsideration. Instead, he allowed me to have all the glory I desired. He truly loved me unconditionally. But the truth is the estate would have never been as successful as it was if it wasn't for his long hours of relentless hard work. His confidence in other human beings that worked the property and the valuable contribution they made brought about fruitful results and new and invigorating ideas. When failure appeared evident, it was your father's persistence, his faith, and commitment that kept Shenandoah going. And when he passed away, Shenandoah was all that it could be. When I look at you, I constantly see him. I guess because of my unfair treatment of your father, I bear a guilt that I cannot escape. Maybe this is why I always appear so angry."

Elizabeth paused and looked aimlessly at the wall. Once more, her eyes were on Pete. "Before the war when Katie and you were beginning to see each other more often, I became afraid. Why, because she was a threat to me. And yes, Katie was correct in her observations and statement when she confronted me on the afternoon that we received the news of your death near Gettysburg. I was so afraid Katie and you would marry and that she'd live at Shenandoah and try to change our way of life. I became so obsessed with the idea of trying to end the relationship between you two. But I failed. And the more I tried, the more I failed and became so frustrated. But in truth, Katie wasn't the threat to me. No my Son, in truth, I was the only threat to me. My Son, I was my own greatest enemy, not Katie McBride or anyone else. I was so foolish and blinded by my own obsessions and hatred that I refused to see something so special, so beautiful between two individuals, something I refused with your father, a love that could possibly last forever. I have become so angry with myself for the way that I've treated you. You should have more in life. So if you want to spend the rest of your life with Katie, then I'll give you my blessing."

Silently nodding his head in acknowledgement, Pete smiled and rose to his feet. At this particular moment, he wouldn't disclose any information to his mother concerning Katie and his relationship. He departed the room as Charles continued to spend time with her.

Pete walked over to Caroline. "How is Hayward?"

"He isn't bleeding. He just needs something to eat and then some rest. Even for his age, Hayward is just as stubborn as ever and strong as a bull."

"My pappy raised me to be that way," Hayward added as he chuckled.

"Good, good," Pete replied as he glanced at Katie. Pete turned and walked quietly to the front door. He opened it and departed.

Caroline noticed the coldness between Katie and Pete. She noticed the somber expression covering Katie's face as she watched Pete leaving. "Is everything all right between you two?" Caroline asked.

"No, it's not." Katie answered in a whispering tone. She wiped her hands on a towel, "Excuse me."

* * * *

It was cool. The sky was clear and the nighttime darkness was filled with stars. Pete was leaning on one of the porch posts and looking toward the heavens. His thoughts were consumed with his mother's slow progression toward recovery. He was thankful she was alive and Charles had the opportunity to see and spend time with her. Now with Charles home, he must begin to plan for his future because legally his brother was the rightful owner of Shenandoah. The sound of the door opening interrupted his thoughts. He paused but didn't turn because he knew it was probably Katie.

Katie paused with her arms crossed to fight off the chill. She silently gazed at Pete recalling in her mind an episode that happened before the war. She vividly remembered Pete traveling to Harpers Ferry. It was in a downpour of rain on a November morning. His intentions were to assist her to safety because the Shenandoah River was flooding the lower area of the town. After a frightening struggle with the rushing water, they returned safely to the homestead. Once they had settled in and had dinner with Charles and Caroline, they went into the ballroom. To the sound of "Oh Susanna," Katie played the piano and Caroline the violin. They sang many of the popular songs, and the conversation between all was rewarding. Afterward, Pete departed briefly to tend to the animals while she walked onto the back porch and gazed at the many stars just as he was doing this very moment.

Seeing the opportunity to speak, she reversed the roles. "Do you believe that you can count all of them?"

"No, no," Pete answered, as a smile covered his face. "As I recall, one time of day I said something like that to you."

"Yes you did," Katie confidently replied as she approached Pete and stood near his side. Continuing in a soft tone, Katie looked up into the heavens. "As I recall, I answered that many of them, just like tonight, were clustered together. It reminded me of how close a family should be." Pausing and looking into Pete's eyes, Katie continued softly. "For you and I, it was just the beginning. Tonight, I just don't know. We are so distant. It is almost as if you can't stand the sight of me."

"No Katie, I don't dislike you. I must admit I am disappointed with our relationship, though…"

Katie abruptly interrupted. "Why, because I spent the evening with Robert Bateman and allowed him to kiss me. I'll admit it wasn't using good wisdom, and you have just cause to be upset with me. But first please hear me out. It all began when an army officer by the name of Bradley Langsten, an acquaintance during the early days of the war, followed me to the Willard Hotel after I saw him earlier at the War Department. It was apparent to me that he was interested in more than just paying his respects. Of course, I refused. While in the dining room of the hotel, he spent the evening gazing at Robert, Father, and especially me. At first, I tried to use Robert to discourage Bradley. And again, I must admit, I was wrong to lead Robert astray by posing as though I was interested in him. Once at the door of my room, yes, I allowed him to kiss me."

Katie began to weep. She struggled to speak as the tears flowed down her cheeks. In a broken voice, she continued. "Vulnerability had overtaken me. I was so lonesome without you. In many ways, I also was angry because you left in a temper when I wouldn't side with you against my father during your angry encounter with him."

Katie gestured with her hands and continued to explain. "With the strain of rebuilding Shenandoah, at times it left you so distant from me. You would go for hours along the river and shut me out of your life. And then when we were in Boston, you tried to convince me to stay. All these things left me so confused about my life and so unsure of our future. I felt so insecure. And then for a moment, Robert made me forget all my troubles. Temporarily, he filled the void in my heart. He wanted more, but I refused. I knew there could be no one but you." As Pete turned and looked, she continued to speak with earnestness. "Once I left his company, I went into my room and brushed my hair. I felt condemned for acting falsely with him, but he reminded me so much of you. The feelings of worthlessness and guilt overshadowed me. It was beyond anything I had ever previously experienced. Not only did I betray you, but more so myself. My love, my loyalty to you. Then as I was thinking of this and of the night we first danced at Shenandoah, I thought of the words to "Lorena." Remember the song we danced to?"

Nodding his head in acknowledgement, Pete refused to speak out of stubbornness. Still, he had been listening intently to every word that came from her lips.

The words went something like this. Katie softly sang with expression in her voice:

"We loved each other then.

More than we ever dared to tell;

And what we might have been,

Had but our lovings prospered well."

Although the words of the song deeply touched his heart, Pete wouldn't respond. He just turned and gazed at Katie waiting for her to continue or leave.

As Pete turned his head and looked at the area where they were rebuilding his home, Katie knew he was making every attempt to shut her out. She continued in a whisper. "As I continued to brush my hair, I noticed a figure standing in the dim light behind me. As he slowly approached, I realized that it was William Pierce whom I hadn't seen since we escaped from Winchester. I couldn't believe it. How did he know where to find me? Probably with the assistance of the desk clerk." Katie continued in a somber tone, "William quickly escorted me from the hotel threatening me with a small weapon if I screamed. And he said that he had employed an associate, who was standing near the entrance to the dining room, to kill my father on his signal, if I didn't comply. At first, I thought it might be Bradley Langsten, but I quickly ruled that thought out. We used the 14th Street entrance. Naturally and out of fear, I did all that was asked." Taking a deep sigh, Katie concluded. "Afterward, we spent some time at Thomas Winesmith's residence. Even though I constantly asked, William never revealed his intentions."

"Katie, I am sorry for all that's happened to you. But you're alive." Pete replied with a calm and composed tone as he continued to gaze toward the area where the mansion once stood. Suddenly, he turned and looked at her. "I am grateful for your help in taking care of Hayward. But now it's time for you to return to Boston and be with your family and start all over. I will take you into town tomorrow to catch the train to Baltimore." Pete silently turned and walked to the door.

"No, Pete. Please," Katie cried as tears flowed freely from her cheeks. She was terrified. The words he had spoken tattered the deepest part of her heart. Placing her hands over her face, and crying uncontrollably, Katie's legs began to give away. Crouched alongside of one of the wooden porch columns, she continued to weep allowing fear over an unexpected future without him rule her thoughts and heart.

Chapter 64

Everyone was exhausted from the emotional experiences and had retired early for the evening. With only the faint light of a candle burning, Charles laid in bed, watching Caroline as she sat before her dresser, brushing her hair. This had always been her nightly habit, and he was always reminded in his thoughts during this time how much he loved her. Tonight wasn't any different. He knew she had many questions that she had been withholding, and he would unconditionally answer each one.

When it was time, Caroline pulled the quilt back and laid beside her husband. Snuggling in her husband's arms, she caressed his bearded face, and stroked his arm.

Charles quietly kissed Caroline's forehead as he rubbed his hand against her arm. "There could never be words to express my deepest agony over your absence from my life those six months that I was on the run. It was the torment and punishment that I deserved for deserting you and my part in the rebellion."

"Oh you're just being too hard on yourself," Caroline said as she cracked a smile.

"No Caroline, I mean it. Look what this war has cost me. Our home and property were destroyed, and now the Unionists want it. And just because we have satisfied the debt, they'll continue to look for another reason to steal it from us. But most of all, I feel so guilty for all that I've put you and Ann through. Many times during the war, I was separated from you and the rest of the family. Now we are financially ruined and your suffering must continue."

"But we have each other."

"Yes we do. And when I look at you, I am always reminded of that important part of my life. We are so fortunate," Charles replied as he looked with a sincere expression at Caroline.

"I know that you have suffered but tonight we are together. And regardless of our losses, we are safe."

"Yes we are." Charles paused and took a deep sigh. "I know you have questions."

"Yes, I have a few. If I may ask, what happened to you once you were able to get out of Richmond?"

Charles was silent. Tears filled his eyes. Finally he broke the stillness. "After we left Richmond with Secretary Breckinridge, we headed west until we came to Farmville. There the Secretary met with General Lee. I don't know in detail what was discussed, but I am sure that it pertained to the necessities of supplies for the hungry army. And also the most honorable way on our behalf to end the effusion of blood between the two armies. I will never forget the last time I saw General Lee. He appeared exhausted with the growing numbers of desertions among the men, which was causing the army to rapidly dwindle in strength. Not only that problem distressed him, but the emotional burden of Richmond surrendering, and Yankees attacking from the flanks and rear of the army. They destroyed what little was left of the ammunition and supplies. The damage was revealing on the old general's face. But through it all, he appeared graceful to all in his disposition. His professionalism and courteous nature was an inspiration to all that he came into contact with."

Charles paused and for a brief moment, he was silent, thinking. He continued to relive his last days with the Confederacy. "After receiving reports of approaching Yankees, we rode out of Farmville early on the morning of April 7th. The Secretary felt it was time to join President Davis, who was in Danville. As we headed toward the Appomattox River, I could hear the sound of gunfire in the distance. For the first time, I became very concerned of capture or dying while trying to escape. Once we crossed the river, we headed in the direction of Pamplin Station. There we came across a supply train for the army. But with our communications severed with Lee's army, we left them and headed south to Danville. Once in Danville, we learned President Davis and his cabinet were heading deeper south after learning of Lee's surrender at Appomattox. We pushed on eluding capture by prowling Yankee cavalry until we finally arrived in the evening at Greensboro, North Carolina. To my surprise, William was the first to greet us. I could tell by his expression that he was greatly shaken and troubled with the news of Lee's surrender and the unexpected future under a different administration. After escorting us into the residence of a Mr. John Woods, he disappeared. There for the first time since the evacuation of Richmond, I saw President Davis. He appeared frail and troubled but still possessed that determined stubbornness."

"He always wanted to exert his energy for a greater Confederacy and only held its best interests in mind. I didn't always agree with his politics, but I must admit, I came to admire him for his vigor and strength," Caroline said.

"I agree," Charles calmly said. He continued his progression of events in a composed low tone. "That same evening Secretary Breckinridge met some of the other cabinet members and they expressed their views. I believe the most important effect on the Secretary, and especially myself, was when we learned through them that Generals Beauregard and Johnston believed that the continuation of the war was futile. And it would be costly in numbers of casualties for our men and possibly less than honorable terms for surrender and leniency. The next morning, President Davis and the cabinet met with the two generals. Everyone was somber knowing this was the end of the Confederacy with Johnston's statement that we should open peace negotiations with General Sherman."

For a brief moment, Charles paused and faintly chuckled. He shook his head. "During the whole proceedings, President Davis kept folding and unfolding a scrap of paper. He gave me the impression that he already had his mind made up on matters. To my surprise, at the end, he asked General Beauregard in a muffled tone his opinion. The General concurred with General Johnston. For the first time, I finally heard the president admit the cause was lost. The words he spoke were as if the ground had trembled beneath my feet. But in the end, President Davis wanted to continue the struggle west of the Mississippi but it was Secretary Breckinridge's desire that he escape from the country while he could. I knew it would only be a matter of time before we were all captured or killed. It was over for me. That night, I was restless and couldn't sleep. The only thing on my mind was escaping and seeing you and Ann."

As Caroline caressed Charles' arm, she glanced at him inquisitively. "If William disappeared, what happened to him?"

"I received lodging at the Beaumont home on the northern side of town. With great physical exhaustion from lack of sleep, weariness of mind, and anxiety to get away, I departed my room several hours before daylight before being noticed by anyone. As I walked onto the porch, William was sitting there on the swing quietly smoking a cigar. He appeared more composed than when we first arrived in the city. As I approached, he sarcastically asked if I was running out while there was still the opportunity. I confirmed his suspicion. William just laughed. He didn't appear angry with me because even he admitted that the cause was lost and we would all probably hang or be imprisoned with President Davis if we were caught. His statement sent chills down my spine. The thought of not seeing you gave me uneasiness. I asked him what he would do. He just shrugged his shoulders and shook his head. His answer was, he didn't know. For him, there wasn't much to return to. I invited him along, but he refused."

"Where did you go after leaving him?"

Before answering, Charles paused and glanced aimlessly at the wall, knowing that Caroline didn't know of William's fate. He turned and stroked Caroline's long blond hair. He looked into her eyes. "I was so frightened knowing Yankees were most likely prowling the area looking for the President. What I will say makes me feel guilty, but it was my hope that he would continue to be their center of attention allowing me the opportunity to escape capture. I had to rely on my instincts just as Father had taught me. It was my habit to travel during the night along the mountains or ridges and hide and sleep during the day. For a little over a week, I had little to eat and fought hunger with determination. It rained and the fields and roads became muddy to the point that it was near impassable at times to continue. My horse succumbed for want of food and fatigue. All along, I desperately tried to maintain my goal of reaching the western mountains of North Carolina, until things calmed down, and planting myself deep within. There I hoped to find men who were friendly to our cause and would shelter me even though they might be paroled."

Charles paused, he noticed Caroline was in tears. "Maybe I shouldn't say anymore."

With witnessing Caroline's anguish, Charles was sensitive to her emotions. Tears filled his eyes. He sniffled as Caroline embraced him, kissing his forehead. "You have been through a lot for all that you believed in. But now it's time for you to get it out. It will always hinder us in our relationship if you don't communicate with me about things that trouble you."

Shaking his head, Charles continued in a soft tone. "All along, I thought I had been traveling westward. In my confusion, I was traveling northwest. The day before I was found I had a brush with a Yankee cavalry patrol. It happened near a little hamlet named Madison. Quite exhausted, I had been sleeping for sometime when I was awakened by crackle of pine needles. When I opened my eyes, I had two Yankees standing over me with their revolvers drawn pointed in my direction. As I looked around, mounted on their horses were five other soldiers. One Yankee sergeant that was mounted asked, 'Is this him?' And from the mist, an elderly gentleman appeared, scruffy and rough looking in appearance. He stepped forward and identified me. It was all over, I thought."

"How did he know who you were?"

"Out of desperation, I had stopped earlier and begged for food."

"Did the Yankees know who you were?"

"I am not sure. If they did, they didn't call me by name. But my greatest fear was that I would never see Ann or you again. They handled me roughly and forced me to walk back toward the old man's cabin. As I looked around, fortunately the sun was descending behind the horizon. Once at the cabin, they tied my hands behind my back and sat me on a chair. When I asked for water, one of them struck me and laughed. Constantly throughout the evening they tormented me."

Taking a deep sigh and showing some anxiety, Charles continued. "Over the next four hours, the Yankees feasted on the old man's whiskey and fell asleep. As for the old man, he went about cleaning up after they had eaten. Lying nearby on a chair was a piece of glass that was broken from a bottle by one of the drunken soldiers in one of his many threats to me. I thought if I could reach it I might be able to cut myself free. Carefully and quietly, I made an effort. In my attempt, I made some noise when a spoon I unintentionally hit, fell off the table and struck the floor. The old man didn't notice nor did he turn around to see what was happening. He must have been hard of hearing. As I took the glass and cut through the rope, I thought that at anytime someone would awaken or that the old man would notice my intentions. I was afraid that I'd be killed. I was fortunate. Once free, I overpowered the old man and he fell to the floor unconscious but not dead. Without hesitation, I raced for the barn and mounted a horse. Once mounted, I headed toward the wooded area with the other soldiers' horses. They never woke and never knew until later, I am sure, what happened."

Caroline deeply sighed as fear covered her face. Her eyes were on Charles with anxiety as she took several deep breaths. "Then they are still looking for you?"

"Yes, even as we speak. But before they find me, I had to see Ann and you. Fortunately, a Confederate veteran, by the name of Maxwell Jennings, who had just returned home, found me the next afternoon. As it was, he was hunting for supper. When he killed the deer, he found me sleeping near some trees surrounded by undergrowth and thickets. After taking me home, his wife fed me. His risk was great for sheltering someone from the Confederate government. Yankee patrols still roamed through the mountains. On many occasions they had to hide me under the floorboards of the cabin. If I were outside helping with the spring plowing, I would have to seek shelter in an outbuilding. Sometimes I would flee for the woods. After three months when it was safe enough to leave, Maxwell acted as my guide, north to Lynchburg. Once we reached the outskirts of Lynchburg, he found me lodging with an elderly gentleman by the name of Johnson McNeil."

"Were you not afraid of someone recognizing you?"

"With my long hair and shabby beard, it was more difficult to identify me. But I continued to be cautious, trusting no one."

Briefly pausing, Charles continued the chain of events after departing Greensboro. "Johnson knew the northern Virginia area very well. During the first two years of the war, he owned a little farm and lived with his family along the Rappahannock River. On many occasions, he helped Confederate agents by providing a safe house and often assisted them as they operated behind Federal lines. After the battle at Fredericksburg in the winter of '62, he had enough and moved his family farther south to the Lynchburg area where they would be safe from the war. I was with Johnson for about two weeks before we headed north to Charlottesville. From there until I got to Warrenton, I was on my own. Johnson was afraid to take any more risks. There, I found a school friend by the name of Andy Logan. Andy had fought as an officer with the 4th Virginia Cavalry under Jeb Stuart. Still burning with anger over the loss of the war and his property, he hid me in his wagon and transported me as far as Haymarket. I had given him instructions as to my destination and my intentions. Once we arrived near Haymarket, he placed me in the care of a former Negro slave that he trusted by the name of Darby. And from there we arrived at the Hammond's within hours."

Charles rose and sat alongside the bed. He appeared restless and edgy as he rubbed his hands through his hair.

Noticing her husband's distress, Caroline rose and placed her arms around his shoulders. "My love, you have been through so much. I don't know how you endured such peril."

Charles glanced over his shoulders. "Neither do I." With his wife's attention, he paused and took a deep sigh. He rubbed his hand over his whiskers. "Once I arrived at the Hammonds, and to my surprise, William was there."

"William! What was he doing there?"

"He was running the same as me. Only he was killing everyone that stood in his way. He had gone mad."

Stunned, Caroline placed her hand over her mouth. "Oh no, not the Hammonds."

"Unfortunately, yes. Apparently, they had asked too many questions concerning his intentions. He became suspicious of them. He believed they were going to give away his plans to the authorities."

"Well, how did Pete and Seamus find Katie?"

"Katie didn't say," Charles said as he glanced once more over his shoulder at his wife.

"No. With Hayward wounded, there wasn't time."

"Apparently, as you may already know, when Pete and Katie were in Boston, her family rejected the idea of financially helping us."

"That part I know and she ended up missing from her hotel room in Washington City."

"Her abductor was William. Katie was there at the Hammonds being held against her will. Once Pete entered the room, William turned the weapon on Katie. Pete complied with William's demand to drop the pistol. Once Milton the family's servant entered the room with rope to bind us, he jumped William. Things got confused quickly. Immediately, William discharged the weapon and the servant fell dead. The gun fell on the floor near Katie. As William approached her to regain the weapon, she shot and killed him."

Caroline was stunned and bewildered over all that she had just heard her husband confess. She stood and paced the floor in disbelief. "That poor girl. What will happen to her next?"

Turning around, Caroline approached her husband and knelt in front of him. She looked up at Charles. "Why in the world would William want to abduct Katie anyway? It doesn't make sense, or does it?"

"I think William was just obsessed with Katie and wanted her love. He couldn't bear the thought of her being with Pete. It drove him crazy. Besides, after losing the war and blaming President Davis for its loss, he had nothing in his life worth holding to. He couldn't return to Norfolk because the estate had been heavily damaged during the summer of '64 with the fighting around Richmond. His political future was totally destroyed. No family, no friends."

"Yes Charles, it makes sense. Before, and after the war began, he always desired her attention. Katie's face began to glow the with mentioning Pete's name, I would notice on many occasions the despair and troubled expression covering William's face. I guess he believed that if he couldn't have Katie's love, then no one could."

With his eyes on his wife, Charles quietly pondered on William's real intentions for kidnapping Katie. There had to be more to it, but what? No one kidnaps someone because of an overly obsessive love for that individual unless they are mad, he thought. Now with William dead, he would never know the real reason. The real secret may lie in the grave.

Chapter 65

Early the next morning, Pete awakened to the sound of birds singing near the window of the slaves' cabin. He placed his hands to his face and wiped his eyes. As he pulled the blanket from his body, he looked out the window at several of the birds perched along the tree limbs. He rose and continued to glance out the window gazing at some wildflowers that were dead from the first frost. The scene resurrected many thoughts of a previous life at Shenandoah before the outbreak of the war. He could still visualize Jeremiah, one of the family's most trusted and elderly servants, laboring in the family's rose garden. He recalled from the servant's own words the pleasure it manifested in his life. Jeremiah was a master designer and many of the guests who visited Shenandoah would often comment and praise his efforts.

It had been a restless night for Pete. He had only slept for several hours. As he walked onto the front porch, his mind was consumed with taking Katie to the train depot in Harpers Ferry. Both of them had changed, and there was more in life they desired but believed that it was too far from their grasp. Issues between them were too complicated. She wanted a family and a relationship he believed that he could no longer provide. Not only was her loyalty questionable, but also after all that transpired during her absence, his trust had vanished. As he looked around the barren estate, he knew there wasn't any money and there wasn't any source for bringing in any funds in the near future. The process of rebuilding Shenandoah into an estate of profitability would take many years and great patience on behalf of the family. The changes that resulted from the abolishment of slavery, and a nation that has been torn by war had left Southern families with a future of uncertainty. Like other families, their suffering was far from over. What would trouble them next?

The family cabin was quiet, and with this stillness, there was a serenity that hung in the air. Katie glanced over to the opposite side of the loft where Ann was still sleeping soundly. She thought of her love for Ann. Ann had been through innumerable sorrows, unbearable tribulations, and great pain over the last several years. She was proud of her because she had learned to endure through these trials and persevere when there was only faith to go on. Ann never spoke a negative word or complained about her living conditions but learned to adapt. Out of everyone in her family, Ann was the only one who accepted what life offered, good or bad.

Katie's struggle with coughing had subsided, but physically she knew something was still terribly wrong. She was experiencing tightness in her chest and some discomfort had begun in the left side of her body. Leaning over the side of the loft, Katie noticed that no one had risen from their sleep. She decided she would rise and stoke the fire and make coffee. As she dressed, she heard Ann move. Katie turned around and looked. Ann's eyes were open, gazing at Katie.

"What time is it?" Ann asked in a sleepy tone.

Smiling, Katie answered in a playful tone. "It's time to get up."

"What will you do today?"

Katie hesitated as she looked at Ann's innocent eyes. "I am returning to Boston."

Surprised and fully awake, Ann sat up. "Why! Why are you leaving? You have just returned home."

Those last words that Ann spoke had deeply pierced her heart. She looked at Ann. "I have to. Thus far, I have never lied to you and I will not begin now."

Pausing and continuing to look at Ann's sad features, Katie knew Ann would not accept her words, but instead, she would grieve. "I just believe with everything that has happened, and everything that has been said, it would be for the best. Your Uncle Pete and I need some time to think matters over between us and decide if we want to marry one day and raise a family. It's an important decision, you know."

"I thought this matter had been settled."

Katie shook her head in frustration. "No, unfortunately, it hasn't." She continued to speak softly, "A lot has happened since I left last month and returned to Boston."

"What has happened that would drive you away from us? What?" Ann tearfully asked.

"You wouldn't understand, and I am not sure at this very moment even I understand. Pete and I are confused, and unsure about the direction that we want our lives to take. You'll discover one day that marriage is a big decision and commitment. It takes a lot of thought and is to be taken seriously. There has to be a sacrificial and unconditional love or it won't work. That is where Pete and I are at in our lives. So we need time to think and to be sure."

Ann shook her head in disbelief. She looked at Katie and collapsed in her arms, crying. "I know he loves you. You must stay."

As Katie stroked her hair, she replied. "But, I can't."

"It won't be the same with you gone. Mother and I will be so upset and it's more than I can bear," Ann cried as she embraced Katie.

"I have always loved you even from the very beginning. Just moments ago, I thought of how proud and honored that I have been to have known you, and seen you grow, and mature the way that you have. You have had a lot to overcome because of the suffering and trials that you've had to walk through. But you have endured the fire. You are stronger now, and I can only hope that all the blessings of God and life are bestowed on you. And yes, I will greatly miss you. Ann, you'll always be in my thoughts and prayers. And who knows, maybe we'll see each other again."

Noise was coming from the lower level. Both Katie and Ann were more composed as they stood. Once Katie climbed down the ladder from the loft, she glanced for the longest time at Hayward lying in the corner. He appeared to be sleeping peacefully and she didn't want to disturb him.

Caroline was kneeling near the fireplace and adding wood to the fire she had just revived. When Katie turned and looked in her direction, Caroline said in a serious tone. "At times during the night, I couldn't help but hear you coughing. Sometime this morning, Pete needs to take you into town to see Doc Marmion and get something to help you."

With her hands clasp together, Katie approached. "Look, Caroline, there is something that I must say."

"Oh, it can wait until later," Caroline replied as she continued tossing another log on the fire.

"No Caroline, it can't. I have something to tell you."

As Caroline turned from the fireplace, she noticed the troubled expression covering Katie's face. "Katie, what is wrong?" she softly asked.

Katie glanced at Ann and then again at Caroline. She slowly spoke, "I am returning to Boston later this morning."

A surprised expression covered Caroline's face. "Why! I don't understand."

"No, I guess you don't. Sometimes I don't think that I do either. But, for sometime now, Pete has been distant from me. Even though I've tried to reach out to him, he refuses to reveal his emotions to me. When I returned last spring after the war ended, we were happy, spending a lot of time together, especially along the river. It was just like it was the day when we received the news that Fort Sumter had been bombarded. We were sharing a picnic lunch and fishing. Later, he opened up to me and began to express his emotions and feelings on personal matters surrounding his life. I really believed we were drawn to each other. When war came, that all changed. With the separation and uncertainty of conflict, he was gone and our correspondences were few. I really believed that I was being robbed and deprived of something that I've always longed and searched for all my life. That's why I came back. I had to know if he loved me and if there was going to be a life with him."

Katie continued in a somber tone. "On the afternoon of my arrival, I found him along the river. He gave me a red rose that he had found near the mansion and told me that he loved me. I remember in turn saying to him that from sabers and roses, a love was born."

"What did you mean?"

"Throughout the war Pete and I endured many trials and separation. It was through these experiences we knew that we loved each other and now that we were together there wouldn't be any more separations. He agreed. Over the months, the relationship was beginning to grow and there was great promise of our dreams being fulfilled, but then, it all began to slowly fade when there was little money for rebuilding and little time for us to be alone. The problems just continued to increase concerning Shenandoah."

Caroline quietly noticed the desponded expression covering Katie's face. "There is still a chance. Charles and I have had our troubles over the years, especially when it came to Shenandoah. Just before you arrived in Harpers Ferry in late summer of '60, we were frequently having disagreements over his negligence of Ann and me. Constantly, he was away, negotiating with clients concerning our horses and cattle. Sometimes he was involved in some scheme of things. And when he was home, he would work on proposals, and at times, wouldn't come to dinner, or he would come to bed late after Ann and I had fallen asleep. I put up with a lot, but in the end, we managed to work it all out."

Slowly shaking her head in disagreement, Katie replied. "This is more complicated. Too much has happened between us over the last three weeks. In my anger against Pete, my desperation for his love, I allowed another man to kiss me, and show his affection toward me, in the attempt of filling the emptiness I was experiencing."

"He knows?"

"Yes. I was honest with him and told him all that happened. Naturally, he felt betrayed. And now, I know I have caused considerable damage to him, our relationship, and I have destroyed any opportunity to work things out."

Before Caroline could answer Katie, the door opened and Pete entered the room. He quietly glanced at both women as he shut the door behind him. Once he turned around, he noticed Caroline's eyes possessed that glassy appearance. Before he could say anything to her, she rushed from the room toward the bedroom, shutting the door behind her. Ann quietly walked outside in great anguish over all that she had heard and witnessed.

Katie quietly watched these actions. She turned her attention to Pete. "I guess you are ready?"

"Yes. I feel the sooner the better."

"Can you just brush me out of your life that quickly?" Katie asked in a pitched voice.

"No, I can't. But I feel that it will be better for everyone."

"You mean you! Well, maybe I was bloody wrong about us when I returned to Shenandoah. Haven't I been through a lot also? You're not the only one you know. I have been kidnapped and abused and put through bloody hell! I even killed a man. How do you think that makes me feel? I'll tell you! It makes me feel worthless even though it was in self-defense. And yet you feel you're the only one that has suffered?"

"I am sorry for all that you've gone through. But, Katie, I can't give you what you want in life. And in reality, that's what our problems are all about. Things have changed since the beginning of the war. We have no money and no way of making any. You will be better off with your family. Leave this area and forget about us."

As Pete turned and stormed out the door, tears began to fill Katie's eyes. "But I can't my love. I can't.

* * * *

The journey into Harpers Ferry was quiet and both maintained their distance from each other. Katie sat beside Pete in the wagon. At times she coughed uncontrollably. Her mind was consumed with her sorrowful departure from Shenandoah. Caroline and Ann pleaded for her to stay despite her indifferences with Pete. She flatly refused. She told them her return to Boston would be best for the family. Even Charles apologized for betraying her trust and the division that he had initiated between Caroline and her during the war. Elizabeth was still sleeping and Katie didn't desire that she be disturbed; so instead, she kissed her on the forehead. As for Hayward, when he received the news, he was without words. His only expression was that he wept like a child.

Like Pete, it would take Katie sometime to recover from everything that had happened over the past three weeks. She resigned herself to the reality that maybe it would be good for her to return home and re-evaluate her life and goals. But it would be difficult putting aside her love for Pete and his family. Shenandoah was her most favorite place on earth. Even though it had been decimated in the latter part of the war, it still was an area of majesty.

As Pete and Katie traveled slowly along Shenandoah Street, Katie glanced in the direction of the river. Many fond memories resurfaced and she gave reflection to each one. Often, while living at Mrs. Stipes's boarding house, she would walk or sit along the river when she was troubled and needed time alone. This gave her the necessary time to regroup her thoughts and reflect on the best answers to the issues in her life.

Katie turned and looked at Pete. "I would like to request one more favor of you before we arrive at the depot."

"All right. What can I do?"

"I want to walk along the river one more time."

Pete quietly nodded his head as he turned the wagon in the direction of Bridge Street. After proceeding a short distance, he brought the team of horses to a halt. He jumped down and assisted

Katie from the wagon. He looked as she glanced at him and faintly smiled. As Katie walked along the water, he recalled this was the same area where she found him after Caroline had broken the news to her that he was leaving home and had enlisted with the 1st Virginia Cavalry. He confided in her all that his mother had done in giving his brother sole ownership of the estate and his deepest feelings on the matter. On that day, she impressed him with her sincerity and compassion. He marveled at her willingness and patience to listen. When he departed, he knew by the tone of her voice and the glow within her eyes that she possessed more then friendly feelings for him.

Katie picked up a few loose stones and attempted to skip them across the water just as Pete and her had done on many occasions. Many memories surfaced. It was in this same area that she first experienced his sensitivity and warmth. It was in this particular area where she first wanted to tell him her deepest feelings for him. She could vividly visualize them sitting on the same log near the riverbank where they expressed their deepest fears and doubts, and also, words of comfort and reassurance. It was in this area where Caroline and she argued over Elizabeth's truest intentions for turning over ownership of Shenandoah to Charles, thus depriving Pete for being as his mother believed, a rebel. One last time she glanced up the river in the direction of Shenandoah. She briefly cried, and then sorrow turned to a smile with the many fond memories of her life with Pete Barker. After wiping her eyes, Katie turned and walked toward the wagon where Pete stood looking.

Once boarded, Pete and Katie headed in the direction of Shenandoah Street. Pete didn't ask Katie her thoughts, but both of them remained quiet. Again, Katie began to cough uncontrollably.

Pete glanced her way. "That cough is getting worse. Before taking you to the depot, let me take you by Doc Marmion."

"No Pete, I'll be all right. I just want to leave as soon as possible," Katie answered as she held her handkerchief over her mouth.

Pete and Katie arrived at the depot. The train had not yet arrived. Pete walked in to the office to send a telegram to Seamus in Washington City assuring him that Katie was safe and on her way to Boston. Hopefully, he would meet her in Baltimore for the journey home. When Pete walked from the telegraph office, he noticed Katie sitting on one of the wooden benches, still coughing. He approached her. "Katie, I can't allow you to leave knowing you're sick."

Katie looked up at him. "No Pete, you have done enough by asking. I just want to go home."

Quietly, Pete nodded and sat next to her. "I sent Seamus a telegram informing him that you were heading home."

"Thank you."

"I don't know what else I can say."

"You don't have to say anything. Enough has been said. Enough has been done. I agree, it's over with between us," Katie replied, as she looked at Pete.

In the distance, the whistle of the train echoed through the valley. As the engine appeared pulling its three coaches, Pete stood and Katie did likewise. Once the train chugged to a halt, he picked up her bags and walked with her to one of the coaches. He was saddened and disappointed.   Just as she, he had high expectations of what might have been in a future with Katie McBride, but now that had vanished.

Once at the designated train coach, Katie turned around and looked into his sorrowful eyes. She believed that she had expressed her deepest regrets for all that had taken place with Robert and her many attempts to accomplish everything within her soul to revive their relationship.   Instinctively, Katie leaned and kissed him on the cheek. As she turned and grabbed her skirt to climb the steps to the coach, she began to collapse.

Immediately, Pete embraced Katie's limp body. He continuously called her name, but she didn't respond to his pleas. Pete was frantic. With haste, he quickly swept Katie into his arms and carried her to the wagon.   While hastening along Potomac Street, the image of the lady near Berryville, who was slowly dying yesterday from unknown causes, still was very vivid in his mind. Constantly they tormented him because he remembered as she was lying on the bed, she uncontrollably coughed and at times blood would follow. Many of the same symptoms Katie possessed.   What concerned him more was the fact that she was unconscious and wouldn't respond to his voice.

Chapter 66

As Pete rounded the corner of High and Shenandoah Street, he raced the team of horses at a fast pace. A Federal soldier near the Provost Marshall's office raised his weapon and shouted for Pete to halt. Ignoring the soldier's command, Pete continued to race the team of horses. After continuing another fifty yards, he cut across the path of another horse-drawn wagon. Ignoring the cursing that flowed freely from the individual's mouth, Pete continued to wheel his team of horses onto Clay Street. In what felt like an eternity, Pete finally arrived at Doctor Marmion's residence, bringing the horses to a halt. Swiftly, he jumped from the wagon and clutched Katie into his arms. She was still unconscious.

Without knocking, Pete raised his foot and knocked open the front door. When Pete entered, the physician was tending to another patient. Quickly Doctor Marmion jumped to his feet. "What is the meaning of all this?"

"Katie needs help. She is unconscious," Pete anxiously replied.

Ignoring his patient, the physician pointed with his hand. "Take her to the back room."

Once in the small room to the rear of the physician's office, Pete carefully laid Katie on a small bed. She was faintly breathing and still wouldn't respond to his voice. Pete was fearful of losing Katie. He felt helpless and wanted to do something but all control of the situation was out of his hands.

Doctor Marmion swiftly followed Pete into the room. The physician knelt over the bed and gently opened Katie's eyelids and examined them. Next, he listened to her heart with a stethoscope while touching her forehead with his other hand. To Pete, Katie appeared lifeless. As the physician continued the process, he looked up at Pete. "Why don't you go out into the other room and have some coffee while I try to determine what the problem is?"

"But I feel like I need to be here."

"There is nothing that you can do," the physician said as he glanced up at Pete. He continued in a stern tone. "I will let you know something as soon as possible. Now go."

As Pete complied with the physician's request, he walked into the office area and gazed out the window. The visions and images of the suffering he witnessed at the lady's home near Berryville continued to torment his mind. He rubbed his hand through his hair. He sighed and attempted to find some way to distract the depressing and troubling thoughts but they continued to overpower him. After some time had lapsed, his anguishing thoughts were broken when he heard the creaking sound of someone stepping on loose floorboards. Swiftly, he turned and immediately noticed the gloomy expression covering the physician's face.

Fearing Katie was dead, Pete swiftly approached. "How is she?"

"Holding her own, I guess." The physician replied as he rubbed his chin with his hand. "She has a fever," he continued, "and for that, I have placed cold cloths on her face in hopes of trying to break or control it from rising anymore." Pausing and thinking, the physician asked, "Has she complained of anything bothering her over the last couple of days? Have you seen any difference in her moods, habits?"

"Since yesterday afternoon, she has had an uncontrollable cough."

"Was she coughing up blood?"

"None that I saw." As the physician walked over to his desk and sat in the chair, Pete followed. More composed, he continued somberly. "Yesterday afternoon, I witnessed a lady suffering from some of the same signs as Katie. The lady was pale, bad cough, and only breathing heavy at the time. She didn't lose consciousness such as Katie. Her servant said the physician had given her some medicine but she had gotten worse since his visit."

Doctor Marmion's expression changed to one of trouble with what Pete said. He took a deep sigh. "All signs point to pneumonia and I am afraid that might be the case for Katie."

"Pneumonia?" Pete paused and continued softly. "That's a death sentence. It killed General Jackson after Chancellorsville."

With a deep sigh, Doctor Marmion tried to be reassuring. "Well Pete, maybe she can fight off this thing. She is young and I assume has always been healthy. But I guess the thing is, does she have the will to live?"

Tears filled Pete's eyes as he turned away. Again, he walked over to the window and glanced out at Saint Peter's Catholic Church. For a moment, he recalled the night when he returned home after the fight at Sharpsburg in the autumn of 1862. The moon was glowing. There was a deep chill in the air. He remembered there was a great interval of time that had occurred since he last saw Katie. Earlier, he was told by the Priest in all probability she'd be at the church as had been her custom in the evening. When he opened the huge doors to the dimly lighted church, there appeared a shadowy lone figure kneeling and praying after lighting a candle. At once, he recognized Katie. As she prayed, her actions and feelings for him struck a deep chord within his heart. He waited patiently until she rose from the alter and made the sign of the cross. Sadness and despair disappeared when she recognized him. Without hesitation, they embraced out of joy. She kissed him and caressed his face, and for a brief moment, made him forget the horrors of war.

After catching up on some things, Pete and Katie departed the church. They went to her favorite area along the river where they built a fire. He could still vividly recall that night as if it had just occurred. Katie shared her two-day experience of hiding in a wet cellar with a Yankee soldier during the heavy shelling by Confederate artillery along the mountains. It was a prelude to the terrifying conflict along the banks of Antietam Creek in which Pete participated. With reservations, Pete spoke of the horrors of war that he had already experienced in his sixteen months of military life. He had the troublesome task of breaking the news to his sister Rebecca that her suitor had been killed at Sharpsburg. This greatly affected him. Katie comforted him as he freely poured out his pain and anguish. That night, he noticed the passionate glow in her eyes, the tranquility in her expression, especially when she told him that she was in love with him. Now she might be dying and never again would he see the glowing light revealed from the eyes that first attracted him. Out of fear of making a commitment and not knowing if she would be a widow before the war ended, he made various excuses in his defense for a way of escape from her emotions.

Pete's thoughts were interrupted as Doctor Marmion stood behind him. "Why don't you go home? I'll send for you if there is any change in her condition."

"No, I can't leave her."

"But there's nothing that you can do for her,"

"No, I don't care how long it takes, I am staying with her."

Nodding his head in agreement, Doctor Marmion turned and walked back to Katie's room.

* * * *

At Shenandoah, Charles had just finished looking in on his mother. She was still sleeping. He glanced in the corner of the cabin and Hayward was doing likewise. Walking over and sitting near the warmth of the fireplace, Charles sipped on a hot cup of black coffee while waiting for Pete. As much as he despised the thoughts of leaving Caroline and Ann, he knew he couldn't turn his back on reality. It would only be a matter of time before a Yankee patrol would discover him, or because of little trust for anyone living nearby, someone he thought, might notify the authorities and gain possibly a reward for his capture. Not only was this a concern, but also, if Federal authorities knew that the family was sheltering him, then possibly, he could still lose ownership of Shenandoah. This would be disastrous for his family, especially Ann. It was still his intentions as before the war that one day she would inherit the estate. As painful as it would be, he decided the sooner he surrendered to Federal authorities, and with his cooperation, the chances would favor a quick trial and maybe less time in prison. If possible, he would like to spend one more day with his family. He knew the sooner that he told Caroline of his intentions, the family could prepare for his lengthy absence.

Charles' thoughts were interrupted. He glanced at Caroline and Ann walking through the front door carrying a pail with milk from the old cow the family owned. "Here, let me take that," Charles scolded. "You should not be doing this."

"With the slaves gone, there isn't anyone to do the work around here. Everyone has to help out," Ann replied.

"Then we will have to hire laborers."

"With what?" Caroline dolefully asked.

Charles paused and nodded in agreement. "I apologize for my ignorance. I seem to forget that things are not as they once were." Pausing again and looking sadly at his wife, Charles murmured, "And they never will be again."

"We are not the only ones that will have to learn to readjust and start over again," Caroline answered. "This county and its people were devastated by the war. Nothing of use remains. Everyone will have to begin anew, not just us."

"Yes. Yes we will," Charles reluctantly answered. "I was just sitting here waiting on Pete to speak to him about running the place while I am in prison. Then after prison…"

"Wait a minute, you're going where?"

"Caroline, I must surrender soon to the Federals and begin to put this nightmare of running from them behind me. It's only a matter of time before they capture me and we both know it means prison. I can't allow the family to be punished for giving me refuge. Surely the Federal authorities will take Shenandoah from us if they find me here."

"I don't care about Shenandoah and if we lose it. I just want us to be together and to put the war behind us," Caroline replied.

"Father," Ann anxiously said, "Mother and I were just talking this morning about all of us leaving this area and escaping west; or the Northern Region, somewhere that is faraway and no one can find us."

"That's right Charles. We could leave tonight before it's too late and the Yankees find us," Caroline added as she looked for some evidence from his facial features for approval of their scheme.

"What about Mother? Who will take care of her?" Charles asked in a concerned voice.

"She has been steadily recovering. Pete and Hayward can manage." When Charles didn't answer, Caroline added excitingly. "They'll understand."

"And this means I will always be on the run and have to live the rest of my life in fear. No, I can't do that."

"But Charles listen. You were part of Jefferson Davis' staff. What do you think is going to happen now that they have caught up with him?" Pausing and waiting for an answer, Caroline continued when her husband didn't respond to her plea. "He'll hang or never get out of prison. Is that what you want? Do you want to put Ann and me through that ordeal?" Looking at Charles, she asked in a pitched tone. "Well do you?"

Approaching from behind where Charles was standing, Hayward softly added. "Mr. Charles, Pete and I'se sort a thought ya git away whiles ya could. Misse Caroline is right ya know. The

Yanks might not be easy on ya. Sir, now is not the time to be mulish."

As he took a deep sigh and looked aimlessly at the floor, Charles again turned his attention to Caroline. "Before the war, I treated many of our friends wrongly, abused their trust in me, and I thought I was rightfully correct, but I was wrong for acting out of what I know now to be only selfishness. Serving under President Davis, I firmly believed was a noble and justifiable cause for our independence in order to preserve our way of life. I really believed I was contributing and there was value to all I was doing. It made me feel proud and honorable. For a while, I actually felt somewhat strange. For once, I had a clear conscious and felt honest. It wasn't like things before the war when I was running Shenandoah. I am sure that you were not blinded by the way I handled the estate's business matters. I am ashamed that I initiated many shady business transactions and continuous wrong doings against our neighbors and acquaintances here in the Valley and elsewhere. Somehow, I managed to erase all of these things from memory until earlier this morning when I looked out the window. You know what I saw?"

"What did you see Father?" Ann asked.

"Someone who is deceitful and deserves just punishment for his sins against those he willfully cheated and stole from for his own glory in life. My greatest evils were committed against my brother Pete and my sister Rebecca. May God forgive me. Mother and I used our friends, by any means, to weaken my brother's position and trust when it came to Shenandoah." After pausing, he continued in a composed tone. "At least there is some honor in surrendering and standing accountable for my crimes. If I die, I die honestly."

"Listen to you," Elizabeth shouted from her bedroom entrance. "We have all done wrong one time or another, but did you ever think that it was because we knew we had to survive. Just like now, you have to think about your own survival. What if old Stanton tries to connect you somehow to Lincoln's murder?" When Charles didn't answer, Elizabeth snapped, "Well, have you thought of what will happen? You must listen to Caroline and Hayward and leave immediately after darkness."

Caroline turned to Ann. "Begin packing lightly."

Turning her attention to Charles, she added, "We just can't take the chance of you being captured."

Over the past four years, Charles had continuously been separated from Caroline and Ann. Many times during a lonely evening abroad in London or in Richmond, the anguish and abandonment was more than he could bear. His mind was torn by the righteousness of this life and experiencing the horrors of alienation all over again. Was his hesitation because he didn't want to surrender the reins of Shenandoah now that he was home? As he quietly walked to the window with the others looking on, he peered through the opening and realized for the first time there was nothing of means and value left to hold to. After struggling inwardly, he determined within his heart that his family and freedom were the most important assets in his life.

Chapter 67

As Pete stood peering out the window, he could see the brick smoke stack still towering over the remains of the armory ruins. Earlier, Pete had dispatched a messenger to inform Caroline and Charles of the events surrounding Katie's sickness at the train depot knowing in all probability Caroline would come. Other than this task, Pete had refused to leave Katie's side. Instead, he quietly sat near her bed, maintaining a constant vigil with an occasional visitation from Doctor Marmion. On the physician's examinations, Katie hadn't responded to his occasional prodding's. She laid motionless in a continuous sleep. In many ways, Pete had some knowledge from his current experience how Katie must have felt when she received the news of his being killed at Gettysburg. The void and emptiness was dominant and ruling within his heart. The indifference and division the two had struggled with over the weeks had racked torment and confusion on his mind. For the first time since their acquaintance in the summer of '60, he knew there was the chance he would lose her to death.

Occasionally, Pete's mind drifted in thought, recalling their times of separation during the war, their times of indifference, constant struggle for survival, and their times of passion. There was something about her character, her calmness in various situations surrounding life, and the qualities that she saw in other persons' performances that challenged him. With all that she had been through, her beauty as a woman still glowed not only naturally but also inwardly.

Pete recalled just before his cavalry regiment went into action at Gettysburg in July of '63, his cousin, Lester Tyler, inadvertently challenged him in their conversation when he spoke of his fondness for Grace Lloyd. War had had caused Lester to reflect on their relationship. Lester added there were words that could not express Grace's absence from his life. His intentions were of the deepest and that marriage would blossom in the future. Pete could still vividly recall that those words had a deep effect upon him, piercing his heart beyond all that he could inwardly withstand. Pete opened his heart to Lester sharing his unquestionable trust for Katie and her sincere willingness to withhold judgment. He explained that often they shared intimate thoughts. He had learned to subdue his pride and allow her to see his inward person. As on that hot summer day, now he missed that oneness of spirit.

At the time of the battle at Gettysburg, he knew he was extremely fond of Katie but was too prideful to admit its reality in his life. Because of his stubbornness, he allowed years then and now to waste away and deprive him of the abundant life he could have shared with her. As he gazed at Katie lying on the bed, it was as though she was gone; he had lost her forever.

The sound of the front door closing gave him the indication that Caroline had arrived. He didn't expect Charles to escort her because it would be too risky with all the Federal soldiers garrisoned at Harpers Ferry. Pete slowly stood and walked toward the bedroom entrance. True to his premonition, it was Caroline.

Immediately, she walked over and embraced Pete. "How is she?"

As Doctor Marmion quietly looked at the two, Pete replied, "She is still unconscious." He continued in a trembling tone. "It is all my fault for not bringing her into town yesterday."

Caroline didn't reply. She stepped aside and quietly walked into the room where Katie was lying. Caroline gazed at Katie and recalled when they first met on the evening after her arrival in town. William had made Katie's acquaintance on the train from Baltimore and it was through him that Charles invited her to William's reception. Even before introductions by Charles, and before a word was spoken by either, her heart willingly reached out to Katie. Immediately, there was something different about her that drew her. It was an evening where she discovered that she and Katie had a lot in common. Both were searching for the true meaning in life at that time. Caroline was impressed that Katie had read and learned some of the Southern culture before coming south to Harpers Ferry. Although from the North, and when times were not without great animosity over fiery social issues, Katie gave the appearance of being humble and knowing her social graces. Katie had received the respect of many guests that attended the reception and conversed freely with all.

That evening, Caroline discovered that Katie was very sociable, most congenial, and possessed a strong determination to be successful at whatever challenged her. She discovered over a short time that Katie was someone she could easily open her heart to and express her deepest emotions. Caroline was one who did not make friends easily. Until Katie, there wasn't a single acquaintance she willingly opened to concerning her life. Over a short period of time, their friendship had become so close that they were inseparable. During that period when Charles was away from home and constantly speaking at rallies throughout the Shenandoah Valley for Vice President Breckinridge during the presidential campaign of 1860, they spent many evenings sharing their personal life and desires.

Quietly turning and glancing at Pete, there appeared a glimmering smile covering Caroline's expression. "I can remember the day after William Pierce's reception when Katie arrived at the estate. I invited her to Shenandoah to tour and see the majestic beauty of the estate. And of course to get to know her better." Caroline paused and briefly chuckled. "After noticing William's frantic behavior when Katie and you were sharing a dance, I decided the next morning to fake a sickness so that you would be the one to escort Katie on the tour of the estate. And I will proudly add, I felt you were the better man for her. After everything that happened here in town that same afternoon…"

Pete interrupted laughing. "You mean when Billy Smith and me got into that brawl. Yes, to this day, every time I glance over toward Potomac Street, I still see him knocking me through the front door of the Wager House and Katie and I hitting the ground. As we both laid in the mud puddle, she was so enraged with anger, she nearly beat me silly with her broken parasol." Pete paused and continued. "So, you were not really sick that day as you would have everyone to believe?"

"No. I wanted to play cupid. I wanted to see if there was something between you two."

"What in the world ever drew you to that conclusion?"

"After Katie returned to the table that evening, there was something her eyes revealed. It reminded me of the glow the night that Mildred Tompkins told me that I had when I first met your brother in Charlottesville." Pausing and turning her attention on Katie, she continued somberly. "The only thing I regret is the coldness and separation I allowed Charles to intiate when he told me William and he were going to England." With her full attention on Pete, she continued. "I could understand him wanting to keep the whole trip a secret and fearing capture if discovered while traveling the seas. I didn't want the same fate for him such as Mr. Mason and Mr. Slidell encountered at the hands of the Yankee navy. Reluctantly, I consented. I did so because my marriage and family were most important to me. After two troubling years with Charles, our marriage was finally progressing and going the way that it should. I just wanted to protect everything that I was experiencing with Charles. Even though I didn't see Katie as frequently as I had been accustomed to, I still had Jeremiah keep an eye on her and see to her safety."

"All this time I didn't know. Old Jeremiah. What do you know," Pete surprisingly replied.

"Oh yes. Even though it gave Charles the appearance that I had turned my back on Katie and was faithful in all he requested, I wouldn't and I couldn't betray the only real friend I've ever known. I felt closer to Katie than at anytime to my younger sister Mary. At times, it was difficult keeping Katie at a distance until one time after we thought that you had been killed during the fight at Gettysburg. Shortly thereafter, Katie and I had a serious disagreement.

"About what?"

"Earlier in the day, Katie paid Mother Elizabeth a visit at the estate to express her condolences. You know Katie's Irish temper. Well one word led to another and somehow Katie believed Mother Elizabeth had only turned over ownership of Shenandoah to Charles in order to influence and control his decisions."

"Yes, I know. A woman having any influence over a business or anything for that matter was considered distasteful. I have heard some say this attributed to the religious fever that had been taking place across the nation prior to the war. Although, I am not sure this is the real reason."

"After learning of your supposed death, I found Katie along the river. She was crying and kissing a picture of you and holding it close to her body. I tried to console her by saying that you had died for a cause that you believed in. Her grief quickly turned to anger. One thing led to another and suddenly we bitterly argued over the accusations that she made concerning Mother Elizabeth and Charles. Afterwards, I didn't see her again until I returned to Shenandoah after the war. And to this day, I still don't know the truth about the accusations against them."

"It's true. Last night after we arrived and Charles and I went into Mother's room, she confessed its truth. She made every attempt to separate Katie and me because of fear. Fear that life with Katie living at Shenandoah would eventually have an impact on the way we lived and it would cause a greater division in the family. She apologized to Charles and me."

Caroline was shocked at this revelation because Charles did not say anything to her when they were alone last night. "I see. And if God is willing, I must make amends with Katie on this." Pausing and quietly walking over to the window overlooking High Street, Caroline continued softly. "All this time I was so wrong about this matter and believed a lie that caused damage to a friendship I cherished beyond any words I can express. I was so furious when I left Katie along the river. I rushed home and confronted Mother Elizabeth. We even argued. The truth was never resolved because Ann overheard us speaking about her father who was still alive."

"I know, I heard from Miss Virginia about Charles' supposed death at Brandy Station. Why?"

Caroline turned and faced Pete. She sighed and hastily replied, "Because I had to. Yankee patrols were constantly harassing us and looking for Charles in order to imprison him for his role with the Confederate government. The only way to buy him time to get him out of the area was to falsify his death."

"Did Katie know?"

Caroline shook her head and answered. "No, not that I know of. She paid her respects earlier in the day after the funeral, but this happened before I said my goodbyes at the old Robinson homestead to Charles." Pausing, Caroline walked to the other side of the bed with her arms crossed. She continued as she gazed once more at Katie. "Regardless of our differences, all is forgiven and in my eyes, she can not do any wrong. She is the closest and dearest friend that Caroline Barker ever had."

With Caroline's last statement, Pete noticed the truest remorse in her voice and a somber expression. He knew Caroline was experiencing condemnation over all he had said about his mother's true intentions, and Caroline truly felt the sting of his words.

Chapter 68

The sun was shining brightly as Charles glanced in the direction where the mansion once stood. He decided to inspect Hayward's workmanship. Once there, he looked around, visualizing the family gathering on the front porch during the evenings of the long hot summer months. Their discussions were both humorous and fruitful. Continuing to look around, he recalled numerous family acquaintances that attended their socials events. Many would never attend another event because they had fallen on the field of glory from Manassas to Appomattox for Southern independence. He walked around the perimeter of where the mansion was being reconstructed with nothing escaping his eyes. He continued to recreate thoughts of all that Shenandoah use to be prior to the war. Now with the conclusion of hostilities, he noticed the last several years of his absence and the effects of the war that had dramatically changed Shenandoah, and maybe, forever.

As Charles stood by the foundation, he noticed the work Hayward and Pete had accomplished in their effort to rebuild the dwelling. He was grateful for their effort. For him, the simplicity he experienced prior to the war had turned into a burdensome task of survival and existence. There were different scenes of his life at Shenandoah that he continued to visualize in his mind. As he recalled good memories and pleasant experiences, he was reminded of a life that he once cherished, now changed to one of uncertainty and insecurities. Even though he had contemplated leaving and beginning life anew somewhere westward, he still struggled with the oppressive burden of Shenandoah and leaving it all behind.

As he was seated on a row of rocks on the foundation, Charles looked in the direction of the cabin and noticed Hayward approaching. Regardless of his attempt to have Hayward killed if caught while helping slaves escape North during the war, he had learned to put all of the animosity behind him. With their daunting experience of the last couple of days, Charles had learned to appreciate Hayward and see the value in him.

"Mr. Charles what ya's doin' out here? If the Yankees come a runnin' down that lane, dey's is gonna git ya. We can't let that happin'."

"I know. And fortunately, I haven't seen any," Charles replied as he slowly stood to his feet and brushed off his trousers.

While Charles was pondering on life at Shenandoah previous to the war, he was unaware of a twenty-five-man Yankee cavalry patrol less than a mile away at Halltown. Having knowledge he was possibly in the area, they had increased their observation of the Barker homestead. During the time that he was sitting on the foundation, several Yankee scouts had been watching his every move through their spyglasses. With assurance that indeed, they had Charles Barker in their sights, the corporal in charge had dispatched his partner to inform Captain Harvey, who commanded the patrol. With orders not to move in or fire if Charles was found at the estate, the soldier continued to intently observe until contacted.

The cavalry patrol was resting their horses along the tracks of the Winchester and Potomac Railroad when the one scout found them. Immediately, the private informed his commanding officer of all they had witnessed. Hastily, the officer along with another soldier mounted their horses and followed the scout. They didn't travel far before they had to dismount and cross the next fifty yards through thickets and underbrush. Once Captain Harvey and Sergeant Major Hardy found the other scout, without hesitation, the officer removed his spyglass from its case.

"Where is Barker?" the officer asked.

"Standing in front of the foundation near the darky," the soldier replied pointing.

The officer raised his glasses to his eyes and was quiet as he searched the area before him. "Yes, yes I see. We do have Mr. Barker." Sheltered by trees and undergrowth, the officer stood. "If I am not mistaken, they are staying in an old cabin behind the ridge."

"Yes sir, I have been there with Captain Brackett," the Sergeant confidently replied.

"All right Hardy, I will have you take ten of the men and gain the rear of the property to cut off his escape in the direction of the river. If you'll use the ridge, you should be able to prevent Barker or anyone else in the house from seeing you. I'll take the rest of the men and scatter them along the front of the property. He'll be surprised and totally surrounded with all routes of escape closed to him. It must be understood that Barker is to be given every chance to surrender himself. Understood?"

Feeling that time was against them, the two cavalrymen hurried around to carry out the task. Retracing their steps, the cavalrymen quickly returned to the rest of the company. Immediately dismounting, Captain Harvey asked for his map of the area from Lieutenant Jenkins. After spreading the map on the ground near the train tracks, the two officers and Sergeant Major Hardy finalized their plans. Anxious to make the capture, Captain Harvey knew that it would take Hardy's men some time to get into position at their assigned location because his column of soldiers would have to travel the greater distance. With their plans complete, Harvey initiated the troop movements. Once he watched the first column mount their horses and disappear, Harvey instructed his men to do likewise.

Fifteen minutes had passed since Hardy's men had departed from the rest of the company. By this time, Harvey's men were receiving final instructions behind the shelter of some trees on the outskirts west of Halltown. Harvey believed that Sergeant Hardy's men must be in position under cover and within sight near the rear of the Barker cabin. Finally the command was given. After leaving the tree line, five of Harvey's men under the inexperienced Lieutenant Jenkins dashed in the direction of the cabin, using Signal Ridge as cover. Five more Yankee cavalrymen moved in an arc under Sergeant McGee in the direction of Barker's Ridge. Harvey and the remaining five soldiers moved in the direction of the entrance to the main road leading directly toward the cabin. Not only with the area of the cabin completely surrounded, the element of surprise would give his men the advantage. On Harvey's hand signal, the Yankee cavalrymen moved forward with speed to execute their plan.

Back at the cabin, Charles had just entered his mother's bedroom. She was sitting up in bed as he entered.

"My Son it is so good to have us altogether again," Elizabeth joyfully said. "My best sleep was last night knowing that my children were home with me."

Walking over to a chair near Elizabeth's bed, Charles took a seat. "Yes, it is good to be home with the ones that I love and value the most in my life."

Elizabeth knew Charles had many thoughts consuming his mind. She noticed the hollow expression and recognized the disturbing tone he used. "Is everything all right? Where is Ann?"

"I wanted her to get away for a bit so she is riding along the river."

"Then if I may ask, what is wrong my Son?"

Shaking his head, Charles despondently replied. "I guess I am still tired from all the running and not knowing what's going to happen next."

"I overheard Caroline and you speaking earlier about escaping and going west. For now Charles, it would be for the best. I firmly believe sometime for any kind of reconciliation to take place, there must be some token of forgiveness on Mr. Johnson's part. I know everyone is quite angry and desiring revenge against the old Confederacy for Mr. Lincoln's murder, but now, we, as a nation must continue on and put the horrors of war behind us."

"I agree, but Mother, I was an aide to President Davis on political and state affairs. My complicity with the rebel government makes my crimes greater in severity than the average soldier's such as Pete."

"Still, you must get away and hide until there is a calmness over the land. Then you can return without fear."

"Tonight after Caroline returns, we will leave. Not to change the subject, but while we are alone, I wanted to speak to you about another matter."

"I know. You want to speak with me about Rebecca."

Tears began to flow from Charles' cheeks. "Neither you nor Caroline realize the guilt I bear because of her death."

"It's all right Charles, I don't condemn you for what happened to her," Elizabeth replied as she rubbed her hand over his dark hair. "Maybe she would still be alive if I had heeded your advice and insisted on her leaving Richmond with us. But when I told her that she could stay, there wasn't anything much that you or anyone else could have done." Pausing and then adding in a murmur, "Not you, but I am the one that must bear the guilt for her death."

"No Mother, I was the one who was negligent. I was the one who fell asleep from exhaustion. If I would have been doing what I was suppose to do, then maybe she would have been alive today and here with us," Charles replied in a raised tone.

While Charles and his mother were speaking, Hayward was looking out the window. In his heart, he sensed a strange and uneasy feeling coming over him. He opened the door and glanced around. Confident they were alone, he next stepped onto the porch, where he heard the sounds of multiple horses racing down the lane. As he turned around, he noticed Yankee cavalry rapidly approaching. Hayward raced into the house and bolted the door.

Hayward grabbed a pistol and rushed over to Elizabeth's bedroom. "Yankee cavalry! Yankee cavalry!"

Charles jumped from the chair and raced to the front window near the door and quickly glanced in the direction of where the mansion was being rebuilt. The cavalrymen were bringing their horses to a halt and some were dismounting and running in separate ways toward the cabin.

Charles looked at Hayward. "Put the gun down."

Suddenly, there were several loud knocks on the door. Charles took a deep sigh as he looked at Hayward. Then turning toward his mother's bedroom, he noticed that she was leaning against the entrance and quietly watching his every move. Again, there were several loud knocks on the door.

"Barker, open this door now or I'll be forced to blow it open." a soldier demanded.

Charles turned and looked at his mother. "It's over."

Again, Charles turned around and slowly opened the door and stepped back. Without hesitation, Captain Harvey entered with three of his soldiers.

"Charles Barker?" Captain Harvey sternly asked.

Charles quietly nodded his head in the affirmative and waited for the officer's next move.

"I am placing you under arrest and taking you to Harpers Ferry where you will be placed in the custody of Captain Brackett, the Provost Marshall of the Harpers Ferry District."

"I understand sir," Charles pridefully replied. Without hesitation, one of the soldiers bound his hands with rope. Charles turned and glanced at his sobbing mother. "Goodbye Mother." He turned to Hayward. "I am sorry for the way that I have treated you. All along you were right and I was wrong. And as for Ann, when she returns from riding along the river, tell her that I promise that one day I'll return."

Hayward silently nodded and followed the soldiers as they escorted Charles from the cabin. Slowly riding down the lane, Hayward noticed the other soldiers rejoining the ranks. Turning his attention to Elizabeth, he re-entered the cabin to comfort her.

* * * *

Dusk was settling over the area as shadows were becoming more prevalent along the mountains. Katie still remained unconscious with Pete and Caroline on opposite sides of her bed. The only activity over the last three hours was when the physician continued his ritual of examining Katie. Every time, he proclaimed her condition unchanged. On his last visit, his daughter, also named Ann, had followed and lit the lamp near Katie's bed.

Caroline stood and walked to where Pete was sitting, placing her hand on his shoulder. "Why don't you return home and rest while I stay with Katie?"

"No, I don't want to leave her. When she wakes up, I want her to know that I am here."

"I will send for you."

"No, but thank you anyway," Pete politely replied. "Besides, I thought Charles and you were leaving tonight."

"I can't run out on Katie," Caroline replied in a compassionate tone. "I must stay until I know her welfare."

"Please go and tell Charles and Ann that I will follow in the next few days. He'll know what you're talking about."

After Caroline finished talking, she walked to the window and glanced out to see what was happening along the street. She noticed the few residents that still lived in town; most had retired indoors for the evening. Just as she was about to return to her seat next to Katie, her attention was interrupted when she noticed a small band of citizens coming into her view along High Street. What could all this mean? Next coming into her sight was a civilian gentleman surrounded by Yankee cavalrymen. With the increasing darkness, it was difficult to make out the figure. Her heart raced and she became quite anxious, knowing the worst event had occurred. "Oh God, they have captured Charles!"

Caroline turned around and raced for the door. "Wait Caroline!" Pete shouted.

When Caroline ignored his plea, Pete quickly followed.

Pete noticed once Caroline was outside, she dashed to the corner of the Mauzy's house where she could get a better view of the Provost Marshall's office.

Caroline gazed intently on several of the soldiers while they assisted Charles from his horse. She looked at Pete. "Oh Pete, it is Charles! What am I going to do? Please tell me!"

As the crowd milled around the office, Pete looked. "We need to go and find out what they intend on doing to him." As he turned Caroline around, he placed his hands on her shoulders. "Whatever they say, let me do all the talking. There is nothing we should say that's going to inflame matters because it will only make things worse for Charles. All right?"

Caroline silently nodded, agreeing with Pete's request. Even though Caroline was quite anxious to immediately proceed to the Provost office, he convinced her to wait until the crowd had dispersed and gone home. Until then, they anxiously returned to be with Katie.

Finally, after some time had passed, Caroline and Pete walked the short distance to speak to Captain Brackett. Once they entered the Provost Marshall's office, Pete could hear the sounds of conversation taking place in the back room. He recognized Captain Brackett and Charles' voices. Being distracted and attempting to catch something that was being said, Pete inadvertently ignored the soldier seated behind the desk.

"Sir, what business do you have with this office?" the soldier asked.

"I want to see my brother, Charles Barker. This is his wife, who would also like to see him."

The soldier snapped. "At the moment, that's not possible. The Provost Marshall, Captain Brackett is speaking to him."

"I am an attorney. I have the right to speak to my client."

"Not at the moment you don't!"

As Pete gave thought of how to handle the matter, Captain Brackett walked through the door. "Well Barker, I am sure I know what brings you to my humble abode."

"We are here to see my brother."

The officer hesitated, looking at Pete's anxious expression. He reluctantly answered authoritatively. "All right. But just for a moment with one of my soldiers present. Any funny stuff and you'll be keeping company with him in the guard house."

"I understand," Pete acknowledged as he looked in the direction of the back room.

Captain Brackett opened the gate along the railing and gestured for Pete and Caroline to proceed to the back room.

Once Pete entered, he saw Charles sitting near a potbelly stove drinking a cup of coffee. In the same room and sitting at a desk was a soldier writing down some information on a piece of paper. Pete turned and glanced at Caroline. Her expression revealed her fear of the unexpected and the concern for Charles' welfare. Pete pulled up a chair for Caroline to be seated.

Afterward, Pete stepped from the back room and noticed the officer removing his sword and sash. "What will happen to him now?" Pete asked.

Captain Brackett turned. "That isn't up to me. I have sent a telegram to the War Department in Washington City informing them that we have captured Charles Barker. Until I hear from them, I will detain him in the guardhouse overnight under a strong guard."

"If you move him elsewhere, would you give Mrs. Barker and her daughter the courtesy of seeing him again before he is moved?"

"You have my word."

Pete turned and walked back into the rear room. "Time is up," the soldier by the desk ordered.

As Pete glanced at Caroline, she was trembling with fear; she was struggling with her emotions as she departed.

"Can I have a moment?" Pete asked.

Before the soldier could answer, Captain Brackett appeared and quietly nodded to the soldier his approval.

Pete walked over and was seated. "Are you all right Charles?"

"I am." Taking a sigh, he looked and continued. "I really didn't think that I had a chance of escaping. Sooner or later, they would have caught up with me. In some ways, it's better this happened so I can get it over with."

"I know, but it's going to be tough on the family, especially Caroline."

"Guilt shreds my heart to pieces when I think of all that I've put her through over these past years. Although she is a strong and a determined woman and can handle a lot, everyone has his or her breaking point. How much more can she handle, I don't know," Charles muttered.

"Caroline and Ann are in good hands; I'll watch out over them."

"Please do. God willing, I will return home. Just now, I told her over and over I would. If she'll only hold to my promise."

"We'll be back," Pete said as he stood.

"Oh, I am sorry to hear about Katie; how is she?"

"Holding her own."

As Pete and Caroline disappeared through the door, Charles broke down and cried. Even though he spoke words of comfort and reassurance to Caroline, he was not sure what his future would be. He could not reveal to her his greatest fears that he might hang for his crimes. He would have to wait and see. As the drama continued to play out, he knew the events that had taken place and those to come from these specific experiences were going to continue to change his life.

Chapter 69

Early the next morning, the brightness of the sun peered through the rear window of the room causing Pete to slowly open his eyes. His first reaction was to glance in Katie's direction. She still was motionless on the bed. As he rose and moved to her bedside, he softly whispered her name. When she didn't respond to the sound of his voice or the touch of his hand on her face, his disappointment was more then he could bear. He glanced at the clock in the room. It was 7 o'clock in the morning. Turning around and again taking a quick glance at Katie, he walked over to the window. Looking in the direction of High Street, he noticed the town was still lifeless other than a few individuals climbing onto the roof of one of the houses to repair it before the commencement of winter.

As Pete quietly observed the men climbing a ladder with their tools, he thought of Charles. Most likely Charles would be transferred from Harpers Ferry to another location where Federal authorities would have to decide if he should be charged for his involvement with the Confederate government. Pete's greatest concern for his brother was how he would adapt to the transition from freedom to captivity.

Upon entering the room, Doctor Marmion placed his hand on Katie's forehead. He glanced at Pete. "I have made some fresh coffee, why don't you go and have some?"

"How is she?"

"Her forehead is still very warm. I will go and get some cold water and lay more cloths on her head. We are going to have a fight on our hands trying to break this fever."

Pete turned once more and glanced out the window. To his surprise, he noticed Caroline and Ann near the junction of Shenandoah and High Street. The first thoughts surfacing in his mind; was Captain Brackett preparing to move Charles from Harpers Ferry? With a quick glance in Katie's direction, Pete swiftly dashed for the door in an attempt to intercept Caroline before she entered Captain Brackett's office.

Just as Caroline was bringing the team of horses to a halt, Pete arrived at the Provost Marshall's office.

"Did Captain Brackett send for you?" Pete asked as he assisted Caroline from the wagon.

"Yes, a courier arrived before daylight."

"Do you know where they are taking him?" Pete asked as he assisted Ann.

"No. The courier wouldn't say," Caroline answered as she began to weep. "If I plead with them, maybe they'll let him stay a few more days."

"I don't think anyone will grant your request."

"Then maybe they'll allow me to go with him until they reach their destination."

While Caroline was speaking, Pete knew she was attempting to cling to any hopes of avoiding separation from Charles. He believed any request on her behalf would be futile and swiftly denied by Captain Brackett. As he looked at Caroline, he knew she would have tremendous difficulties accepting the reality that Charles might be imprisoned for many years. Without his brother's presence, he knew he couldn't leave Shenandoah and expect Caroline to manage the property on her own.

Caroline, Ann, and Pete entered the Provost Marshall's office. All but Pete was immediately escorted to the rear room where Charles was waiting to say his farewells. Pete remained in the front office with Captain Brackett. He wanted to give Caroline and Ann as much time as possible with Charles. Once they disappeared through the door, Pete turned his attention to the officer. "Where will you take my brother?"

"I have orders from Secretary Stanton to send him to Baltimore under a strong guard. Possibly, he will be held at Fort McHenry."

With tears in her eyes, Caroline paused as Ann dashed forward and embraced her father. Caroline didn't know how Ann would manage emotionally without her father. Still, Caroline was thankful he was alive and also for the brief time they spent together.

Looking into Ann's eyes, Charles smiled. "I am so proud to be your father. I could never ask God for another blessing because he has given it to me. He gave me you."

"Father where will they take you? How long will you be gone?"

"Ann, I don't know. But no matter where they take me or what they do to me, I will never be far from you. Nothing can separate us because you will always be in my heart."

From a basket containing her personal effects, Ann removed an item and handed it to her father. "Here, I want you to take this picture of me. And every time you look at it, I want you to know how much I miss and love you."

Once more, Charles embraced Ann. "I will come home to you." With tears in his eyes, he gazed into hers. "And when I do, I will make up for everything I have put you and your mother through these past four years. There is just one thing that I ask of you."

"What is that Father?"

"In the deepest part of your heart, I just ask you to forgive me for being so negligent of your needs and absent so often from your life. I was so selfish and only thinking of my own personal interests when I left home for Richmond. I know now that I lived in hope and not reality. From the beginning of the war, I didn't really believe we could defeat the Union army in the field; instead I hoped and prayed for a compromise. It cost me. Although I still believe in our cause for independence, I didn't stop and realize the commitment required of me: the sacrifice of those closest to me, my family."

Nodding in agreement, Ann quietly looked into her father's sorrowful eyes once more before departing the room. Once out of his sight, she released her emotions in her uncle's arms.

Finally, Charles approached Caroline and placed his hands on her cheeks. He looked into her eyes. "I know the sorrows and pain you bear…and right now what you're going through because I too feel it to a point to where I don't know if I can go on. Caroline, I never intended for things to turn out this way between us. Everything I did, I only did because I wanted the best for all of us. Maybe, I demanded too much of life and my expectations were unrealistic. I don't know."

"My love, I know you had our best interest at heart. And you had great dreams and expectations and I am thankful."

"Sometimes we require too much of life and there are times we will do whatever is necessary to achieve our purpose. Even if it is by means of dishonesty and deceitfulness. For me, I am as guilty as hell, and now I must pay the price by sacrificing many good years that I could have spent with Ann and you."

"I don't care how long you are away, I will be waiting for you until you return."

Captain Brackett walked into the room. "We have to go now. The train is due in ten minutes."

Once more, Charles looked into Caroline's eyes. It was extremely difficult for him to begin the process of separation. With a sense of desperation, he embraced Caroline, passionately kissing her. When they broke their embrace, Caroline could not withhold her emotions.

"It will be all right. And as I promised Ann, I will return," Charles said in a reassuring tone.

Slowly turning, Caroline walked to the door of the room still sobbing. On Captain Brackett's command, one of the soldiers approached Charles and placed shackles around his ankles and wrist. With the clinging sound of the metal, Caroline turned and looked. Quietly, she ran from the Provost Marshall's office.

Once Charles appeared in the front office with Captain Brackett and the guard, he gestured to speak with Pete. The officer nodded his approval. "I guess this is it."

"I know."

"Pete, I haven't always treated you fairly and with the respect I should have. For one thing, I now know I always felt I was the better one. My pride had blinded me and allowed me to be greatly deceived, but look at you and now look at me. You are the better man because you are a man of integrity and honesty. Please accept my apologies for my sins."

"I hold nothing against you. You will always be my brother," Pete replied as he stretched forth his hand.

Charles looked at Pete's hand and slowly grasped it. "I am honored to have you as my brother. I truly am. Until I return, will you please look after Caroline and Ann?" Pete silently nodded in agreement. "Reassure Mother that I am all right and send my love to her. As far as I am concerned, Shenandoah is yours for the taking. You deserve it, not me."

"No Charles, just as father would have wanted it, Shenandoah is ours."

Silently, a smile covered Charles' face as he nodded in agreement and turned to depart with Captain Brackett. Once outside the office, several soldiers assisted Charles onto the back of the wagon for the short trip to the depot. He quietly complied. Pete, Caroline, and Ann watched as the wagon slowly drifted in the direction of Shenandoah Street. In the distance, Pete could hear the whistle of the train locomotive as it was approaching the Harpers Ferry depot. As he observed Caroline embracing Ann, he made the commitment to rebuild Shenandoah to its former glory.

* * * *

After Charles' departure, Pete returned to Doctor Marmion's house. As he quietly sat on the side of Katie's bed gazing into her lifeless face, his heart was heavy with burden and his mind troubled over the issues of his life. He stood and glanced out the window in the direction of Solomon's Gap. His eyes were on the Short Hill Mountains towering over the Potomac River. Glancing across the crest of the mountain, he noticed the peculiar rock formation where Katie and he had rested after escaping from Winchester. He recalled some particular memories, especially all she revealed about William Pierce and his accusations of her spying for the Federals. Before departing he recalled asking if William's charges were justifiable. She answered, "Would it make any difference?"

Those words continuously troubled him.

As Pete continued cleaving to his thoughts, he heard a soft muffled voice.

"Where am I?"

Surprisingly, Pete turned around and glanced at Katie. She was looking in his direction. His heart was relieved and filled with excitement. "You are at Doctor Marmion's house."

With tears streaming down his cheeks, Pete approached and began to speak, but Katie placed her finger over his lips. "Let me speak. I have always loved you and could never see my life apart from you. Yes, we have had our differences and struggles in the past, and even now we face many trials. But I know because of our love we can work through our problems and with each other's strength, we can overcome anything. My life isn't in Boston with my family but with you at Shenandoah. Shenandoah is my home and always will be."

Pete wiped his eyes. "I have put you through hell these past weeks since I rushed from your family's home. I should never have left you, but I was hoping you would stay with your family. I underestimated you.

"Yes, you did."

"And I know why I did it. It wasn't anything that your father or Seamus said. But they gave me the excuse I needed to try and escape your love for me. Before the war, I lived a life where there was never any demands placed on me by a lady. For some unexplainable reason when you came along, I was continuously drawn to you. This is why I looked for every reason during the war to return home. Just to see you....to give you security and assurance that I was all right but more to be with you because I didn't know when the end might come. As much as I tried to escape it all, it became more difficult. I couldn't get you out of my mind. Continuously I saw your face. And every time there was an engagement such as Antietam, I knew once you received word of the battle, you'd worry as to my welfare. Then once you returned to Boston and later to Shenandoah after the war, I didn't want to be separated from you again. Our relationship became more demanding and the prospect of marriage and a family, not to say all the other issues we faced, the pressure became too much for me to handle. But this sickness threatened to take you from me. There are no words to describe the emptiness and despair I experienced." Pete paused and took Katie's hand and continued. "Out of all the ladies I have been with and known in my life, you are the first to make an impact upon me. After all that has happened in the last four days, my heart can never be separated from you again no matter what risk I must take."

Katie raised her arms. "Just hold me for a moment."

Pete gently embraced Katie. He could feel the warmness of her tears mingling with his. He clutched her close to his body desiring not to let her go. His eyes were looking on the warming glow hers reflected. He caressed Katie's hair and gently kissed her lips.

"Once you can leave here," Pete said, "I am going to take you to Shenandoah where we will live and one day grow old with many children and grandchildren."

Again, Pete passionately kissed Katie embracing her body gently against his. Once more tears flowed freely down his cheeks. Within his heart, any reservations he possessed had vanished. Only death would separate and cause their relationship to cease.

Chapter 70

Thaddeus and Margaret McBride had just walked into their drawing room after a late dinner of scrod. Thaddeus poured a brandy and with a smile, quietly handed it to his wife. She thanked him and then turned to walk over to the blazing fireplace. After being seated in a chair, she opened her book, "The Child of the Island" by the British author, Caroline Norton and began flipping the pages. After pouring his drink, Thaddeus walked over to sit on the sofa and placed his spectacles on his face. Some important business papers from the bank for a special board meeting the following day consumed his attention. Without a word, they were deeply absorbed in their own personal thoughts. The only sound was the echo throughout the large room caused by the continuous crackling of the logs burning in the fireplace.

Time had passed rapidly as the clock chimed nine times. Thaddeus looked up at the clock and removed his spectacles, contemplating on retiring to his bedchamber for the evening. When he began to speak to his wife of his intentions, he heard a loud thumping against the front door. Thaddeus was astonished; who might be calling this late in the evening? He stood as Robert, the butler, approached the door to answer the call. To his amazement, Thaddeus noticed Seamus entering and being greeted by Robert. Without hesitation, he quickly approached Seamus as he was giving Robert his coat and gloves.

"My Son, it's good to have you home." Taking Seamus by the arm, he escorted him into the room. "Come and stand by the fire and get warm."

Immediately, Margaret laid down her book and stood. "My Son, thank God you are safe." Swiftly, her joy turned to bewilderment. "Where is Katherine?"

"Well Mother, four days ago, I received a telegram from Pete Barker at Harpers Ferry that Katie was leaving on the morning train for Baltimore. Naturally, I proceeded to that city and waited for her: but she wasn't on the train. Once I found the telegraph office, I fired off a message to Barker for an answer why she wasn't there. Uncertain as to why, I didn't receive an answer. For sometime, I waited until the next train arrived. Katie wasn't on that one nor had Barker answered my telegram. I took it that Katie was going to stay awhile longer."

Margaret held her hand to her face. "Oh, dear. I hope something didn't happen to her."

"Now, now, my dear," Thaddeus replied as he poured a brandy for his son. "When I was in Washington City, she appeared in the most anxious manner to hurry to Harpers Ferry."

With a troubled expression, Margaret sighed. "Really, I had high hopes after all she had gone through she would want to return home and begin a normal life once and for all. That Barker must have some kind of magic over her."

Thaddeus walked over and handed the drink to Seamus. "From the sound of your telegram, Katherine must have been put through bloody hell with those rogue agents."

"Yes she was. Physically, they bloody abused her. They bloody held her captive against her will, and who knows what else, but in the end, she got her revenge."

"How is that?" Thaddeus anxiously asked.

"Katie's captors allowed her time by herself to clean up in the upstairs of the house in the afternoon. Knowing this from a servant, Barker and I devised a plan where I would search that area of the house, and once I found her, I would lead and protect her to safety. Well, it didn't bloody workout that way. While I was in the upstairs area, Barker was going to surprise her captors. As our luck would bloody have it, Katie was being held downstairs where some bloody rogue agent was holding a pistol aimed at her head. After entering the room, Barker was commanded to drop his weapon or Katie was going to be killed. Naturally, Barker had no other choice. By now, I was upstairs struggling with the other associate." Seamus polished off the brandy and placed the glass on a table by the sofa. "As I understand from Barker, our luck changed. Some servant who worked for the Hammond family was sent to secure some rope to bind Barker to a chair. Afterwards, from all I understand, the servant was quite upset because these bloody rebel agents had killed and buried those that he had been faithful to all those years. When the servant was close enough to the agent holding the gun on Katie, he surprisingly lashed out at the agent and almost overpowered him. When they hit the floor, Barker attempted to intervene. The agent had dropped the gun near Katie. Before Barker could get to her, Katie raised the pistol and shot her abductor, killing him."

"Oh no!" Margaret cried. "My poor, poor girl."

"Katie shot and killed a man?" Thaddeus asked in amazement.

"Father, she didn't have any bloody choice in the bloody matter. That crazy man would have killed all of us if given the chance."

"And you said these people were rebel agents?" Margaret angrily asked.

"Yes Mother."

"Then tell me Son, was she really spying for our cause while in Harpers Ferry?"

"Father, it's possible. A little over two years ago when I received a furlough and went to Harpers Ferry, she never confided in me about such activity. As you well know, it was common practice among civilians who were loyal to one side or the other side. But my feelings are that she didn't."

"Yes, I know, but surely she has speculated to you why she believed she was abducted."

"Only, something to the effect that William Pierce was obsessed for her love. Apparently, she became acquainted with him on the westbound train to Harpers Ferry in the late summer of '60. It was through him, Katie became acquainted with the Barkers, who were good friends with Pierce. Especially Charles Barker. Other than this, Katie was too distressed to speak much about her experience with Mr. Pierce. At the time, seeing her emotional condition, I didn't see the need to pursue the matter any further."

"I guess it makes sense. And I guess that puts to naught that silly idea that my Katherine was some kind of a spy," Margaret replied in a confident tone.

"You said the rogue Katherine killed was a man by the name of William Pierce?"

Seamus turned his attention toward his father and nodded his head in agreement. By the grave expression covering his face, he knew he was in serious thought. "Father?"

Thaddeus approached Seamus shaking his head. "Yes, yes, I remember now. In '62, Charles Barker and Mr. Pierce were sent abroad by the Rebels to help Captain Bulloch negotiate some contracts for the Confederate navy. So as far as I am bloody concerned, he got what was coming to him. Now maybe she can hopefully come home and put all of this nonsense behind her."

"I am not too sure that will happen."

"Seamus, what do you mean?" Margaret quickly asked.

"Yes Son, I thought the matter was settled," Thaddeus added.

"When Katie didn't appear at the train depot in Baltimore, I knew for some strange reason she would continue to stay in Harpers Ferry."

"With Barker, I assume?"

"Yes."

After answering the question, Seamus quietly listened to his mother and father angrily displaying their frustrations over what appeared Katie's refusal to return home. He sank deep within his own thoughts. He attempted to blot out the exchange of words taking place in his family. His parents still possessed a very strong animosity toward Pete Barker. He understood their reasoning but was disturbed that they were too prideful to at least give Pete credit for risking his life to save their daughter from harm. He became angrier as the verbal onslaught continued. To get away, he walked to the window and stared out into the nighttime darkness. Looking aimlessly at the gaslight lamp along the street, he continued his thoughts. The experiences he was compelled to face with Barker had destroyed his pride and allowed humility to rule and rein in his life. His parents didn't have the opportunity nor did they experience the horrifying encounters in the quest to free Katie such as Pete and he During those days in Virginia, while pursuing Katie and her abductors, Seamus had learned to appreciate and respect Pete, seeing him in a different light. It wasn't only for his deep convictions that he admired Pete, but mostly as an individual, someone with feelings and emotions that desired a normal life such as he did. After all of the fiery tribulations they encountered to bring Katie to freedom, he knew he had developed a bond with Pete, especially for saving his life in Washington City.

As his parents continued to manifest their displeasure, Seamus was getting angry. "Neither of you went through the hell that Barker and I had to face to see to Katie's safety. It was Barker and me who were shot at, not you. We were the ones who risked our bloody lives to see that she would continue her life. You really want to know what the bloody problem is here? I'll tell you. We have all been too selfish and blinded by our blasted bloody pride and hatred for Barker to consider Katie's feelings when it comes to her life. And whether you like it or not, she may just stay in Harpers Ferry."

"What are you saying?" Thaddeus interrupted.

"I am saying that if Katie and Barker want to have a life together and raise a family, then they have my blessings. As for me, the war finally ended five days ago at Leesburg, Virginia when we freed Katie. Not at Appomattox. It's bloody fruitless to continue this struggle and live in this type of hell. I am ready to move on with my life. And that means if I want any kind of a relationship with Katie, then I will have to put the war behind me and try to find some peace. And I suggest that both of you consider doing the same thing as I am doing. If we don't, we might lose her altogether, and personally, I don't want that to happen. Do you?"

"No, I can't forgive what those rebels did to our boys!" Margaret cried.

"Or is it a different reason Mother why you will not try?" His eyes were fixed on his mother waiting for an answer. When she remained silent, Seamus continued. "For that matter, if Katie does marry Barker, I will use any and all of my financial resources to insure that Katie and Barker maintain ownership of Shenandoah."

Margaret quickly raced from the room in tears as Thaddeus approached his son, shouting. "You must be bloody insane! Why the man stands against every principal that we have stood for!"

"Yes Father, he does but we won the war. The Negroes have their freedom and the Union has been preserved. But just as Barker has realized, it's time to move on and begin to put the past behind us."

Thaddeus began to point his finger at Seamus and continued his rage, "Seamus McBride, you need to think of what you just said and reconsider your position. Tomorrow, you will send Katherine a telegram insisting that she return to Boston immediately."

Seamus remained quiet, attempting to quell the indignation against him. As he watched his father abruptly depart the room, he could understand his parent's fury and dissatisfaction against him. His convictions and beliefs concerning Katie and Pete, and a new beginning in life were quite different, and radical. It would require some time for them to adjust to his new attitude on life.

Chapter 71

Several months had past and Katie had completely recovered from her sickness. Her relationship had prospered with Pete and she was confident he was committed to a future and family. This was a special day for Katie because she was about to enter into matrimony with Pete. For four long years, she had patiently waited, endured many trials, and struggled through many tribulations to reach this important event in her life. She was standing near a mirror in one of the rooms of the Catholic School where she was once a teacher until the early days of the war. Ann was assisting her preparations by placing small pink and red roses in her hair. Katie thought of her hopes and dreams that now were becoming a reality. As Katie was completing her arrangement, there was a faint knock at the door. She looked at Ann and nodded her approval. Ann slowly opened the door as Katie turned around. Quietly gazing stood Katie's mother. Katie was surprised her mother had accepted her invitation to come to Harpers Ferry for this special ceremony.

"Mother, my heart is filled with joy that you could share this day with me," Katie said as she approached and embraced her.

"I have heard so much about Shenandoah, not only from you, but also from Seamus. So, I had to come and see for myself."

"Did Father and Seamus come?"

"Yes, they are in the church waiting."

"Here young lady, let me help you arrange these roses," Margaret said to Ann.

"Mother, what made you change your mind?" Katie asked in an inquisitive tone.

"You are my only daughter." Pausing she placed the last rose in her daughter's hair. "And yes I still have my opinion about matters, but it would be selfish of me, and prove nothing at all if I didn't show up for my daughter's wedding. Now would it?"

"Yes, it would."

Margaret turned to Ann. "Young lady, would you mind if I spoke to my daughter in private?"

"No ma'am," Ann politely replied as she turned and departed.

Margaret turned her attention to her daughter. "Katherine, I am still not convinced that you marrying Mr. Barker is the right thing to do."

"But Mother, why?"

"Katherine, please hear me out. Maybe in time I will be proven wrong. But you must do what you feel is right." She paused and walked over to the window and looked down in the direction of the Shenandoah River. "In my life I have made many mistakes by doing something I thought at the time was right but later discovering it was not using good wisdom and understanding on my part. There are things I have said and done I can never take back even though I wish I could. But now, you have to make up your own mind and do what is best for you."

"What made you change your mind?"

"When Seamus returned home several months ago, I swore I'd never forgive those rebels for the atrocities they committed against our boys. But that was all an excuse and a poor one to use. In reality, I didn't want to face the fact you were not going to return home. Instead you were going to stay in Harpers Ferry and marry Mr. Barker, making this area your home. No demonstration of ill feelings or words on my part now, I know, will change how you feel. I just hope and pray you'll be happy and not regret it later."

"Mother, even though you feel as you do, I understand and respect those feelings. No one knows when they enter this type of union what to expect even though we all have our expectations of what it should be. Marriage is a risk just like everything else in life. But it is a risk I am willing to take because of my love for Pete. And unless I take that risk, that step of faith, I'll never know what might have been if I didn't."

With a serious expression covering her features, Margaret nodded in agreement and quietly followed Katie to the church. Once they arrived at the entrance, Margaret paused. "This is your day. I want you to be happy." Leaning forward, she kissed Katie on the cheek and entered the church.

On the inside of the sanctuary, Margaret noticed Seamus and her husband sitting toward the front of the place of worship. She walked down the aisle where she knelt and prayed. Then she rose and lit a candle. She turned to rejoin Thaddeus. Margaret noticed Caroline standing near the front pew opposite of where Thaddeus and Seamus were seated. She was startled by Caroline's facial features, her resemblance, her smile, and especially her eyes. There was something familiar that struck a chord in her heart. Glancing at the area near where Caroline was standing, Margaret's heart began to race as she noticed and recognized another lady from her past sitting nearby.

Caroline turned her attention to Margaret and noticed her constant gaze. Immediately, she smiled and approached Margaret, "I am Caroline Barker."

"Oh, I am so sorry I was staring at you. I was admiring your beauty," Margaret laughingly replied.

"Oh thank you."

"I am Katherine's mother, Margaret McBride."

"Katie, I mean Katherine has told me so much about you. I am so overwhelmed with joy that Katherine and Pete are going to be married and live at Shenandoah." Her joy and emotions were revealed in her expression and tone. "The very first time we met at Shenandoah, I have always been drawn to Katherine. We have so much in common concerning our interests and how we see life. She is the closest and dearest friend I could ever have. I am so fortunate and blessed by her. And my daughter Ann thinks there is nobody like Katie."

Immediately Margaret looked into Caroline's eyes and noticed the warm glow that they reflected. Her heart was captivated and it was all she could do to withhold her feelings because she was certain in her heart.

"I only desire Katherine's happiness," Margaret said.

"Please come and meet someone who is special to me."

Margaret quietly complied, allowing Caroline to take her hand and escort her for the introduction. Fear began to rule Margaret's heart as she struggled to repress her emotions.

"Margaret McBride, I would like for you to meet my mother, Anna Shultz."

"Anna, I am honored to meet you," Margaret replied in a cordial manner.

Astonished, Anna still recognized Margaret after all the years.

"And I am honored to make your acquaintance on your daughter's special day," Anna softly replied.

It was close to the time for the wedding to begin when Caroline was called away to speak to Katie. Margaret watched

Caroline walk down the aisle to the entrance of the church. She turned her attention once more to Anna. "After all of these years, I can still recognize her the same as the day when she first came into this world when my eyes observed her beauty."

"And of course I am sure, you recognized me."

"Yes, how can I forget."

"We gave Caroline a good life and she married into a good family. Does she know?"

"No, I just met her," Margaret paused with a deep sigh. "It's strange how sometimes fate will work in mysterious ways and bring people together. And of all things on an important day such as this. Who would have guessed such a thing?"

"I beg of you not to say anything to Caroline. It would damage the trust we have worked so long to build and maintain. She is so sensitive and loyal and something like this would destroy all that I've strived for in her life."

"No, as much as I would like to tell her that I am her real mother, I will not say anything. I too have considerations. Like you, it would tarnish my marriage to Thaddeus and my son might even disown me because of my dishonesty. And the damage it would do to Katherine would be unspeakable. Just as Caroline, she is very loyal and sensitive in nature. The damage would be un-repairable."

Pausing and looking at Caroline speaking to Katie at the rear of the church, Margaret continued. "I am so grateful you kept the name I gave her. It was so aristocratic and possessed a majestic quality about it. As all mothers, I had great dreams and hopes for Caroline, but when I realized I couldn't keep her because I was unable to provide for her needs, all those dreams and hopes vanished. As you know, I have an ugly past that's difficult to live with. Many times I have tried to drown myself in my own pride and deceit to blot it all out. But you know, it continues to torment me. Over the last 27 years I have lived in constant fear that Thaddeus would discover the truth and banish me from the house. He is a good man but very prideful. I guess this is who Seamus gets it from."

"We all have our troubles that we try and shelter from the ones we love, and we all suffer in some way the penalty of our actions. And I guess all these years without Caroline and not knowing where she was has been punishment enough."

"Yes, more than I can express in words." With her eyes on Anna, Margaret continued softly, "You do not have to worry about me revealing our past. It will stay with me until the day I go to my grave."

Margaret and Anna didn't realize, but Ann was standing within a short distance of the two ladies and overheard everything that was said. Ann understood the seriousness and the consequences of maintaining their secret. As she looked toward the rear of the church, she inwardly rejoiced, knowing that Katie and her Mother would be together, and share the unity of love after such a long and difficult separation that life had dealt them. Suddenly, Ann noticed her Grandmother Elizabeth being assisted into the church by her mother to be seated next to her Grandmother Shultz. Everything was ready as Ann took her seat beside them.

It was 2 o'clock in the afternoon when Caroline began to play on a borrowed violin Felix Mendelssohn's "Midsummer Night Dream." The few-invited guests stood and turned their attention to the rear of the church. Katie was escorted by her father to the altar where Pete and his best man, Hayward waited. Katie and Pete were plainly dressed for the occasion since there wasn't any additional money for clothing. Once Caroline finished playing the song, she laid the instrument down and quietly stood alongside Katie as her matron of honor.

Father Costello began to speak from the scriptures of I Corthinians, Chapter 14. As he spoke of unconditional love and commitment required in a relationship, Pete and Katie looked at each other. In his heart, Pete knew he had finally met someone who unconditionally loved him for who he really was. The days of excuses and running from the one person who had the most to offer had finally ended, and he would seal the relationship with the entirety of his love.

When Father Costello asked Pete and Katie to face each other, Katie looked into the warmness of Pete's eyes. When she repeated her vows, she spoke softly and with emotion. As she spoke her remaining vows, she knew her love for him would never cease to exist. Persistence and love had rewarded her. It had been placed through strenuous trials and tribulations of fire and still it burned brightly.

In the front row, Margaret continuously gazed at Caroline and pondered on all the lost time they could have shared together.

Even though she would never reveal the truth to Caroline or the rest of her family, she took consolation in the fact that Katie and Caroline would be together. Their natural attraction had bonded and cemented their love the same as if they had grown to maturity together. Finally, two sisters stood side by side in life. Inwardly, Margaret was sorrowful that she couldn't reveal the truth to them. Then too, she knew her hell in life was the lie that she willfully chose to live. The consolation was that she had discovered her oldest daughter after all of these years and now through God's grace would put the animosity that the war caused behind her. In the future when Katie traveled north, Margaret would invite Caroline and her family to Boston, and at times, she would visit Shenandoah. She turned and looked at Ann, her granddaughter and momentarily pondered on all she experienced and endured through the horrors and troubles of the war. She determined she would do everything within her ability to assist in a normal life for the young lady, and would play a role in her future.

Finally, after Pete and Katie finished exchanging vows, they smiled and kissed. As they walked to the entrance of the church, Caroline again played the violin. Family and friends filed toward the entrance to the church where Pete and Katie warmly greeted them. Their life together of hopes of a happy future, dreams of peace, and expectations of an abounding and successful life was now in its genesis.

* * * *

Later in the evening, Pete rode alone over to the crest of Barker's Ridge. As he gazed across the estate, he pondered on all of his future plans for Shenandoah. He visualized cattle and horses roaming freely across the pastureland; his children competing in equestrian games; and a business that was just as prosperous as before the war. His thoughts were interrupted by the sound of an approaching horse. Turning and looking, Pete noticed Seamus galloping in his direction. Pete wheeled his horse around as Seamus arrived.

Seamus stretched forth his hand. "Again Johnnie, I want to congratulate and welcome you into the McBride family." Quietly, Pete smiled as Seamus pulled a small bag from his coat pocket. He removed the contents, "Do you remember this?"

"Yes," Pete surprisingly answered as he gazed at the stone. "It is the ruby that I swapped you for food and coffee the day after the fighting at Antietam. I never thought that I would see it again."

"Well Johnnie, in good conscious I can't keep the bloody jewel." He stretched forth his hand with the precious stone. "Here, take the bloody thing, it's yours."

"But I gave it to you in a fair trade."

"No, no, I have no bloody use for the thing."

Pete took the stone from Seamus' hand. "Thank you so much for returning it to me. What this means to me I can't put into words."

Seamus wheeled his horse around. "Well Barker, for me as I hope for you, the war is over. And Barker, if you need anything or if the Unionists in this area give you a bloody fit over this place, then send me a telegram. I will do anything to help Katie and you." Looking around one last time, Seamus continued, "You know Johnnie, Katie is right about this place, it is one of the most beautiful spreads I have ever seen."

"It will always be home."

As Pete looked, Seamus saluted and galloped off toward the Charlestown Pike. Once he disappeared, Pete rode to a different area of Barker's Ridge where the sun was beginning to set in the western sky. He gazed across the rolling slopes and considered the best use of the land. It was some of the most prosperous grazing land on the estate. His mind played with the idea of giving it to Hayward to begin his own little spread. This heart fulfilling desire would give his best friend the ability to share in the ownership of a farm such as he had dreamed. With this idea, he rode off until he came to his special area along the river. After dismounting and walking to the riverbank, he began skidding some stones across the water's surface. With a thought, he turned and glanced toward the ridge where a rider was swiftly approaching. A broad smile covered his face. It was Katie coming to join him. He patiently observed and waited until she brought her horse to a halt.

"I see you have the same thing in mind as I do," Katie said in a tone of enthusiasm.

"Eventually, I knew you would come," Pete replied as he assisted her from the horse.

"You did, huh?"

"Yes," Pete replied in a serious voice. "I was over along the western side of the ridge looking at some property I want to give Hayward for his loyalty and his valued friendship."

"It's been more than a friendship. From all I have seen over the years, he has been like a father to you. And I know beyond a doubt he has loved you as such. Besides, I have felt many times you see him in that role, providing for that need in your life. I really believe he cherishes that honor."

"Regardless of the color of his skin, I have seen his heart and know it is as pure as God could make anyone on this earth."

"Before riding out here, he told me he only wanted our happiness and prosperity. And the only thing of importance he could give us was his love. I assured him that was more than enough. He just smiled and walked away singing a song of love." Katie paused and looked across the river to the opposite shore at some deer grazing. "Shenandoah is so beautiful and majestic. I never want to live anywhere but here. This is where I want to raise our family."

"I agree, even if we only live in the cabin." Pete turned and placed his hands on Katie's shoulders. He looked into her eyes. "Our life together is just really beginning. When I thought you were dying, my life and all of my dreams were fading and dying with you. More than anytime over the last four years, I realized just how much you were a part of my life and how much I needed you. And I missed the most important necessity in my life, your love."

"Had I not collapsed at the train depot, I would have returned to Boston. Somewhere in my heart I knew you still loved me. But I knew too, that you were struggling with pain and anguish over my acts of unfaithfulness with Robert. In time, I knew if you really loved me, you would have come to Boston just as I returned here to Shenandoah after the war. All this has taught us one thing."

"And what's that Mrs. Barker?"

"In spite of all the differences and trials we have been through over the last four years, there is nothing but death that can separate us. Through the worst that life has to offer, we still have been drawn together by our love. My love and commitment will be yours forever. And again I will remind you of the words I spoke to you here at this exact place six months ago. From SABERS AND ROSES, a love was born."

Epilogue

Ann Barker closed the diary she had been reading and expounding on for the past hour. Ann wiped the tears from her eyes, as she silently gazed in the direction of the mansion. Many good and prosperous memories lingered in her mind. She could still vividly visualize her mother and herself riding across the field just to the west of the mansion where the terrain posed many challenges for competition. It was a time for building important family relationships and a time to receive the nurturing love she so cherished. Occasions such as this with her mother, Ann missed more than anything else in her life

On the more tragic side of her life, Ann could still recall the afternoon when she gazed out her upstairs bedroom to the sound of beating drums and the patriotic whistling music of the fife. Throughout the day, thousands of Confederate soldiers were walking in ranks toward Halltown for the fight with the Yankees at Harpers Ferry. She paused and pondered on how many soldiers had sons and daughters at home who were waiting for their return. By the conclusion of the war, how many were actually fortunate to escape the wrath of battle? Often soldiers, both blue and gray, occasionally visited Shenandoah either to inquire of her father's whereabouts or to steal what little possessions they had. Neither side were respecters of private property when it came to meeting their own personal needs.

Ann's experiences from the war had taught her how to survive the most difficult situations and to exercise patience and unrelenting determination when needed. Many times over the years, she attempted to blot out the horrors of the war and its aftermath. Through its experiences, she had learned its lessons and matured, learning many valuable qualities that she would need to overcome the many challenges that she had faced in the future.

Suddenly, there was the sound of an automobile horn. Ann looked around and noticed the vehicle had stopped and a middle-age gentleman had rolled down the window on the driver's side.

"Is there anything I can do for you folks?"

"We are sorry if we are trespassing," Bill replied as he began to point in the direction of the mansion. "But this is Miss Ann Barker who use to live in the house over there."

"Barker, huh?" the gentleman replied as he rubbed his chin. "Oh yes, my father purchased the property from you in 1929, just before the depression years."

Danny escorted Ann to the gentleman's automobile. Immediately, Ann recognized the gentleman. "Well if it isn't Elmer Potts. As I recall I sold this place to your father, Leroy a little over 30 years ago. At the time, you were just a small lad of about 12 years of age. And if I am not mistaken, you were one of my students at the Harpers Ferry School."

With a smile, Elmer answered. "Oh yes, it has been many years. If I am not mistaken, I had you for the second grade?"

"Yes, and also the sixth."

"Your memory is quite good."

"Your father had some questions concerning the failing grade I gave you in arithmetic. He came to the school after class one afternoon and we discussed your attention problems."

"Yes, it was quite troublesome for me," Elmer laughingly replied.

"Well at that time your father inquired about purchasing some property from me. He wanted to purchase three hundred acres of land along the river. Since I was alone and unmarried with little money, Shenandoah had become a financial burden with no hopes of a resolution. As difficult as it was to admit, for sometime I had been contemplating the sale of Shenandoah. I mentioned something to the effect that I'd like to sell the whole place. Without hesitation or thought, your father purchased the remaining one thousand acres."

"You must miss the old place." Danny said in a curious tone.

"More than words could ever express."

Elmer listened to the sad words spoken and he noticed the somber expression covering Ann's face. "Would you like to see the house and the property again?"

"It would be good for you Miss Ann," Danny enthusiastically said.

Ann looked in the direction of the house. Memories continued to race through her mind. Her heart raced with excitement over the prospect as she silently nodded her approval.

"Well then, follow me," Elmer said as he rolled up the window of the car and proceeded slowly down the lane.

Danny assisted Ann to their car. As he was opening the door, Ann mumbled, "All that I see, it's like living the youth of my life all over again."

Danny was puzzled by Ann's statement but he didn't respond nor pursue its meaning.

As Bill slowly accelerated the automobile, Danny's curiosity continued to dominate his emotions. "Miss Ann, earlier you said your father had been sent to prison. Without being too nosey, how long was he gone?"

"Son, maybe Miss Ann doesn't want to talk about it," Bill suggested before Ann could answer.

"It's quite all right. My father was sent to Fort Warren in Boston harbor for a four-month duration. At the time, President Johnson believed it would not be beneficial for the officials of the former Confederate government to be charged with crimes of treason, and then tried by a jury, and sentenced to lengthy prison terms or death. The nation had been through enough division and strife to last a lifetime. The conflict had been costly beyond anyone's comprehension, and had troubled every household, both North and South, in some way. In order to bring about speedy reconciliation, all of the officials that had been captured were released. The exception was Jefferson Davis. He remained in prison at Fort Monroe, Virginia for two years. He was released and never tried either."

"Then your father returned home?"

Ann's face glowed brightly as she answered the lad's question, "Yes, just as he promised before leaving the Ferry. Once he returned, my father and uncle worked together to resurrect the glory Shenandoah once enjoyed. Within four years of the conclusion of the war, my Uncle Pete and Hayward along with additional hired laborers completed the mansion that's before you. It's not quite like the first one, but as you can see, it is majestic and was home to the whole family just the same as before the war. The agreement between my father and uncle was that my father would maintain the business end of running the estate while my uncle would maintain control over everyday operations. We picked up where we left off prior to the war by breeding horses and cattle for the army. But not without difficulty. Since my uncle and father were loyal to the Confederate government, it took Thaddeus McBride's intervention to secure its success. After my uncle and Katie were married, her father ran for the United States Congress and won. He didn't only serve just one term, but six additional terms before his son, Seamus was elected to his seat from the state of Massachusetts."

"Wow!" Danny loudly exclaimed.

"Later in years after reconstruction ended, there was a move for my father to pursue a representative's office, but he firmly declined." Ann changing the subject, continued, "Just as that fateful night in May of 1864, I can still see Yankee cavalry galloping along this lane on a mission to burn our home. As much as I have tried, I can still see within my mind that horrifying night. Like others in the South, we must know the cost of war and its tragedies."

As the automobile pulled into the circle in front of the house, Ann commented, "This is like the days of old when all of the carriages and buggies arrived for a social function."

After Danny assisted Ann from the car, she looked at the mansion. It was similar to the former. The stone, white column double veranda, two level structure stood erect among the many trees.

"It hasn't changed much," she said.

Once Bill assisted Ann up the stone steps, she slowly entered the mansion. With only some moderate changes, it was still the same as when she sold the property. The layout of the house was the same as the former. The library was off to the left of entry and the parlor to its right. In the rear was the drawing room and dining room. The rooms were spacious. The flooring was of oak and the ceilings were high. She thought of how her uncle had kept his promise to her grandmother and rebuilt the mansion much the same as the former.

After walking through the downstairs of the mansion, Ann paused near the huge spiral stairway. Quietly, she gazed at a room off to the left of the upper level. "Do you want to go upstairs?"

Ann looked at Elmer. "Would it be all right?"

"Sure, it's perfectly all right," Elmer replied.

With Elmer and Bill's assistance, Ann struggled to the upper level. "I want to go over to this room," she said.

The door was open and Ann paused before entering. Many thoughts raced through her mind on the revelation that occurred in this room. She slowly entered and noticed the same bed and furnishings. They were still in their exact place. She peered out the window and noticed the old cabin where it had all begun. It was still standing, although in a dilapidated condition. Again gazing intently at the cabin, her mind returned to late afternoon in 1927.

Ann was in the library looking through some old books, determining those of importance she cherished, and those books that could be given away to the local library. Her mind was on her ailing Aunt Katie, who was in the front bedroom on the upper level. For several days, she had been struggling with a re-occurrence of the illness that almost robbed her of life in the autumn of 1865. Now many years later, it was only Katie and Ann who were left from the family. Often they would spend the evening beside the fireplace reminiscing of the events and the life that transpired at Shenandoah during and after the war. Sometimes they would look at photographs of friends and family through a steroview and laugh and cry over precious memories.

Ann's thoughts were interrupted when she heard the bell ringing from Katie's room. She put aside some boxes of books and dashed to the upper level to her aunt's room. Once she entered, Katie slowly turned her head and looked at her niece.

"Is everything all right or do you want me to call for the Doctor?" Ann asked.

Shaking her head in disagreement, Katie gestured for Ann to be seated. Ann complied with the request. "I will not try to fool you with excuses and useless words. I know death is at the door as probably you also expect."

"No, no," Ann cried.

"I have always been honest with you and now is no exception. When I was taken sick this past time, I knew it would be the end of my life. And it is something we both must accept, especially you my love."

"Don't say that. Please."

"No Ann, we must. Besides, I am tired and weary of life. I just want to go and be with my Pete. Ever since his death in the winter of 1924, my vigor and vitality for life has vanished. I feel so empty. There has been nothing worth living for other than being with you," Katie replied as tears streamed down her cheeks.

"Aunt Katie…"

Katie interrupted Ann and continued, "But before I go there is something I must share with you that I have kept secret for all these years. No one has ever known. Not even my closest friend, your mother or my beloved Pete. It is knowledge I have held and closely guarded all these years and I have been terrified by its truth and impact on this family if it was ever disclosed."

"What is it that could be so important?"

Katie gazed out the window at the cabin. "I had a large part to do with the destruction of Shenandoah during the war."

Ann was so shocked and devastated that she was speechless. Not out of anger, but of sorrow. Her expressions told the story of her despair.

Katie continued in a whisper. "I never had the intentions of coming to this area and falling in love with your uncle or anyone else for that matter. In 1860, love and a family was the furthermost thing from my mind. But that all changed after I met Pete." Taking her niece by the hand, she continued, "Ann, I was a government agent sent to Harpers Ferry to spy and relay information back to the War Department in Washington City. Throughout those four years, I had done things until this day, I still feel so guilty and worthless about that sometimes I feel degraded as a human being. It was a constant strain to juggle my work with trying to win your uncle's love. Never did I attempt to extract information from him at anytime because when I was with him, the war didn't exist because I surrounded myself in a world of fantasy. But William Pierce and your father's suspicions were correct but couldn't be proved because there were never any associations to my affairs."

Laughingly, Katie freely spoke. "Who would have suspected a woman of being an enemy agent?" Pausing and coughing, she continued, "Now concerning Shenandoah. For months I was gathering information on residents living in the area who were sheltering or supplying Confederate partisans. At the time, your grandmother and mother were doing just that. I struggled within as to what I should do with the information. By this time, like many, I just wanted the war to end and my brother and your uncle to go home safely, regardless of the circumstances or sacrifices to be made."

"But this was our home. We too did what we thought was right."

"I know, and we'll probably never see eye to eye on the rights and wrongs of the war." Katie looked and sighed. "My desire to keep my activities secret was so intense that I killed a double agent in Winchester in the autumn of 1864. He was going to reveal my identity and intentions to the Provost Marshall in Winchester. His name was Arlen Pierce."

"William's brother?   My father nor my mother ever said anything about Mr. Pierce having a brother."

"I didn't know until it was too late. I was assigned by General George Sharpe, who was chief of all tactical operations for the Union army, to discover the identity of the agent who was operating in the Shenandoah Valley. Since the Ferry was all but deserted in the summer of 1864, and being suspicious of any new people arriving, I immediately imposed myself on him when he arrived. I wasn't fooled for a moment of his false identity as a traveling merchant. After a bottle or two of whisky, he had a loose tongue and was willing to do anything in order to have his way with me. But after getting the information I wanted, I refused and escaped his grasp after he passed out on the floor. It wasn't until I went to Winchester in the early autumn of 1864 that I ran into him again. Of course, he had eluded capture and was behind Confederate lines. Unintentionally, I ran into him in that city while visiting the McDonalds. Arlen Pierce was the only person to discover my identity and know my intentions. And unfortunately, he died because of it. Once I escaped with your uncle's help from prison in Winchester, William figured it all out. Since William knew the truth, he met the same fate at my hands. I could have wounded him, but instead, I deliberately shot him to death"

In a determined tone, Katie softly continued. "No matter what the circumstances, I would have killed him at the first chance to protect my secret. My earnest intentions were, no one would, or should ever know my complicity of gathering information during the war. And even if someone would have stepped forth and troubled this family, I would have done whatever I had to in order to protect my secret and marriage." Pausing and smiling, Katie humored. "No one, not even my family during the war knew I was spying. Maybe it was the best-kept secret, I don't know. But I have shared this with you to clear my conscious before I die. Even now, there isn't a day that goes by that I don't feel guilty. When I use to look at your uncle's face and witnessed the suffering and disappointment he endured with fighting to maintain this estate from the hands of the Unionists, it devastates me because I knew I was the cause. No one knows as much as me concerning what your uncle was going through trying to hold on to this place and rebuilding all that had been destroyed by my actions." Katie paused and closed her eyes.

Ann was terrified over the scene. She touched her aunt's arm. Katie opened her eyes. "Please Ann, forgive me for sinning against you and your family. Please."

"I do Aunt Katie. I have loved you too much to ever let something like this stand between us."

"Because of this sickness, I was never able to bear children," Katie said as she struggled to breathe. Tears filled her eyes as she continued in a whisper, "But from the very first time that I laid eyes on you, I've loved you as my own."

"I know, I know," Ann softly answered as she wept.

Once again, Katie looked at Ann and then in the direction of the cabin. A peaceful smiled covered her face. Ann was amazed at its glow. This was the first time since Pete past away that Katie possessed such an expression. Suddenly when Ann's hopes were resurrected, Katie closed her eyes and the last breath of life departed from her body.

* * * *

An old spotted hound below the window where Ann was standing began to uncontrollably bark. Ann was startled as she attempted to focus her attention on the present. She turned and looked at Elmer, Bill, and Danny. "No one in my family ever knew the truth about Katie McBride."

There were expressions of astonishment from all they had witnessed and heard Ann share of Katie's final days at Shenandoah. Without a word, Ann quietly walked by the threesome and continued her tour of the house. Finally, she stepped onto the back porch and paused, gazing in the direction of a grove of trees about a hundred yards from the house. She held her left hand against her cheek and whispered. "I want to visit my mother's grave."

Ann slowly approached the small family cemetery where the Barkers were buried. She knelt and quietly prayed at each individual gravesite. When finished, Bill assisted Ann to her feet. She looked at him.

"After Katie married my uncle," Ann said, "my mother and her became closer and enjoyed a richer more prosperous relationship than anytime before or during the war. Sometimes I think they might have known they were sisters. Never did I at anytime give any indication or hint that I knew the truth. When my mother passed away in the summer of 1910, Katie grieved for many years afterward. But my uncle's love and strength sustained her through a very difficult time in her life."

"I see your father passed on in 1895," Danny added.

"Yes, he did. After he returned home he fulfilled his promise of making up for all the time we were separated during the war and while he was at Fort Warren." Ann pointed to the ridge near the house. "On many occasions, we sat on a fence such as that one and shared the most inward thoughts of the heart. Life at Shenandoah was full of hope and love abounded abundantly following the war years. We all had learned a difficult lesson from the war. But the real prosperity rising from the horrors of the war was that the division between family members had ended and the real and meaningful relationships in life had just begun and would grow and flourish. At no time did I ever see my Grandmother Barker merrier then after the war. Up until she left this world in 1877 her time was totally dedicated to the family and its emotional prosperity."

Ann paused and slowly allowed her eyes to gaze around the estate. She brushed the hair from her face. "As for the McBride family and the Barkers, we reconciled our differences and went on with life, visiting each other quite often. The turmoil we experienced after those first months following the war were quite troublesome for my family and then Katie's revelation. It was as though some kind of Northern Fire had rained down on us Barkers. I really believed the two families would be bitter enemies and never give reconciliation an opportunity to manifest. Like many, we learned to put the continuous animosity, and the deep division behind us. Maybe I was the last with putting the war behind. Although, after all of these years, I guess I can finally say that I have laid the matter to rest."

As Ann turned and walked away from the cemetery toward the house, Danny asked, "What about Hayward?"

"My Uncle Pete offered Hayward five hundred acres of the western pastureland to start his own homestead. Hayward refused the offer. Instead, he chose to follow his heart's desire and headed to Oregon. Over the following ten years we heard from him twice. At the time, he was settled into a small homestead and living alone. And then after the second letter, we never heard from him again. I found out some years afterward that Hayward had died in the summer of 1881."

Finally, Ann and the others reached the front corner of the house. Again she turned. "I will see all of you soon."

Later that same evening, Ann Barker departed this life and joined those she loved and cherished. Ann had lived through one of the most dramatic eras in history and its aftermath. The lessons Ann and her family learned through those dark, gloomy days of Civil War, and the traumatic aftermath known as the Reconstruction Era were valued and cherished more than anything else in life. In spite of their many differences, they had learned the importance of forgiveness, the blessings of reconciliation, and the need to go on with life. Shenandoah and its memories have faded with the passage of time. Like many who experienced the tragedies of war, just as the Barkers, they learned the valuable lesson of persistent endurance.